SHADOW

OF THE

WOLF

SHADOW
OF THE
WOLF

Tim Hall

David Fickling Books

SCHOLASTIC INC. / NEW YORK

First published in the United Kingdom in 2014 by David Fickling Books, 31 Beaumont Street, Oxford, OX1 2NP. *www.davidficklingbooks.com*

The publisher does not have any control over and does not assume any responsibility for author or third-party websites or their content.

This book is a work of fiction. Names, characters, places, and incidents are either the product of the author's imagination or are used fictitiously, and any resemblance to actual persons, living or dead, business establishments, events, or locales is entirely coincidental.

Library of Congress Cataloging-in-Publication Data

Hall, Tim K., 1977- author.
Shadow of the wolf / by Tim Hall.—[First U.S. edition].
pages cm
"First published in the United Kingdom in 2014 by David Fickling Books."
Summary: Two events change young Robin Loxley's life forever—he encounters a wargwolf in the woods and returns home days later to discover that his family, believing him dead, have left the village, and six months later he meets the young and rebellious Lady Marian.
ISBN 978-0-545-81664-9
1. Robin Hood (Legendary character)—Juvenile fiction. 2. Maid Marian (Legendary character)—Juvenile fiction. 3. Werewolves—Juvenile fiction. 4. Sherwood Forest (England)—Juvenile fiction. 5. Great Britain—History—Medieval period, 1066-1485—Juvenile fiction. [1. Robin Hood (Legendary character)—Fiction. 2. Werewolves—Fiction. 3. Sherwood Forest (England)—Fiction. 4. Great Britain—History—Medieval period, 1066–1485—Fiction.] I. Title.
PZ7.1.H3Sh 2015
[Fic]—dc23
2014035621

10 9 8 7 6 5 4 3 2 1   15 16 17 18 19

Printed in the U.S.A.   23
First edition, June 2015

For Lizzie

First, forget everything you've heard.
Robin Hood was no prince, and he was no dispossessed lord.
He didn't fight in the Crusades. He never gave a penny to the poor.

In fact, of all those Sherwood legends, only one holds true: Robin
was blind.

No, even that's not right. Truer to say: Robin Hood didn't see with
his eyes. Perhaps, after all, he was the only one who saw clearly in
this place of illusion and lies.

Forget, too, all you know of Marian.
She was never a nun, or an abbess. Much less a damsel in distress.
She was the Destroying Angel. The most desperate and deadly of
them all.

Look around you. And listen. A wasted world now, shrunken and
burned.
A howling winter and a silent spring.
But it's all still here, lurking amid the mist.
A world of gods and monsters, rolling their final dice.
A time of heroes and demons, and the horror that shadows both.

The world of Robin Hood . . .

Prologue

R obin Loxley placed more wood on the fire. He breathed into the heart of the flames and they crackled fully to life. He used his knife to scrape away embers for cooking.

A twig cracked. He looked up. His father was coming back across the clearing, carrying more strips of flesh. He came to Robin's side and laid the meat across the cooking stones.

"Just wait till Hal sees," Robin said. "And Thane. They've never made a kill this big, have they?"

His father looked for a moment into the trees before turning back to the fire. "It was a fine hunt," he said. "A superb kill. Here, eat some more, you earned it."

Using the flat of his knife he lifted a strip of cooked meat. Robin took it carefully and sat back and ate. His father went back to the carcass, a hulking shape at the edge of the glade. He began working at it again with his knife, and Robin felt a fresh swelling of pride. It *was* a superb kill: a large male with eight tines to its antlers—perhaps not a fully mature hart but certainly an older buck. It would provide meat for months— for the whole village—as well as the farm tools they would make from its antlers, the strong rope from its sinews, and all the other useful pieces.

He put more wood on the fire. He listened to the forest,

loud on all sides: the skittering of clawed feet, sudden wing-beats and distant killing shrieks. He realized he had no idea what hour it was. All day the sun had sulked behind dense cloud, the light little more than a gray wash. And now, as the mist began to thicken, it was growing so dark it could almost be dusk. But it couldn't possibly be that late. Nobody would stay in Winter Forest after nightfall. Not even Robin's father.

He looked to the edge of the clearing. Through the mist, in his dusky hunting cloak, his father could almost be a piece of the forest, man-shaped. Like Robin his clothing was stuffed with grasses and his skin was rubbed with mud and moss to mask his scent.

Now his father was cleaning his knife on the grass. And when he stood and turned, he was holding the buck's bloody, steaming heart, still impaled with Robin's arrow. He carried it back to the fire.

"Are we going to eat it now?" Robin said. "The heart is the hunter's part, you always said. Or is it an offering? Are we going to bury it beneath the Trystel Tree?"

His father didn't answer. He was sawing away the shaft of the arrow and then stuffing the heart into a hemp sack. He put the sack to one side, blood beginning to patch through the weave.

Movement nearby. Something darting through the undergrowth. Robin's eyes went after it. He thought it was a stoat, or a pine marten, but it was difficult to tell—all shapes were beginning to merge. Something else flicked past on dark wings.

Dusk *was* drawing in, wasn't it?

"Robin, don't be nervous," his father said. "There's nothing here for you to fear. That's what my father used to say, when he taught me my wildwood skills. He said I would never have to be afraid of the cold, or hunger, or rely on another

2

man to offer me shelter. I could move freely in the world and survive anywhere, even here. That's why I've been teaching you the same skills. And you're a better apprentice than I ever was. You're in your element. Don't fear it."

As he spoke he lifted his prized hunting bow. And now, to Robin's disbelief, he was pushing the bow into Robin's hands.

"I want you to have it," his father said. "Take it, it's yours."

"How can I? You need it."

"I'll cut another. This one is too good for me. It always was." Robin had been trying his best to resist, but his father's arms were thick as tree trunks, his hands tough as roots, and he kept gently but firmly insisting, and finally Robin had no choice but to take the gift.

He turned the shortbow in his hands. It had been polished over and over with hazelnut oil to such a fine finish he could see his reflection in the heartwood. The grip was antler bone wrapped in soft worn leather.

"This gift means something, Robin. It means I'm proud of you. Proud to call you my son." Something caught in his father's voice and made Robin look up. He was staring at Robin intently and his eyes, dark as oakwood, were glistening in the firelight.

"What is it?" Robin said. "What's wrong?"

His father looked away. He cleared his throat. "It's nothing," he said. "I'm fine. Smoke in my eyes, that's all. And I'm tired—even if you're not. That was a long hunt. We'll rest before heading home."

He stood and moved Robin's hunting pack so it could serve as a pillow. Robin hesitated at first, but then he lay out flat and rested his head. They must be closer to the forest edge than he imagined. There must be plenty of daylight left. No harm in a short rest.

His father sat at his side and started to stroke Robin's hair. At the same time he began to murmur some words, his voice enfolding Robin like a blanket.

"Don't be afraid . . . in your element . . . fought them all, but fear of the unknown . . . what more could we have done . . . so sorry . . . winter-born . . ."

It was hard to hear what the words were, and anyway, they were muddled and strange—like one of the nonsense rhymes his mother sometimes sang at his bedside. But whatever he was saying, the sound of his father's voice was reassuring.

"Everything in our power . . . so sorry . . . find you I promise . . ."

And as he spoke he continued to stroke Robin's hair, in a way that never failed to lull him to sleep. And it was warm here near the fire and the aspen leaves were making a hushing sound and Robin was tired and fully fed.

And his father was still murmuring those words. He was still stroking Robin's hair . . .

And Robin's eyes were closing . . .

They opened again a heartbeat later.

Robin blinked. He kept blinking, trying to clear the blackness from his eyes. The world had disappeared. There was no edge to the clearing; no branches or leaves above.

There was only this: a single speck of light, hanging in the void.

He realized it was the remnants of their fire, burned down to embers.

They must have fallen asleep. Both of them.

"Wake up!" Robin hissed. "Please, quickly, wake up!" Nobody stirred. A silence at his side. An emptiness.

He sat up slowly, a sickly feeling spreading from his groin. The wind blew and he shivered.

4

He whispered: "Where are you?"

In reply came the distant hooting of an owl. A branch cracked and fell, somewhere close.

Robin crawled, on hands and knees, around the firepit, searching with his fingers for his father's things. His hunting pack, his knife, even the sack containing the animal's heart. All of it gone.

"Where are you?" he shouted. "I'm here! Come back, please!"

He stood and shouted again and he listened to his voice dying in the mist. He sat and hugged his knees, gripping his father's bow to his chest. *He'll come for me. I was asleep and he heard a noise and he went to investigate, but he'll be back. He'll be back.*

A sound like a distant scream—Robin forced himself to think of an owl, hunting. Another noise like something being dragged through the wet leaves—Robin's heart hammering, harder and faster.

He stared again into the blackness. He began to pick out shapes. Something nodded its head and he told himself it was a sapling. He watched a yew tree, its outline rippling in the wind. To Robin the movement looked like rising and falling. Like breath. The needles looked like fur.

It's here, it's watching me, I know it is.

A gust of wind and the mist swirled and moonlight found the forest floor. From the corner of his eye he saw something else. More movement.

There was somebody there. Kneeling at the body of the buck.

His father.

Of course. He's caching the meat. To return for later. He's been here all along, of course he has!

Robin got shakily to his feet. He groped his way in the dark, edging toward his father.

"Why didn't you answer?"

No reply. A twig snapping loudly underfoot. The boughs groaning high above.

"Why are you doing that alone?"

Robin moved closer, almost close enough to touch. The wind making the leaves skitter.

"Why didn't we get help? Why are we still here?"

Still his father hadn't turned or said a word. He was just crouching there, working at the carcass with his knife. Except, was he using his knife? It looked like—

The mist swirled once more and moonlight spilled through the trees. Robin saw the kneeling figure more clearly.

He saw this was not his father.

This was an even bigger, broader man, with hulking shoulders. A man wrapped in some kind of animal pelt.

And when he half turns, still crouching over the carcass, the man's eyes are amber and his mouth and teeth are glistening with blood . . .

Robin running. Lurching away from those eyes and running, blindly into the darkness and the mist, gripping the shortbow in both hands and holding it out before him, stumbling over roots, falling, picking himself up and running again, breathless with the fear of it.

Running harder. The branches bare bones, snapping; the forest screeching, clawing at him with thorns.

From somewhere shockingly close comes a human noise— a woman's laugh. Followed by words, whispered on the wind: *Not yet. Too soon.*

And then a face looming from the darkness—a small child, grinning, her eyes flashing golden, like a hawk, or a vixen.

Robin doesn't dare look back, but he knows the Wargwolf is there too, its lower jaw hanging slack, its breath mixing with the mist, its lantern eyes burning.

Robin running and falling and running, trying to shout for his father but fear blocking his throat.

Around him the wind swirls and seems to form those words:

Not yet. Too soon. He must suffer the wounds.

Another cackle of laughter.

Stumbling and falling and getting to his feet and staggering on. Running now so long and so far that the night is beginning to lift and sunlight starting to sift through the trees . . .

Still Robin runs and he keeps running until the last of his strength leaves his body and he falls to the wet earth, senseless with fear and exhaustion, blackness closing its fingers around him and blocking at last the laughter snaking through the mist.

Part One

Winter-born

Six months later

I. The Village

Robin crouched in the long grass, gripping his hunting pack, his father's shortbow strapped across his back. He kept his hood raised. He had smeared his face gray-green with a mixture of ash and dyer's weed.

He peered into Wodenhurst. The village was waking, shutters opening, spilling voices still hushed from sleep. Nearby a baby was crying, and farther off came the creaking of the waterwheel and the barking of a dog. It was a cold, bright dawn, woodsmoke hanging hazy above the roofs.

He looked toward his old home, standing square and solid at the top of Herne Hill. From this distance it looked exactly as it always had, and just for a moment he imagined he could walk into that house and there his family would be sitting: his brothers with their boots pulled off, their feet stretched out near the fire; his mother, at the window, softly singing of a journey home; his father leaning close, listening intently.

The next moment the illusion was shattered: Warin Felstone ducked out of the house. He pushed back his shoulders, arching his spine, before walking down into the village. Next emerged his wife, Mabel, and then their children, Narris, Richard, and Ida, the two younger ones pinching each other and squabbling.

So, the path was clear. The frosted grass crunched as Robin left his hiding place. He darted through High Field, running low to the ground. He looped around the orchard and the croft, and he came to the front of his old home. He went inside and hurried through the silent, gloomy house.

He went to the sleeping chamber he once shared with his brothers. It was cold and dark. He opened the shutters—a gust of wind whipped in, scattering the floor rushes. He went to a far corner and knelt on the packed earth. He took out his hunting knife and he began to dig.

The hole widened and deepened. He was so intent on his work that at first he didn't notice someone had come to stand in the doorway. The figure moved to the window and his shadow fell across Robin.

Warin Felstone was holding an adz in one hand, an ax in the other. He propped the tools against a wall and crossed his arms. "Narris thought he saw you lurking," he said. "How long is this going to continue, Robin? What if your father could see you now, the way you're living? Look at me when I'm talking to you. And you can start by telling me what in Woden's name you're doing."

Robin continued digging. Mabel Felstone came bustling into the room, short of breath. "Mother's mercy, Robin, it's true. How long since we've set eyes on you? I was beginning to think you'd caught your death, it's grown so cold. Or, worse, the bailiff had gotten his hands on you. Hold still, let me get a proper look—check you're not wasting away. What's all this on your face? So long spent in those woods you're turning green."

She licked a thumb and reached through the curtain of Robin's long, mud-matted hair. She rubbed at his cheek. Robin pushed her hand away.

"We've been patient," Warin said, coming away from the

window. "But it's time to start putting this behind us. This stupid feud with Narris and the rest, I've told them it has to stop, but I can't do it alone. You have to start showing them you belong. The first step is to get you pulling your weight. We need every pair of hands. On top of everything else the storm damaged the spirit fence, and the Walking will come around, soon as we know it."

Mabel took her wimple from her head and used it to wipe at her eyes. She clasped one of Robin's hands in both of hers.

"We miss them too, Robin, you know that, don't you? It's been hard for every one of us since . . . since they left. But sooner or later life has to carry on. Please say you'll come back, live here with us. This is still your home, as much as it is ours."

Robin pulled back his hand. He took from the ground a small pinewood casket—his woodsman's cache. Inside was a fresh bowstring; two boar-tusk bodkins; a spare flint for his strike-a-light; a whetstone to sharpen his knife. When he had buried these things, the previous spring, it had been only to keep them hidden from his brothers. But now, with winter approaching, these objects could prove vital. He put each one in his hunting pack. He stood and raised his hood.

"This isn't my home," he said. "And you're not my parents. You can't tell me what to do."

As he spoke he was already moving toward the wall, and before Warin could stop him, quick as a squirrel Robin leaped into the window and squeezed through and jumped down to the ground. He moved swiftly around the house, scattering the magpies that were in the orchard, squabbling over fallen fruit. He headed down into the village, following the twisting lanes between the homes.

People were emerging and setting about their work. Pagan Topcroft and Stephen Younger and the rest of their oxgang were armed with sickles and were heading for Far Field.

William Tanglefoot was hobbling around with the ducks, casting feed. Agnes Poley and Matheu Plowless were going to help repair the spirit fence, walking up toward Woden's Ride carrying sharpened stakes and the sun-bleached skulls of sheep. A few of these people looked at Robin as he passed. One or two shook their heads, or turned away as if he wasn't there. Robin didn't care; he kept his hood raised and went on his way.

He walked beneath the granary and the hayloft, standing on their struts. He passed between the smokehouse and the slaughter-shed. And all the time he was passing beneath the great arching boughs of the Trystel Tree. The ancient oak, covered in burns and lightning wounds, wrapped in vines thick as rope, rose from the center of the village. It spread its limbs so low and so far and so heavy through the lanes that many of the villagers had used them as top-beams for their barns or the rear walls of their homes.

Joylessly, through habit only, Robin leaped onto a low branch and walked along it, toe-to-heel, his arms outstretched for balance, the way he had done so many times with his brothers—Mogon's Well and Cooper's Corner passing beneath his feet. The branch came to rest and he jumped off. He crossed the creaking bridge that ran across Mill Pond.

He was passing the boundary stone, leaving the village, when raised voices stopped him. He looked back and saw Swet Woolward and Alwin Topcroft, heading this way. At their head was Narris Felstone, gripping in his solitary hand a fencing post, scratching at his ear with the stump of his left arm.

Robin didn't feel like tangling with Narris and the others today. He turned and broke into a run. Ahead of him Silver River glistened as it wound into the valley. He followed its course, two otters barking at him before diving out of sight, herons taking flight, a fox watching him from the far bank.

At Bel's Bridge he stopped and looked back. Narris and the others had followed no farther than the boundary stone, content to strut there back and forth, still watching Robin, laughing among themselves.

Work had begun now at the spirit fence—the *whump-whump* of hammers drew his eyes up to his old home, and up farther, to Woden's Ride, where the villagers were working at the forest edge. He couldn't help looking higher still, to the shadowy movements stirring above. There, looming over Wodenhurst, dwarfing even the Trystel Tree, was the black-green mass of Winter Forest, stretching up and away with the hills, its highest reaches lost in low cloud. The wind was picking up, making the wildwood churn. He listened to its whooshing roaring noise, and he stared, transfixed . . .

For three days and three nights he had wandered lost in the wildwood, shivering in the rain, running from visions in the mist. He remembered little of the ordeal—scattered impressions only—the half-glimpsed face of a young girl; an uncanny laugh.

But he did remember, all too distinctly, finding at last the path he had followed with his father, stumbling along it and finally breaking free of the forest.

And then staggering down into Wodenhurst, and drawing close to his home . . .

Finding it dark and deserted. His family vanished.

"They were heartbroken," Mabel Felstone told him tearfully, in the days that followed. "Your father came back alone, silent with grief, near madness. Those who get lost in Winter Forest are never found, you know that—never until now. They thought you were gone forever. Your father blamed himself, and it was more than he could stand. They left that same day, taking a few things, barely saying a word to any of us. They left to start afresh—is all I can think—to try to forget."

17

None of this made much sense to Robin. He couldn't begin to understand why his family would leave without him, or how his father had let it happen. He told himself he didn't care *how* or *why*. His family were no longer here; he didn't know how to find them. Nothing else mattered.

He managed to turn away from Winter Forest. He stepped onto Bel's Bridge and balanced across the frosted, moss-covered log. He entered Summerswood, following the man-made hunting paths and crossing the open rides.

His stomach was growling. He went to his shelter, and his smoking frame, where he had left strips of cured rabbit meat. He reached inside the frame eagerly. But the meat was gone. He checked the soil for the claw marks of a badger; he looked for signs of a clever crow. But no, as he had suspected, this had been a human thief. Nearby he found proof: footprints, child-sized. Who had been here? Who was it, kept stealing his food?

He foraged for hazelnuts and blackberries and butterball mushrooms. He returned to his shelter and sat outside it and ate his meager meal. He took the whetstone from his pack and sharpened his knife. In the distance the sound of hammers had stopped: The villagers must have gathered at the foot of the Trystel Tree, sharing bread and ale. There was a clink of metal, and a cheer: Narris Felstone and the others, throwing horseshoes on the common ground.

I hate them all. I wish they were dead. It was a terrible thing to think, but sometimes he couldn't help it. She was a liar, Mabel Felstone. She didn't miss Robin's family. None of them did. Listen to them now, as if nothing had ever happened, and nobody had a care.

Robin was vaguely aware that today was his birthday. Today he turned eight years old. It wasn't important. A cold wind was blowing through Summerswood; leaves were falling like rain. He needed to cut twine and collect pine branches to build his shelter warmer. He needed to start stockpiling food. One day his father would return, of that he had no doubt. And when he did he would see Robin had needed nobody's help, and he would be proud.

Robin finished his meal. He tested the keen edge on his hunting knife, then he took the blade and set about his work.

II. The Greenwood

Robin woke knowing someone was creeping close to his shelter.

He sat up, very slowly, and crouched on the balls of his feet. He tried to peer through the weave of the walls. He saw little in the dim dawn light. But he knew who this was outside: Narris and Swet and the rest.

He closed his eyes and listened. How many of them had come? What did they carry with them this time?

Twice in recent months Robin had woken to the smell of something foul dripping through the roof of his shelter and the sound of Narris and the others running away, laughing. After each attack Robin had retreated deeper into Summerswood. He had coated this new shelter in brambles, so from afar it looked like any other blackberry bush.

But he had not been careful enough. The boys from the village had found him. They were being very quiet—barely a leaf cracking—a single twig snapped—it was more of a *feeling* Robin had that they were skulking, very close.

He sensed them drawing nearer, nearer—

He burst from his shelter, throwing himself on the nearest intruder, grappling their legs, Robin's head colliding with their stomach—a winded cry of surprise and alarm—the two of them sprawling together to the earth, Robin scrapping wildly and silently and whoever it was fighting back, scratching and biting and hissing at him through bared teeth and then screeching a high-pitched wail and finally spitting out words, furious and garbled.

"Gedoff lemeego stoppit leggo gedoff leggoff!"

Robin understood several things at once: the intruder was alone; it was not Narris Felstone or anyone else from the village. It was a stranger. It was a girl.

He eased his grip. The girl slipped out of his grasp and sprang away and crouched there, her back arched, poised on bare feet and fingertips, fixing Robin with a dark fierce glare.

"You hit me!" she shouted. "How dare you—who are you— what are you doing in my woods I'll have you thrown in jail and you'll stay there living on bread and water for the rest of your life which in any case won't be very long because I'll have my father's knights chop off your head and put it on a spike so everyone can see what happens to a filthy stinking wretch who dares put his hands on a duchess—which is practically a princess—how dare you, you hit me, you've *drawn blood*!"

This went on for a long time, the girl ranting and raging, barely taking a breath, until she sounded ready to choke. And then, abruptly, like a summer storm parting, she fell quiet. She stood upright. Her top lip was bleeding. Her tongue appeared and licked it clean.

"Who are you?" she said. "Where did you come from? I'd think you were a woodwisp, appearing out of thin air, but you can't be, because wisps can't be touched." She came forward and lifted a finger and prodded Robin in the chest. "What are you, then? A wildling, raised with the fawns? Yes, that's it. You can't talk—you know the language of the birds but no human words. So, this is where you were hiding. You've even got a bed, sort of—what's it made of, ferns? I slept under a bush,

21

with tree roots and stones and even a toad. I don't know how animals stand it, living in the woods."

The girl had moved past Robin and was peering into his shelter. She was wearing an elegant dress made of some fine material, but it was scuffed with dirt and torn on thorns. Her tawny-brown skin was heavily scratched. Her hair, dark as a forest hawk, was tied in two ragged braids and fell almost to her bare feet. She turned and looked at Robin and he saw her hazel eyes were mismatched: one flecked gray and one flecked green.

"You're the thief," Robin said. "You're the one who steals my food."

"So, you *can* talk, after all. Did you lurk near homes at night, piecing together what you heard? Yes, that's it. I know all about wildlings. My mother used to read me a story about . . . Wait, what do you mean, *steal*? I didn't steal anything. These are *my* woods, and anything in them belongs to me. Including you, now I come to think of it. And anyway, I—"

The girl froze and fell silent. She was scowling. Robin heard voices in the distance. The clattering wings of a wood pigeon. Two men, on horseback, were heading in this direction. They were moving down one of the wide rides that sliced through Summerswood.

The girl turned and ran. Robin found himself following. She darted through a coppice of lime trees. She went to hands and knees and crawled through a hole in a deer fence and into the timber enclosure beyond. She fled across this open ground, between pine saplings sprouting in uniform rows. Robin caught up with her at an old standard oak. She was scurrying into its branches. Robin climbed. He found the girl at the top, in the tree's flattened crown.

"This is Oldcastle Oak," she whispered between breaths.

"Yesterday I defeated its garrison and claimed it as my own. You're lucky I let you come up. You can stay only if you promise to be quiet, and if you help me defend, if we come under siege. Now, shush."

The horsemen drew closer. A voice became clear. "Come on out, Lady Marian, he's not angry, not yet. He sent us with this. Look what we've got. Your favorite, Mistress Bawg says. Capon, foxwhelp. Honey and spice. It smells so good, you'd better hurry, or I'll eat it myself."

Robin could see the riders clearly now. They wore blue tabards embroidered with the image of twin crows, their wings outstretched. They moved closer—close enough to smell the pie one of the men was holding.

"Lady Marian, that's enough," one of the men called. "Your father goes back to Aragon any day now, had you forgotten. How displeased will he be if he doesn't see you before he leaves? I wouldn't like to be in your shoes, next time he returns."

Between their shouting, Robin heard the men muttering among themselves.

"As if we need this, again, and now of all times . . ."

"Bigger things to worry about . . ."

"Playing wet nurse to that precious little . . ."

But their words were becoming harder to hear, their shouting growing faint once more as they passed Oldcastle Oak and kept going, following a hunting trail west through the wood. Robin raised himself to his knees. From this height he could see the entire length of the valley. To the north, Wodenhurst, huddled on its hillside. And on the southern slopes the Delbosque manor, its whitewashed towers shining pink in the morning sun.

"Is that where you come from?" he whispered, pointing. "Do you live there?"

"I did, once, but not anymore. I'm never going back."

"Never?"

"No, never. Never ever never."

She fell quiet. More horsemen were entering Summerswood. From somewhere unseen came the barking of bloodhounds. Robin told himself he should leave this tree immediately and find his own hiding place. One of his earliest memories was of the day the lord's bailiff had come to Wodenhurst, and with him were three of these men-at-arms, with the twin crows on their tabards. They came dragging Narris Felstone by the hair. The bailiff said Narris had been caught trapping squirrels in Summerswood and he made all the villagers watch while he punished Narris with the loss of a hand.

Today these dangerous men were out in force—all of them searching for this girl at his side. Being anywhere near her was lunacy. But Robin looked at Marian and he didn't move.

He watched yet more riders entering the wood.

He said: "I know a better place to hide. Somewhere they'll never find us."

Without waiting for a reply, he scampered down the tree. He heard Marian following, close behind. He headed out of the greenwood and then led the way, toe-to-heel, across Bel's Bridge. A wet wind blew in their faces as they ran up the valley and squelched through the marshy land to the south of the village. They arrived at Hob's Hollow. Robin pushed inside and Marian followed.

Hob's Hollow was a low, damp place, full of moss and rotting logs. Tucked between two hillocks, it was permanently cast in deep shade. Even in summer, when it was hot outside, to enter this place made your skin prickle with chill. In autumn the mist never burned away.

"Perfect," Marian said, rubbing her arms, squelching around in the grotto. "The perfect hiding place. I bet there are haunts and specters—children who wandered in and were never found. I *felt* one! It passed straight through me! Turn around, touch the ground, something borrowed, something found . . ."

Robin shushed her. "We have to be quiet." He waded deeper into the bog, pushing through spear grass and lance thistle taller than he was. He hauled himself up onto a slimy boulder. This raised stand made a good place to watch from, and to listen. The valley was loud now with the sound of people calling for Marian. Not just men's voices, but women and children too.

"There are dozens of them," Marian said. "They're *all* out looking. Servants and laborers and *everyone*!"

"We have to be quiet," Robin hissed. "Rub mud on your arms, it will help hide your scent from the dogs."

Marian made a disgusted face as she scooped mud from the edge of a green-gunk pool. But she did as Robin said, spreading the mud on her arms and legs.

The sounds from outside were coming through dull and heavy. People calling, and the barking of bloodhounds. Two buzzards mewing high above.

They hid there, wrapped in that cloak of mist. They waited.

It was a long wait. The search went on all day. Calling on his hunter's patience, Robin sat still and quiet, ignoring the hunger twisting in his stomach.

Marian found it more difficult to wait. She whispered constantly, telling Robin the names of the people she heard searching, and which of them were her sworn enemies and who were allies. She poked around in the grotto, finding a lizard and bringing it for Robin to see but dropping it and not being able to find it again between the roots and the rocks.

Only once did she stop talking and the silence made Robin look back. Marian had plucked a mushroom from the base of a tree and she was chewing.

"No, stop!" Robin hissed, springing from his rock. "Spit it out, spit it out."

Marian coughed in surprise and she kept coughing and she spluttered the mushroom onto the ground.

"Spit it all out, every bit," Robin said. "Look at the gills and the cap. That's a destroying angel. Eat that and you'd be dead by morning. Don't you know anything?"

Marian was silent, looking at Robin, wide-eyed. She scraped the last of the deadly fungus from her tongue. She went and sat on a moss-quilted log, hugging her arms.

After a while, she said: "I know more than you. I know what *penumbra* means, and *chthonic*, and I know how to spell *metamorphosis* in Latin, French, *and* Spanish, and I know how many ducats you get in exchange for a pound. I bet you don't know any of that. All you know is stupid woods stuff. Anyway, I knew that was a destroy angel, I just forgot."

Robin wasn't looking at her. He had gone back to sit on his boulder.

The day drew on. Marian sulked and fidgeted, and began again to explore Hob's Hollow. Her stomach rumbled. They waited.

"Look, they've gone," Marian said. "Every one of them. We've won."

The day was coming to a close, a damp gloaming seeping into the hills. The raucous call of rooks and crows, squabbling over the best roosts.

They left Hob's Hollow cautiously. Marian was right: The final horseman was a dot in the distance, heading back to the manor house. Marian was moving in the same direction. She broke into a run.

"Where are you going?" Robin said.

"Home."

Robin stopped. Marian kept running.

"What do you mean . . . home? But . . . we hid. All day. And now . . . they'll catch you."

"Can't be helped," she called back. "I need a bath or I'll start to smell like you. And I'm famished. Suppertime. They didn't catch us, that's what counts. We won!"

Her words had become faint. She kept running. Robin watched her become small in the distance, joining Packman's Furrow, then starting up Lord's Hill, and he watched her dwindle farther until finally she faded into the gloaming and was gone.

III. The Tower

"Come on come and look quick I've got something to show you just wait till you see!"

Robin was prowling the valley with his bow, shooting at crows. Three days had passed since Marian had blazed through his life, and he hadn't caught a glimpse of her since. But now here she was near Bel's Bridge, springing from a copse of ash trees.

"Come on, quick," she said again. "You won't believe it—it's perfect and it's all ours—so much better than those woods with the toads. Somewhere they'll never find us ever ever *ever*."

He knew where she wanted him to go. He looked at the Delbosque manor, lurking there on the hillside. His memory showed him images of men-at-arms and what they had done to Narris Felstone.

Marian came closer, padding along the riverbank, barefoot. She gleamed in the sunlight: Her tunic and cape were embroidered with gold moons and stars; glass flowers clipped in her hair.

"Look, I brought you this," she said. "You proved yourself gallant and brave. This is your reward." In her outstretched palm was an object wrapped in an oiled cloth. Robin took it and unwrapped it and inside was an arrowhead, made of jade, patterns swirling through the black-green rock.

"Jade protects a person from fire," Marian said. "And from drowning, did you know that? This gift seals our friendship, now and forever. Now follow me, we're going to explore—a place even I haven't been—it's probably *full* of treasure."

She could wait no longer. She turned and ran toward the Delbosque manor.

Robin unstrung his bow and strapped it across his back. He caught up with her.

"Why do you live in the woods?" she said, as they ran. "Don't you have a family?"

Robin thought about his answer; everything he rehearsed in his head sounded wrong. Finally he said simply: "They're gone."

"I thought so," Marian said. "You and I are the same. My mother died. Father cares more about his stupid lands in Spain than he cares about me. He left again this morning, good riddance, and he took most of my enemies with him. But there are still sentries to avoid, and bandogs big as this, taller than I can jump—watch—and Mistress Bawg is always on the prowl so we have to be quick and silent, like shadows."

They climbed Lord's Hill, the manor walls looming above their heads. And nearer still—close enough to hear the flutter-snap of flags flying on the towers. Marian darted off the main path and headed east, circling the manor. They came to a section of wall that had partially collapsed. An elm tree, growing close, had reached its branches into the gap.

Marian went to the tree and began to climb. Robin told himself not to follow—this was far enough—turn around now and go back to Summerswood. But it was no good. Marian whispered for him to hurry, and then hissed, "Come on, slow goat, keep up!" and Robin found himself raising his hood and going to the tree and clambering up. Marian was waiting atop the wall, her head moving side to side, watchful as a wildcat.

"This is our only way in or out," she whispered. "But it's near the sacristy, and the coffers, so there are always guards here, no matter when. Look out for the Castellan most of all, Gerad Blunt, you'll know him from his limp, he's tough and mean."

She slipped over the side, using cracks between the stones and creeping vines to lower herself to the ground. Robin scrambled down after. He tried to concentrate on following Marian and watching for men-at-arms, but he found it difficult not to stare at his surroundings. Within its walls the manor was the size of five villages, or ten, maybe. There were ponds and lawns and walled gardens. There were evergreen bushes clipped into the shape of strange birds. He couldn't make sense of everything he saw. Standing in a courtyard was a machine, built of wood and iron, that looked like a giant catapult snare. And there were ladders on wheels that ran up into the air and led nowhere.

Marian must have seen him staring. "This is nothing, what you can see up here. Belowground it's ten times as big. There are tunnels and dungeons and a labyrinth. Together we'll explore it all, and learn its secrets."

For all its size and grandeur, the manor was far quieter than the village. So far Robin had seen only two people: a man with a long-cart, heading for the main gate; a boy raking something from a path in the distance. Neither of them appeared to notice Robin and Marian as they darted through a covered bower, across a lawn.

And then the manor became even quieter. They crossed into an area that looked completely deserted. Buildings here stood shuttered and dark. Cobbles gave way to cracked tracks, sprouting grass. The only life here was a jackdaw digging for worms in an old flower bed.

"The Lost Lands," Marian said. "It wasn't always like this. These buildings were full of people, once, when my mother was alive. She had her own maids and servants, and jongleurs and acrobats. When she died they all left. Nobody comes here now—they say it's haunted. And it is. I've seen shades and specters myself. Now, here we are, what do you think of this?" They had arrived at a tower. It had been abandoned, rubble dumped across the entranceway. Timber struts had been wedged against one wall, and it appeared to lean slightly. It looked something like a face: two arrow slits for eyes, a curved buttress for a nose.

"Look there, see," Marian said. "A murder hole, where you throw rocks and pour oil on attackers. But now it's our way in, and all these stones get us halfway up." She was standing atop the rubble and pointing to the underside of the buttress, where there was an opening.

Robin went and joined her. He crouched and she clambered onto his shoulders. After several attempts, and a few falls, she managed to haul herself up into the buttress. Her head disappeared and then her stomach and then her feet, swallowed into the darkness above.

"We did it, it worked!" her muffled voice came back down to Robin. "And it's not a murder hole at all, it's for bringing in provisions without opening the door. There's a basket and a winch, wait, here it comes."

A rusted cranking sound and an iron basket descended from the tower. Robin climbed up the chain, hand over hand, his feet against the wall. He pulled himself through the gap. Marian was grinning, her gray-green eyes bright in the gloom.

"A castle of our own! They'll never find us here, and if they do they'll get rocks on their heads. Come on, let's explore."

*

The farther they ventured through the tower, the fiercer Marian's excitement burned. The chamber on the first floor—where they had come in—had once been a storeroom, it seemed, and was full of crates and boxes and bottles. There was also a cistern, for storing water. Through a barred window sunlight glittered across cobwebs and sparkled on dust. A wooden staircase wound down into the dark. Robin took two tallow candles from his hunting pack and lit them using his strike-a-light. He handed one to Marian and her flame bobbed down into the gloom, the steps creaking faintly beneath her weight.

At ground level they found a kitchen, of sorts. There was a sink and a hearth and a big brass bath. There was a stack of seasoned firewood.

"From the outside it looks like a fortress, for soldiers," Marian said. "But inside it's more like a house, for normal people. Look, there's a cauldron for cooking, and knives and spoons. Why would they leave all this behind?"

They climbed the spiral staircase back up, and up farther, to the top story. Here was a sleeping chamber. At its center stood an open-frame bed, stacked with quilts and furs. There was a second hearth, lined with mosaic tiles. The walls were plastered white and painted with fabulous scenes. One mural showed a figure, half man half stag, being torn asunder by a pack of hounds. Another was of a boy-bird, flying toward the sun, feathers falling from his wings.

"Icarus," Marian said. "And Perseus with his winged sandals, see, and that's the gorgon's head and Theseus there with the Minotaur and Diana and Actaeon and . . ." She went from one mural to the other, pulling away cobwebs thick as wool, telling Robin what story was depicted in each. Above one of the paintings were words. When Marian saw these she fell silent, frowning.

Finally she read: " 'Flamenca's Tower.' Why does it say that? Flamenca was my mother. But she lived in the main house, with me. What does that mean? And look, these are her books, I recognize these."

She had entered a curved antechamber that connected with the main solar. Here was a writing desk beneath another barred window. And there were caskets containing clothes and trinkets and several large manuscripts, bound in wood and leather. Marian went back into the solar carrying one of the books. It was almost as big as she was. She thumped it down and heaved it open. Its gold-leaf letters shone.

As she turned the pages she grinned. "Pyramus and Thisbe. My favorite! And Orpheus and Eurydice, my *favorite* favorite!"

In her excitement she went to the bed and stripped off its quilts to reveal the leather straps beneath. She climbed onto this springy mesh and she began to jump, sending up clouds of dust.

"A castle," she was saying as she bounced. "A castle of our own and a fiefdom to rule and books full of stories! Come on, see if you can reach the ceiling—bet you can't."

Robin watched her and he thought: *I bet I could.* And he was climbing onto the bed and he was bouncing too, his fingers almost, *almost* touching the ceiling, the two of them jumping and stretching and Marian saying: "I saw that, you smiled, so you can smile, after all!"

From the solar a ladder and trapdoor led into the crown of the tower. Robin and Marian stood up there, looking out. Night had long since fallen. Elsewhere in the manor candles were being extinguished. A lone sentry stood with his lamp above the main gates. A few final prayers were being said and then silence.

They went back into the tower and crawled into their den. It had been agreed, without it being spoken, that the bed was for bouncing. They made camp instead on the floor, laying out the feather mattress and the furs. Over the top Robin had hung blankets to create a tent, not unlike his shelter in Summerswood. They lay inside on their stomachs, being careful with a storm lamp they had found in the basement, and in that cocoon of flickering light Marian opened one of her mother's books.

"First, Heracles and his labors. No, no, even better— Theseus and the Labyrinth, this is my *absolute favorite* favorite, ready . . . ?"

Marian read of Theseus and Ariadne and the Minotaur, while Robin listened, enraptured. Next she read of Jupiter and Ares and all the gods of Olympus and of the heroes forced to endure their games. Until this moment Robin had little idea what wonders existed beyond this valley, and now here those wonders were, unfolding, worlds within worlds, and he felt he was soaring above it all, looking down upon glittering golden cities and mystical mountains and magical desert realms.

Marian read deep into the night, until she was tripping over the words and her head began to make forward nods. She closed the book and extinguished the lamp. But it would be hours yet before they slept. Instead they lay on their backs and whispered in the dark, taking turns to yawn, and they were still whispering when the birds began calling in Summerswood, announcing the arrival of dawn.

IV. Robin and Marian

"Look what I found," Marian said. "Just the thing for you."
They were in the storeroom, searching through the chests and the boxes. Scattered around Marian were myriad objects: a candelabra, a brass speaking horn, a checkered game board of some kind.

Now she was holding up a hunting cloak. It was made of Turkish cloth, thick woven against the cold and the damp of the woods. It was the deep gray color of dusk. Robin shrugged out of his own ragged cloak and pulled on the new one. It slumped off his shoulders and fell farther than his feet, pooling a little on the ground.

"Perfect," Marian said. "Time to cast off your wildling disguise. It's up to me to make you civilized. Robin, look at all this treasure, and it's all ours!"

He opened a cedar chest. Inside were mantels and kerchiefs and capes, and buried at the bottom was a book—this one small and unadorned. As soon as he lifted it out Marian was at his side, taking it from his hands. She laid it open and lifted her candle. Her mouth fell open.

"What is it?" Robin said. "More stories?"

She turned the stiff, browning leaves. Here and there

Robin saw drawings: horned men, feathered women, scaled beasts. Marian licked her lips.

"It's . . . potions," she said. "It's . . . spells and charms and . . . poisons! This must have been my mother's too, she knew all about these things. Listen to this: 'Curse of the Pharaohs. A hedge-witch conjuring, possessed by the ancients. May he who is cursed suffer chill and itch and sores and mental fits, may he lose his wits, his home, his possessions, may he not walk the ground lest his feet become fire, may his humors boil and his vapors congeal . . .' It goes on that way for a whole page. Our enemies beware!"

She continued studying the grimoire, her breath misting in the candlelight. They had slept clean through the daylight hours and now the sun had set and the air was growing cold. Robin went to the basement to collect firewood and carried it to the main chamber. He used his hunting knife to whittle kindling and soon he had a blaze crackling in the hearth.

A squeaking noise caught his attention. He went to the window. A lumbering figure was approaching the tower. The squeaking noise was their lantern, swinging on its chain.

"Someone's coming!"

Marian darted up the stairs and came quickly to his side.

"It's Bawg," she whispered. "Don't make a sound."

Mistress Bawg was an enormous woman, her breasts and stomach wobbling as she walked. Her lantern squeaked on its chain. In the other hand swung a wicker basket.

"Lady Marian," she called. "I know you're in there, you may as well show yourself. No reason we shouldn't be civil. A girl like you, the way you were raised, and no more manners than a scullion. No? Very well then, if you're still intent on your little game, no harm in it I suppose, while your father's away. But be warned, Father Titus is on the warpath, it's been so

36

long since he's seen you—I hope for your sake all that Latin hasn't seeped out of that pretty little head. And understand this, once I'm sleeping there'll be no second chance—you'll get no hot bath or warm bed—you'll be on your own till morning. Very well then, I'm going, don't say I didn't try. I'll leave this here, though it's more than you deserve. There's enough for your new friend, should you feel like sharing. And now I'm going, good-bye, I'm not standing out here all night in the cold . . ." She waddled away, leaving the basket sitting on the ground.

"Leave it," Marian said. "It's a trap, trying to lure us out."

They went back into the sleeping chamber. Robin charred the end of a stick in the fire and they used it to draw games of nine-man-morris on a bare patch of wall. They turned to other games and distractions, trying to ignore the parcel. But it was impossible. Their curiosity burned. Finally Marian went to the window to keep watch while Robin crept down and retrieved the basket. Inside was a loaf of rye bread and two tubs of jam and a pot of honeyed figs. They sat by the fire and shared this nighttime breakfast.

"Bawg is still our enemy, never forget," Marian said, between mouthfuls. "No matter what bribes she brings. Anyway, we don't need her help. I know a secret way into the pantry and the kitchens. We'll feast like a king and queen, you'll see."

"And we can go to Summerswood," Robin said. "Set traps and hunt. I can show you how, if you want."

Marian wiped at her mouth with the back of her hand, smearing jam across her cheek. "Yes, that's exactly what we'll do. I want you to show me which plants are good to eat, and how to read claw prints, and all the rest of it. In return I will teach you to speak French." She sat up straight and adopted a serious expression. "You and I are the same, Robin Loxley, I knew that the moment we met. No one else cares about us, even if they pretend they do. We will survive, and prosper, but we must be quick and brave and clever."

She turned her attention once more to the grimoire. She pointed at a page. "Here's an unction called 'night owl.' The perfect thing for us. It helps you see in the dark. We need hart's tongue fern, do you know where that grows?"

Robin nodded.

"And devil's berries. What are they?"

"The fruit of deadly nightshade. There are hundreds in Hob's Hollow. I can show you tomorrow."

"Let's go now," she said, jumping up. "There's a moon to see by, look, and there are no prying eyes. Prowling time for the hobgoblins!"

She scampered from the tower and slipped out of the manor, Robin close behind. He took her to Hob's Hollow, and then to Summerswood, collecting all the ingredients for her concoction.

They looked around for what to do next. Robin pointed toward Wodenhurst and they went back up the valley and crept into the darkened village. Robin led the way to the orchards. In the moonlight the apples shone like silver coins. They went from tree to tree, plucking the fruit. They jumped at every rustling of a branch, but the villagers went on sleeping, and Marian went on grinning, and they slipped away unseen, their clothes bulging with apples and pears.

"After dark the whole world belongs to us," Marian whispered. "We will go where we like, take what we need. Now, follow me, and stick close, we are going on a long and dangerous journey."

They left the village far behind and traveled deep into the valley, following the moonlit course of Silver River—two explorers charting unknown lands, stopping now and then to crunch on fruit and to race sticks in the eddies. They discovered ancient barrows and firefly grottoes and even a forgotten lake, claiming them all as their own. And still they pushed on. A traveler's moon cast its blue light and purple shadows, showing them the way; everyone else lay oblivious in their beds; the whole of the night was theirs.

V. The Walking

This time with Marian—this grand adventure—lasted far longer than Robin expected. For weeks they roamed the valley and explored the manor, scurrying across the roofs, crawling by candlelight through the crypts and the cellars, emerging with whatever treasures they could find.

But then came the night Robin woke with a twisting emptiness in his stomach, and he knew all this had come to an end. He sat up in the dark den, listening to the moaning of the wind, knowing he was alone in the tower. All that remained of Marian was a single glass flower, lying on a pillow. He told himself he knew this would happen—he knew sooner or later she would return to that grand manor house, and to her servants and maids and cooks—yet the twisting in his stomach only grew worse.

He crawled out of the den and pulled on his boots, preparing to go back to Summerswood. But then he noticed the trapdoor was open, wind fussing around it, making it rattle. And there were other sounds, faint in the distance: shrieks and whistles and bangs; people shouting and clapping their hands.

He climbed into the crown of the tower. Night had fallen, the sky was thick with cloud, yet it was so bright out here it could almost be noon, a giant hunter's moon gilding everything in its reddish hue.

Marian was there, at the edge of the parapet. "Lazybones," she said. "Thought you were going to sleep till Doomsday. What's funny? Why are you smiling?"

Robin said nothing, only stood alongside her and looked out. From up here, on such a bright night, Winter Forest appeared to stretch away forever, lost on the very edges of sight. It was a great storm of colors: evergreens and browns and reds. Streaks of smoke and bone and old blood and rust. Even where the branches were bare it was black in its depths. It was like the ocean—the way it was described in Marian's mother's books—churning and roaring in the wind, throwing up a spray of leaves. Above it boiled a sea of cloud: its dark reflection.

Robin looked toward Wodenhurst. At its northern boundary—where village ended and wildwood began—three huge balefires burned, as they did at every full moon. The light from the fires danced across the spirit fence: a row of stakes topped with animal skulls. Along this perimeter the villagers patrolled, ringing hand bells, beating sticks against pans, blowing reed whistles, entreating the Wargwolf and all the other gods of the forest to stay in their domain.

"Summerswood and Winter Forest were joined once, did you know that?" Marian said. "And Bearwold too, in the next valley, and every other coppice and copse, all across the land—they were all part of Sherwood. My mother told me. Now Winter Forest is the only true wildwood left. Sometimes it spreads overnight, trying to reclaim what it lost, and it swallows villages whole. One day Sherwood will circle the whole world, the way it once did. What do you think of that?"

Robin didn't answer. Movement deep in the wildwood had caught his eye. Movement that seemed to have nothing to do with the wind . . .

It was a rippling line, distant at first, but zigzagging closer. Robin watched the tips of the trees shudder. Hot needles were stabbing at the back of his neck. His heart raced. The dread wave was heading for the forest edge, snaking ever closer to Wodenhurst . . .

Thankfully the clouds were spreading thicker and were beginning to defeat the moonlight, the valley fading to black. Robin lost track of the movement through the trees.

He became aware that Marian was watching him intently.

"What happened to your parents?" she said. "Are they dead?"

He shook his head.

"Where are they then?"

He didn't answer. He stared at the phantom flickering of the balefires.

"Are they coming back?" Marian said.

He nodded. Marian pinched her lower lip. "And when they do . . . ," she said, "what will happen then? Where will you live?"

He looked at her. "With them, of course. With my parents and Thane and Hal. In our house, at the top of Herne Hill."

Marian turned her back and went farther along the parapet. In Summerswood two owls hoo-hooed back and forth.

After a while, Robin said: "You can come too. Come and live with us, in our house."

Marian turned and glowered. "To grub in the dirt with the swineherds? I'd rather be dead. I'll stay right here and I'll be glad, a castle of my own, and if you ever try to come back, you'll get rocks on your head, and if you're going, why don't you go now then, leave and never come back, I'll be fine on my own."

She fell quiet, and she was scowling, and Robin found himself growing angry.

"Anyway, why do you care?" he said. "Soon you'll go running to Mistress Bawg and your servants and cooks."

"I won't!"

"That's what you said before. You said you wouldn't go back but you did."

"That was different. A duchess—which is practically a princess—cannot very well live in the woods, with the toads. Now we have a home of our own. Mother hated that house and everyone in it and so do I and I'm never going back there, no matter what, even if—" She fell silent and looked up, blinking. She held out both her palms. "Robin, I think . . . Yes, look, it's snowing!"

She came back to him. She opened one side of his cloak and burrowed inside. The snow drifted, then swirled, then pelted them in great gusting waves. Marian squealed and darted for shelter, and the pair of them scrambled through the trapdoor, pulling it closed.

Robin stoked the fire and they sat near it, wrapped in blankets. Marian's scowl had disappeared and she was grinning as they listened to the snowstorm howl outside. Very faintly now they could hear the villagers, still patrolling at the forest edge.

"It won't make any difference, will it?" Marian said. "They'll keep at it, until first light?"

Robin nodded.

"I wouldn't like to be them," Marian said.

Robin fed the fire and the flames crackled. The timbers of the tower creaked and groaned, stretching themselves between the stones, the way they always did when it was cold outside and warm within.

Marian sat up straight and turned to him. "If you don't go back to the village," she said, "I won't go back to the house. Agreed?"

Robin looked at her and nodded.

"That means," she said, "if I never leave you, you'll never leave me. Promise?"

He nodded again. And what happened next came as a shock to them both. Before he realized he was doing it, without even really meaning to, Robin found he was leaning across and quickly kissing Marian on the cheek.

She shrieked and twisted away. "No, no, no! You must *never* touch another person with your lips. It brings down the worst of all possible luck. My mother told me that. You have to kiss properly, like this." She put two fingers to her lips, then placed the same fingers to Robin's forehead, between his eyes. "Now you . . . Robin, I said 'now you.'"

Robin's face was burning and he couldn't meet her gaze. He put two fingers to his lips and hurriedly brushed them across her brow.

"Better," Marian said, before going to the window and looking out. "It's getting even thicker! It's going to settle ten feet deep. I remember once, when Mother was alive, nobody could leave the grounds for weeks, and everyone was out in the gardens, even Father, and we built lords and ladies and snow angels and we skated on the ponds and . . . you'll see . . . just as soon as this wind stops we'll begin . . ."

For two whole days the blizzard raged. They were confined to the tower, playing endless games of nine-man-morris, Marian hopping around, seething with impatience.

Finally the wind eased. The third night lay still and crisp. They tumbled from the tower and clomped about the Lost Lands. Beneath cold clear stars they built a knight out of snow. A birch branch served as his lance. His greathelm was a cooking pot.

"Follow me," Marian said. "We'll look in the old forge for armor, and then we'll—"

44

She shrieked. Robin saw the night move, and he heard the *crump-crump* of boots, and he heard Marian shout, "Robin!" and he began to run, but two huge shapes shifted in the starlight and descended on him from either side, clamping him tight around the chest and throat. Robin kicked and twisted in the grip. A heavy gloved fist hit him on the back of the head. Robin kicked more furiously. The man thumped him again, harder, and Robin felt dizzy.

"Plenty more where that came from," said the man on his right-hand side. "I should be indoors, with a mug of spiced wine and something to warm my bed. Instead, I'm out here in the snow. Here, have one for free." He hit Robin a third time and the world blurred, water welling in his eyes.

The guards dragged him into a courtyard. There were more men-at-arms there, standing beneath a hanging lamp, and two of them had hold of Marian, a hand clamped across her mouth.

"Midwinter always makes me think of Daneland," a gray-haired guard was saying. "Remember that, Hawkman? Five years ago, was it, six? A blizzard so thick you couldn't see your hand in front of your face."

"And more barbarians than there were snowflakes," another man said, scratching at his bulbous stomach. "I'll never know how we made it home from that one."

"And now look, here we are, chasing after children. What happened to us?"

"You got old, and I got fat. Just be glad we're still good for something."

The guards fell quiet. Another figure was approaching. He had difficulty dragging his lame leg through the snow, but even so this newcomer seemed more fearsome to Robin than all the other men-at-arms put together. When he pushed back his hood his face in the lamplight was lined and hard, his big square jaw crisscrossed with scars. Here was Gerad Blunt, the Castellan.

"What now?" said the one who had hit Robin. "Do we really dangle this one down the well?"

"I'm going to presume she was joking," said the Castellan.

"She'll let us know. She's on her way over."

Soon Mistress Bawg came into sight, plowing through the snow, her lantern jerking from side to side. She came close to Marian, reached down, pinched her arm, then her stomach, then her leg, while Marian writhed and made muffled noises beneath the guard's hand.

"There never was enough flesh on your bones," Mistress Bawg said, pinching again, and twisting. "But you're not starving, and there's color in your cheeks, that's something. I swore to anyone who would listen this weather would drive you home—we only need wait once winter came. Should have known better, of course, once you get an idea in your head. But you're keeping warm, I've seen the woodsmoke from that tower, and yes, I suppose you look healthy enough. Very well then, thank you, Harold, Cuth, you can let her go."

The men-at-arms released their grip and Marian sprang free and began shouting. "That house is not my home, and you are not my mother no matter how much you want to be— my mother was young and beautiful and you're ugly and mean and you'll never—" She fell quiet, looking around her at the men-at-arms. She pouted. "What do you mean, 'let her go'?"

"What were you expecting?" Mistress Bawg said. "Should I drag you back to the house, kicking and screaming, force you into a hot bath and clean clothes, bring a feast to your room while you insult me and call me names? Should we carry on that way until next you manage to escape, then start all over again? Well, no thank you, I've had enough of that. I won't spend my life chasing after you, and these men have better things to do. So go on, get on your way, you're free. I'll bring you a basket from time to time, but that's all. Until your father gets back, you're on your own."

Marian stood there, scowling. She narrowed her eyes. She pointed at Robin. "What about him?"

Mistress Bawg crossed her arms. "Yes, what to do about this one . . . what to do with Robin Loxley? Don't look so surprised, child, of course I know who you are. That village isn't so far away. Lucky for you I don't believe the half of what I hear or else . . . well, suffice to say we're civilized people this side of the river." She moved close to Robin, dropped her voice to a whisper. "But you had best listen to me closely, Master Loxley, for the sake of your own hide. We each of us, in this world, have a part to play, and a path to tread. All too soon, before we know it—"

"Whatever she's saying, it's all lies," Marian said. "Don't trust a word." She was circling closer, trying to get within earshot while maintaining a safe distance.

"When Marian's father returns . . . ," Mistress Bawg continued whispering to Robin, "whether that be in a month, or a year, or five, she will embark on a path where you cannot possibly follow. The wisest thing you can do is get over that wall, this instant, leave this place and . . . I see, I'm too late, aren't I? You're not even looking at me, you're looking at her. I'm wasting my breath."

She rubbed at her face with her knuckles. "Well, in any case, at least it's been said, and now you can't say you weren't warned. So then, Master Loxley, since you're here and you're clearly staying, you can make yourself useful. I mean what I say: I'm finished playing her games. But it's more than all our lives are worth if she doesn't stay safe and well. And like it or not she's my responsibility."

She glanced again at Marian, circling closer, before turning

47

back to Robin. "So here's what we'll do: I'm going to pass that responsibility to you. That's quite a thing to ask of a boy. I know plenty of grown men who wouldn't be up to it. But I think you're older than you look, in a manner of speaking, and I sleep better at night, in fact, knowing you're by her side. So I want you to be brave, and guard her from harm. That means saving her from herself, more than anything—she can be her own worst enemy. Do you think you can do that for her? Can you promise to be Marian's champion?"

Robin looked at Marian. He nodded.

"Fine. Go on then, the pair of you, disappear. Keep out of mischief, as much as you can manage, and stay this side of the river, I don't want you getting mixed up with . . ." Her words were becoming difficult to hear because the guards had loosened their grip and Robin and Marian were already bounding away through the snow.

Mistress Bawg was as good as her word. Whole weeks passed, and then months, and Robin and Marian were left alone.

"She's admitted defeat," Marian said. "This is our home. Our enemies know we will defend it to the death."

This is our home.

Marian said things like that often. Yet still there were times, as that first winter gave way to spring, when Robin was sure she would abandon the tower and go back to the comfort of her old life. There was the night she stumbled and burned her arm in their fire, and she swore and ranted at Robin as if it were entirely his fault. But Robin made a soothing balm from primrose petals, the way his father had taught him, and he treated Marian's wound and soon she was placated.

On another occasion their tower became infested with wasps and they both suffered several stings. Robin put damp wood shavings on their fire and wafted billows of smoke into the rafters, driving the insects away. Each little crisis they met one way or another.

Spring turned to summer; they went to Silver River for midnight swims. Summer gave way to autumn; they foraged for fruits and berries and staged grand woodland banquets. And still they were left alone, to follow this life of their own devising, rulers of their own nocturnal world.

One night Robin woke with a sickly, panicked feeling, as if he had forgotten something of utmost importance. Finally he understood: He had not thought of his family for days. They were no longer his first thought on waking, nor his final thought before he slept.

He closed his eyes and summoned a memory of his brothers, teaching him to swim at Mill Pond. He started to do this every night: He would bring to mind the sound of his father's laugh, or silently recite the words to one of his mother's songs. He would never allow himself to forget, no matter how long they were gone.

But it was increasingly difficult to *remember* to remember: His life with Marian was a constant whirl of challenge and adventure, of stories and dares and quests; not to mention the vital work of keeping themselves warm and fed. No wonder his old life, at the top of Herne Hill, was beginning to fade, just a little.

This is our home.

Slowly Robin came to believe it was true. The tower *was* home. And as the seasons turned, this life with Marian—this feral existence roaming the valley and the manor—there were times when this felt like the only life he had ever known.

Part Two

Summer's End

Four Years Later

I. Forever Days

Robin climbed the slope to take another turn on the rope swing. Below him Titan's Lake gleamed golden in the late-summer sun. He took hold of the rope, stood as far back as he was able, the branch creaking high above.

He swung out over the water, let go, came splashing down in a tangle of limbs. Marian laughed, and when he got back to the bank she was still laughing.

"You're all arms and legs," she said. "Look, like this, watch me." She climbed to the rope, swung over the lake, turned gracefully in the air, arrowed into the water like a diving kingfisher. She swam back to the bank and stood in the shallows, wringing her hair. "See," she said. "Easy."

Robin climbed the slope once more, swung out, came down on his back, with an even bigger splash. He went again and again to the swing, trying now to make each landing worse than the last, playing up to it while Marian laughed.

"I wasn't born for the water," he said, standing waist deep. "Not like you. You're half fish."

"Take that back!" Marian rushed into the lake, swept a wave over Robin's head. He was making fish faces with his lips. She charged at him, splashing wave after wave.

"Truce!" Robin said. "You're not half fish."

"Well, you're all toad."

They clambered out of the lake and flopped down on the bank, the last of their energy used, too hot now to move. Never had they known a summer this hot. Week after week the valley had scorched beneath a molten sun. It was too stifling to sleep indoors—during the day even their tower became like an oven—so temporarily they had given up their nocturnal ways and they spent most of their time here, at Titan's Lake, dozing in the dappled shade, stirring now and then to engage in a flurry of games, cooling off in the water and stretching out again to doze.

Robin looked at Marian, twisting lazily to get comfortable, catlike. Gold coins of sunlight dripped through the leaves and lay across her neck and her shoulders. She was wearing only a thin shift, which with the water had turned almost transparent.

She caught him staring and he looked away, heat rising to his face. He glanced at her again and now she was watching him, smiling slightly, pillowing her head on her hands.

"What?" Robin said.

"Nothing."

She rolled over on her back, closed her eyes, still smiling. Robin looked across the lake. Above its surface a layer of gnats shone in the sun's rays: It looked like a second, enchanted lake, shimmering above its twin. On the far bank, ponies stood in the deep shade, flicking their manes. He lay out flat and watched the light sparkling emerald through the leaves. This was a moment he would remember for the rest of his life: the feeling of warm breeze across wet skin; the sound of crickets in the long grass, and the skylarks high above.

He must have dozed off because when he opened his eyes Marian was at his side, on her stomach, propped on her elbows, her face close to his.

"Do you ever wish . . . ," she said, "you could pick one day to last forever? Did I tell you what my mother used to say about Winter Forest? She said sometimes it spreads overnight and swallows villages whole. The people are all in there somewhere, in the wildwood, still collecting water from the well, digging in their crofts, children playing snitch—they live the exact same day, over and over. Well, I was thinking, does that sound so bad? I might even be glad, if that happened to us. Imagine if it was today we lived, again and again. What would you . . . ? Robin, you're not even listening! What are you thinking about? What could be more important than listening to me?"

Movement across the lake had caught Robin's eye. The ponies had raised their heads, all at once, their ears flicking up. One made a sudden movement that startled the others.

"What's up with them?" Marian said.

Finally they heard what had unnerved the ponies: a creaking, rolling rattle. A wheeled vehicle, moving through Summerswood, passing close to the lake.

Marian sat up straight, mischief already glinting in her eyes.

"Let's go and see," she said. "Could be easy pickings."

They pulled on their clothing and Robin collected his shortbow and hunting pack and Marian hoisted her knapsack and they ran up the bank and crept along a high ridge, scanning the ground below.

There, moving through a tunnel of trees, rocking violently on the woodland road, was a two-wheeled litter. The driver was Hadden Sloop, a stableboy from the manor, and riding in the litter was a plump old man and a skinny youth: Father Titus and Elias Long. Marian took one look at this and she licked her lips. She turned to Robin and they both smiled and nodded.

"Not like those two to venture so far from home," Robin said.

"And all alone," Marian said. "Not a single guardsman. How they'll come to regret that. Stay out of sight. I'll whistle when I'm in position."

She pulled from her knapsack two glass phials, each containing a brown powder: a mixture of crushed pepper and rosehip seeds and various other irritants. She scampered away, and a few moments later Robin heard a whistle. He took from his hunting pack the speaking horn they had found years before. He put the horn to his lips and he spoke through it and his voice boomed.

"Hold your horses, if you value your lives."

Hadden Sloop tugged at the reins in surprise; the litter came to a shuddering halt.

"We have you surrounded," Robin said. "Lay down your blades . . . if . . . if you carry blades."

"Who's there?" Father Titus shouted, standing. "Show yourselves!"

"Mercy . . . Mercy on our souls," said Elias Long. "I told you, Father, didn't I say . . . there are bandits in these woods. The same ones what robbed old man Jones."

"Bandits, here? How dare they!" Father Titus shouted. "How dare you molest us, here? These are Guido Delbosque's lands. He'll have you hanged, drawn and quartered. Where are you going, boy? Get back here!"

At the mention of bandits, Hadden Sloop had sprung down from the driver's perch and now he was sprinting away into the woods.

"Give up your gold," Robin said, trying not to laugh, "and we will spare your skins."

As he spoke, he watched Marian crawling along a branch directly above the litter. She unstopped her phials and Robin watched the powder filter through a sunbeam before clouding around Father Titus and Elias Long. The priest and his acolyte coughed and sneezed and rubbed at their eyes.

"What's happening?" wailed Elias Long, gripping the priest's arm. "I'm blind!"

"Outrage!" bellowed Father Titus. "You will pay for this violation, in this world and the next. Unhand me, Elias, comport yourself!"

While the horses fussed and the two travelers wept and cursed, Robin and Marian crept close to the litter. With his hunting knife Robin sliced the cord of the purse that hung at the priest's waist. Marian darted in and grabbed a sack that lay at Elias Long's feet.

"Lord Delbosque will hear of this," Father Titus continued to splutter. "He will hunt you down like dogs. He will have you torn limb from limb, he will—"

"No more talk of Guido Delbosque," Robin said, through the speaking horn. "Everyone knows his ship sank, and he was drowned. These woods belong to us now."

"What . . . what do they mean?" said Elias Long, weeping. "But . . . but this whole thing . . . the reason we're leaving . . . only this morning, the message you received—"

Father Titus jabbed his companion with his elbow. "Quiet, Elias, we will not speak with these ruffians. They are lower than beasts. They will be apprehended, and they will be punished."

Marian was watching Elias Long quizzically now. She came to Robin and whispered in his ear. Robin lifted the speaking horn to his lips.

"Elias . . . I mean, you, the younger one, what were you going to say? Tell us about the message."

"Tell them nothing!" Father Titus shouted. "They will writhe in Hell for this sacrilege, this assault on God's loyal—"

"Tell us!" Marian shouted. "Tell us what you meant this

instant, or—" She clapped a hand to her mouth. She looked at Robin.

"Lady Marian?" Father Titus said, squinting, his eyes streaming. "Lady Marian, is that you? What in God's name—"

Marian picked up a willow switch and used it to whip the rumps of the horses. The animals bucked and pulled and the litter lurched away, the priest and his acolyte bouncing along in their seats, wailing and coughing and cursing.

"Now you've done it," Robin said. "Wait till this gets back to Bawg."

Marian frowned, staring after the dwindling litter. "I don't think we need worry about that," she said. "I don't think we'll ever see Father Titus again."

"What do you mean?"

"You heard what Elias said: 'The reason we're leaving.' And you saw the amount of stuff they were carrying. I think they were going for good. Where would they go? And what did they mean about Father?"

"You don't think . . . ?" Robin said. "He can't be . . . ?"

Marian said nothing, only frowned in thought. Robin watched her and got a horrible feeling in his stomach. It couldn't be true, could it? Marian's father had been gone almost four years. At one time they had heard many rumors of his imminent return, but they always turned out to be false. And in recent times the rumors had all been of a different kind: Lord Delbosque had drowned at sea, or he had died of plague, or been poisoned by one of his debtors.

"It's probably nothing," Marian said, turning to Robin. "If Father was coming back, why would that make Father Titus leave? He's lived at that house forever, he married Mother and Father, and he baptized me. He's part of the stonework. No, if he's leaving that only proves one thing: Father is dead and buried. Forget it. Let's count our loot."

Robin opened Father Titus's purse and tipped it toward the ground. Two clipped shillings fell out, together with a glass bead and five acorns.

"Next to worthless," Marian said. "A dummy purse. He must keep his real one tucked away in his folds. And this lot isn't much better." The sack she had stolen contained a priest's alb and a few other clothes, along with a small Psalter and a liturgical bell. "A few things we can sell, I suppose," she said. "But at this rate it will take us a hundred years to earn our passage. We'll have to do better next time."

As they made their way home, through the lengthening shadows, Marian said: "Even if Father Titus does go back to the house, do you think he would ever tell Bawg and Blunt what really happened? Robbed by the two of us! He'd tell the whole world it was bandits, a giant horde of them, armed and desperate! I almost hope he does return so we can hear him tell the story."

Robin laughed at this, but it was hollow laughter, because he couldn't stop thinking now about Marian's father—what if he was still alive, and planning to return? What would that mean to this life of theirs? Would it spell the end of everything?

II. The Return

He didn't have to wait long to find out. The very next day, at dusk, they were walking home from Titan's Lake when they again heard rolling, rattling sounds. This time the noise was farther away, yet deeper—this was not a solitary litter.

Their eyes met, briefly, then looked away. Without a word they ran through Summerswood. By the time they reached Chiron's Rise and gained a clear view up the valley, there was a cloud of dust approaching the Delbosque manor. Emerging out of the dust were horsemen wearing blue tabards, and following them was a covered carriage, painted red and gold. Above it flew a blazon bearing the crest of the double crow.

At first Marian stood motionless, glaring at the carriage. Then she groaned and slumped to the ground and hugged her knees. She looked at Robin, then put her face in her hands.

Robin watched the lord's retinue snaking into the valley. Following the carriage were packhorses pulling wagons and litters. Servants walked alongside or trailed behind.

After a while, he said: "Maybe it won't make any difference. Bawg left us alone in the end, didn't she? Maybe he will too. We'll stay out of his way and everything will carry on just the same."

Marian made no reply. He sat next to her and they stayed there, in silence, watching more men-at-arms and carts appear at the head of the valley. They sat there while the sky darkened and the gnats came out in force, bobbing their dance of dusk.

Marian sat up straight, took a long breath. "So then, that's that," she said. "We're leaving."

"What?"

"You don't know what he's like, Robin. He's cruel and vindictive. He'll try to keep us apart, at the very least. If he's staying, we're leaving."

"But . . . to go where?"

She looked at him. "Everywhere. Isn't that what we've always said—how one day we'll go to all the places in the stories, Troy and Rome and Carthage? How we'll sail the five seas, and find the World Tree, and all the rest of it. How troubadours will sing tales about us, about our travels and our victories."

"Yes . . . 'one day,'" Robin said. "But . . . right now . . . just like that? You said yourself we'll need money, to pay for passage."

"We'll have to manage. You're skilled, I'm clever, together we'll get by. He hasn't left us a choice."

Robin looked toward Wodenhurst. "I . . . I can't just go," he said. "What about my family? What if they come back?"

Marian snorted. "I'm not even listening to that. They're not coming back. You've known that for a long time, you just don't want to admit it. There's only you and me, the way it's always been, and we will do what needs to be done." She stood and ran toward the manor.

"Where are you going?" Robin said, running to keep up.

"To the tower, of course. We can't leave empty-handed. We'll need cured meat for the road and spare clothing, and we'll take a few things to trade or sell. We'll pack light, travel fast, but at the very least we'll need—"

She stopped and stared. She pointed. Something was happening, down there on Packman's Furrow. One of the wagons had cracked an axle on the sun-baked road, had toppled into a ditch, sending trunks and chests tumbling, spilling their contents. And it was those contents that made Marian and Robin stare: countless tiny things, glittering in the dusk.

"Are those coins?" Robin said.

"Whole cartloads of them, by the looks of it. And those bigger objects, silver and brass plate, see? Wherever he's been, he's brought back a king's ransom."

They ran on, darting up the blind side of Lord's Hill, out of sight of the retinue. They reached their elm tree and climbed up onto the crumbled battlement. The normally hushed manor was busy and loud, wagons and carts being unloaded. The thump of trunks and baskets and the rumble of barrels and people shouting, all of it echoing off the curtain walls. Hanging lamps were being lit as the twilight faded.

Most of the activity clustered around the Great Ward. For now their path to the tower looked clear. Marian moved forward, about to break cover. Robin touched her arm—she froze. A postern gate had slammed open and there was movement in the shadows.

"Believe me, he's going to do it," a voice said below. "Tonight, maybe. But soon, for sure. None of them are biting."

Another man coughed, cleared his throat. "He won't. He wouldn't go that far. He's bluffing."

"I'm telling you. You weren't with him. You've never seen a man so desperate. Or so frightened."

Robin peered through the branches. Two men were walking past at the foot of the wall. One had a heavy limp and was built like an aurochs: Gerad Blunt, the Castellan. The second

64

voice belonged to a smaller man, with sandy brown hair, who Robin couldn't name.

"What, you think he'll stand up to him on his own?" said the unknown man. "The crow facing down the wolf? Remind me to be far away from here if it comes to that."

"No argument, he's in a corner," said the Castellan. "But even Delbosque wouldn't . . . his own daughter . . ."

"I'm telling you . . . know what they say . . . the winter-born . . ."

"Those damned words, makes no difference . . ."

"Will be worse . . . what's more . . ."

"Refuse . . ."

" 'Course you will . . ."

The words became harder to hear as the speakers moved away. A door slammed and the two men disappeared into a guard tower.

Robin's heart sounded loud in his ears. A sickly feeling churning in his stomach. Something he had heard . . . a phrase one of the men had used . . . he could barely even hear them and yet . . . something dark had stirred in his memory . . .

"Come on," Marian said. "They're gone."

"Wait, Marian, I—"

But she had already slipped over the side of the wall, was scampering to the ground. Robin followed. She drew ahead, moving in a half crouch, running a wide arc around the iron-studded doors of the sacristy. She turned left past the bakehouse. For a moment Robin lost her from view and so he didn't see it happen.

He only heard a screech and a scream, and then shouting.

"Leggo geddoff lemeego!"

Robin ran. He leaped up onto a hay trough and from there up onto the roof of the bakehouse. He looked down and saw what was happening. It was Mistress Bawg. Over the years she had grown steadily more massive, and now she was a mountain of flesh. In one hand she held a drinking bladder; in the other she gripped Marian, twisting her arm behind her back, hauling her away across the East Ward.

"Now, now, Lady Marian, quiet down," Mistress Bawg was saying as Marian howled. "You've had a good run. You could hardly go on living that wild life forever. You knew this day would come, sooner or later. We each have our path to tread, no good wishing different. Where's that shadow of yours, then? If he's got any sense, he's made himself scarce."

On the roof of the bakehouse, Robin had taken his bow from his back and looped the string into place. He removed an arrow from the quiver at his hip.

Marian was yowling; Mistress Bawg still twisting her arm.

"Come now, Lady Marian, there's no use kicking. Change is coming for all of us, and we don't have to like it. My goodness, look at you—I've barely seen you to notice—growing up already. I hope for all our sake—"

Mistress Bawg screamed, throwing up both her arms.

Without giving it a second thought, in one fluid motion, Robin had nocked the arrow, drawn, sent the shot flying toward Mistress Bawg. The arrow struck its target dead center—impaling the drinking bladder. A loud pop and liquid bursting out, splashing across Mistress Bawg's legs. She dropped the bladder and let go of Marian in the same shocked motion.

Marian ran and Robin jumped down and went with her, the sound of Mistress Bawg wailing behind. They fled though the manor, taking less care than usual with their route, passing too near the sacristy—disturbing a bandog, the animal snarling very close, its chain rattling before pulling taut. Running on, escaping into their darkened corner of the grounds and clambering into their tower and pulling up the chain ladder and sprawling breathless on their backs.

Marian was rubbing her arm, where Mistress Bawg had twisted it. She made quivering sounds, and Robin thought she was crying. But then he realized she was laughing. Her laughter grew louder. Robin smiled, and then he was laughing too.

"The look on Bawg's face!"

"Our best escape ever!"

That was all either of them said, because what little breath they had left they were using to laugh.

III. Invaders

Dressed in gray and black, their hoods raised, they crept out of the Lost Lands and into the main manor. They skirted a pool of light cast by a hanging lamp, then dashed across a well-lit courtyard.

Robin glanced up. He counted four—five—sentries already patrolling the battlements, their spear tips glinting in the moonlight. "Are you sure this is a good idea?"

"We need to know what's going on," Marian whispered back. "Look, there goes another wagon. Are they all loaded with coin? Where did it all come from? They're headed for the coach house. Maybe we'll find answers there."

A noise—just in front and overhead. Robin ducked behind a fire barrel, taking Marian's arm, pulling her alongside. They held their breath against the stagnant standing water and they listened to the creaking sound.

It was a sentry, crossing a wooden gantry. They waited for the man to move away, his lamplight swinging on its pole and chain. They stood and continued past the small mead hall. From inside they heard a barked word and a door thump and something smashing against stone. In the distance Robin thought he heard somebody crying.

"Why is everyone so frantic? And so . . . angry?"

"Something strange is going on," Marian whispered. "Some of the guards haven't even unsaddled their horses, look. Maybe he's not staying. Perhaps he's only passing through. Either way, we need to know. Come on."

They crept into a covered bower. They took cover amid the foliage and peered toward the coach house. Two guards stood near its entrance, but their backs were turned, their heads bowed. And now a third man was coming to join them, glancing over his shoulder. The three men stood whispering before moving away together.

Robin and Marian slipped out of the bower and across to the coach house. Another pause to check for danger. Then inside. Almost complete darkness. Robin took two candles from his hunting pack and he lit them both and he gave one to Marian.

They moved around and cast their light and looked in wonder. The barrel-vaulted coach house held three carriages and several long-carts and one big dray, several of them still stacked with chests and strongboxes. Some of these were bound in iron and locked, but others they could heave open. When they did the contents gleamed, and Marian gasped.

"Look at it all," she whispered. "There's gold and jewels and gems and . . . It's a dragon's hoard! And here, look, furs and tapestries and satin and silk . . ."

Robin picked out something made of silver and gold, fashioned into the shape of a hand. And here was another glittering ornament, in the form of a human head. Part of the skull was made of glass, and through this window he could see a lump of something grayish, like very old bread. Why make such an exquisite case and keep something worthless inside?

"That's a real chunk of brain in there," Marian whispered, coming to his side. "And the other one holds finger bones—

pieces of dead saints. These are powerful relics, and worth a fortune. But they're too bulky to take with us. Look for coins."

Robin put the hand and the head reliquaries back in the chest and shut the lid.

"Has he sold something?" Marian said. "You could buy a whole kingdom in exchange for what . . . Quick, look at this."

She had lifted the lid of another chest. Robin climbed up alongside. A dull gleam and the smell of iron. He moved his candle closer. The chest was stacked with spears. The shafts were as thick as Robin's arm; the blades when he touched them were wickedly sharp.

Elsewhere they found hauberks and bucklers and another stack of spears.

"Far too many weapons for his men-at-arms," Marian whispered. "It's like he's equipping an army. Why would he need—"

A noise at the entrance to the coach house.

Without a word, in unison, they extinguished their lights. Another flame was moving in their direction, between the carriages.

"Who's there?" a voice said. "What's happening here?"

The lantern moved farther into the coach house. Footsteps. The clink of keys against a belt.

"Show yourself. Who is it?"

But Robin and Marian had already gone: They had slipped silently to the wall and crept around the guard in the dark and vanished into the night.

"Pssst, Burram, it's me, over here."

Burram Fletch froze, cocking his head. He lifted his lantern and peered along the battlements. A soft hiss where he drew his sword.

"Who-who's there? I-i-i-identify yourself. G-George, is that you? Identify yourself or—"

Marian hissed again: "It's. Me. Over. Here."

Burram Fletch crept toward where Marian and Robin were hiding, in the shadow of a guard tower.

"L-L-Lady Marian? Wh-what are you doing? You shouldn't be up here. If B-B-B-Blunt catches you, at a time like this . . ."

Burram came fully into view, his lantern shaking slightly on its chain. He was by far the youngest of the men-at-arms, no more than eighteen years old, and he always had a nervous manner, especially when talking to Marian. But tonight he looked more anxious than ever.

"You sh-sh-shouldn't be creeping around, n-n-not on a night like this," he whispered, before pointing at Robin. "As f-for him, I ought to s-s-sling him off this wall myself."

"We only want to know what's going on," Marian said. "We just saw Cuth Forrester and Harold Stint and they could hardly stand up they're so drunk. Why is everyone acting so strange, and seem so desperate? I told myself: 'If there's one person who'll know, it's Burram Fletch.'"

Burram stood taller, puffed out his chest. His lantern tipped toward them.

"It's th-th-th . . . ," he stammered. "It's th-th . . . it's the Sheriff."

Marian took a sharp, audible breath. A gust of wind whispered along the wall.

"What do you mean?" Marian said. "What about him?"

"He-he-he's coming. Here. In person."

"Why?"

"W-w-well, as to that, I-I-I'm not certain. All I know is, your father looked for help. He w-w-w-went to all of them: Durrell, de Roye, every h-house he counts as a friend. He offered a fortune, but they all said no, e-e-every one, and so we're on our own, and I'm not scared, you understand, I'm r-r-ready, come what may, but s-some of the others, they . . ."

"He's here," Robin said.

Burram stared at him.

"The Sheriff," Robin said, pointing. "He's coming up Lord's Hill."

Burram dropped his sword and it clattered off the battlements—he spun to look and his lantern cracked against stone. "Wh-wh-where? I-I don't see anything! Wh-wh-wh-where?" Finally he turned back and looked at Robin and gritted his teeth. "S-s-silly boy. I ought to drop you off this wall . . . do-do-don't let me find you here when I get back." He took his cracked lantern and disappeared down the staircase, looking for his sword.

Marian glared at Robin. "You wouldn't joke if you knew about the Sheriff." She walked off along the battlements.

"What do you know about him?" Robin said. "Have you met him?"

"Not met, exactly, not face to face. But I remember his visits well enough, although I was young. He used to come here often, when Mother was alive. She was terrified of him—she used to hide me in the cellar until he'd gone away. And then afterward—this is what I remember most of all—afterward I wouldn't see Mother for days. She'd lock herself in her chambers, refusing to see a soul, not even me, and Father too was at his worst during those times. I never even saw the Sheriff, in the flesh, but just thinking about him makes me feel all cold inside."

She fell quiet. Robin watched his feet. They were making their way along the curtain wall, circling close to the main house. The night was growing darker, the moonlight dimmed. Robin looked out toward Winter Forest. Black swaths of cloud were bunching there, a storm gathering, the heat of the summer about to break at last.

Marian stopped and put her hand on Robin's shoulder. "Listen," she said. "Hear that shouting? That's Father's voice. From behind the house, I think. He's furious about something. Time we learned what all this is about."

They wound their way down from the battlements. They crept across the Great Ward and reached the main house. One wall was thick with creeping vines. They used these to climb, Marian scampering up first and fastest, Robin following behind. They clambered up the steep roof. Some of the slate tiles were loose, there was a thirty-foot drop, but they were well practiced at this and soon they were scuttling and sliding down the opposite slope, and dangling and dropping onto the family chapel. Here they stopped and listened. The argument was louder now, although the words were still difficult to hear.

"My father's father . . . served this house five generations . . . some orders I can stomach easier than others . . ."

They wriggled closer.

"Ready to ride away, tonight, and take their chances."

"Then you've got to stop them! That's your task. That's what you're for!"

They reached the edge of the roof and peered over. There, in a lamplit cloister, was Gerad Blunt, the Castellan. And with him, pacing up and down, was Guido Delbosque, Marian's father. In Robin's imagination this powerful lord was a towering, gleaming figure, matching the bronze statue of him that stood in the West Ward. The real man Robin now saw was far less impressive. He was a head shorter than the Castellan, and his face in the lamplight was red as a berry, ripe to burst. His hair was slicked back and the oil had run, leaving a glistening trail on his neck.

Lord Delbosque stopped pacing and lifted a shaking finger. "You've got to stop them!" he said again. "Scuttling away like rats. Cowards!"

At the word *cowards* the Castellan pulled himself up to his full height, loomed there in the half-light like a bear. Lord Delbosque stopped pointing.

"Those men you're talking of . . . ," the Castellan said. "Some of them have served with me two-score years. And we haven't always stood watchdog at your gates. Together we've fought Franks in the northern forests, dug Picts out of their mountain fasts. We've marched through Baltic blizzards, Vandals snapping at our heels. I will tell you this: Not one of those men is a coward."

Lord Delbosque started spluttering a reply. The Castellan raised a hand, cut him short.

"It's simple enough, as far as I can see. You have left yourself just two options, each as ignoble as the other. Come to me when you've made your decision. I will see it done, for our fathers' sake. But there the chain is broken. I will never take an order from you again." The Castellan turned, dragging his lame leg; he clomped from the cloister and was gone.

Lord Delbosque pushed one fist to his forehead. "Craven. They jump at every shadow, fearing it's him. Do they think I'm made of the same soft stuff? I'll show them. The Delbosque element is fire, and I intend to prove it."

At first Robin thought the earl was talking to himself, but then he noticed there was a third man in the cloister. He moved into the light, his cane clicking on the cobbles. A stooped, silver-haired figure whom Robin didn't recognize.

"The Castellan was wrong," the old man said. "There is a third option. There is Sir Bors."

"Never."

"But, sire, at least consider. He could be here in three weeks. Four at most. If we can only hold our nerve until then. In his letter he mentioned them both. He said the boy too is—"

74

"Never! I don't care what Sir Bors wants. I don't care about their damned war. What is the boy to me? I'll send him his head in a sack! But if he ever again mentions my daughter . . ."

Marian stiffened at Robin's side. She tugged at his cloak. He slid with her away from the edge of the roof. Below them the conversation had paused, and when the earl spoke again it was so quiet Robin could barely hear.

"How could she allow it? Was she unaware?"

The old man made some answer that was unclear.

"And what of the boy, should it come to that?" Again, the reply was too soft to hear.

"Leave me now, Hapax. Make the preparations. We must be ready, either way."

A door creaked. Silence. After a while more footsteps moved away and they knew Marian's father had gone.

"Who was that other man?" Robin whispered.

"Hapax Gaul. The Chamberlain."

"And who were they talking about? Who is Sir Bors?"

"Never heard of him." She looked back toward the cloister, scowling. "I hate not knowing what's happening. But in any case, it's his concern, not ours. This time tomorrow we'll be far from here. It's too dark to set off tonight—those clouds are getting thicker. We'll leave at first light. Agreed?"

They clambered down from the chapel and slipped back into the Lost Lands and they climbed into their tower, the way they had done a thousand times, and the way they would never do again.

IV. Desperate Measures

They sat in their chamber, wide awake. Marian hugged her knees, her knapsack fully packed between her feet. Robin gripped his shortbow and his quiver. They waited and they waited and finally the first fingers of gray light reached into the tower.

Marian went to the window. "The storm is *still* building," she said. "It's going to be a monster. We shouldn't set out in the middle of a tempest, should we? But the moment it passes we'll be on our way. We won't wait a moment longer."

They sat again in silence. After a while Marian reached out to him and locked her fingers with his. "I know it's going to be sad," she said. "Leaving our home. I'm not ready to go either, not really, no more than you are. And what's more, I'm scared. But I know it's the right path, and the time to begin." She squeezed his fingers tighter, leaned closer. "And just imagine it . . . Think what lies ahead! All the places we'll see and the stories we'll hear and everything we'll make of our lives! We can make a new home, wherever we choose. And when we feel like it we'll get up and go on again, and then we'll pick a new place, and call *that* home—anywhere and everywhere, that's where home will be, so long as we're together. You and me versus the world, the way it's always been."

Robin stood and moved about their chamber. There was something he had been meaning to do for some time. He rummaged through all the trinkets they had found and stolen over the years: He threw aside a cracked drinking ewer, a folding travel altar, a necklace of acorns. He found what he was looking for: a stonemason's chisel. He carried it to the basement. From his hunting pouch he took the jade arrowhead Marian had given him when they first met. He placed the arrowhead on a chopping block. He used the poll of their wood-ax as a hammer, bringing it down on the haft of the chisel. The arrowhead cracked the first time neatly down the middle. Using cradle knots he tied willow twine to each half.

As he carried the twin amulets back to their chamber, he heard a drumming sound, growing louder—the rolling rumble of hooves. Marian was already climbing the ladder, into the crown of the tower. Robin followed.

They stood at the edge of the parapet, blinking in the dawn light, and they watched a cloud of dust drawing down the valley. A poisonous hush had spread through the manor. It was so quiet Robin could hear the odd word drifting from the servants' quarters. He thought he heard somebody saying that name they had heard last night: *Sir Bors*. Somebody else hissed, very clearly: "No, it's him, he's here!"

Armed riders became visible. There were four of them, wearing bloodred cloaks and black steel breastplates. Stark against those breastplates was an image, embossed in red lacquer. It was difficult to see at this distance, but the emblem looked like a wolf, its teeth bared.

"The Sheriff's Guard," Marian said.

The soldiers disappeared from view as they drew close. Gerad Blunt came limping along the battlements and climbed into the barbican tower. He was shouting something, but

Robin couldn't make out the words. The gates remained closed and bolted.

"It looks like Burram was wrong," Marian said. "The Sheriff isn't with them. Either way, this will work to our advantage. While Father's distracted, we'll slip away, and he won't even notice. What's that you're holding?"

Robin held up both palms, revealing the twin arrowhead amulets. Marian smiled and bit her lower lip. She tipped her head back and gathered up her hair. Robin reached behind her neck and tied the cord. She took the second talisman from him and tied it so it hung at his chest. When she'd finished she stayed there, pressing lightly against him. She turned her eyes up to meet his.

"Robin—don't you see?—we shouldn't be sad, or frightened. This isn't the end. This is the beginning. Of everything."

She put two fingers to her lips, then touched them to Robin's forehead. She moved away, biting her lip. She came back, stood on tiptoes, kissed him properly on the chin. She opened her mouth wide and rolled her eyes in mock shock. Then she was dancing away, glancing back, grinning.

"I've thought of more things we need, I'll go and pack. Just think of it, the whole world, ours to conquer! As soon as the storm clears we'll be on our way. Look at that sky! Don't stand up here too long."

Their eyes met once more through the closing trapdoor, and she was gone. Robin put a hand to his chin and in spite of everything he found he was smiling. Yes, she was right, of course she was. Whatever was happening here, this was no place for them, not anymore. They should go their own way, build a life free from the whims of Mistress Bawg or Marian's father or anyone else.

Maybe . . . maybe they would even find them, out there somewhere. He and Marian would be passing through a village and someone would hear the name *Loxley* and would remember meeting Robin's father. Robin would follow their trail, from place to place, until one day he would find them, and they would be amazed and overjoyed and proud beyond words that Robin was alive and had managed to track them down!

Robin was pulled from his reverie by raised voices near the main gates. Dust was rising—the Sheriff's soldiers riding away, shouting as they went. A knife of lightning stabbed at Winter Forest, quickly followed by the first crunch of thunder.

He turned to go into the tower. But then another noise caught his attention. He peered toward the stables. Horses were being saddled and yoked, and vehicles were being prepared. One was Lord Delbosque's own gilded coach.

Is he leaving again, already? Was he only passing through, after all?

The main gates opened with a clanking of wood and a rattling of chains and the Chief Porter waved a litter out and away. A second litter followed, a little quicker, its wheels bouncing across the cobbles.

Yes, he's leaving! They all are. But why now, straight into the teeth of the storm . . . ?

And stranger still: It wasn't only the lord's traveling staff who were on the move. Here was Mistress Bawg, her great bulk shaking as she clambered onto a waiting carriage. And there, crossing the Great Ward: Igiotte Hutte, the Seneschal. Where were they all going?

Then Robin saw the strangest sight of all. Gerad Blunt was moving between the kitchens and the servants' quarters. He was rolling a barrel and he kept tipping it so a black liquid pulsed out. It was bubbling hot, like pitch. The Castellan went to fetch a second barrel and continued dribbling the stuff onto the timber struts of buildings. As he worked he kept shaking his head.

Elsewhere there were sudden movements, and sounds of alarm, and from somewhere close a thump and perhaps a cry of pain. Thunder stirred through it all, masking the details. Robin listened hard. He stared into the storm-dark dawn, not yet ready to believe his own eyes . . .

Marian's father came into view, unsteady on his feet. He was naked to the waist, and he held a flagon, spilling wine. In the other hand he was waving a flaming torch. He came swaying toward Gerad Blunt.

He can't be, thought Robin. *His own home* . . .

The Castellan spread his black trail; Lord Delbosque staggered to meet him . . .

A flare of lightning, freezing the scene.

Robin strapped his father's bow across his back. He hurried through the trapdoor.

"Marian, you need to see this. Something is happening out there. Your father, it looks like he's—"

But Marian wasn't there.

"Marian!"

He raced down the spiral staircase, shouting for her as he went. He saw something protruding into their tower, poking through the buttress. A ladder. He scrambled down it to the ground. He found Marian's knapsack, lying open, spilling its contents.

"Marian!"

Robin running, through the abandoned lanes, into the main manor. Into a great rush of bodies and noise and panic. Already wafts of black smoke and the smell of burning pitch spreading through the manor. Servants and maids running for the main gates, being barged out of the way by men on horseback.

Robin racing toward the main house, plunging deeper into the chaos, people and animals rushing past on every side. Two bandogs, free from their chains, snapping at each other and at people as they raced to escape the flames. A clattering of wings from the dovecot—the birds spiraling into the storm. A child crying in her mother's arms.

Robin weaving through it all, shouting for Marian, coughing and disoriented, colliding with someone rushing from a side door, stumbling, staggering onward.

Thunder tearing the sky, the vibration of it in the earth. A wall of rain sweeping in, hissing against the flames. Lightning flared, and through the glare and the thickening smoke—there—Marian's father. The earl staggering aboard his carriage.

And then the briefest glimpse of a smaller, dark-haired figure . . . kicking and twisting . . . being dragged into the vehicle by two heavyset men . . .

"Marian!"

Robin ran for the carriage. Something hit him hard from behind and he went to the ground. Boots thumping by on both sides. He struggled to his feet, scrapped his way past two men carrying a strongbox between them. He ran, gasping for breath, across the Great Ward, past the manor house.

"Marian!"

Running and fighting and scrapping, blind now in the smoke. Groping and kicking and coughing, and finding himself at the main gates. Stumbling out.

There, at the foot of the walls, he slumped to his knees. Because below him, rattling down Lord's Hill, still gaining speed, was Lord Delbosque's coach, fading in and out of view through the columns of rain.

Around Robin the last of the servants were emerging, coughing, shouting names, gripping their few belongings. Flames were soaring above the curtain walls, reddening the storm. A yawning splintering sound, followed by a resounding crash, sparks rushing into the sky.

Robin was oblivious to it all. He stayed there on his knees, rainwater running down his neck, the inferno raging at his back, watching the carriage dwindle, thinking of Marian inside, and knowing for the second time in his life that he was now truly and utterly alone.

V. Shelter from the Storm

R obin stood, at dawn, amid the remains of the Delbosque manor. Here and there ash still blew, eddying around his feet.

He pulled his cloak close as he picked his way between crumpled stone and blackened timber. His eyes followed the faint tracks of a fox. He knelt to examine the hardened footprints of crows. The scavengers had come no doubt to look for corpses amid the ashes. Was that why Robin had resisted coming here himself, in the weeks since the fire, in case he found signs that Marian had not been stolen away, after all, but had died that day in the flames? He dared to look closely now and he found only a dog's skull and tiny bird bones, nothing girl-sized.

He went to where their tower had stood. It was toppled, its timbers poking through masonry like splintered bones. With his foot he turned over an object left strangely intact. It was one of Marian's mother's books, its cover charred but its pages still gleaming with pictures of monsters and gods.

He closed his fingers around the amulet at his chest. He squeezed tighter, felt the jade cutting into his palm, and he kept squeezing. Why had he been left behind, twice over? Why had Marian's father done this, and where had he taken her?

He looked up the valley. He knew where he could go to vent his anger. He went to the edge of the manor, where he had left the willow bough, hung with the hare he had shot in the warrens. He hoisted the yoke and settled it across his shoulders, then followed Packman's Furrow, climbing toward the village.

"You're not welcome here, turn around."

"Crawl back to your den."

They had appeared from behind the threshing barn and now stood above Robin on Marsh Ridge. It was Alwin Topcroft and Lagot Reeve who had spoken, but as usual it was Narris Felstone who stood as their leader. All three carried short heavy sticks.

Only three of you, Robin thought. *Three is barely even a fair fight.*

They looked thin and sallow, these older boys. In recent years scorching summers had been followed by autumn floods: Time and again the villagers' crops had failed. Robin, in contrast, had grown tall and broad, his big hunting cloak no longer slumping from his shoulders.

"And you can leave that," Narris said, pointing his stick at the hare. "We set snares. Our bait had gone but there was nothing there. Now here you are with our catch."

Robin continued across Mill Bridge to the bank of the pond. He laid the hare on the ground. "Here it is," he said. "Come and take it."

Narris ran his tongue across his lips. He was gripping his stick so hard his knuckles had turned white. Lagot and Alwin were stepping back.

"Let him go, Narris," Lagot said.

"We don't want his food," Alwin said. "We don't want anything he's touched."

Narris scratched at his face with the stump of his left arm. "It's not that easy. He's a thief. Thieves have to pay. No matter what." He raised his gaze, looking to the far side of the pond. Robin saw him nod.

So, there are more than three of you, after all.

He turned just in time to see Swet Woolward and Harmon Byeford rushing him from behind, thumping across Mill Bridge. And then they were coming at him from both sides, Narris yelling and leading the charge down Marsh Ridge and even Alwin and Lagot shouting and swinging their sticks now that they could see it was one against five.

Robin lashed out at his nearest assailant and he felt his fist connect with bone and in the next instant his world had shrunk to kicks and blows and the taste of blood and the feeling of hard earth and finally a cold deep churning and gasping for breath as his world turned over and swirled red and black.

At least three of the others had ended up in Mill Pond with him. By the time Robin pulled himself to the bank they were helping each other out of the reeds and were dragging themselves up through the village. Narris was limping, and it sounded like Alwin Topcroft was sobbing.

Robin was bleeding freely from a cut on his forehead; one hand was numb but the fingers still flexed. *Barely a scratch. They weren't even trying.*

But then he noticed something: his father's shortbow was no longer strapped to his back. He looked for it and saw they must have taken that too, along with the hare.

Now Robin's rage was rising.

He stalked up into Wodenhurst, looking for Narris, looking for his bow.

As he moved through the lanes, beneath the boughs of the

Trystel Tree, he was met by silence, and by faces at windows, and children who came out to look before being dragged back inside. And finally, at the top of the village, he was met by a circle of armed men and women.

Pagan Topcroft was there, as nervous and ratlike as his son, gripping a mattock; and big Nute Highfielde, dumb as an ox, holding a threshing flail; and mean Agnes Poley, with her wildfowl net. There were eight or nine of them, and dizzy as Robin was he didn't put up much of a fight before they had him in the net and were dragging him through the dirt.

"He could have crippled my son," Pagan Topcroft was saying.

"I saw the whole thing," Agnes Poley said. "He attacked them with a stick."

"He tried to steal their meat," another voice said. "Food that could feed the whole village and he wanted it for himself!"

"Put him in here, where an animal belongs."

"Where's my bow?" Robin shouted, thrashing within the net. "Give it back!"

They thrust him into an empty cowshed, slammed the door and bolted it and left him there in the dark, dripping wet and bleeding and cold.

Hours later, a voice at the door of the cowshed.

"Robin, it's me. And Mabel. Just us. We're coming in."

The door opened. Warin and Mabel Felstone moved inside.

"I've brought you some of Narris's clothes," Mabel said. "They'll be a bit small for you now, but you should get out of those wet things."

Robin was shivering, but he didn't reach for the clothes. He remained sitting against one wall, his hood raised. Warin came close and laid Robin's shortbow on the ground.

"He shouldn't have taken it," Warin said. "I don't know who threw the first stone, and I don't care. I just need this stupid war to stop. Here, I brought you this too. I've been using it in the coppice. But I've been thinking, your father would have wanted you to have it." He gave Robin a bone-handled knife in a buckskin sheath. It was his father's old woodsman's blade, serrated on one edge, slicing steel on the other.

"Why now?" Robin said, lowering his hood. "Why are you giving me this now?"

Warin removed his skullcap and gripped it in both hands. He and Mabel glanced at each other.

"We've . . . I've come to a decision," Warin said. "You can't come here, to Wodenhurst, anymore. And Summerswood isn't far enough. Every time you fight with those boys it gets worse. The ferocity, when you get like that, it's frightening. It will end with one of you being killed. Unless I end it now."

"Warin is right," Mabel said, shuffling her feet in the straw. "I wish there was another way, but you're not a child anymore. There are scores of people in the city, of every sort, I've been there myself. You could find a place in the city, and build a life. You could—"

"I am leaving," Robin said. "But not because you want me to. I'm leaving because I hate this place and everyone here. I'm going and you'll never see me again."

Warin exhaled heavily.

"Well . . . that's . . . good," he said. "It's . . . for the best."

He looked at Mabel. She shuffled her feet, didn't meet his gaze.

"Well then, I suppose it's now or never," Warin said. "We've put this off too long. Robin, there's . . . something we need to tell you. Before you leave. The people here, they . . . we . . . haven't always told you the full truth. Out there, wherever you go, you will meet more fear, and more anger, of that I have no doubt. Wherever the road takes you, I want you to know—"

He was interrupted by sudden noises from somewhere down in the village. The barking of a dog, the jabbering of guard geese. The sounds grew louder. Children were running to look before being called away.

Warin left the cowshed. Robin followed, blinking into the sunlight.

As his eyes began to adjust he saw armed riders. A dozen square-shouldered men, swords and axes slung behind their saddles. The man in the lead was the most enormous person Robin had ever seen. He wore a bearskin that was as matted as his black-gray bush of a beard. The pommel of a broadsword protruded from a baldric at his back. His fingers were thick with rings. *Warlord*, Robin immediately thought of him, he looked so much like a Viking raider from one of Marian's books.

"You should leave," Warin said, turning to Robin. "Now is the time. Whatever this is, it's our burden. You've no part in it."

Robin kept watching. Stephen Younger was bustling his family back inside. Pagan Topcroft was calling for his daughter. Everywhere doors were closing and there were shuffling feet and whispers.

Most of the warriors had stopped near the mill, but the warlord and three of his thegns were continuing up Herne Hill, the hooves of their destriers slipping in the soft soil.

"Robin, go," Warin said, sounding angry now. "This is for your own good, as well as for ours. Do you understand what I'm saying to you? If you ever come here again, I cannot be responsible."

Still Robin didn't move. He watched the warlord say something to Robert Wyser, and he saw Robert point an unsteady finger toward Warin Felstone, headman of the village. The riders continued up through the lanes, the breath of men and horses heavy in the sunlight. The warlord grew and grew until he was towering over Warin.

Warin went to one knee, twisting his cap. "My lord, we—"

The warlord lifted one hand; Warin fell quiet.

And it was then that Robin understood: The warlord had not come to stand over Warin Felstone.

He had come to look down upon Robin.

And when he spoke it was to say Robin's name.

"Robin Loxley. I am Sir Bors. I have been searching for you for some time. I have come to offer you shelter, and guidance. You needn't ask why. There will be a time for questions, and answers. For now it is enough you should understand this: You are being offered an extraordinary gift. Have the sense to accept it with good grace."

Sir Bors. Robin's mind was racing. He had heard that name before . . . Lord Delbosque and the Chamberlain had spoken that name, the night before the fire. What part did this man play in all that had happened?

"You will come to my house, to live as my ward," Sir Bors continued. "You will be taught many skills and be shown the path to a useful and rewarding life. You are unlikely to see this valley or these people again. Say your good-byes. Gather any belongings you might have. We have some distance to travel before nightfall. It's time to leave."

Robin's instincts were telling him to run. He knew this valley; these men on their lumbering mounts would never catch him. He could hide until this daunting man went away.

But then he looked around him at the villagers—these people who had treated him with fear and anger and suspicion ever since his parents disappeared, for reasons Robin barely began to understand. Then he looked up at Winter Forest, the wind whispering dark secrets at its edge.

Not yet. Too soon. He must suffer the wounds.

Suddenly he wanted desperately to be away from this place. Wherever this man Sir Bors took him, anywhere would be better than here. And so, when one of the thegns reached down a huge hand, Robin found himself lifting an arm to meet it, and the man was hoisting him onto the rear of his horse. And before Robin had time to question his decision, or even think too closely about why any of this was happening, the horse was turning and he was being carried down through the village and across Mill Bridge.

He didn't look back, but he felt the villagers watching him. With every beat of the hooves he was leaving them and Winter Forest farther behind, and with that idea came great relief. But there was also sorrow. Because he was heading into the unknown, the way he and Marian had always dreamed. But he was doing it alone. Without her. And it was this idea, as Robin was carried away from his childhood home, that pricked hotly behind his eyes and made him fight hard to keep the tears from his cheeks.

Part Three

The Path of Angels

Three Years Later

I. Running the Gauntlet

Robin's world turns over, black and green.

It spins again, more violently. A rushing roaring in his ears.

Something—someone—thuds into his chest and the last of his breath bursts from his lungs, the bubbles rushing for the surface. He kicks after them—this is his final chance, if he doesn't reach the air now, he'll drown—he comes up against a crush of bodies, thrashing limbs, and he is pushed even farther down, and he is gripped by panic.

I'm going to die. Right here in this moat.

He kicks and scraps and thrashes. His foot connects with something solid and he thrusts himself upward. His head breaks the surface—he can hear shouting and coughing.

Gasping for air, swallowing water, choking, he grabs at the bridging ladder. He gets a handhold. But then looming above him is an indistinct figure, ghostlike through sunlight and water. Something all too solid in the man's hands—a quarter-staff—cracking down on Robin's fingers, jabbing at his head, thrusting him away from the ladder.

Down again, and down farther. The world turning.

Another body falling on top of him. Clawing at each other. The boom of underwater shouts.

And down still deeper, all light fading to black.

He's made a mistake, and now it's too late. He's killed us all.

Two hours earlier this had been a peaceful place: an abandoned garrison fortress, set on its own wooded hill, the crumpled walls growing over with vines. But the peace had been shattered, the doves taking flight from their roosts as twenty-four young men in full plate armor began a grueling endurance course.

Long ago the fortress had been undermined, and tunnels still ran beneath its foundations. The first stage of the course ran through these crawlspaces, Robin and his fellow squires clanking through them on hands and knees. Meanwhile bachelor knights fanned fires at every exit, sending heat and smoke billowing into the warrens so the squires inside were coughing and disoriented and desperate to be back at the surface.

Once they struggled free of the tunnels they found grappling hooks waiting—they were made to scale a thirty-foot wall, knights standing at the top, bombarding them with rocks. Next they ran ten circuits of the fortress, their muscles burning, the summer sun beating down, Sir Derrick—their combat instructor—barking at them to move faster.

And then, after all this heat and smoke and pain, Sir Derrick ordered them to the moat, and they were stripping off their plate armor and attempting to cross, bachelor knights swinging quarterstaffs so that each one of the squires was knocked from the bridging ladders before they could make it halfway across.

And that's where Robin finds himself, unable to see farther than his outstretched hand, his green-black sphere turning over once again. Even without his plate mail, his leather under-armor feels impossibly heavy, dragging him down to these black-green depths.

But then, abruptly, the panic drains away. He feels he is watching all this from afar. For a moment this is frightening—is this how it feels to be dead?—but when the fear passes he finds he is calm. With a new clarity he is aware of the other squires and their wild thrashing in the dark. In their desperation they are all trying to clamber aboard the two nearest crossings. And all the bachelor knights are there, defending.

Robin kicks clear and takes measured swimming strokes away from this mass of roiling bodies. He gets his head above water and gasps air. He keeps swimming, free of the tumult, ignoring the next bridging ladder and the next and heading for the one at the farthest edge of the moat. Here there is no one. With the last of his strength he drags himself from the water, staggers across the ladder and onto the bank, collapsing onto his knees, wheezing and wiping the gunk from his eyes and nose and coughing it all up onto the grass.

The final few squires had been dragged from the moat. They all stood in a line, bent double, fighting for breath. Robin fished something slimy from beneath his jerkin. The foul taste of the water rose again in his throat. But at last it was over. He could almost laugh with the relief of it. Once again it was peaceful out here in the late-summer sun, doves returning to perch on the fortress walls, crickets chirping in the long grass.

Sir Derrick strode up and down the line of squires, his bald head gleaming. "This is the beginning of a momentous week," he said. "You are excited. Apprehensive. That is to be expected. The squires' tourney offers you a chance to shine in front of Sir Bors. It offers a chance to strut like peacocks in front of girls who have traveled from far and wide. And then comes the tournament proper, bringing you face to face with your idols. I know you think of me as a monster. But I was your age once. I remember these feelings. In coming days there will be jousting, feasting, war games. A glorious prize to be won. What young man would not be thrilled by the prospect?"

He paused to swipe his willow switch across the calves of Rex Hubertson, who was lying flat on the grass. Rex staggered to his feet.

"But," Sir Derrick said. "*But.* I am here to remind you that a warrior's life is not pomp and pageantry. It is not waved handkerchiefs and lavish banquets. These are pretty distractions, merely. For a fighting knight real life is a mouthful of mud and pain that has sunk into your very bones. It is an endless trek beneath a Moorish sun. It is the sight of your own blood in the snow and knowing you cannot go on, yet you must. In the coming days I want you to remember these facts. I want you to remember that a warrior's life is spent toe-to-toe with death."

Sir Derrick stopped at the end of the row, where the last squires to be dredged from the moat were coughing on their knees. He pointed at Egor Towers.

"You. Take the lead. Back around the course. In reverse."

"But . . . ," Egor said, "I'm not . . . I can't . . . I can barely . . . breathe . . ."

Sir Derrick lifted one foot, laid it on Egor's shoulder, launched him backward into the moat. He went to the next squire, kicked him into the water. And the next. Farther along the line, Robin and several of the others looked at one another. As exhausted as they were, they were not going to wait to be shoved.

Robin made a dash for the far crossing, ducked a quarterstaff, managed to stay on the ladder halfway across, but then hit the water. And so it began again. Robin's world condensed to churning black-green slime and grasping weeds and bursting breath.

The squires dragged themselves, on foot, back toward the manor. They had survived a second running of the gauntlet, and a third, and now they had barely enough strength left to lift one stride in front of the other. Most of the squires were silent, but Bones and Irish were muttering at Robin's side.

"Tyrant. Pure luck none of us drowned."

"Or choked to death, in those tunnels."

"We should go to Sir Bors. The man is a lunatic. Loxley, what think?"

Robin didn't answer. From this ridge, looking across the hills, he could now see Sir Bors's domain, stick figures patrolling the battlements, pennons flapping in the wind. At the south gate, beneath the vast flanking towers, a dray was arriving, carrying crates and barrels. Lower down, on the river, a barge stood at the landing stage, waiting to be unloaded. On the display ground, at the foot of the east wall, carpenters were erecting the spectator scaffolds, the rasping of saws and the *klonk-klonk* of hammers reaching the squires even at this distance.

Robin remembered thinking, a lifetime ago, that the Delbosque manor was massive and magnificent. But it was a mud hut compared to Sir Bors's domain. Here was a fully functioning citadel, home to scores of craftsmen and merchants and clerics and military men. And today, with the tournament approaching, the citadel had never been busier. Each competitor brought with him grooms and pages and body servants, and was trailed by players and tinkers and bards. Many of these camp followers had to shelter under canvas, a separate town of tents growing outside the curtain walls. Even now another knight was arriving, a herald scampering to the Tree of Shields and hanging it with the man's coat-of-arms.

Watching all this, dragging one foot in front of the other, Robin was only vaguely aware that Bones and Irish were still moaning. Other squires were sharing a joke at Sir Derrick's expense. Robin felt no reason to complain. These were the best kind of days: the times their tutors worked them so hard it was impossible to think of anything else, or to remember. He imagined that when he finally collapsed into bed he would be too tired to even dream. Although on that front he had often been wrong.

Ahead of them the manor continued to fuss and scurry and thump. The squires continued to moan. Robin dragged himself silently and gratefully toward his bed.

II. Brothers-in-Arms

Robin woke suddenly in the cold and the dark, his heart racing. A hand was shaking his shoulder. He looked up into a scowling face, a bare outline in the gloom.

"Marian?"

"Ha, you wish," Bones said, scratching himself between the legs. "Who's this Marian? The girl of your dreams? Keep her there then—don't inflict her on the rest of us. You shouting on one side, Rowly snoring on the other, I've a mind to . . ."

Bones was crawling back under his blankets, his muffled complaints fading to silence.

Robin sat up on his hard wooden cot. He reached underneath for his clothes and his boots. He got up and groped his way across the spartan chamber, picking his way between the other sleeping squires and reaching the doorway. He walked up the steps and emerged into the gray light of the courtyard.

It was not yet dawn but already the citadel was waking: hearthboys yawning as they crossed the courtyard with armfuls of firewood; maids emptying chamber pots. The sentries in their watchtowers began the first of the day-calls—"Prime hour. All clear"—the chant beginning over the main gates and working clockwise round the battlements.

Robin filled a bucket from the well, stripped off his night-clothes, washed himself, wincing at the fresh bruises covering his muscles. The water was very cold and was helping to dissolve the memory of the nightmare. In his sleep he and Marian had been running from the Wargwolf, its lower jaw hanging slack, trees bending from its path the way a cat moves through grass.

He ducked his head fully in the bucket. By the time he'd rubbed the water from his eyes Bones was there, yawning and scratching at his groin and filling his own bucket from the well.

"Rowly's getting worse with his snoring," Bones said. "He's an animal, trapped in a man's body. I'd get more rest sleeping in the swineshed." He splashed water on his face, rubbed at his eyes. "Nightmares again?" he said. "Want to talk about it? No? Good, because I don't want to hear it. Not at a time like this." He leaned closer, dropped his voice to a whisper. "Listen. Here's something to lift your spirits. I didn't get a chance to tell you yesterday. I've made an alliance."

Robin raised his eyebrows.

"Well, not *made* exactly," Bones said. "*Making*, I should say. But it's just a formality. Six of us! Think of it, the ultimate company."

"Who are they?" Robin said.

"You'll see. We're meeting this morning, first light. Who would you like it to be? Come on, let's get the other two, drag them out of that pit. This is our day. This is when it begins, I can feel it!"

The four of them waited beneath the north tower, on the slope that led down to the moat. Robin stood motionless, leaning back against the wall, his hood up, watching Bones pace back and forth. Rowly had sprawled his big frame on the grass. Irish was on one knee and was digging in the soil with his knife.

"They're not coming, are they?" Irish said.

"Can't believe I missed breakfast for nothing," Rowly said. "Loxley, you've always got some food stashed away. What can you offer?"

"They'll be here," Bones said. "They're being cautious, that's all. They can't wait to come over, you'll see."

He didn't look as confident as he was trying to sound. He continued to pace in the shadow of the tower, twisting fingers through his blond chin-beard. The citadel was rousing to full wakefulness—the echo of voices and the clopping of hooves and creaking of carts. Time was running out.

"Forget it," Irish said, wiping and sheathing his knife. "They're not interested. Let's get back and—"

"There!" Bones said. "Here they come. Look. Yes, yes, this is it. Have I let you down yet?"

Sauntering out of the north gate were Joscelin Tarcel and Ayala Baptiste. Robin was impressed. These two would be perfect. Baptiste had only been at the academy a matter of months, but already he had earned himself the nickname The Beast. He was almost as big as Rowly, and equally fearsome in the combat yard. Joscelin Tarcel, quick on his feet and crafty, was an excellent skirmisher.

"What about it, eh?" Bones whispered. "Think of it. The Beast standing defense with Rowly. Tarcel joining the rest of us in attack? I could almost feel sorry for the others."

"You will forgive our tardy arrival," Tarcel said, as they approached. "My friend Baptiste refuses to do business on an empty stomach."

Rowly made a snorting noise.

"But now time is short," Tarcel said in his slight Frankish accent. "Let us dally no longer. The Enterprise of Champions is not known for the size of its war chest, so we will not be talking of coins."

"It would be insulting to us both," Bones said. "We offer a richer reward. Victory."

Tarcel glanced at The Beast, who stood behind, expressionless. "You hear this, Baptiste. Victory. And look what we have here . . ." He pointed to Irish. "Fyn MacDair. As good a swordsman as you will find, and peerless in the joust . . ."

Next he pointed to Rowly. "Ifor Rowland. The Destroyer. A formidable weapon in the melee, so long as somebody points him in the right direction . . ."

Rowly looked puzzled, clearly not sure if he was being praised or insulted.

"Robin Loxley," Tarcel continued. "All but guaranteed to win the archery stage, and quicker than most running the gauntlet. And lastly Jack Champion. The famous Bones. He brings brains, and a certain rough guile. Join our skill and strength to their ranks, Baptiste, and we would stand every chance of claiming the coveted prize."

"So it's agreed," Rowly said, standing, rubbing his big hands together. "We'll go out there tomorrow and smash the rest to pieces."

Tarcel looked at him and smirked. "No, we will not be joining you. Must I inform you why? Very well. Baptiste is the son of a Sicilian duke. My family, as you certainly know, stretches back to the Roman kings. In years to come, in real theaters of war, should we ever find ourselves on the losing side, Baptiste and I would prove prize assets. A ransom would change hands, our blood would remain unspilled. But you two . . ." He pointed first at Robin, then at Bones. "A peasant and an almschild. The pair of you, in defeat, would be worth less than stray dogs. You would be slaughtered with the foot soldiers and left for the crows. Why would we devalue ourselves, even at this stage, by allying with the likes of you?"

Until this moment Baptiste, whose English was still poor, had shown little sign of following the conversation. But now he smiled.

Bones was clenching and unclenching his fists. "So you came out here purely because it amused you."

"Not at all," Tarcel said. "We meet in good faith, to negotiate. As you know, my company, unlike yours, has a full complement of six combatants. However, two of our number are proving . . . less than satisfactory. It occurs to me their ideal replacements are here. Ifor Rowland, the son of a marcher baron. Fyn MacDair, descendant of a Celtic prince, no? Talented both, and high-born, yet wedded to these scullions. The pair of you, I'm sure, would be more at home—"

"You snake, you slimy crawling—" Bones moved toward Tarcel; Rowly held him back. "You're going in the moat," Bones said to Tarcel, struggling. "Let go of me, you big aurochs, let me get my hands on him, he's going for a swim . . ."

"You see, Baptiste," Tarcel said. "Master Champion attempts to play the nobleman, but now he shows his true colors. We will be hearing from you shortly, squires Rowland, MacDair."

Tarcel and Baptiste, still smiling, turned and walked away. Bones twisted in Rowly's grip and swore. Robin moved forward and put a hand on Bones's shoulder.

"Don't give him the satisfaction," Robin said. "Can't you see how much he's enjoying himself. He wasn't serious. He knows no one can split the four of us."

He looked at Rowly, who was now staring out over the moat, and at Irish, who was digging in the earth again with his knife.

"Right?" Robin said. "He's just trying to unsettle us. He knows we stick together."

Rowly nodded.

"Yes, sure, correct," Irish said.

Bones looked at all three of them, each in turn, but said nothing. They went together back to the north gate, and walked through the manor to the armory, none of them saying a word.

The squires spent that morning in the near hills, endurance training with Sir Derrick. Beneath the sharp sun he made them run up and down the slopes, carrying one another pig-a-back. Then they tied ropes from the beech trees and Sir Derrick made them climb these, over and over, using only their arms.

When he had finished with them, Sir Derrick strode away without a word, leaving the squires sprawled in the grass. They were about to drag themselves back to the manor when Sir Gilbert, their tactics tutor, came hobbling up the hill, carrying a sack across one shoulder.

"It's too hot to go back to that stuffy chamber," Sir Gilbert said, scratching at his potbelly. "We'll sit up here beneath the mulberry trees, eh, what do you say? I've brought bread and cheese and we'll drink from the stream."

Gratefully Robin took his place in the shade, amid the chirping crickets and the slow bees. He broke bread with the other squires and they looked across the hills to the citadel.

"No need to stare into dusty old books, not today," Sir Gilbert said. "There's plenty to learn right here. An opportunity to practice your heraldry. See that banner, above Murdak Tower. Two foxes, rampant, on a blue and black field. Whose device is that?"

"Morton Durrell, of the Marches," said Rex Hubertson.

"Yes, very good. A fierce lord of the borderlands, by all

accounts. He should be one to watch in the joust. And there. Embattled walls. Blasted tree. Yellow and green."

"Tristan de Roye," said several squires in unison.

"Very good, very good. The Count is a man of great means. His lands stretch across three realms, in Saxony and the German Empire . . ."

While the lesson went on, Bones leaned across to Robin. "You don't think they'll do it, do you?" he whispered. He nodded toward Irish and Rowly, who were sitting a little way apart, their heads bent together.

"Of course they won't," Robin said. "Tarcel is playing games. He wants you to think they could even think it."

Bones looked to where Joscelin Tarcel was sitting with Baptiste and two of his other lackeys. Tarcel glanced over his shoulder and smiled and turned to say something to Francis Tutt.

"I don't care if we win," Bones whispered, twisting fingers through his chin-beard. "So long as we score more points than that pampered bunch of—"

"Master Champion," Sir Gilbert said. "Since you have so much to say, perhaps you could inform us whose colors are those, at the far end of the west wall . . ."

The lesson continued and the afternoon stretched away. Robin watched the pavilions rising, blue and yellow, on the display ground, and he felt the excitement and the nerves building. All the other squires were feeling the same, he could tell, and even Sir Gilbert was excitable as a child.

"Listen," Sir Gilbert said. "The herald's horn. Another competitor arrives. Who can tell me who this is, flying the serpent and the cross? Yes, correct, Sir Stephen Coldacre, the famous crusader, and a hunting companion of the Lionheart no less . . ."

It was a glorious afternoon, the skylarks pouring down their song, every blade of grass bending beneath the weight of an insect. A knight came out to exercise his war-horse, galloping up and down the lists, man and mount coated in steel, the thunder of hooves so heavy Robin thought he could feel it in the earth, even at this distance.

"See here, yet more guests," Sir Gilbert said. "A prize for the first of you who . . . Ah, no, I see I'm wrong. My eyes are not so sharp as they once were."

Robin looked to the road below and what he saw there caused a cold shiver at the back of his neck. Winding their way up from the river were four horsemen, but these were not earls or dukes. These were common soldiers, dressed all in black, apart from their crimson cloaks, and the image of a wolf's head livid red against their breastplates.

"The Sheriff's Guard," said Egor Towers. "What are they doing here?"

"You know what I hear about the Sheriff," said Richard Warbrittle. "He feeds his horse on human flesh."

"He flays peasants to the bone . . . ," said Henry Winchester. "Wears their skins as clothes."

Several other squires joined in, their stories increasingly lurid.

"The man is a lunatic . . . declared war on the forest gods . . ."

"Thinks he's a demigod himself . . ."

"Born in the wildwood . . . raised by wolves . . ."

"Quiet down," Sir Gilbert said. "That's quite enough. I don't want to hear you talking that way, even in jest. You realize, I hope, that such tales were told of the Sheriff's predecessor, and the man before him. Each sheriff must don such legends, it seems, along with his robes of office. But such stories belong at the fireside of peasants. I don't know the Sheriff personally, but I'm sure he deserves our respect. So then, a big day tomorrow. Get yourselves to the dining hall, eat as much as you can beg or steal, then rest well. Ah, now, here comes another banner. The double dragon. Sir Arnold of Aragon, a modest mercenary once, in the pay of the Pope, but now risen to great heights, and a paymaster himself . . ."

As they walked back to the citadel Sir Gilbert went on talking. Robin wasn't listening. He was watching the Sheriff's soldiers. Three now stood this side of the moat, while one was waved across the drawbridge. Robin realized his jaw hurt, he was gritting his teeth so hard. The sight of those scarlet cloaks had stirred all the old anger and the heartache. The fire at the manor; Marian's father stealing her away. Why had he done it? What part had the Sheriff played?

"I said, what if it isn't just a game? What if he's got to them somehow?" This was Bones, talking away at Robin's side. "I mean, how much does friendship count for, weighed against a prize like that? If we lose those two, we're finished, before we even begin. What's up with you, Loxley? Are you even listening?"

They walked into the sump of Saddle Hill and by the time they crested the next rise the lone soldier had reemerged and all four horsemen were riding away.

Irish and Rowly moved over to join Robin and Bones.

"There's something we need to tell you," Rowly said.

Robin snapped out of his reverie. He and Bones stopped and stared at the other pair. Irish scratched at the back of his neck. Rowly looked at the ground.

"It's about tomorrow," Rowly said.

"We . . . well, we've been talking," Irish said. "And we've decided . . . we think, maybe, the best thing for all of us, at this stage . . ."

He paused and he and Rowly turned to each other with serious expressions. But then one of them smiled and made the other laugh and then they were both laughing.

"The look on your faces!" Irish said. "You thought we were going to do it."

"What kind of rats do you think we are?" Rowly said.

"I knew it!" Bones said, slapping them both on the back. "I knew you never would. That's what I've been saying to Loxley all along. Didn't I say, Loxley, friends like us are worth more than all the gold in Rome."

"We *were* talking," Irish said. "But only about how to wipe the grin off Tarcel's dainty face."

"Yes, yes!" said Bones. "That's it, that's what I've been saying, and on that front I have a brave and splendid plan. It cannot fail. Listen, what do you think of this . . . ?"

He put his arms around the shoulders of Irish and Robin, and as they walked he began to outline his strategy, and soon Robin was sharing his own ideas and arguing with the others, the painful memories fading from his mind, the Sheriff's Guard all but forgotten.

III. War Games

Robin gripped his shield and his greathelm, and he waited with the other squires on the display ground. Around them the murmur of the crowd continued to swell. The spectator scaffold was almost full, noblewomen and their daughters talking beneath their hands, pressing kerchiefs to their powdered cheeks. There were people too all along the curtain walls and perched on barrels and hanging out of trees. Bones raised a hand toward a serving maid from one of the taverns. He clashed his shoulder against Robin's.

"Molly Shrievner is over there. No secret who she's come to watch. Look, Loxley, she's waving her kerchief! Go and fetch it. The luck of a pretty girl is worth a spare sword arm."

The noise of the spectators rose farther, then faded to whispers. Sir Bors had emerged from the east gate. Following him were two household knights, wearing their silver cloaks, their tabards embroidered with the emblem of the golden arrow.

Sir Bors reached the spectator scaffold, climbed its steps, the terraces creaking beneath his weight. He reached the top and turned and fixed the squires with his iron gaze. At first he said nothing and the quiet around him became silence, broken only by a single sneeze from the curtain wall, and a squire dropping his greathelm and scrabbling to pick it up.

Finally the overlord's voice boomed. "You young men stand here today at a threshold. Before the week is out, the bravest and best among you will have embarked upon a new life, leaving your less able brothers behind." He lifted a tabard, emblazoned with the golden arrow. "Those of you who earn this symbol will tread an extraordinary path. On campaign, at my side, you will travel to Byzantium and Baghdad and all the golden cities of the east. You will see sights you never dreamed and taste new fruits and know the satisfaction of hard and necessary work. You will endure danger and discomfort, plenty of it. But you will also know glory and reward. You will return to these shores with a name to speak loudly and with stories to tell with pride. That is the world that awaits, should you summon the strength to step across this threshold. So be quick and resolute, compete with skill and valor. Good luck."

Sir Bors left the scaffold, and as he walked away the noise of the crowd rose again to a hiss and then a rumble. The squires talked among themselves, huddled in their companies, and they donned their greathelms and swished their hardwood swords through the air or clashed together their shields. At Robin's side Rowly hoisted their battle banner: winged Pegasus on a blue field. He slid the pole into a baldric at his back and snapped the clasps shut.

Meanwhile, Sir Derrick had come forward and was striding between them all, shouting. "Remember, a knight fights with his head, just as much as with his sword. You all have war chests, so use them. If you see an opportunity to agree terms, do so. Never risk a battle with blades if it can be won with cold coin or warm words. Captives can be ransomed, traded, or sold, and this year even company banners can be bartered.

Those companies with only four or five squires should be looking to bolster—"

He was interrupted by the blaring of trumpets—the Master of Ceremonies had cut the tourney rope and the spectators were cheering and the squires were off and running.

Robin and the other three headed east, then south, as they had agreed, down to the river and across the ford and into the wooded hills beyond. They climbed the steep slope and came to a halt not far from the tournament bounds. Rowly unclipped their banner and waved it three times above his head, showing the judges that this was to be their home ground.

"Are we sure about this?" Irish said.

"It's the perfect tactic," Bones said. "Go after the strongest team, before they can blink. It's the last thing they'll expect."

"There's a reason for that," Irish said. "It's madness."

"Most companies will start cautiously, won't they?" Bones said. "They'll work up alliances, not take any chances. Tarcel's lot will be different. They'll go on the hunt straight off."

"But leave Rowly here on his own?" Irish said.

"You run along," Rowly said. "I'll be fine."

"Look at him," Bones said. "He's a one-man fortress. And we can't do it with less than—"

"We talked about this," Robin said. "We made the decision. Now we're just wasting time. Rowly, don't let go of that flag."

With that, Robin was clanking back down the slope. He heard Irish and Bones following. They made their way along a ridge above the river. Below them they saw John Pendergast and Gordon Levett and the rest of the Society of the Silver Star. When they spotted Robin and the others they moved off in the opposite direction, their starred standard snapping on its pole. In the distance rose the sound of wood clashing against steel and the cheering of the crowd announcing the first battle joined.

"Tarcel's troupe, it's got to be," Bones said. "Going for one of the weaker banners. Their territory won't be far from here."

"How do you know so much about Tarcel's tactics?" Irish said. "If I didn't know better, I'd—"

"Up there," Robin said. "See them?"

"What did I tell you!" Bones said. "And only two!"

Above them, their armor flashing in the sun, were Robert Benhale and Ayala Baptiste, the latter carrying their black-tailed banner.

Without a word they parted ways, Irish going straight up the slope to attack from the east, Bones circling around to the west. Robin advanced from the south, drawing his ashwood sword as he made his way through the field, thick with nettles and blackthorn. He felt conspicuous and noisy, as he always did in plate armor, his hunting instincts objecting. Crows scattered from his path, croaking. Jackdaws took wing and cackled their alarm.

And now Baptiste had seen him. He hefted his whalebone battle-ax and charged down the slope. The distance between them shrank. Robin raised his shield and the ax came crashing down, and at the last instant Robin relaxed his shield arm to cushion the blow. The ax came down again; Robin felt the impact in his bones. He made no attempt at a counterattack; he went on meeting each strike with his shield, letting Baptiste think he was getting the better of this.

Behind Baptiste the second skirmish flared with the singing of wood on steel, and within moments Robin thought he heard someone clatter to the ground. And then Bones and Irish were charging Baptiste from behind and their attacks were raining down and Robin's sword too was ringing off the big squire's greathelm and Baptiste was turning and roaring and from nowhere a judge was blowing his whistle and quick as that it was done.

"Three clean strikes to the head," said the gray-robed judge, moving down the slope, pointing at Baptiste. "You're taken captive. Same goes for you, Benhale. That's enough of that. They knocked you off your feet, fair and square. Get yourselves to the hostage pen."

Robert Benhale had taken off his helm and thrown it to the ground and was kicking it. "I told them, I told them . . ."

Baptiste unclipped the banner from his back but refused to let go and Robin and Bones had to wrestle it from him and the judge had to blow his whistle some more and make threats and eventually Baptiste released his grip. Robin slung the banner under his shield arm and the three of them ran with it through the fields toward the river.

"Two hostages and twenty points already," Bones said. "Not to mention a prize banner."

"The banner will be worth nothing unless we get it to the victor's stand," Irish said. "Can't you run any faster, what's up with your leg?"

"Benhale caught me a lucky hit to the knee. I'll be fine. Don't slow down for me."

They forded the river and started up toward the display ground. The crowd waved flags and pointed to see a captured banner. Robin held it upright and ran with it, preparing to plant it in the victor's stand, a mound of sand piled in front of the stands.

But then he slowed and drew his sword, and the other two did the same. Squires were charging at them from both sides and in a storm of steel and wood they found themselves in the middle of a melee. There were fighters from at least three companies here, including Joscelin Tarcel and the remainder of his gang, intending to reclaim their standard. Others were scavengers, looking to steal the prize for themselves.

Robin crashed his shield into a squire and thrust him aside;

he bounced off another opponent and managed to break free of the ruck. Bones was shouting at him, "Go!" and Robin went, sprinting clear of the tumult, heading for the victor's stand.

Only fifty paces to go—forty—but then Joscelin Tarcel stepped into his path. He stood there in his elaborate armor, with its velvet coat and tassels. Through the jagged scar of his mouth guard he was gritting his teeth and forcing a smile.

"We can reach agreements, you and I," Tarcel said. "Think what I might do to improve your station."

Robin's sword crashed into Tarcel's shield. He swung again, putting all his weight into it, wanting this over before any of Tarcel's cronies could break free of the melee. Tarcel took a step back and Robin pressed the advantage, driving his opponent toward the victor's stand. He kept swinging and Tarcel kept giving ground and Robin kept attacking. He readied the banner, thinking he could reach the stand and plant it even with his opponent still on his feet.

But then a glimpse of something caught Robin's eye.

A dark flash at the top edge of his vision.

He forced himself not to look. He swung his sword; Tarcel retreated.

He kept his eyes fixed on his opponent; he attacked.

But there it was again, gleaming darkly, impossible to ignore. Something—someone—high up on the scaffold.

He looked up.

A young woman stood there, staring back. She wore a scarlet-and-gold gown, the flared sleeves hiding her hands, which she kept clasped at her middle. Her hair, swept across one shoulder, fell as far as her waist and was so lustrous in the sunlight it was almost iridescent, like the feathers of a starling.

Her eyes, even at this distance, even beneath a light veil, were luminous eyes of gray and green.

Marian.

It was enough to make Robin drop his guard completely. And the shock only ran deeper as he saw that Marian was flanked by two household knights, and that between one of these men and her something shone dully like iron, like . . . shackles . . . as if she was standing there a prisoner . . .

Robin registered all this in a heartbeat, but in that heartbeat Joscelin Tarcel made his move. He glanced toward the scrum to check no judges were looking this way, then he stepped forward and performed an attack called the Lion's Claw: an underhand sweep, arcing toward Robin's chin. It was a strike banned from the tourney field: a technique Sir Derrick said could break necks, even with training swords.

Robin didn't see the attack; the first he knew of it was the sound: a sickening clanging crunch. His head jolted back. Pain shot through his skull. There was a spinning blackness and he couldn't see. He could barely breathe. He stumbled backward, both his sword and the banner dropping from his fingers.

He regained his footing. He used his sword hand to thump down on his greathelm. The visor slid back over his eyes and he could see. The chin strap stopped choking him and he could breathe.

The display ground spun. In front of him were two Joscelin Tarcels, stalking toward him, each raising their swords for the killing blow.

In pain, enraged, Robin's instincts took over. He made a lurch right, as if stooping for his sword, then bounced off his right foot, swerving left just as Tarcel's sword arced past. Robin abandoned his own weapon and charged at Tarcel, barreling into him with his shield, his helm smashing into Tarcel's chest. Tarcel stumbled backward and Robin kept charging and spitting fury and butting with his helm. Tarcel was driven backward, faster, and he was losing his balance even before he thumped into the victor's stand. He went sprawling across the mound of sand. Robin threw himself on top of him, beating his gauntlets on his chest. Tarcel made sucking sounds through his mouth guard and Robin went on smashing his fists down, over and over, the sound of it echoing around the display ground . . .

"I said, that's enough!"

Sir Derrick took hold of Robin's gorget and used it to haul him backward to his feet. Whistles were blowing and all other fighting was coming to a halt. Robin struggled with his greathelm and eventually pulled it free.

Sir Derrick came and stood very close, his breath sour. "So, Loxley, still determined to be the back-alley brawler? I thought we hammered that out of you long ago. Just goes to show, you can take the boy out of the hovel, but you can't take the hovel out of the boy." He turned and swept an arm around the circle of squires. "What is the single most important thing we've tried to teach you boys? That to win at any cost is not to win at all. The most dangerous opponent you will ever face is yourself. Sacrifice self-control, give way to fear and fury, and you may win this battle, but the war is lost. Get out of my sight, Loxley, you're a disgrace. The Enterprise of Champions are disqualified from today's events, with zero points."

Robin wasn't listening. He was scanning the spectator scaffold, looking for Marian. But the platform where she had stood was now empty and there was no sign of her anywhere else. She and the household knights had disappeared.

IV. The Prisoner

"**W**hat are you doing here? You know this is out of bounds to squires."

James Wringfield, a household knight, was standing sentry at the foot of the guard tower. As he spoke he puffed out his chest bearing the emblem of the golden arrow.

"We're taking food to the prisoner," Robin said, raising the packet he was holding. "Marian Delbosque."

"You're doing what?" Wringfield said. "Where's the usual . . . Ah, I see, you've heard about our captive and you'd like a look for yourselves. She's an eyeful, it's true. You're not the first I've turned away."

"What's it all about?" Bones said. "All those lectures the Old Boar gives about honor. And now he's taking young ladies hostage?"

James Wringfield shrugged. "He doesn't tell us anything. He's been acting odd of late. All I know is, no one goes in this tower, no one comes out, until I'm instructed otherwise."

"Listen, Wringfield," Bones said. "You and I used to fight in the same company. Until you defected."

The knight looked at the ground. "An offer I couldn't refuse. You would have done the same."

"My point being, we were friends," Bones said. "I like to think we still are. I want you to do my other friend here a favor. He says he knows this young woman, and only wants a word."

"If the Old Boar caught you, we'd all be in the mire."

"He's in the Great Hall, entertaining his guests," Bones said. "You can hear him from here. Nobody will know. It won't take long, and then we'll disappear—right, Loxley?"

Robin nodded. James Wringfield tapped his foot, looked around him. "As a matter of fact," he said. "Maybe there's something you can do for me. You know Leira Coot, don't you? Well, I've been wondering . . ."

"Yes, yes," Bones said. "Maiden Coot is a very good friend of mine. I can certainly help you out there. Let us discuss it while Loxley wastes no more time . . ."

He was pushing Robin into the guard tower. James Wringfield reached back and barred the way.

"If I whistle, come running fast," the knight said. "And if she asks anything of you, don't listen. She could talk a river into running uphill. She persuaded Jonah and Richardson to take her to watch the squire's tourney, would you believe, and afterward there was hell to pay. So when she opens those big eyes and whispers her words, block your ears, got it?"

He moved his arm and Robin continued into the guard tower. The daylight was fading. He took a flaming pitch torch from the wall to light his way. He climbed the stone steps, feeling light-headed. He continued up and the dizziness grew worse; he told himself it was the blow to the head he had suffered, but he knew it wasn't.

On the first floor were two chambers. Robin peered into each and found them empty. They were comfortable places, luxurious even, full of carpets and tapestries. Only the heavy locks on the doors marked them as jails.

On the second floor were two more chambers. From inside one candlelight flickered. He hesitated, battling a bizarre urge to turn and go back down the steps. Three years had passed. Thinking back, Robin barely recognized that boy who had lived with Marian in the tower. What would she think of him, now? And how about her—would she be the same person he remembered? He pushed these thoughts away. Here was *Marian*. He had no reason to be nervous. He had dreamed of this over and over, their reunion.

He moved slowly to the oak door. At head height was an open guard hatch, crossed with iron bars. He put his face to this hatch and looked through.

And there she was, kneeling, her back to him, her hair and her gown pooled on the floor. He didn't make a noise, but Marian sat up straight. She put down an object she was holding. She stood and turned and came to the door. Their eyes met.

Neither of them spoke. They just stood there, staring.

Eventually Marian put two fingers to her lips and reached up and her hand came through the bars and her fingers came to rest on Robin's forehead.

"Found you," she said softly.

She pulled her hand inside and they went back to just staring. Long moments passed before she spoke again. "Don't you have anything to say? Aren't you going to say you're happy to see me? How you missed me, at least, after all this time. I always did most of the talking, didn't I, you were always the quiet one. But now you're not saying a word. All you're doing is staring. Don't you talk at all anymore?"

Robin was trying to speak but thinking too hard about which would be the right words, and all the things he had planned to say had been building up beneath his tongue, so he ended up saying nothing at all. From within her clothing Marian pulled her half-arrowhead amulet. She pushed it to her lips and went on looking at him.

Eventually he managed to force words across his tongue. "Where . . . ?" he said. "Why are you . . . ? What are you doing here?"

She tipped her head sideways. "I came to find you, of course, what else? I'm here to rescue you."

All the tension broke then and Robin laughed. "Rescue me? From what? And how, exactly? You're . . . in there. Under lock and key."

Marian huffed. "I've got out of tighter cages than this. I've put up with this one so long as it served a purpose, but now you're here, we can begin. Robin Loxley, it's you, it's really you, here you are in front of me, and I've got a thousand things I want to say and I can see you feel the same but all that will have to wait because we need to be quick. We can say it all on the way."

"On the way?"

"We're leaving. Tonight. I'm not safe here, and neither are you, no matter what he says. The Tree of Shields, near the display ground, I'll meet you there. Midnight. I want you to bring—"

"Wait, hold on, you're not making any sense."

"Robin, are you being deliberately stupid, or did that sword knock out the last of your brains? We. Are. Leaving. The two of us. Tonight. We'll have to go back there, first, we have no choice, but then we'll be on our way to the coast and—"

"Back . . . ?" Robin said.

"Yes, you know where. It can't be helped. I need more answers. I need to find out . . . Listen . . . What's that noise?"

A whistling from the foot of the tower.

"I have to go," Robin said. "I'll be back, just as soon as I can."

"What? No! Don't come back here. I said, meet me—"

"Marian, I'm not sure what you're talking about. But you

have to know I . . . I can't go anywhere. We're not allowed far-ther than . . ."

He trailed off. Marian had moved away from the door but now she came storming back, her expression dark. The shad-ows from the bars striped her face. Her eyes narrowed to gray-green slits.

"What did you say?"

"I . . . I can't leave the citadel," Robin said. "Not yet. Not until—"

Marian made a growling noise. "No, no, no! I found you, after all this time, and I came all that way and if you knew what I had to go through, and I've made plans and it's all arranged but we can't wait, we have to go tonight and you made a promise and now you're saying you can't go even though what you mean is you *won't* go, how can you be so . . . !"

She growled again as she moved away to kneel once more on the carpet. Robin saw now what she had been holding: It was a mortar, full of small red things, perhaps berries. She started crushing them with a pestle. She crumbled something else, like bread, and added that to the mixture.

"What are you doing?"

"Helping myself," she said, the pestle cracking down hard. "The way I've always had to help myself because everyone else is too scared, even you, even the one who promised to always fight for me, the one who would stand up to anybody. And now after all this time apart I was stupid enough to think—"

The thunder of boots on the stairs.

"Loxley!" Bones hissed. "Loxley? Come *on*! Didn't you hear the whistle? The Old Boar, he's here! Wringfield is run-ning a distraction, but we have to—"

He had reached Robin and was tugging at his arm, but as he did so he looked into the prison chamber and Marian looked up and Bones stopped and stared. Marian went back to her work and Robin heard her say: "I can't wait for you, I can't. He's coming and it's not safe, not even here, *especially* not here, all of them together. You'll have to follow, I know you will, you don't have a choice, our fates are tied, we've always known that . . ."

And then her words were becoming faint because Bones was hauling Robin away and hissing at him "Come on!" and Robin was calling over his shoulder, "I'll be back. Soon." And then he and Bones were running down through the guard tower and slipping away to safety, everything Marian had said twisting in his mind.

He passed a fitful night, turning and kicking. At some point he must have slept because he woke to sudden sounds drifting down the dormitory steps.

He crept up and lurked in the courtyard, listening. He heard Sir Bors shouting, and the clatter of boots and the thumping of doors and horses being led out of the stables, and Sir Bors shouting even louder, and the east gates cranking open.

Robin headed toward the Inner Court. He saw Turnstall Smith and Duncan d'Orris, two household knights. They were talking quietly together and laughing.

"What happened?" Robin said.

Turnstall Smith glanced over his shoulder. "You heard about the hostage? Well, she's a hostage no more. She escaped."

"The funny part . . . ," Duncan d'Orris said. "She told Wringfield she was sick. Mixed up some paste and stuck fake pustules on her face. And he bought the whole thing! He took her to the apothecary, and while she was there she slipped away."

"The Old Boar is not pleased," Turnstall said. "Wringfield better get used to the smell of latrines. What's wrong with you, Loxley? You've turned gray."

Robin left the knights and he paced back and forth in the drizzling dawn. What should he have done? He should have taken her seriously when she said she would escape. Then what? Gone with her, as she wanted? Told Sir Bors what she was planning? Pleaded with her to stay?

You had a chance, he told himself. *Now she's lost to you, and you may never see her again.*

Something occurred to him and he went to the Inner Court. This time there was no sentry at the guard tower. He went in and climbed to the second floor. The door to Marian's jail stood open. He went inside. Her absence hung heavy in the air and the idea that she had been here so briefly and was gone was torment. He searched the chamber and when his eyes adjusted to the low light he saw something gleaming in a corner. He knelt and peered closely. Here were words, scrawled in berry juice. He traced the shapes with his finger and eventually he managed to read: *Follow the Path of Angels.*

Marian had left this for him to see. She had given him another chance.

Below her message were more scribbles, but these words had run into one another and were impossible to read. So then, that was all there was: *Follow the Path of Angels.*

It was a cypher. And for now Robin had no idea what this meant. But he remembered what Marian had said—*we'll have to go back there*—and he knew where she was headed.

And he knew he was supposed to follow. Back to the dark places of his past.

V. The Decision

It was another sunny day and almost everyone was outside, watching knights practice and spectators arrive. The babble of excitement reached Robin only faintly as he made his way along the deserted hallways.

He found Sir Bors in the Chancery. It was stuffy in this wood-paneled room, hung with tapestries, and the overlord looked uncomfortable in his robes of office, wedged behind an oakwood desk. The Cofferer and the Chief Clerk fussed around him while a notary chased the end of a pipe roll that snaked across the carpet.

Robin approached and stood waiting. At last Sir Bors raised his huge head, and just for an instant Robin imagined he saw something flicker in his eyes—something like resignation—as if Sir Bors had been expecting this moment and dreading it. But as quickly as it came the expression passed and when Sir Bors spoke he was as gruff and imperious as ever.

"Well, boy, what is it? You squires. This estate administers six market towns, twelve hundred oxgang of plowing land, fifty fighting knights, plus twenty-four boys with blunt swords who think the entire place revolves around them. Well, boy? Spit it out."

"I need permission to travel—"

"No. Was that all? Right, get out." Sir Bors lowered his head and searched across the desk and snatched up two parchments and held them over his shoulder for the Chief Clerk. "This one and this one," he said. "Closed seal. And make sure they're copied first."

Robin stood there. The overlord raised first his eyes, then his head, very slowly.

"I need to go home," Robin said. "My . . . old home. To Wodenhurst. I hope to be back in a few days. A week at most."

The Chief Clerk was gathering up documents and inkwells and moving away from the table. The Cofferer had already edged out of the rear door. But Sir Bors only looked at Robin, studying him with those hard gray eyes.

"Have I ever been unclear about my rules?" he said. "Have you ever doubted that primary rule, in particular? You will pass the boundary to these lands twice in your life: once an undisciplined boy; the second time a man prepared. All or nothing. There is no other way. We have had boys staying with us when their fathers have died, and do you think they were permitted to attend the grave? I'm asking you a question, boy. Did they visit the grave?"

Robin shook his head.

"Right. So. Get out. Now."

"I made a promise."

This time two huge fists came down and the desk jumped and everything went flying to the floor. "Get out of my sight!"

Robin left.

Only later did he remember he was also going to ask—to *demand*—that Sir Bors tell him the full truth of all this. Why had Marian been here? Why had Robin and Bones and the other low-born squires been brought here in the first place?

Why would Sir Bors make Robin a ward, alongside lordlings like Joscelin Tarcel?

You will be told all, the day you step up to the Household Guard. That was what the overlord had told Robin, when he had first arrived. But it wasn't good enough. Seeing Marian had brought all this to the surface. Robin had spent his entire life being pushed around. Never told the whole truth. Sir Bors was as bad as anyone. Worse. Why should Robin go on blindly doing as he said? Wasn't it time he took control of his own life?

"Bones, do you ever think about leaving?"

Bones hooked his gardbrace back on its stand. He glanced over his shoulder at Geoff Pike, the Armorer, to check his back was turned.

"Leaving?" Bones said. "This place? Of course I don't. Some days are tougher than others, we all know that. But why would I want to leave?"

"I'm not talking about *wanting*," Robin whispered. "I'm talking about . . . family. And home."

"We don't have families, except each other. This is our home, until this is over."

"You're just repeating what they tell us. But it's not true, is it? You must have somewhere. Someone. Waiting."

Bones looked at Robin and twisted fingers through his chin-beard. "Don't tell me, this is about angel eyes, isn't it? That princess in the tower. She really is something to you then, you're not just dreaming it? Well, you can forget her. She's not worth it, not even that one. At the very least she'll have to wait."

Robin took a cuisse plate from his stand, began rubbing nut oil into the joints.

"I said she'll have to wait, won't she? Loxley, look at me.

You can't be thinking . . . you cannot actually even be starting to think—"

"Keep your voice down," Robin whispered, glancing over his shoulder.

Bones leaned in; his voice became a hiss. "But seriously, listen, look at all this stuff. Look what you've won. And think where you came from, and one day it'll be *Sir* Robin, greatest knight in the realm. *That's* your future. It's golden. How could you even start to think . . . how could you possibly ever want—"

"I told you, I'm not talking about *wanting*! I should have known you wouldn't understand."

Squires were turning to look at Robin.

"Quiet, down there," Geoff Pike said. "Robin Loxley, don't make me hand out penalty points. The last thing your company needs."

Robin filled a bowl with water and lemon juice. He began polishing his hauberk, one chain link at a time, concentrating on that, letting his anger subside.

"I know you can't mean it," Bones whispered. "We all have tough days. A shock to see your childhood girl again, I'm sure. But you need to focus. We're not out of the running yet. The gauntlet this afternoon, then archery tomorrow. Win both of those and all will be forgiven. And I've been talking to Irish about Tarcel. We've thought of the perfect revenge, just listen to this . . ."

That night Robin lay awake in the dormitory, trying to weigh one thing against another. But his every thought returned to her. His skin shivered with the memory of having been close to her once more. His head thumped with the idea of her being out there in the dark, all alone. In the end it didn't feel like making a decision at all. A path had opened ahead of him, and he could already see his footprints upon the soil.

Around him all waking sounds were fading. Bones had stopped whispering strategies; Rowly was snoring; Irish silent. Farther off was the muffled click of dice rolling on straw, but soon this too ceased. Robin sat up and reached under his bed for his hunting pack. He put inside some dried meat and oatcakes he had stolen earlier from the dining hall. He packed his father's woodsman's knife and some tallow candles and a drawstring pouch containing almost a pound in silver coins. Last of all he reached into his hiding place near the wall and took out his jade amulet. He tied the cord around his neck.

He sat on the edge of his bed, wishing he could at least say good-bye to these friends of his. For the first time in years he felt tears pricking behind his eyes.

Come on, keep moving, he thought. *She needs you.* He stood and left the dormitory. He went across the darkened courtyard and into the maze of alleys known as the Warrens. He ducked beneath the servants' quarters. He continued past the aviaries, the hunting hawks tipping their heads and watching him blindly, their eyes stitched shut. In the distance, clear on the night air, he could hear singing and laughter, and the playing of harp and drum—some of Sir Bors's guests, feasting through the night. At a time like this, no one would notice a solitary squire, slipping away.

He reached the armory and went down into the sunken chamber. He lit one of the candles and went to his own stand. He took the goatskin boots and pulled them on. He put on some of his under-armor: the padded aketon jerkin, and leather wrist bracers; over the top his finest black embroidered surcoat. Finally the hunting cloak he and Marian had found all those years ago. It was now a little tight around the shoulders, but still the perfect thing for the road. He took the shortbow that had once belonged to his father and he slung it, unstrung, across his back. He shouldered a quiver of arrows.

Everything else—the hauberk, the longsword, the greathelm—
he left on the stand. Those things would only slow him down.

He left the armory and crossed toward the stables, a bright
blue traveler's moon showing him the way. He moved slowly.
Perhaps he was still suffering from yesterday's blow to the
head, because the world was fuzzy at the edges and the ground
felt uncertain beneath his feet.

Ariadne snorted and stamped a foot when she saw Robin.
He put a hand on her forehead and led her out of the stables.
Harold Muster, the old porter, was asleep in the east guard-
house, as he usually was. And here was the postern gate, often
left unwatched at night. Robin crept toward it, carefully slid
the bolt across, eased the gate open, squeezed Arry through.

The warm summer breeze. The land spread out in darkening layers.

Here he was outside. All this real and really happening. No
going back.

He was feeling dizzier than ever. So when he saw a phantom horseman, standing against the manor walls, he told
himself it was just another trick of the dark. It was just the
moon, casting shadows from the Tree of Shields. *You're imagining things. Get out of here, before you have time to change your mind.*

He turned away from the shadow-shape and he climbed
onto Arry. He spurred her into a trot and he forced himself to
think of Marian and he did not dare look back.

VI. The Scroll

By the time he reached the river he knew he was being followed.

Bones. He must have noticed me missing. The idiot. He'll get kicked out if he's caught.

He forded the river and spurred Arry into a canter—she was a good night horse and Robin was a better rider than Bones so it shouldn't be difficult to leave him behind.

But already his pursuer was splashing through the ford. The thundering of hooves. The breaking of a branch. And quickly as that Robin was caught.

He brought Arry to a halt and he looked up at the horseman towering over him. This wasn't Bones. This was the shadow-figure he had seen beneath the Tree of Shields.

"I hoped you would turn back of your own accord," Sir Bors's voice rumbled. "But you are clearly beyond making a measured decision."

"Why was she here?" Robin said. "Why did you take her prisoner?" He startled himself, talking this way to the overlord. But something inside him had snapped, and now there was no holding back.

Sir Bors studied him with those cold-steel eyes. He took a long breath before he spoke. "Marian Delbosque was here for her own protection. And for yours, no less. I knew I was taking a risk, bringing the two of you so close, but I was left little choice. And I didn't think even she would be this rash. Listen carefully now, Robin, and know I have never told you anything so true: Leave this place and you will be heading into worse danger than you—"

He was interrupted by shouting from the direction of the citadel. Robin looked back and saw three tiny figures, one of them attempting to turn his horse, another slipping and struggling to stay in the saddle.

"I wondered if they would be fool enough to follow," Sir Bors said. "Your actions threaten to cost your friends dearly, as well as yourself. Come with me now, back inside."

Still Robin didn't move. "I won't abandon her," he said. "I won't leave her all alone. I made a promise."

Sir Bors sat straighter in his saddle, the leather creaking. "I also made a promise, to myself," he said. "And the promise was this: I would not send you to face the world until you were prepared. If I let you ride away tonight, I will have failed."

Robin couldn't raise his eyes from the ground. "I am prepared."

"No!" Sir Bors shouted, startling Arry. "No, you are not. What do you think has been happening here? We had more to teach you than how to swing a sword and ride a war-horse. When you came here you were driven by a rage that could have scorched the earth. That fury was hurting others, but it would have destroyed you, in the end. We've tried to tame it, direct it, but the work is only half done. That raw anger is still there, I can see it, clinging to you like a shadow."

Sir Bors looked back at Bones and the others, drawing closer. Two guards had now emerged, holding flaming torches.

"We don't have much time. I need to stop those three compounding your mistake. If they cross that river, I'll have no choice but to cast them out. This is your final opportunity, Robin. Leave this place and there will be no second chance. You must understand that. You will be dead to us."

Until this moment Robin had been weathering a storm of sorrow and guilt and elation and a numb kind of doubt. But he had not been scared. Now, as he looked back at the citadel, watch fires flickering there on the battlements, and he looked once more into the unknown night, he felt fear stir for the first time and he felt it settle deeply in his bones.

You will be dead to us.

What if he couldn't find Marian? What was she running from? What waited out there for her, and for him?

But still he didn't move. He kept Arry facing away from the citadel. "Before I came here," he said, "Marian was my life. There was nobody else. Nothing else. She was . . . everything. You can't forget something like that, even if it would be easier if you could."

He took a breath, meaning to say more, but he didn't know the words to even begin. He looked at the ground. He felt Sir Bors studying him.

"So be it," the overlord said finally. "There can be little purpose in forcing you to stay. Deep down I knew this day would come—I only hoped I would have more time." As he spoke he took from beneath his tabard a rolled parchment. The wax seal was his own crossed spears and battle boar. "I wrote this for you the day you arrived," he said. "I wanted to know, if I failed to return from campaign, that the truth would not die with me. Where you're going there are people who will lie to you. They were already lying to you, before you came here."

Robin only stared at the scroll and did not reach to take it.

"When you read these truths," Sir Bors said, "I want you to remember what we've tried to teach you: The greatest enemy you will ever face is yourself. Submit to fury and to hatred and you will become the monster you are fighting against."

"Loxley! Loxley, are you out here? Loxley!"

"Stop there! Stand your horses."

Bones and the others were drawing near, followed by the guards.

Robin took the scroll with an unsteady hand.

"So then, be on your way," Sir Bors said. "By first light I want you far away from those three. Stick to the back routes— the main roads are becoming more lawless by the day. Farewell, Robin Loxley."

Without another word he turned and headed back toward the citadel.

As Robin rode away he tried not to listen to his friends calling to him in the dark. He tried not to hear Sir Bors's words, echoing through his thoughts. *You will be dead to us.*

He forced himself to think of Marian, out there somewhere, alone, and he kept his eyes fixed ahead, on the dark and unknown road.

VII. The Road

Robin ignored Sir Bors's advice and he kept to the major roads because they were quicker. While the night lasted it looked like a good decision. He saw nobody.

Around midnight he rested Ariadne, resisting the temptation to take a break himself, stomping back and forth to stay awake. He rode on, the landscape passing in blue and purple layers—open farmland and rolling hills, calm and quiet. He began to feel relaxed and then almost heady with the freedom of the road. Where the ground flattened and straightened he coaxed Arry into a gallop and he felt the wind bringing him fully awake, his cloak streaming like a banner.

But now, as dawn broke and a light rain started to fall, he began to see danger at the roadside and he slowed his progress to a walk. Just after sunrise he crossed a crumbling stone bridge and there beneath were three cutthroats. They had murdered a man and had stripped him of his clothes and now they were driving a sharpened stake through his heart. The killers froze and watched Robin cross the river.

A little farther on he thought he saw metal gleam from a thicket on the opposite side of the track. Only when he rode over it did he see the outline of a heavy rope buried in the leaves. This was a garrote line—the bandits would raise the rope to knock a traveler from his horse. Robin didn't know why they didn't bother with him: Perhaps they were waiting for a bigger catch, or lying in ambush for somebody specific. Whatever the reason, Robin was relieved to ride on unmolested.

In those early hours he saw plenty of other life. A bishop's carriage, escorted by armed riders. A tavern, travelers gathering thickly there for safety in numbers. A stonemason's wagon, pulled by a dozen oxen.

But as the day went on these signs of life became fewer. For many miles now he had seen nobody, not even bandits. Even the occasional village he passed was deserted, and Robin began to feel like the last person alive. At a crossroads he passed a row of stakes, each mounted with a human head. Their mouths were open and crows had pecked out their eyes. A warning to robbers, perhaps. But it seemed to Robin these dead mouths were urging him to turn back before he fell off the edge of the world.

But more unnerving than any of this was the forest. It had accompanied Robin his entire journey, at first only visible in the distance, but increasingly tight against the road, sometimes now spilling over the road so he was forced to ride through gloomy tunnels.

He knew now it was true, what Marian had told him when they were young, that Sherwood Forest was vast, and that different parts of it had different names and very different natures. Where it ran closest to Sir Bors's manor it was known as Thorpe Wood. There it had been tamed, large parts of it cleared for timber, the rest crisscrossed with hunts and enclosures. The farther Robin rode west, the wilder Sherwood became. Now it loomed over him, tangled and ancient and black in its depths. Here was the true wildwood. He turned again and stared into the trees. He was *sure* this time he had caught the edge of movement—something tipping its head—but he kept staring and there was nothing but old man's beard bobbing in the breeze.

Stop imagining things, he told himself. *There's enough real danger on this road without inventing horrors.*

He stopped to give Ariadne another rest. While she drank from a stream he sat with his back to the forest. He couldn't resist taking Sir Bors's scroll from his backpack. At first his fingers only picked at the seal but refused to break it. What would these words reveal about his parents? Why had Sir Bors felt the need to shield him from these truths? His fingers went on bothering the wax.

At last he forced himself to break the seal and unroll the parchment. He stared at the writing, but initially he saw only meaningless swirls. He started again, forcing himself to take his time. During their years living in the tower, Marian had been teaching Robin to read and write, but she had never been the most patient of tutors, and at the academy Robin had proved better suited to physical pursuits than book study, so reading for him would always be a laborious task. What made this doubly hard was Sir Bors's script: It was an erratic scribble, the letters lurching about the page like dying spiders.

Robin tried once more, tracing the lines with his finger. A few phrases lifted themselves from the babble.

A silent spring, he thought one part read.

And another: *tearing of an angel's wing . . .*

So far none of it made much more sense than Marian's cypher. Did Sir Bors really write this nonsense-riddle?

One line looked like: *A son in darkness, a daughter chained.* There was something that might have said: *Fenrir's lust.* Then several words he couldn't read, then: *winter-born.*

He read this last phrase over and over. Where had he heard that before? Why did reading it make his heart thunder?

He looked up. He had been concentrating so hard on the scroll he hadn't heard the armed riders until they were almost on top of him. There were four of them, wearing black half-armor and bloodred cloaks. Stark against their breastplates was an image of a wolf, its teeth bared. The Sheriff's Guard.

Robin went to Ariadne and kept his hand on her muzzle. Three of the horsemen looked at him briefly, then turned away, continuing along the road, slouching in their saddles. The fourth soldier held Robin's gaze. He was around Robin's age, or a little older. Visible beneath his skull-helm was a shock of hair, orange as a wasp. His cheeks were dotted with scars, each one in the shape of a teardrop. He searched Robin up and down. He looked at the scroll in his hands. Finally he turned away and continued after the others.

Robin rolled the scroll and put it back in his pack. There would be time to decipher it later. His most pressing task was to find Marian. He swung into the saddle and continued on his way, overtaking the soldiers at a canter and leaving them far behind.

At last, as the day drew to a close, he saw landmarks he recognized. Here were the standing stones known as Merlin's Dancers, and the overgrown mound of Beowulf's Barrow. He skirted Thuner's Fold, where he used to go with his brothers to shoot at crows.

And then finally, on the hillside, wrapped in mist and drizzle, was Wodenhurst. From this distance it appeared silent and still, huddled around the Trystel Tree, cowering beneath the wildwood.

Robin passed well wide of the village, following Packman's Furrow into the valley. He splashed through the shallow river and climbed Lord's Hill and approached the remains of the Delbosque manor.

He reached the boundary and tethered Arry to a tree. He walked among the collapsed buildings, grasses growing thick between the crumbled stone. He found the husk of the tower he and Marian had once called home. He stood there in the eerie quiet, and he almost believed he could hear her voice, reading to him in their den, whispering as they tumbled out on one of their adventures. But then these memories were swept away by thoughts of fire and panic.

Why would she come back here, of all places?

He looked for signs that she had been here in recent days but found nothing. And by now he knew he was just wasting time. Putting off the inevitable. Because he had become quite certain where Marian's trail began: what she meant by *follow the path of angels*.

He suspected too where the trail would lead, and he dreaded the idea.

In any case, there was no more he could do tonight. The rooks were already squabbling in their roosts and the sky was darkening into bloodred strips. He went back to Arry and they wound their way back up the valley, heading for the village.

Much of Wodenhurst was exactly as he recalled, only smaller. His brothers had taught him to swim in Mill Pond, and back then it seemed large as a lake; now Robin thought he could probably jump across that patch of water. Some of the sounds were the same: the lonely creaking of the waterwheel, the *clink-clink* of Gord Moore working late in his forge. But then the hammering stopped. Robin felt eyes searching him. Candlelit faces at windows.

He stroked Arry's neck and continued up through the lanes, beneath the limbs of the Trystel Tree. He couldn't help imagining what he must look like to the villagers, returning this way, dressed in these clothes from Florence, riding this courser worth more than all the livestock these people had ever owned.

Children came out to look. But there were too few children. Where were all the people? Half the houses looked deserted, their thatched roofs stripped bare by their neighbors.

The villagers went on staring. And by the time he reached the common ground the voices had started.

"It *is* him."

"She said he'd return."

"You shouldn't have come back here. This is no place for you."

"Keep riding. You don't belong."

He thought he recognized the voice of Agnes Poley, and Matheu Plowless, but nobody came fully into view so he could not be sure. He began to regret coming back here. He didn't need the shelter, not really; he could sleep wrapped in his cloak somewhere off the road until it was light enough to follow Marian's trail. So why had he come back? To be reminded? To try to remember?

He came to the top of the village and stopped in front of his old home. He barely recognized it. The stone walls stood whole but now the timber door was off and propped against the barn and most of the shutters were missing or hung loose.

Narris Felstone was in the croft, repairing a fence post. His hammer hovered. His mother, Mabel, came out of the house and she froze, staring. Robin looked for signs of Warin Felstone, and Richard and Ida, Narris's younger brother and sister.

Mabel saw him looking and shook her head. "Times have been hard," she said. "For all of us." She looked back up at Robin. "I'll fetch fresh straw for your bedding. I'll put something in the pot. We'll get you comfortable. This is still your home, and always will be." She went back into the house.

141

"Nobody wants you here, you know," Narris said, scratching his face with the stump of his left arm.

Robin ignored him. Of all the things that looked smaller than he remembered, Narris Felstone looked the smallest of all. He led Ariadne to the barn, made her as comfortable as he was able, then went into the house. Mabel brought a bowl of nettle soup and she and Robin ate in silence. She gave him bedding and he laid it in front of the hearth.

When Mabel and Narris were sleeping Robin tried once more to make sense of Sir Bors's scroll. It was impossible by the light of a single candle. He put the parchment back in his pack.

He couldn't help thinking of his friends competing in the tourney today without him. He couldn't help listening to the memories scuttling in the corners of this house. Eventually, he slept.

VIII. First Blood

He woke to a muffled thud and a crash and a wailing noise. Panicked geese and the barking of a dog.

He went out of the house and stood in the croft. He saw four soldiers wearing bloodred cloaks, swaggering across Mill Bridge on foot. The day had dawned a sickly yellow, and at this distance it was difficult to tell, but he suspected these were the four rangers he had seen yesterday on the road. Each had a different weapon slung across his shoulder: a crossbow, a flail, an ironwood club, a boar-spear. Two of the soldiers were shouting something, but their words were swallowed up by Winter Forest before Robin could hear what they said.

He watched one of the men go into a house and come back out dragging old Robert Wyser by his hair. Another swung his bludgeon and Stephen Younger went to the ground, curled in on himself. William Tanglefoot, his hobble more pronounced than ever, was trying to move quickly across the common ground, a ranger flicking at him with his flail.

Mabel Felstone and Narris came out of the house and stood beside Robin.

"Why are they doing that?" Robin said. "Why are they here?"

"Same reason *you* are," Narris said. "That girl of yours. She attracts all the unwanted guests. Like flies around—"

Mabel slapped Narris on the back of the neck, stopped him short. "They've been here before," she said. "The younger two in particular are terrible boys, and vicious. Each time they come back they get worse."

"Supposing I was to go down there," Narris said to Robin. "Tell them exactly who you are. Tell them you and Marian used to stick closer than a bee on honey. Maybe they'd even give me a reward."

Mabel slapped him again on the neck. "You'll do nothing of the sort."

"Why should the rest of us suffer?" Narris said. "I bet he knows exactly where she's hiding. He must know she's near, or he wouldn't have come back here."

"What Robin knows or doesn't know is none of our concern. We brought this on ourselves and you know it."

Robin continued to watch the Sheriff's men. He could see now they were indeed the soldiers he had seen on the road. The one he remembered most distinctly—the young man with wasp-orange hair—was standing over Robert Wyser and brandishing a pair of wool shears.

Shouldn't Robin do something? How many times had Sir Bors lectured them about honor and duty—about defending those unable to defend themselves? He put one end of his bow on the ground and deftly looped the string into place. He rested his right hand on the quiver at his hip.

"Robin, you should go," Mabel said. "Before they see you. This is our burden, not yours."

Robin watched the soldiers prowling through the village, kicking out with their nailed boots, leaving women and children bleeding. He took an arrow from his quiver.

"You, come down here with the others. Don't make me come up there and get you." This was the short ranger with orange hair. He had finished with Robert Wyser and he had turned and was shouting up at Robin and Mabel and Narris.

"Go," Mabel said, pushing at Robin. "Sneak out the back and down to the river. We'll say you were a stranger, passing through. Hurry."

The ranger who had shouted was already coming up Herne Hill.

Shouldn't Robin stay? Shouldn't he help protect the weak?

You're not here to fight the whole world, he told himself. *You came back here for Marian, remember. In any case, these people hated you, cast you out. You're not their defender.*

The wasp-haired ranger was drawing near.

"My horse. . . ," Robin said to Mabel, "she will be valuable to you, if you care for her. If I don't return, take her to market. You should get ten pounds for her, at least."

"Go," Mabel said quietly.

Robin tucked the arrow back in his quiver. He headed for the rear of the house.

"You, stop!" the ranger shouted, then Robin heard a war horn.

He slipped down the blind side of Herne Hill, into Lower Field, and around the marsh. He remembered this valley's nooks and its running routes and sightlines, and within moments he had bolted away and hidden himself from view.

He crouched in Hob's Hollow, listening to the rangers on the hillside above. By their shouting, it seemed all four of them were now hunting Robin. No matter how little he owed Wodenhurst he was glad to have lured them away. Through the undergrowth he looked up to Woden's Ride and he saw two of the red-cloaked figures moving there, heading in the wrong direction. Were they really here because of Marian? Why? He needed to find her, and quickly.

145

He moved around inside the grotto, his boots sucking in the mud. He dug through the mulch and turned over rotting logs. He found nothing, but kept searching—he was certain now this was where her trail began.

Follow the path of angels.

The memory of it was burning, perfectly clear: It was the day they first met, and he and Marian were hiding here in Hob's Hollow while her father's retainers searched nearby. Marian was chewing a deadly fungus—a destroying angel—and Robin had leaped from his rock and saved her life. That was what she meant by angels. She meant here. He was sure of it.

He kept digging and crawling and looking and eventually among the reeds he found an ice skate, made from the shin bone of an ox. He was right: Marian had been here. She had left this for him. This was a cypher trail, of the type they used to lay for each other when they were children. A trail only Robin could possibly follow.

He took the skate and left Hob's Hollow, scanning the fields and hedgerows, looking for any sign of the soldiers. They had disappeared. In fact, it was strangely peaceful now in the valley as he headed for Summerswood. Two otter pups played in Silver River; a single buzzard mewed as it wheeled above.

He crossed the river and entered the greenwood, its paths cool and quiet, a solitary blackbird singing as Robin crossed a broadleaf glade. He followed the hunting paths to the far southern edge of the wood. He walked down a familiar slope—past a tree still hung with a rope swing, now green with age—and he arrived at Titan's Lake.

An ice skate.

He and Marian had spent many summer days here at Titan's Lake, but they used to come here too in the winter, whenever the lake froze over. They came here to joust, using ash branches for lances, wearing knights' helms they stole from a dusty trophy room in the manor house. They wore skates like the one Robin now held in his hand. He stood at the water's edge, and in spite of everything he couldn't help smiling. He remembered Marian—her greathelm comically large, lolling from side to side—unable to skate in a straight line, laughing uncontrollably.

He went to the place beneath a willow stand where they used to store the knights' helms. They were still there, dented and rusty. Inside one was a jagged rock. He tossed it into the water and walked away from the lake.

A rock.

This clue meant Oldcastle Oak. Many times as children they had stood in its crown throwing rocks against attacking rooks and crows. He went to Oldcastle Oak and after much searching he found a chess piece sitting on a branch.

He followed this trail most of the morning, some of the clues difficult to find and hard to decipher, others pointing the way as clearly as a raised finger. He found a swan's feather, a drinking ewer, a glass bead, a clipped shilling, and he followed the trail zigzagging through Summerswood and out to Silver River and back up the valley.

And with each new clue his heart beat harder and faster, fear building in him cold and heavy, because every waymarker was now leading him closer to Winter Forest. He stared up at it, looming ever larger, churning in the wind. Above the tree line crows spiraled, thick as flies. And still he drew closer, as he knew he would. He was certain now, where this trail ultimately led—where Marian would consider the safest place to hide from the Sheriff's men.

He followed the clues back to Wodenhurst, and near Mill Pond he found a snakeskin: This related to a prank they had once played on Narris Felstone while he lay sleeping in his bed. So then Robin had to return to his old home, at the top of Herne Hill. He climbed through the village, every pair of shutters now closed, not a whisper from behind walls, no sign even of a stray cat stalking the goslings. After the noise and fury of dawn, it was as if the village was feigning death, praying not to be noticed. The only movement was a light mist, seeping out of Winter Forest and slithering down Herne Hill, snaking its tendrils between the homes.

He arrived at the top of the village and searched beneath the window of his old room. He found the weathered skull of a sheep.

An animal skull.

The spirit fence.

He dropped the skull and continued up Herne Hill, through the thickening mist, until he reached Woden's Ride, his heart thundering, his fear complete.

Here he was, standing beneath the vast dark wall of Winter Forest. Above him it twisted in the wind, making its dry roaring noise. At his side Silver River glistened one last time before being swallowed into the gloom.

And there, on the riverbank, was a sailing boat, woven from reeds, with an acer leaf as a little red sail: the type of boat he and Marian used to float on the river, pretending they were Argonauts on their way to Babylon and Troy.

The reed boat was pointing upstream. Meaning Robin was meant to follow its course.

Into Winter Forest.

Into the place he had not been since he was seven years old, when he had woken to find himself alone, his father vanished.

He stared into the blackness. He saw berries glistening like demon eyes, thorns glinting like teeth. He imagined he heard a child's voice, drifting out of the depths.

Where are you? I'm here.

He realized it was his own voice, echoing down the years.

Come back, please.

And for the first time he thought: *I can't do it. I can't follow her. Not in there.*

In front of him was the spirit fence, its posts topped with the skulls of goats and sheep. The barrier was meant to stop anything leaving the forest, but to Robin it was one more dire warning not to enter: *Nothing and nobody should cross this point.*

He tried to persuade himself he must have made a mistake somewhere along the trail. Marian wouldn't really go in there, alone. She must be hiding somewhere else—he would have to retrace his steps and start again. But then he saw a dull gleam—something half buried in the grass. He knelt and turned the object. It was a pair of manacles on a heavy chain— the kind of shackles he had seen restraining Marian on the display ground.

She's been here, he told himself. *You're on the right path. No good lying to yourself.*

"So then, what have you found?" a voice behind him said. "What do you think of this, eh, Scutter? I told you it would work—sit tight and let this one pick up her scent."

Robin turned, furious with himself. He had been so obsessed with Marian's trail, and his own fear of the forest, he had stopped watching for the soldiers. There were two of them, coming up Herne Hill, emerging out of the mist. They must have been hiding in Wodenhurst the entire time. The ranger who had spoken was the short one with wasp-orange hair and scarified cheeks. Behind him was an older guard with a whip at his belt.

"A peasant called Narris told us about you," said the orange-haired guard, aiming his cocked crossbow. "He said you'd know where the girl is hiding. I removed these from his mother to make him talk. But, you know, the funny part, I didn't need to touch the old hag. Her son couldn't wait to tell us. If Scutter here hadn't been holding him so tight around the neck, he would have blurted it out, no questions asked. Still, no harm done."

Removed these from his mother.

The wool shears were tucked in the ranger's sword belt. They were stained red where the blades met. Robin's stomach turned as the ranger threw something that hit him wetly on the chest and fell away in two parts. Two red-and-white things. He didn't need to look to know they were fingers.

His hand went to his quiver.

"Put those on the ground," the wasp-haired ranger said. "Your bow too. You can lie down, your hands behind your back. We're going to have a talk, see what it is you know."

"But, Edric, shouldn't we wait for the others?" the bigger ranger said. "Hold this one until he arrives? What if they're telling true, back at that village?"

"Are you scared of one boy?"

"Yes. No—I mean, the winter-born, though. You know what they say. What the instructions were. We should wait for him to arrive with Jadder Payne."

Winter-born. There was that phrase again—the one Robin had read in the scroll. Why had the soldier directed it at him? Who did they think Robin was? He was born in the autumn, not the winter.

"I don't need to wait for anyone," Edric said. "This will be *my* triumph." He gestured at Robin. "Didn't you hear me—I *said*, lie down on the ground."

Robin didn't move.

The *kaw-kaw* of crows, turning blackly above.

"He's deaf," Edric said. "I need to unblock his ears. A crossbow bolt should do the trick."

He took a step. Robin didn't flinch.

The ranger came forward again.

"We need to be careful," the one called Scutter said. "You know what the man said. He wants—"

"Quiet," Edric said. "This one will learn to obey. Filthy shire-folk. How dare they—"

The soldier had taken another step, stumbled. His crossbow fired. The quarrel whispered past Robin's leg and embedded itself in the soil.

For a moment both soldiers just stared at the crossbow bolt. In that moment Robin stooped, picked up the manacles, moved forward, swung the chain. The iron bonds cracked the younger ranger across the side of the head.

A sickening crunch. The soldier slumped.

The second ranger had turned and slipped in the mud and was picking himself up and running back toward the village. Robin watched him go. He forced himself to look at the soldier called Edric, motionless on the ground, his legs sprawled at an odd angle. His skull-helm was too big for him and the manacle had caught him beneath that and now blood pumped thickly from above his left ear. Robin had no doubt he was dead.

He had killed a man.

He bent double and was physically sick. No amount of training with Sir Bors could have prepared him for this.

He stood and breathed and tried to think. It had all happened so quickly, and now a man lay dead.

What should he do? Bury the body?

No, you don't have time. You didn't want this to happen. He left you no choice. It wasn't your fault.

He looked toward Wodenhurst. The mist was pouring so thickly now from the forest he could barely see even the Trystel Tree. From somewhere in the valley he heard a war horn. The second ranger must be summoning help.

Robin looked at the dead soldier and he knew he could not stay here. He thought of the citadel, and Sir Bors, and he knew there was no going back.

You will be dead to us.

The war horn blared once more and was answered by shouting.

She needs you, he told himself. *You've come this far.*

He turned and walked past the spirit fence and pushed through the clawing branches into Winter Forest. Immediately the world turned darker, the air colder. He kept going, pushing through the thicket, all sounds from outside fading to silence.

He clambered on, keeping the twisting river on his shield side, following its course upstream as it snaked between mossy boulders and beneath fallen boughs. He battled with thorn bushes and hanging vines, thick as rope. The riverbank became steep and he had to drag himself forward on hands and knees.

A hot tingling in his spine, cold sweat at the back of his neck. He was angry at himself for feeling this way. When he had been lost in here, all those years ago, he had been a child, with a child's fears. Now he was practically a man and he had killed a man, and anyway, it was just as Sir Gilbert used to tell them back at Sir Bors's estate: *There are no monsters except those which men create.*

He hurried on. From somewhere close came a high-pitched squeal. A stoat had found an underground den and was busy killing whatever was home. Overhead a buzzard screeched.

He stopped, suddenly sure he was being followed. He crouched, his every muscle tense, listening intently for the tiniest sound. He heard only the chattering of a squirrel, a jay cackling in alarm. He convinced himself he was imagining things. He clambered on, but still with the feeling he was being watched.

There are no monsters except those which men create. But that was easy for Sir Gilbert to say. Easy to think that way from the safety of the citadel, surrounded by farmland and towns, the wildwood cleared for miles around. Here it was different. You felt it the moment you entered this ancient place. A crossing over. A changing of the rules.

He continued along the steep bank, the river sometimes wide and marshy but here narrow and twisting and overgrown. The smell of yew needles and of mist; the skittering of clawed feet and the trilling of water over stones. All of it perfectly distinct, fear amplifying each smell and every sound.

He told himself to stay alert and to keep calm. It wasn't working. A knot of fear had lodged itself in his throat, a sickly sensation spreading from his groin—all the feelings of a lost child. But the worst thing, as he continued to slip and fight his way along the riverbank, was the sensation of something tugging at him. Something *insisting*.

He stopped and looked away from the river, peering into the darkest reaches of the forest. They were terrifying, those infested depths, but they were also somehow . . . enticing. Occasionally, when Robin and Marian stood at the top of their tower, Robin would look down and he would feel the disturbing urge to jump. It was as if he had once had wings, and a part of him yearned once more to fly. This feeling was similar. He looked into the boundless wildwood, he felt dizzy and afraid, yet at the same time he desperately wanted to fall into that black abyss, to walk away from the river and keep walking. As if to do so, to lose himself utterly in the wildwood, would come as a great relief. Would feel almost like . . . *coming home.*

He stood there, fighting the sensation. Eventually his breathing slowed and he continued following the river. At times it disappeared underground and he followed it by the marsh y patches left on the surface. Or it paused to form pools and beaver lakes and he took long detours around their edges.

The mist thickened. Outside the day had been brightening toward noon, but here it was so dark the world might have slipped back into night.

Movement caught his eye. A glimpse of dark hair, flying . . .

Marian?

There it was again, and footsteps through dry leaves. He left the river and set off in pursuit.

He glanced behind him. What was she running from? He fought the urge to call out, concentrated on keeping her in view. There she was, disappearing now down a slope, visible again on the far side of that willow stand.

The wildwood became more tangled. Robin battled onward. He slipped on mossy logs and he stumbled on rocks and he pushed thorns from his eyes and he ran and kept running.

Suddenly this felt familiar. So many times they had done this in Summerswood: Marian running barefoot, Robin trailing in her wake, the pair of them caked in mud and scratched from scrambling up trees. And the familiar feeling was so warm and good that Robin felt mad with it and wanted to laugh. And now he was able to move quicker because a badger path had opened up before him, cutting through the undergrowth. He checked his footing and he ran and he glanced up and he ran faster.

But he didn't seem to be gaining on her. It was difficult even to keep her in view—mere flashes of her hair between the bark and the moss.

Except, was that a young woman's hair, or was it feathers? A kestrel darting through the trees? An owl hissed in the distance and through the mist it sounded like someone rasping for breath. A vixen bounded through the leaves, making a noise exactly like a person pursued . . .

Robin stopped, all the good and warm feelings draining away.

He looked and he listened.

He admitted he had not been following Marian at all.

He could not hear the river. How far had he come? He turned slowly and retraced his steps. He began to hurry, and then to run, still not seeing the river, panic rising, running faster, thorns slicing his skin.

To his right, from the darkest shadows, he was sure he heard a scream, followed by a laugh. He crouched, his breathing sharp and shallow. He had heard a woman's laugh, hadn't he? Or was this more deception—the screech of a jackdaw and the cackle of a jay?

He hurried on, pushing through brambles, slipping and regaining his feet and charging forward, and arriving finally back at the river. He stayed there for a long time, his hands on his knees. He looked once more into those black infested depths.

He continued on his way, the trilling sound of the water merging with the thundering of blood in his ears. A dreadful idea was playing over and over: *I thought I was following Marian along that badger path. I wasn't. What if this entire trail has been an illusion? What if I left the academy for nothing and she isn't here at all? What if I'm here, in Winter Forest, alone?*

He told himself to trust what he had seen—the clues Marian had left and the shackles he had found.

She's here. She's close.

He clambered on. Up another steep bank. The skittering of claws as squirrels headed for higher boughs. The alarm call of a jackdaw, guarding its nest. Hisses and cackles on all sides.

Eventually the ground flattened out. The river paused to become a small lake.

And that was where he found her.

First he spotted a campfire on the bank, and then a pile of clothing, and then . . .

Marian had her back to him. She was sliding into the water. Through dead branches and swirls of mist he watched the curve of her back submerge, then her shoulders, her hair fanning out on the surface, her head ducking under. She popped back up, gasping at the cold.

Robin managed to clear his throat.

"Marian . . ."

She turned, glared, strode out of the water. She didn't cover herself with her arms; she didn't blush or show the least concern she was standing there naked. She just shouted.

"Where have you *been?* How could you leave me here all this time all alone, you always were a slow goat but I never dreamed even you would take *this* long! You had better have brought the things I asked for or I am going to be *really* mad . . ."

IX. A Darkening Path

Marian was dripping wet, clothed only in mist, and she was *still* shouting.

"A few simple clues—I couldn't have made it much easier—I told myself over and over you'd be here any moment because there's no way you'd leave me in this place all alone, but I kept waiting and waiting, sitting here and listening and thinking the worst and *still* you didn't appear. What did I do to deserve you!"

Abruptly she stopped. She gave a violent shiver, glanced down at herself, bit her lower lip. She went to the fire and wrapped herself in a blanket, then came storming back to Robin and threw her arms around him.

"I *knew* you'd come. Sir Robin of the Hood, my champion from the very first. Come by the fire. Sit. Closer. Just until I dry off. Then we're leaving. Robin, thank goodness you're here, I didn't mean what I said about you being slow—well you *are* slow that's true but it's not your fault, you were born that way—I'm not angry, only I've been scared and so lonely, you can't imagine what it's been like, the sounds in this place!

"That's why I went in there to bathe, I had to do something other than just sit and listen, and I was beginning to wonder if you'd come at all, but of course you would, you never let anyone or anything stand in your way stubborn goat, I knew you'd come when I needed you most. And now I'm gabbling like a goose because it's the strangest feeling being this close to you and the most wonderful feeling too—here we are, properly together without a door between—and you're exactly as I remember but different at the same time.

"And I suppose one of us has to say something—all you're doing is staring, the same as you did before. You always were the quiet one—I knew you'd grow up the silent brooding type—and haven't you grown up, strong and handsome, look at you, a prince in those clothes. And anyway, you're probably in shock, that's why you're not speaking. I don't suppose you expected to see all that exactly. But honestly don't you have *anything* to say? Have you given up speaking this time for good? All you can do is stare."

She fell quiet and looked away and bit her lip. Robin was getting his breath back, his heartbeat still loud in his ears. Marian had dragged him close to her fire and they sat there, an arm's length apart, her hair steaming in the heat of the flames. He had a thousand things he wanted to say, but everything he rehearsed in his head sounded childish or stupid or wrong, and all of it building up behind his tongue, the same way it had when he saw her again in that jail cell. So he just went on staring. She swept her hair across one shoulder and turned to face him and stared back. Neither of them blinked. From a long way away an owl screeched. The fire popped and cracked and fizzled. The wind stirred and leaves skittered.

Eventually Marian said: "I need to get dressed. Turn your back like a nobleman. Not that I've got anything left to hide, you've seen it all now in any case. You should have seen the look on your face!"

She wriggled into underclothes and a kirtle. But before she

even finished dressing she reached for Robin's backpack and looked inside. And again she started shouting.

"Where are the things I asked for? The rest of the code, didn't you read it? I wanted peasants' clothes, and as much money as you could steal. How much is here? Ten shillings? Less? God's bones, Robin Loxley, if I didn't love you so much . . ."

She trailed off, raised a hand, and pinched her lower lip. She looked away. The forest now had become very quiet. Robin listened to the snap-crackle of the fire and he watched the blue-edged flames lick the wood. He could imagine he was back at the citadel, in his dormitory bed, and he was dreaming all this.

Marian pulled on a velvet supertunic; a fur-lined cape. She tied her jade amulet round her neck, then pressed it to her lips. "What's this on your clothes?" she said. "This is blood. Whose blood is this?"

Robin looked down at the splatter of crimson on his tunic and the sight of it cleared his head and made everything come into focus, sharp as a knife edge.

"It's a soldier's blood," he said. "One of the Sheriff's men. I'll tell you about it. But first I need to know what's going on. Why are they chasing you? Where are we going?"

She looked at him quizzically, her eyebrows knitting. "We're going to Castile. You know that's where my mother was from, I must have told you a thousand times. I wrote to her family and it's all arranged, they'll take us in. We won't be safe, exactly—we could run to the ends of the earth and it wouldn't be far enough—but it will have to do, for now. It was all there, written on the wall. The message wasn't *that* hard to decipher. I'm beginning to wonder how you made it this far. Have you at least got a proper knife? Give it to me."

Before Robin understood what she was doing she had taken his father's woodsman's blade and was using it to saw through whole handfuls of her hair, leaving long snakes of it lying on the ground. When she had finished she put the knife back in Robin's pack.

He stared at her. All he could do was stare. Perhaps it was the shock of seeing her with short hair, but suddenly it seemed this was not his childhood friend but was instead some beautiful stranger he had met out here in the savage wood. He stared at the curve of her neck, the line of her jaw, the gleam of her gray-green eyes, as if seeing it all for the very first time.

"Marian, what's happening? Why are those soldiers chasing you? And who do they think I am? What do they mean by winter-born?"

She tipped her head. "Where did you hear that?"

"One of the rangers said it. What does it mean?"

"The same as warg-child. Or sylva-spawn. It's all part of the same thing. He's got it all wrong, but he thinks—" She fell silent and became perfectly still, steam rising from her hair.

Robin said: "What do you—"

"Ssshhh, quiet. Listen." She took his hand and gripped it so hard he felt her nails pierce the skin. "I hear them," she whispered. "They're coming." She fixed him with that big dark glare. Her voice became a hiss. "They must have followed you!" Then she was up and running. Robin grabbed his backpack and his bow and his quiver and he scrambled after her. She weaved between trees, clambered over logs and boulders. Robin kept pace. Several times he glanced behind him but he saw nothing except the dark wood, lurking.

"There's nobody there," he said.

She kept running. Robin saw they had left the course of the river. They were running blind through the forest. Fear gripped his throat. That sickly feeling spreading from his groin. The feelings of a lost child. "This is stupid! We'll get lost in here."

She ran on. All he could do was follow. Up steep slopes and down into stream beds and through blackthorn bushes, battling their way through the undergrowth, brambles and branches fighting back. She stopped and crouched in a gully beneath an overhanging willow. They crouched and breathed hard and they listened.

"There was no one there," Robin said.

"It was them," she said, scowling. "I know what men in nailed boots sound like when they're trying to be quiet. And I know a stupid goat when I see one and so I know how they found me. But we've lost them for now. Come on, we need to keep moving." She hauled herself over a fallen beech trunk.

"We'll get lost in here," Robin said.

"No we won't. We're heading north. It feels like we've come a long way into the forest but we haven't. We're following the tree line."

Robin peered through the mist and he saw she was right: He could see the horizon. The edge of the forest was a few hundred paces away and they were walking parallel. He could have sworn they were heading west—it was so difficult to orient here. They walked and they walked, hacking and fighting their way through the undergrowth, the forest cackling and shrieking at them as they went.

Robin said: "Sir Bors told me he took you captive for your own protection. And for mine. What did he mean?"

Marian said: "When it gets dark we can leave the forest and head across open country. We'll steal horses and be at the coast by morning. Then we'll be on our way to Castile. My mother's family are expecting us. You can continue your training there." She pushed her way through a thicket of hawthorn, gritting her teeth as it clawed at her skin. "I have to make preparations too," she said. "And one day, when we're ready, we'll come back. And we'll kill him."

Robin looked at her. "What do you mean? Kill who?"

"The Sheriff."

She strode on, not meeting his eyes. At least she was calmer now. She had always been a blaze of energy, but now, of all times, they needed to keep clear heads.

"Start again," Robin said. "I need you to explain. What's happening? What does it have to do with the Sheriff?"

She stopped and peered back, narrowing her eyes. They walked on together.

"There's so much to tell you," she said. "I forget how little you know. The things I've learned. It's taken me a long time, but I've uncovered the truth. It was the Sheriff. All of it. He's shadowed us our whole lives. He's the reason my father burned the manor, and our tower. My mother's death wasn't an accident—the Sheriff caused it. And he killed your parents, and your brothers."

Robin stopped. There was a moment of absolute silence. Memories flooded through him, red raw, of the time his family disappeared.

They were heartbroken, Mabel Felstone had said. *They left to start afresh—to try to forget.*

He ran and caught up with Marian. "Why are you saying that? My family could still be alive, somewhere. After they left the village, nobody knows where they went."

"They're dead. It was the Sheriff." She ducked beneath a low branch. Something hissed a warning in the undergrowth. "The Sheriff came to Wodenhurst. He destroyed your family. He did it because of you, because of what the villagers told him. And he didn't just kill them, he—"

"No, no! Why are you saying this? You don't know anything about it. That day in Winter Forest, when I was hunting with my father, I fell asleep and he must have heard a noise and so he went to investigate and he couldn't find his way back to me

162

and that's how I got lost. My family thought I was gone forever and they were heartbroken, so they—"

"I know what the villagers *told* you. I know what they *wanted* you to think. They wanted to believe it themselves, because it was less shameful than the truth. But it was all lies. In the first place, your father didn't hear a noise. It was no accident—he left you in the forest on purpose."

Robin stood still and there was another moment where the world stopped, every sound drifting to silence, the mist hanging motionless.

They were already lying to you, before you came here.

He caught up and walked at Marian's side. "It was an accident," he said quietly, defiantly. "My father blamed himself and it was more than he could stand so they left to start a new life, nobody knows where. That's the truth. Sir Bors said there would be people who would lie to me, but I didn't think it would be you."

"You don't have the first idea about the truth," Marian said. "I understand now what it was like at that academy. They pretended they were training you to be men, but really they wanted to keep you as children. They gave you sticks and told you they were swords. They hid you away from anything sharp or frightening. Time to grow up now, Robin. You're back in the real world. Open your eyes and admit what you've known all along. Your parents and your brothers are dead. Your father left you in the forest on purpose. What's more . . ."

She trailed off and glanced into his eyes and twisted her mouth. She walked on. Robin stopped and let her go. He pulled his cloak close and he watched her fading into the mist. He wanted to stand here until she had disappeared. He wanted to go no farther down this dark path.

It's not too late to turn around, to go your own way, he told himself. *Wherever you end up, it has to be better than this.*

Marian had become a vague gray shape. She faded farther.

Robin told himself to remain where he was, but even being this far from her caused a painful twisting in his chest. He thought of never seeing her again and the idea was torment. He ran and caught up.

"Here's something *you* don't know," he said. "You can't lie to me because I'm holding the full truth here, in my pack. Sir Bors wrote it all down for me. I can read it any time I like."

"Go on then."

"I will."

"Go on then."

They had ducked beneath a fallen bough and were crawling through a muddy ditch. A jackdaw took flight, croaking its alarm. They stood and looked at each other.

"Go on, read it," Marian said.

Robin looked away. The sun was just an outline. The trees shifting shadows in the drifting mist.

Marian said: "You won't read it, because you're scared of the truth. And you're scared of what it will mean you have to do."

They clambered on in silence. After a while, Robin said: "Whatever the scroll says, it isn't important. Whatever happened, it was a long time ago. You can't fight the past, Marian, no one can. That's the most important thing I learned from Sir Bors: There are battles that can't be won."

Marian was striding away and Robin wasn't even sure she was listening. But then she stopped and turned and she was shouting.

"What have they done to you? The past isn't gone. You can't just give it up. It's a part of you. This nightmare will follow us forever, no matter where we go, unless we fight and fight until it's destroyed."

Robin hung his head. "I shouldn't have come back."

"Then why did you? I'd be better off alone. I've been uncovering the truth, and making plans, and now I'm ready and I can see what needs to be done and I thought you'd be ready too, when the time came. You used to fight harder than anyone—it didn't matter what or who stood in your way—I saw you stand up to Bawg and Narris and his whole gang, and you weren't even afraid of the Castellan. But then Sir Bors gave you a blunt sword and let you pretend to make war and he kept you hidden behind his walls, and now you want to carry on hiding—hiding even from the truth because if you hear the truth you'll have to do something about it and you can't because it wasn't some accident or hand of fate that did this to us, it was the Sheriff and the Sheriff is strong and frightening and you're weak and scared just like your father!"

All this was becoming too much for Robin. Two days ago he had left a place he felt safe and respected, abandoned people he had come to think of as brothers. Today he had killed a man. And now he had come deep into the place he feared most in the world.

All of it for Marian. All for her sake.

And still he didn't know why those soldiers were chasing her or why Sir Bors had taken her prisoner or where she had been these past years, but rather than telling him any of this she was just shouting at him and saying things he didn't want to hear about his family. And so when she turned and stomped away Robin felt his anger surge and he found himself running to catch her and physically seizing her by the shoulder and spinning her around.

"Marian, listen to me! Just stand there and don't say a word and for once just listen. I need—"

That was as far as he got because she glared, then gritted her teeth, then launched herself at him, throwing her arms around his neck, pulling his face toward hers, pushing her lips to his, kissing him, and gripping him harder and kissing him over and over. The sweet heat of her breath, the darting softness of her tongue.

She stopped, breathless, and lowered her head. She stayed there, pressed against him. She whispered something, but the words were muffled against his chest, and the blood was thundering in his ears, so he didn't hear what she said.

She stepped away. Her eyes turned to meet his. Her tongue appeared and moved along her lower lip. She continued through the forest. She had become small in the distance by the time Robin followed.

He caught up and they walked side by side, their eyes fixed on the ground. Every sound loud in the silence between them. The snapping of a twig. Robin's feet sucking in the wet earth. The clattering wings of a wood pigeon. They walked and they walked, Robin ordering his thoughts, trying to recall all the questions that had been burning through him only moments before, but now, in spite of everything, able to think of nothing except the taste of Marian on his lips.

He became acutely aware of her smell, the sound of her breath, her every movement—lifting a hand to push a strand of hair behind her ear. He watched her from the corner of his eye, and after a while he saw she was smiling. They clambered on and the smile widened.

"Robin, the look on your face, when I came out of that lake! I wish you could have seen it, your mouth flopped open like a fish! I've only seen one other person look so shocked ever—Bawg, when you shot an arrow at her, remember?"

Robin smiled. "I did not shoot at *her*, I was aiming for the drinking bladder. If I had wanted to hit Bawg, I couldn't have missed."

"She got fatter by the year, didn't she? By now I wonder how big she is."

They fell quiet and walked on, watching their feet. Long moments passed before Marian said: "Isn't it strange how things turn out so differently from how you imagine. You can picture a moment over and over in your head—exactly where and when and how it will happen. And then the moment comes, out of the blue, and nothing you dreamed was anywhere close to the truth."

"You mean . . . ," Robin said, "like the way we used to imagine our future? How we said we'd sail the five seas and go to Troy and Carthage."

Marian looked at him and grinned. "We would visit the pharaohs," she said. "And the Crusader Cities."

"We'd steal the Crown of Thorns . . ."

"Learn the songs of mermaids and ride a unicorn and . . ."

"Trade treasure with kings."

Robin looked around them at the wildwood, flexing its talons of shadow, and he looked at the dried blood on his tunic and he remembered the Sheriff's henchmen terrorizing the village. *You're right*, he thought. *This is not the future we envisaged.*

"Actually . . . ," Marian said, "I didn't mean our adventures. I was talking about something else. I meant how I imagined the first time we . . . I can't believe I'm telling you this . . . but for years, even when we were living in the tower, some nights, I'd lie awake and I'd think about . . . kissing you. Properly. And the way I dreamed it you . . . What am I thinking? I *am not* telling you this!"

They clambered on, a slight smile playing around her lips.

After a while Robin said: "At the citadel, I used to imagine the day I would see you again. It was going to happen years in the future. I was a knight of the realm by then, and I was returning to England, sailing into port with fifty bannermen and a hold full of gold and . . ." He trailed off, stared at his feet, kept walking.

"Tell me!" Marian said, bounding to his side, slipping her arm beneath his. "You can't be embarrassed in front of me. And we can't have secrets, we tell each other everything. Come on, continue. I can see you on that ship, standing at the prow, battle-weary but proud! And where was I, what did I look like? Tell me! How did we meet?"

"You didn't tell me yours."

"We'll both tell. You first."

"It's your turn."

"You owe me! You left me out here all alone, and now you've got to make amends—the very least you can do is tell me this daydream of yours." She pulled him to a halt, reached her hands behind his neck, stood on tiptoes. "Robin Loxley, you are so infuriating, tell me the rest this instant, or I swear I will never let you kiss me again, not so long as we—"

She looked toward the horizon. Her grip tightened at the back of his neck. He heard it too: faint noises of a struggle, from the east—from just beyond the forest.

Marian let go of him and stepped away, staring toward the commotion. She hesitated, then moved toward the noise. Robin followed.

They crept toward the wildwood edge, the sounds of destruction growing louder as they went. They reached the tree line and crouched still and looked out. There was a village, a short distance outside the forest, halfway down a steep slope. Crashing about the village were the Sheriff's militiamen. Robin counted at least nine, ten of them, the wolf-head emblem livid against their chests. He watched them turning over carts, pulling apart animal shelters. He saw a dog, speared through the belly with a crossbow bolt. Three soldiers armed with ironwood clubs went into one hut. Two of the red-cloaked figures came back out, dragging an unconscious man. From inside the hut came a woman's screams.

And then Robin's eyes were drawn back up the slope. Above the village a solitary figure sat, dressed all in black. He had his head bowed and his face was hidden beneath a hood. He picked at his fingernails with a knife while his stringy black mare bit lazily at the bark of a tree. Marian was looking at this man too. Robin felt her freeze and go tense.

One of the rangers ran up to the hooded figure and was saying something. The man in black sat motionless. The soldier returned to the village. Then the man in black raised his head and turned to look up at the forest. He lowered his hood.

The right side of the Sheriff's face was that of a normal, healthy man of middle age. The left side of his face was burned, or melted perhaps, the skin folded down like hot wax, his sandy beard and hairline growing only in glistening clumps. The socket of the left eye hung red and loose. His intact eye was a startling bright blue.

He looked along the tree line. His gaze reached Robin and stopped.

Robin could *feel* it. He was *sure* the Sheriff was looking directly at him.

But then he turned away and lowered his head and raised his hood and went back to picking at his nails with the knife.

Marian let out a long breath.

She was tugging at Robin's sleeve, then she was up and running through the forest. And Robin was following. The sounds of destruction behind them growing faint. And the pair of them were silent and they were running and running and neither of them looking back.

X. A Time of Running

"Now you've seen him," Marian whispered. "Now you've seen your enemy."

They were the first words either of them had spoken for hours. After seeing the Sheriff they had continued north through the wildwood, running when they had the strength, walking when they didn't. Now it was dusk and they were crouched at the tree line, watching the fields turn purple and then gray. They were listening for sounds of horses in the open or for anyone in the forest behind.

"That's the man who did this to us," Marian whispered. "Now you've seen him. Now it can begin."

Robin said nothing. He was thinking about the Sheriff. He was thinking about all Marian had said, and about the scraps of sense he had managed to lift from Sir Bors's scroll, an awful possibility beginning to form in his mind.

The dusk grew darker, then lightened to silver, starlight frosting the hills. Marian moved out of the forest. Robin followed—a surge of relief, free of the wildwood at last. They walked in silence, across plowed fields, stubbled and sticky underfoot. Scrub, wild and uninviting. They kept off the road, not even using the droving paths, but searching always for the hardest route, to make pursuit more difficult, clambering over collapsed walls and through sharp thickets.

They hurried on, the North Star showing them the way. All the questions were rising once more in Robin's mind but for now he remained silent, partly for fear they would argue again. Getting far away from the Sheriff's men, only that mattered for now. They walked and they walked and they didn't talk.

It began drizzling, then raining hard. They sheltered against a hillside, beneath an overhanging rock. They sat a few paces apart, and in the space between them the air felt the way it can before a thunderstorm: tense and taut. Marian pushed her jade amulet to her lips and studied the horizon. She glanced at him, then stared once more into the night.

"I talked to you," she said, not meeting his eyes. "Every day we were apart. Does that sound strange? I would ask you sometimes if I was doing the right thing, and if it was something hard I had to do, you would be there, urging me not to give up. And I heard your laugh, other times, and saw the look on your face. In a way you were with me, no matter what. Maybe you think that sounds stupid. Or mad."

She took a breath, apparently about to say more. But whatever it was remained unsaid. It rained harder and a sharp wind blew. Robin stood and took off his cloak and draped it around Marian's shoulders. He went and sat again by himself but then she wriggled closer and threw the cloak around them both and pushed herself against him. When they touched the charged air broke and Robin felt it shiver through his skin—he held her close and it shuddered into his bones. He could still feel her kiss, imprinted on his lips.

Soon the rain eased and she was getting to her feet and Robin was pulling on his cloak and they were off again, walking and walking through the night. Marian looked back across a land that was bands of purple and gray and black. She pointed.

"Lanterns," she said. "He's on our trail."

Robin looked and saw a distant flickering. "Could be a campfire," he said. "Travelers, stopped for the night."

"It's him. He's following."

"You thought they were tracking us through the forest, but then we saw him and his rangers in that village, so they couldn't have been."

She turned and headed across a fallow field.

Whenever Robin looked back he thought he could see that spectral orange glow in the distance. And he was beginning to think it could be four distinct spots of light. Surely they were only campfires?

He hurried after Marian.

The nocturnal world. Eerie quiet punctuated by points of noise. The spectral wail of foxes. The rustle and screech of a pine marten hunting. Something dashing across their path, its eyes flashing.

Onward, tracing the course of a valley, keeping to the lower marshy parts, rather than the exposed road on the upper slopes. Twisting through a copse of trees, following the narrow trail dug out by sheep. Disturbing a boar and both of them jumping at the snort and the crashing off into the undergrowth. The wind picking up. Sometimes now choosing the paths to make the walking easier. Finding an old Roman road, crumbled and uneven but at least firm underfoot. Robin looking back and again thinking he could see those four orange lights. And thinking this time, yes, they were moving. *She's right. They look like lanterns. They're drawing closer. Aren't they?*

Trying not to think about that. Taking his bow from his

back and stringing it and concentrating on Marian and on the path ahead.

From a distance the village appeared dark and silent. Perhaps even deserted. As they crept closer they could hear pigs snuffling and people coughing in their half sleep the other side of thin walls. A restless, nervous feel to this place. They crept amid the wattle-and-thatch huts. There was a barn that looked like it might house horses. Robin slid the bolt. It made a grating sound.

A dog started barking; guard geese jabbered.

Robin and Marian crept around the barn, hid in the shadow of the building.

Movement. Whispers. Two people appeared. The blade of a scythe catching the starlight. The men moved slowly around the barn.

Robin and Marian circled the building in the other direction. They slipped back out of the village, continued along the path they had left.

It was almost dawn by the time they reached the next village.

"We can't carry on in the daylight," Marian whispered. "We'll have to find somewhere to hide. Tonight we'll try again to steal horses and continue to the coast."

The village was surrounded by a ditch, to keep out wild pigs. They crawled into it, hopped over the wettest part and crept into the village. There were ten or twelve houses, gathered around a common green and a Trystel Tree. There was a garlanded wellhead and a stream whispering beneath a wooden bridge. There was a granary, set high on stilts. Marian climbed the ladder and Robin followed. Several times the ladder creaked and he froze but the village continued sleeping.

The granary was dry inside and the walls were made of tightly woven willow poles so this was a good place to hide through the daytime. Against the walls were the storage urns for the grain but there was space between them to sleep. They stretched out on the hard floor, an arm's length apart. Between them Robin felt that thunderhead tension once more. Marian shuffled back and forth, trying to lie comfortably. Finally she twisted around and put her head on his stomach. When she spoke her voice was already becoming drowsy.

"I didn't mean what I said—about being better off without you. And it was silly of you to say you shouldn't have come back. You had no choice, don't you see? It's not enough to say we belong together. I *am* you, just the same as you are me. Our fates are tied, we've always known that."

She shuffled position again, putting one arm across him and laying her head on his chest. It was almost painfully exhilarating where their bodies touched.

"You don't mind me using you as a pillow, do you? Not that you're very comfy—nothing but muscle—like lying on a sack full of rocks. I know I've been horrible to you. It's only because I've been scared, and being scared makes me angry. You understand that, I know you do."

Her hand found his and she knitted their fingers. Her voice dropped to a thinner whisper.

"In that forest, all alone, you don't know what it was like. The noises at night. Singing and footsteps and . . . other things. The stories we were told about that place. I don't want to believe them, not anymore. But the things I heard, and thought I saw . . . Perhaps, sooner or later, all the stories come true. All the monsters made flesh."

Robin was feeling delirious through lack of sleep and the exhaustion of running through the night. He knew Marian must be feeling the same. She gripped his hand tighter.

"My mother used to tell me a story about a nymph called Arethusa. I must have read it to you, do you remember? Arethusa spent her whole life running from a river god—she was running and running but never getting away. One night, terrified and desperate, Arethusa hid in a savage wood. She hid there and a thick mist came and covered her. The river god stalked her—she heard his footsteps—and she broke out in a cold sweat. More and more sweat poured from her skin. The sweat became a spring, then a stream, then a river. A goddess had taken pity on her and was trying to save her—she was transforming her into water. Arethusa flowed away as a river and she thought she was free. But the river god saw her and turned himself into water too and he mixed his current with hers and she was caught. Every time I heard that story it scared me more. Can you think of anything worse? A nightmare you can never escape because it flows into you. It *becomes* you. Well, I think it's coming true. I can feel that man in my sweat, on my skin, in my hair . . . I could run forever and never get away."

She paused, gripping Robin's hand.

Then she said, in a different voice: "And that's why, one day, we will have to kill him. I've come to see that as clearly as anything I've ever known. It's the only way I'll ever be free. And the same is true for you. He's shadowed you, and he always will—until he's destroyed. There's so much you need to know, I can barely think where to start. When you hear it all you'll see what needs to be done. You can't seal up the past and pretend it never happened."

She yawned heavily, then fell quiet. Robin listened to her breathing.

After a while he said: "When we were living in the tower, and we planned all the places we'd go and the things we'd see—*that* was our future, the life we should have had, until it was stolen from us. Well, don't you see, we've been given a

175

second chance. We should be looking forward, not back. We'll go to Castile, if that's where you want to go first. And afterward to Arabia and Rome and Baghdad. Our story was interrupted. We can continue where we left off."

He paused. She said nothing.

"After the fire . . . ," Robin said, "you could have been anywhere in the world. I didn't even know if you were alive or dead. Can you imagine what it was like for me, seeing you again, on the tourney field? And now we're here. We're together. Now . . . nothing else matters."

But he knew she was no longer listening. Her breathing had changed, become slow and heavy. In her sleep she murmured: "Strong and handsome. My champion. Knew you'd come."

He felt her breath on his neck. He felt her soft warmth rise and fall. He breathed the smell of her, and he felt her kiss, forged on his lips. He stared at the roof of the granary. The dawn approaching. Motes of dust beginning to show in the air.

He senses it won't take long now for them to reach the shore. They are in a boat with a bright red sail, and on the horizon is an exotic trading port with flat white roofs and silver domes and golden spires. He is aware he is dreaming. He hasn't yet fallen asleep, but already he is dreaming. He can taste the salt in the air; he can hear the raucous call of gulls. And now they are sailing back to England and Robin is wearing a silver cloak and holding a golden sword, and his father and Sir Bors are both there on the shore, looking at Robin, seeing all he has become . . .

Robin's eyes are closing . . .

They open again a heartbeat later.

He is sure they were closed no longer than a heartbeat. Yet somehow full daylight is slicing through the woven walls, and the quiet of Marian's breathing is being shattered by hammer-blow sounds from the ground below. And Marian is rising to her knees and her eyes are wild and scared.

Horsemen are coming into the village. Ten, twelve riders at least. The thunder of hooves coming to a halt and the sound of men in mailcoats as they dismount. The crump of nailed boots.

And then Robin hears a voice, and he has no doubt this is the Sheriff speaking.

And the Sheriff is saying Marian's name.

XI. The Cage

The Sheriff spoke softly, but his voice carried clearly on the breeze.

"We are searching for a young woman. Her name is Marian Delbosque. Anyone found harboring her will be dealt with severely. I will remind you all that lying to me is punishable by the loss of a tongue. Who is the headman here? Come and stand before me. Prime Marshall, direct your men."

Robin and Marian crawled across the granary and pushed their faces to the latticed wall. Hazily, through the narrow gaps, they saw the Sheriff, sitting on his black mare. Alongside the Sheriff sat a gray-faced man, thin as a knife. And climbing down from their horses were a dozen soldiers, each of them gripping a stabbing sword or an ironwood club.

Robin saw with shock that one of the rangers had scarified cheeks. Here was the young man they called Edric—the soldier Robin thought he had killed. Beneath his skull-helm a reddened bandage showed. This ranger went about the village in a fury, kicking a stray dog, swinging his club at anyone too slow to get out of the way. Other soldiers were thrusting spears into hay bales, kicking over water troughs, crashing through homes.

Then came a new noise: the creaking of a ladder.

The ladder that led to their hiding place.

Marian had turned still as stone. Robin pulled her to her feet. He took her to the rear of the granary. The largest of the ceramic urns were four feet high. Most were full of grain, but a few were empty. He helped Marian climb inside one of the urns, then he clambered inside another and ducked out of sight.

The ladder creaked more heavily. A soldier lumbered into the granary, followed by a second man. For a moment neither of them moved, waiting perhaps for their eyes to adjust to the gloom.

Robin had grabbed his backpack and now he gripped the handle of his woodsman's knife. Sir Derrick had taught the squires to use their environment as a weapon: to be aware that sunlight will dazzle; that uneven ground will keep an assailant off balance; to use concealment and shock to their advantage. All of which told Robin he should attack these rangers now, while they were on unfamiliar ground, while they were half blind, coming in from bright sunshine. Wasn't that Marian's best chance of escape, while Robin kept these men occupied?

No, there are too many soldiers below. You can't fight the whole world. Keep your nerve . . .

He held still, listening to his heart thump, and the sounds of his breath, loud in that constricted space. The men came farther into the room, the whole structure lurching beneath their weight.

A tapping sound—Robin thought it was one of the men prodding at the urns with his club.

Then a crash—an explosion of pottery and grain. The soldier grunted and swung his club again and a second vase shattered. The pattering of grain through the mesh floor.

The men continued pacing, tapping at the urns, then destroying them, one after another.

No choice now. Robin would have to fight.

Tap, tap.

He gripped the knife, braced himself for the moment his urn smashed.

Tap, tap.

The noise now very close. He only hoped they would reach him before Marian . . .

Tap, tap.

But the next crash never came. The tapping stopped.

"Just grain," one of the rangers said.

"In a granary?" the second man said. "Who'd have thought? Waste of time. How long has it been? Mark her down as the one that got away."

The men turned and the granary lurched and the ladder creaked and they were gone.

Robin listened to the other soldiers, still searching the village. A dog barked, yelped, then whimpered. Someone was crying, and someone else pleading. Finally came a quiet word from the Sheriff, followed by barked instructions, and the rangers were mounting their horses.

The Sheriff and his henchmen were riding away.

We did it. She's safe.

They climbed out carefully. Robin moved to the wall and put an eye to the lattice and he watched villagers picking themselves up, helping one another.

"We should stick to the plan," he said. "Stay here until dark."

Marian was staring into space.

"This is probably the safest place for now," Robin said. "They won't look in the same place twice."

Marian nodded, just once.

"As soon as the villagers are asleep we'll go and find horses," Robin said. "We'll put miles between us and the Sheriff."

Marian was hugging her knees and saying nothing. Robin went to her and put his cloak around them both. They sat in silence and they waited.

All they could do was wait. There was no chance they could sleep again now. The lances of light through the wall became brighter, then softened. The motes of dust began to fade, rain clouds darkening the sky. A light drizzle falling on the granary roof.

They waited. Marian rested her head on Robin's shoulder. But then she sat up straight and an expression crossed her face: not a look of fear; more of puzzlement and disgust.

Robin heard it too and in the next instant horses were riding fast into the village.

No, no! Why are they coming back?

They pushed their faces to the wall and peered through the lattice. Marian's fingernails sank into Robin's flesh. There was the Sheriff on his black mare, and beside him the skeletal man. And with them were the twelve red-cloaked soldiers from before. Behind them, more slowly, came packhorses pulling two carts. On one of these carts was an empty cage. On the other were four more rangers, carrying backpacks and lanterns.

Four rangers who had clearly been tracking their quarry on foot.

Robin thought of the points of light that had followed them across the fields.

Marian's nails dug deeper. "They *did* follow you! They've been following you since the start. You led them to me!"

Robin put his hand over her mouth. "I need you to stay calm," he said. "We hid last time, didn't we? We'll hide again. We'll get through this, but only if we don't panic."

181

He put one eye back to a gap in the weave. The Sheriff was sweeping his piercing blue gaze around the village.

"Headman," he said. "Come and stand before me."

A white-haired man shuffled forward. A big soldier with a patch over one eye grabbed him by the scruff of the neck.

"We came here looking for a young woman," the Sheriff said. "You assured me you had not seen her. And yet my Chief Rider tells me he followed her and a boy through the forest. He tracked the pair to this village. He says the signs go no farther. I am going to ask you one last time: Where is she hiding?"

The old man didn't make a sound; he only raised his hands, shook his head.

The Sheriff lifted one finger.

The one-eyed soldier took a step back, swung his ironwood club. A loud crack. A red mist rose against the drizzle. The ranger hit the headman again and again, where he lay on the ground. The soldier's back was facing the granary so Robin could no longer see the old man, but he could see the soldier swinging his bludgeon, over and over, until it was making a noise like somebody churning butter. People were sobbing.

The Sheriff peered around the village. On his left side his lips were burnt away, exposing the teeth, so it looked as though he was grinning.

"When a vixen goes to ground . . . ," he said, "she leaves us no choice but to smoke her out. Marshall Rogue, see it is done thoroughly."

Soldiers went into homes, came back out with burning brands from cook fires. They used the brands to set alight the thatched roofs. Villagers pleaded and cried and fought— rangers pushed them aside or beat them down.

One soldier passed below the granary. Smoke snaked through the mesh floor.

182

Marian headed for the ladder. Robin held her back. She struggled. He held her.

"Listen," he whispered. "We've got one chance. It's been raining—the thatch is damp. There's going to be a lot of smoke, and panic. That could work to our advantage. We wait until the smoke is thickest and then we slip away. The ditch, at the edge of the village. We run for that. We hide there. But we have to stay here as long as we can stand."

Marian's eyes were desperate above his hand. She managed a single nod. He pulled his spare tunic from his backpack and wrapped it around her nose and mouth. He pulled his cloak over his shoulder and wrapped it around his own face.

The granary was filling with smoke; Robin pushed Marian to the floor, to find the clearest air. Heat was washing up in waves, flames beginning to lick around their feet. Wind whistled through the village, making the fires roar.

The granary lurched. A splintering, cracking sound.

Robin could hold Marian no longer—she struggled from his grasp, darted to the doorway, and disappeared over the edge. Robin counted ten breaths, allowing her to get clear, before he followed.

He was halfway to the ground when the ladder collapsed. He landed heavily, pain shooting through his skull and his ribs. For a moment the world dimmed and he couldn't move, he couldn't breathe, but then everything swam back into focus and he sucked a breath and struggled to his feet. He staggered through the smoke, holding his side, heading for the edge of the village.

He couldn't see Marian—she must be somewhere ahead.

A flash of red; a shout of pain and a crash; an acrid stench. He ran clear of it all and fell down into the ditch, jarring his injured side, gritting his teeth and managing not to cry out.

He splashed around in the mud, first one way, then the other, looking for Marian.

No sign of her.

He battled the urge to run back into the flames—fought the instinct to stand and shout her name. He peered again into the village, but the smoke was swirling thick and blue and he could see nothing.

The wind was blowing to the north; he crawled south, looking for clearer air. He kept crawling, still fighting for breath. He raised his head from the trench.

Anger and fear surged.

Above him, sitting calmly on their mounts, were the Sheriff and the gray cadaverous man. They had moved to the common grazing ground, on raised land to the south of the village. Robin had crawled very close. Close enough to see the ruined side of the Sheriff's face weeping in the heat. The Sheriff dabbed at it with a handkerchief as he turned and said something to the skeletal man.

Robin ducked down and crept backward, to stay out of their sight line. He raised his head once more. Now the Sheriff was staring into the village. Robin looked and saw soldiers coming out of the smoke, coughing and trying to calm their horses.

Last to emerge were the pack animals pulling the two carts.

And on the back of the second cart was the cage. And inside the cage was Marian.

Stay calm, Robin told himself. *Nothing rash. Stay hidden.* If he was going to help her, he had to plan carefully and stay in control. But he looked at Marian in that cage—her wrists tied and a gag between her teeth—and he felt hot rage pushing at the back of his skull. Even in the worst, darkest days after his parents disappeared—even following the fire at the Delbosque manor—he did not remember feeling such fury.

184

The prison cart was being led past the Sheriff; he no more than glanced at Marian before turning to talk again to the thin man with the gray face. The cage came to a stop at the far edge of the common ground. Robin followed its progress, crawling through the ditch, keeping his head down. He was trying to think clearly, and to plan. Now that they had Marian the soldiers had forgotten about him—that was why he could creep so near. So then, he would remain hidden: He would follow the soldiers, wherever it was they went. Once darkness fell and there was just one man on guard, then Robin would strike, and find a way to set her free. *Until then, patience. Put aside your anger—it will not help her.*

Yet even as he was thinking this, his knife found its way out of his pack and into his hand. He slipped the blade from its sheath, laid a finger on the serrated edge.

He crawled closer. Two soldiers, standing very near, would have seen him if they had looked down, but they weren't looking because they regarded Robin as merely a boy and no threat. How he would make them regret that . . .

But only when the time is right. Think of the hunt: A hasty shot will ruin everything. Patience is the key.

He slid the blade back inside its sheath.

But then he watched another soldier approach the prison cart. It was the wasp-haired ranger called Edric. Robin was close enough to see the blood dried on his neck; the teardrop scars on his cheeks.

This ranger glanced at the Sheriff—one hundred paces away, his back turned—before he started circling the cage. He began making slow noises with his tongue: *la, la, la.*

He was staring at Marian, circling her.

La, la, la.

Robin felt such rage he wanted to scream.

His bow was still strapped to his back, but his quiver had

185

been lost somewhere along the way. So then, there was only this knife, hot in his hand.

Don't move. Remember what they taught you: Sacrifice self-control and you may win this battle, but the war is lost.

But the young ranger was reaching into the cage . . .

La, la, la.

And Robin was pulling the knife from its sheath . . .

La, la, la.

"You, Edric, get away from her."

An older ranger was striding toward the prison cart. A tall, dark-featured man. Here was the leader of the squad who arrived in the village last—the man who had tracked Robin from the start.

"I said, move away from the prisoner."

Edric stayed where he was, raising a finger to his bloody bandage and scratching beneath. "Look, she's a ravishing little thing," he said. "Think I'll volunteer for first watch tonight."

"This is the last warning you'll get," the older soldier said. "Men—*boys*—like you make me sick. We have to see this work done, but we do not have to like it."

"Are you squeamish, Will Scarlett? Something tells me you're not going to be Chief Rider very long."

But as he spoke the soldier called Edric was moving away from the cart.

"Ranger Cragg," said the one called Will Scarlett. "Keep one eye on the prisoner, the other on Edric Krul."

As soon as Will Scarlett walked away, Edric Krul moved once more toward the cage.

"Krul, you heard the Chief Rider," a third ranger said. "Keep away from her."

The younger soldier ignored him. He picked at the scabs forming above his ear. "Where's your friend?" he said to

186

Marian. "Did he run out on you? Shame. I was looking forward to meeting that one again. At least you're here to console me."

He circled the cage and made that noise again with his tongue.

La, la, la.

Robin's wrath rose, hotter than ever.

La, la, la.

The ranger was reaching through the bars.

The fury burning at the back of Robin's skull.

La, la, la.

Marian shrinking away from Edric's fingers, her hands tied.

The look in her eyes . . .

La, la, la.

The soldier reaching . . .

Robin launched from his hiding place, his knife heading for the young ranger's throat. In that same moment the third ranger stepped toward Edric Krul to haul him away from the cart. Robin's knife gashed the second man's arm—he cried out and stumbled away. Robin lunged again at Edric Krul, but he was scuttling out of range.

And now other soldiers were coming at Robin, their cudgels raised.

Shouting, and a war horn, and more men running.

Robin spun and met his nearest assailant, stabbed the man in the side, finding a gap in his half mail. He turned the man, using him as a shield while he pulled the knife free. He slashed another ranger across the nose; he crashed his knee into a third man's groin.

He moved in a half crouch, feinting right and left, keeping his opponents off balance, using the knife-fighting techniques he learned with Sir Bors. At the same time he was a redraw scrapper again, brawling with Narris Felstone and

Swet Woolward and the rest, kicking and punching and butting heads.

But today neither measured skill nor berserker fury would be enough. He was surrounded by a circle of armed men. Every time he struck with his knife a soldier backed away and a man behind him advanced to swing his club.

A heavy thud in Robin's back—he staggered, winded. He retaliated but his attacker had already retreated to a safe distance. A glancing blow to the side of Robin's head, sending a blinding flash through his eyes. Another hard hit from the side.

He made a lunge at Edric Krul but he scuttled backward once more, out of striking range. He was grinning, this young soldier, keeping his distance and grinning . . .

A shooting pain in Robin's ear, his vision blurred.

And then, unbelievably, his knife dropped from his fingers. It tumbled, very slowly, and stuck upright in the earth. Robin stooped to pick it up, and missed. He tried again, and failed. Either the ground kept getting farther away or Robin's arm had become too short.

He watched red spots fall great distances. A wet throbbing at the back of his head.

The world turned, lurched, dropped out of sight.

Blackness.

And when the blackness cleared Robin found he was on his back, looking up. He tried to stand but he couldn't move. There were four soldiers each using a knee and all their weight to pin his arms and his legs.

Standing above him was Edric Krul. He had lost his skull-helm and his orange hair was wild and there was blood running from beneath his bandage and coating his scarred cheeks. He gripped a spiked mace. Leering, he raised it above his head.

188

"Leave him."

This was the older soldier called Will Scarlett. He took hold of Edric's mace and pulled it from him and shoved the younger ranger away.

Will Scarlett hung his head. "Haven't we done enough here?" he said.

And then Robin, still blinking rapidly, was looking up at another face. Ruined, weeping skin, exposed tendons in the neck. The Sheriff had walked his horse across, and he was now staring down at Will Scarlett.

"Why the delay?" the Sheriff said. "This young man attacked officers of the Sheriff's Guard, which is tantamount to attacking the Sheriff himself. The prescribed punishment is death."

Without looking at the Sheriff, Will Scarlett said: "He's not much more than a boy. We have what we came for. We could afford to show some leniency."

The Sheriff tipped his head, the left side of his face grinning, and he looked directly at Robin for the first time. As he did so his expression changed. His intact eyebrow raised, just a fraction. There was a look in his clean right eye that was something like recognition.

An expression that seemed to say: *I know you.*

"What have we here?" the Sheriff said, so quietly he could be talking to himself. "Perhaps we have been more fortunate than we realized. Perhaps we caught this one just in time."

He glanced at Marian in the cage, before staring once more at Robin.

"You think the boy should be spared, Chief Rider? It would be remiss of me to ignore your advice, today of all days. Yes, you are quite right, this is a time for clemency."

Will Scarlett was looking up at the Sheriff now.

"I am minded to be merciful," the Sheriff said. "Let the

boy live." And the Sheriff was turning away, pressing his reddened handkerchief to the ravaged side of his face, walking his mare back across the common ground.

Robin struggled to stand, but the soldiers kept him pinned.

The Sheriff passed the thin, gray-faced man. He did not look at the man and he did not look back at Robin. He only spoke in a quiet, dispassionate tone.

"Jadder Payne," the Sheriff said. "Exact a lesser punishment. Bring me the boy's eyes."

Will Scarlett used his cloak to wipe the sweat from his face. He walked away, hanging his head. Robin struggled harder, but he was held fast.

The skeletal man climbed down from his horse. He opened his cloak and underneath was a holster full of surgical blades, each one containing a miniature reflection of the village in flames. From the holster he took a lancing knife. A soldier handed him a burning brand and Jadder Payne held the knife over the flame and began to heat the steel.

The cart carrying the cage was lurching into motion. Robin caught a final look into Marian's eyes. He couldn't read her expression, but he remembered her last words: *You led them to me!*

And now she was moving away. The Sheriff and his escort too were leaving. Injured soldiers were having their wounds tended before being helped onto the spare cart.

Robin watching all this in a daze. Feeling no fear now, only confusion—all this too unreal for him to be afraid.

This is just another nightmare. Any moment now this will end. I'll wake with Bones shaking my shoulder, telling me I've been shouting in my sleep.

Yes, in a heartbeat he will wake, and the sun will be shining and the crowd will be cheering and it will be the first day of the squire's tourney. Everything since has been one long fever dream.

But then the skeletal man is looming over Robin, and he is crouching on one knee and holding Robin's chin in a grip that is stone cold and all too real. And in the man's other hand is the hot blade, moving toward Robin's face, and the rest is pain and darkness.

Part Four

Wyrdwood

I. Mercy

Narris Felstone didn't want to kill Robin Loxley. He hated the idea.

But he knew they were going to make him do it. He knew he would have no choice. Anyway, wasn't it more cruel to leave Robin alive?

Yes, think of it as a mercy, Narris told himself. *Think of the runt of the litter, too weak to compete for food. Put it out of its misery. Think of it that way.*

It had started when a lone soldier walked into the village, leading his horse by the reins. This was not one of the vicious boys from before, but an older man, and clearly a soldier of high rank. Lying across his horse, apparently lifeless, was Robin. The soldier stopped near the common green, lowered Robin to the ground. The ranger hung his head, climbed into his saddle, and did not look back.

Robin made a pitiful figure huddled on the ground: his fine clothes were tattered and smoke-blackened; a cloth pack and hunting bow were still strapped across his back. His hood was raised, but underneath Narris could just make out those dreadful wounds, puffy and weeping.

The villagers formed a circle around him. It seemed to

Narris the circle was growing tighter, a crush of bodies shuffling inward. But then Narris's mother was there and she was pushing through the crowd and with her good hand she was helping Robin to his feet and she was leading him away. Narris followed his mother and Robin back up Herne Hill, while the other villagers watched them, silently.

His mother sat Robin in a corner of the central chamber of the house. And that's where he had stayed, ever since. Narris led him twice a day to the latrine, and Robin ate the meals placed in his hands, but other than that he didn't flinch. He didn't speak. As if he were made of stone.

To look at him made Narris shiver. Those cauterized crosses where his eyes used to be. You couldn't tell if he was awake or asleep, sitting upright against the wall. Nighttime would come and the firelight would flicker across his face, and then the flames would die and Narris would go to his bed, and still Robin sat there in the darkness, just the same, silent and still.

Every few days they would get visitors to the house. Narris stayed out of sight but he heard what they were saying. Agnes Poley or Eva Topcroft would say: "You heard what Old Ma warned, all those years ago: Such a child would bring disaster. The forest wants him. Twice it has been denied. Look around you, Mabel, see what he's caused."

And Narris's mother would reply: "Listen to yourselves. This village isn't dying because of a curse. It's dying from shame."

"He keeps returning, like the pox," another of the villagers would say. "Loxley should never have interfered."

And Narris's mother would say: "Robert Loxley was worth ten of any one of us. You all know what you did. What you didn't do. Shame on you. Shame on us all! Hasn't this poor boy been through enough?"

196

But as the weeks passed it seemed to Narris his mother's arguments were growing less fierce. Were the villagers wearing her down? Or could she stand to look at Robin no longer? Could she no longer bear the accusing look in that dead stare?

Narris thought he knew what was coming, and he loathed the idea.

One evening, as he was returning from the fields, he stood outside the house, listening. His mother sighed, and said: "And who would do it? You?"

Edith Younger said: "Your son and Robin hated each other. Narris would do it with pleasure."

It was November. The blood month. The time when the valleys shriek with pigs being slaughtered for winter stocks, while in the wild old toothless creatures sense they won't live to see another spring.

November, the month when everything dies . . .

Narris had been meeting with the village elders beneath the Trystel Tree. They had been deciding what to do about Robin Loxley's horse. They could no longer afford to feed such a beast. And nobody was willing to brave the road to take it to market. In any case, the larders were practically empty. There was really no choice to be made. The horse would be slaughtered, and its meat would provide a lifeline during the year ahead.

Narris returned home to find his mother staring across the room at Robin. She raised her good hand, beckoned Narris close.

"Winter is coming," she whispered. "Stocks are low. The others are right: We must feed the strong. Take Robin to the forest and leave him there."

*

197

Narris led Robin up Herne Hill and out of the village. Robin stumbled occasionally but he held onto Narris's arm and followed without question. They reached Woden's Ride, the wildwood towering black and fierce ahead. Without allowing himself to pause, feeling his heart quicken, Narris hurried across the spirit fence and pushed into Winter Forest. It was broad daylight, and weeks before a full moon, but still it made Narris's skin crawl to be here and he ventured less than a hundred paces before he dared go no farther. He sat Robin between two beech trees. Fallen leaves had soaked the ground crimson, as if Narris had already done the deed.

Leave him there.

Narris knew what that meant. He hefted the woodsman's ax, felt the weight of it, watched the light run along its cutting edge.

This was deeply unjust. Why did he have to do it? Certainly, he and Robin used to fight. But fighting with someone is very different from killing them. Besides, what harm was Robin to anyone now? How old was he? Fifteen? Crossing into manhood, yet look at him, helpless as a baby. Perhaps the villagers were right: Better to put him out of his misery.

Narris gripped the ax, raised it above his head. Steadied it with his stump.

Robin's head was bowed, his neck exposed. One clean strike and it would be over . . .

But what if the strike wasn't clean? What if Robin shook and kicked and bled yet refused to die, the way that runt pig had done the time Narris missed the vital spot? He remembered chasing after the spurting, slippery runt and finally finishing it off with a knife.

What if?

He lowered the ax.

He had suspected this would happen. He pulled a

sheepskin from his pack and wrapped it around Robin's shoulders. He laid a small packet of food at Robin's feet and made sure he could find it with his fingers. Narris took the ax and went back home.

He returned to Robin's camp every few days with a small amount of food. Sometimes he would sit with Robin for a while.

"It's getting colder," Narris said. "You're going to have to make your own fire. I remember you were a fine woodsman, when we were younger. I'll wager you can learn it all again by touch. Here, I found your strike-a-light so you've always got a spark."

This is ridiculous, he thought. *What am I doing? A blind boy can't live out here by himself. What if the snows are heavy and I can't reach him with food? What happens when he runs out of dry firewood?*

Winter was coming, and winter would kill Robin just as surely as a blade. The difference was that winter would allow his death to linger.

Kinder to end it now.

Narris raised the ax, felt it shaking, steadied it with his stumped arm. He studied the vital spot on Robin's neck.

One clean strike. Perhaps he wouldn't even feel it . . .

"I will kill him." Robin's voice was cracked through disuse.

"What?" Narris said, lowering the ax.

"I am going to kill him," Robin said. "The man who took Marian, and did this to me, and whose men hurt your mother. The Sheriff. Next time you come, bring my bow."

Narris didn't know whether to cry or laugh. This pitiful figure—this man-boy who wouldn't even be able to find his way back to the village—he was going to kill the Sheriff! He put down the ax and rubbed at his eyes and cleared his throat.

"I can't stay long," he said. "Mother's not well. But it's getting colder. We have to build you a better shelter. You tell me how and we'll do it together. So, how do we start?"

Every time Narris visited without the shortbow, Robin reminded him to bring it next time. Eventually Narris took the bow and a quiver of arrows and he placed them in Robin's hands and that seemed to satisfy him.

Robin also asked for his backpack so Narris found that in the house and brought it to his camp. Narris had already searched the pack. It contained tallow candles and a drawstring pouch containing some silver coins. Narris had taken those things for himself. They were no use to Robin now. The backpack also contained a scroll, its broken seal in the shape of two spears, crossed below an armored boar. Narris found himself taking this parchment and tucking it inside his tunic. He would take it back to the village, ask Robert Wyser what the writing said. But then he looked over at Robin, crouched over scraps of moss and kindling, trying to ignite his fire, and he felt an odd pang of guilt. He put the scroll back where he found it.

Now Robin was shuffling around on hands and knees, running his hands through the leaves. He had dropped the flint from his strike-a-light—Narris could see it clearly against the graying litter. He picked it up. He tossed the flint and caught it while he watched Robin search.

Eventually Narris said: "Here. I found it. Give me the firesteel. I'm going to tie them together and I'll tie both to your belt. So you don't drop them again."

"I could have done it," Robin said. "I would have found it."

"I know you would. But there, it's done now."

He looked around him at the forest. Berries had been huge this autumn; ash leaves had fallen early: sure signs that this winter was going to be harsh. Narris had only two options, and he could not shake the feeling it was *more* cruel to leave Robin alive.

It had snowed for the first time overnight. The snow wasn't deep, but it was enough to make up Narris's mind. At dawn he followed the path toward Robin's shelter. Droppings were bright against the snow and steam rose from holes in the ground, marking where animals snored in their burrows. The cold bit sharply in the stump of Narris's left arm.

He carried with him no food; only the ax. He would do it this time. Without pause or question. The villagers were right: This was the only way. *I'll be doing him a mercy,* Narris thought. *Putting him out of his misery.*

Death was on its way. Better the swift blade than the creeping cold.

He reached Robin's camp between the beech trees.

But Robin wasn't there.

His little shelter had been crushed and the embers from his fire had been scattered. A chill went through Narris. Had something been here, and taken Robin? Or scared him deeper into the wildwood? He stared into the shadowy depths of the forest; he listened to its uncanny cackles and shrieks and wails.

Well then, that was that. It was out of his hands. Whatever had happened to Robin—whether he was already dead, or dying in the wildwood—that was the end of it. With sadness and relief, Narris folded the sheepskin. He tucked the ax under his arm and he hurried out of the forest.

II. Echoes

In Robin's new black world a single image appears, over and over: a lancing knife, descending toward his face, drawing closer and closer, not stopping even when the hot point of the blade disappears inside the jelly of his eye. The blade digs deeper, he relives the searing pain. It stops and there is a moment of relief. Then the cycle begins again.

Something else repeats in his mind, equally torturous. The voice of a young woman: *They* did *follow you! You led them to me!*

Since the fight with the soldiers, a year could have passed, or a day. This moment it could be midnight, or midday. Time no longer moved. Why would it? There was no future for it to move toward. True, Robin heard certain temporal clues: the tolling of the bell in the village; the rhythmic creaking of the waterwheel; the *clink-clink* of Gord Moore hammering in his forge. But these things no longer marked the passage of time; they were mere echoes of a past life. Spirits sent to taunt him over all he had lost.

The waterwheel moaned: *She's. Gone. Too. She's. Not. Coming. Back.* Gord Moore's hammer spat: *It. Was. Your. Fault.*

Sometimes Robin heard people speaking. But whoever these phantoms were, they had merely stolen the voices of people he used to know. One sounded like Mabel Felstone, but she said things Mabel would never have said. One day Robin overheard her saying: "Take Robin to the forest and leave him there."

And he felt the man who was not Narris Felstone helping him to his feet and leading him out of the house and away from the village.

So Robin found himself in Winter Forest. It was colder, but otherwise it was the same here as it had been in the house. He was still locked in this black coffin, haunted by the image of the lancing knife and the young woman's voice.

But slowly his mind began to clear and Robin realized it was different here, after all. Here there were signs that life was moving forward as it always had and always would. Stags bellowed and grunted, the crack of their antlers echoing through the trees like battling monsters. The otherworldly wail of young foxes fighting for a territory of their own. And everywhere the sense of autumn desperation: the snuffling scratching noises of creatures eating and burying the last glut of food before the dearth of winter. Birds flitting after the final flush of insects.

Robin sat and listened to all this and time juddered back into motion. And that was when a new image appeared in his mind. It was of a man with a ruined face, dressed all in black, and there was an arrow buried in his chest.

This did not happen in the past. This must be waiting in the future. The future existed. Suddenly everything that had happened made a strange kind of sense: his parents disappearing; the fire at the manor; Robin training with Sir Bors; Marian in that cage. All these events were waymarkers leading to this single future event: the man in black with an arrow in his chest. Robin was going to make this happen. He didn't know when; he couldn't begin to imagine how; but this was a fact.

As this understanding dawned, Robin became aware of something else: Narris Felstone intended to kill him. He could not allow this to happen. Not now.

So Robin said: "I will kill him. I am going to kill the Sheriff."

It worked. Narris laid down the ax. Next time he visited he brought food and drink, and eventually he brought Robin's bow.

Robin rolled a small ball of moss in his palms. For the thousandth time he flicked the flint against the firesteel of his strike-a-light. Once again the spark didn't take. A cold wet wind blew across his face and all around him the ground was sodden and for a moment he wanted to give up—this was impossible.

No, he told himself. *You made fire with your father countless times, in conditions far worse than this. In swirling snow and thunderstorm. Back then you could have made fire with your eyes closed. So, you can do it now.*

He flicked the strike-a-light. This time he smelled smoke. He breathed on the moss and kept breathing until it was smoldering hot and he could no longer hold it in his hands. He lowered the moss onto wood shavings he had whittled with his knife. Gradually, carefully, he added more twigs to the hissing fire, breathed on it, coaxed it fully to life.

He wanted to stand and shout the triumph of it. But he concentrated on keeping the fire fed, while ensuring it could breathe. It had taken him a long time to get to this point—his fingers covered in burns, his stomach churning with hunger. But it was worth it—the feeling of doing this thing for himself.

When the fire was robust enough he pushed two stones into the flames and after a while he removed them with a stick and spread them with the oat paste Narris had brought. He smelled the oatcakes cooking and again he felt that sense of achievement.

He had cooked a meal for himself.

It wasn't much, but it had begun.

Robin was sitting in his shelter, arranging sticks on a fire he had built at its entrance. He heard footsteps through the wet leaves. Narris had returned. Robin felt him slide into the shelter. They sat in silence. Rain dripping through the roof.

"Why aren't you saying anything?" Robin said. "What's wrong? Have you brought the ax again? You don't need it."

No answer. Narris's slow, steady breathing.

"I'm learning to survive," Robin said. "You don't need to kill me."

A hand reached to touch his shoulder. Robin listened to the *churr* and *chack* of a nightingale, and from somewhere far off the hooting of an owl.

"It's after dark, isn't it? You don't normally come here this late."

Still no answer. Robin turned his head. There was a smell like freshly skinned rabbits. A musky aroma like a dog with wet fur.

You're not Narris. Who are you?

Whoever it was took their hand from Robin's shoulder. They edged out of the shelter and got to their feet. They stood there for what felt like a long time.

Finally, a woman's voice said: "Kill you?" She laughed softly, then said: "After waiting so long?"

She laughed again, then turned, and her footsteps faded through the leaves.

More footsteps. This time they brought Narris's voice.

"Spiced beer. And sweetmeal, so you can make flatbread. Don't expect much more where that came from. I have to get back. Mother's getting worse. Here, your fire is going out." He bent to blow on the embers.

"Leave it," Robin said. "I can do it."

"Fine. But snow is on its way, Robert Wyser says. Next time I'll try to bring another blanket—anything we can do to make your shelter warmer."

"I'm taking care of it," Robin said.

Narris left without another word. And by the time he could visit again, Robin would be far from here, and far beyond Narris's aid.

III. Hunted

During the night something had happened to the sound of the world. It had become softer, more muted. Robin put a hand out of his shelter and felt snowflakes on his palm. His eye wounds wept in the cold. Birds had woken more anxious than ever, scurrying desperately after berries, calling frantically to one another.

And there were other noises this morning. Sounds that didn't belong. They were faint at first, but growing clearer.

A cough. A snort. A metallic rustle and clink.

These noises stirred fear in Robin. They evoked awful images in his mind: red cloaks, studded boots, spiked clubs.

A branch snapped, close by. A man laughed.

Marian's words turned over in his thoughts: *A nightmare you can never escape because it flows into you. It becomes you.*

He scrambled from his shelter. He slung his unstrung bow across his back. He searched wildly for his backpack—found it, hooked it over his shoulder. He turned away from the menacing sounds and stumbled away. He tripped immediately, fell hard on his knees. He got up, ran again, arms outstretched before his face.

"Look, what's that?" a man shouted.

"A vagrant," another voice said. "Or an outlaw, all the way

out here. Might be a price on his head. Best take him in. Better than going back empty-handed."

A snapping noise, *kittissh*.

"After him. Yah, yah."

Robin stumbled through the blackness. He ran hard into a tree, fell to the ground, tasting blood, spitting out a tooth. He dragged himself up, shuffled forward in a half crouch.

The snapping noise again, *kittissh*. A stinging pain at the back of his leg. He stumbled over roots, fell once more, crawled on hands and knees.

"Then get off your damned horse," one of the men was saying. "Get down on all fours like him if you have to. Just bring him to me. Now."

Some of the rangers had dismounted and were coming up behind Robin.

"What *is* it?" one of them said.

"A wildling?" said another. "Look at the way it moves. Is it blind? God's teeth, it *is*—look at the cuts across its eyes."

"Deaf, dumb, blind—I couldn't care less. Grab it and let's go. I *do not* want to spend the night in this place. Two more traps to check and then home. That thing almost got us lost in here."

A hard blow to Robin's ribs. He curled in a ball around his pack, gasping for breath. Another kick to his back. He felt something being tied around his waist. The rope tautened and he was hauled to his feet. He was dragged, stumbling, and collided with a tree. He was pulled in another direction and fell down and landed hard on his left arm. The soldiers were laughing.

"Watch this, watch this," one of the men was saying.

"This way, over here, through these thorns."

Robin stumbled and fell and was dragged up and fell once more.

"That's enough," another man said. "Stop jacking about. You can have your sport when we're out of this Godforsaken forest. Treadfire, bind its arms. Tie it behind your horse. Let's get moving."

Where he lay, facedown in the snow, struggling for breath, Robin felt a soldier binding his arms behind his back.

IV. Wyrdwood

From somewhere high above and far away a fearsome noise began. A grunting, bellowing sound, impossibly loud—like the roaring of fifty king stags.

A ranger was saying: "Treadfire, bind its arms. Tie it behind your horse. Let's get moving."

As the noise shook the trees and the pressure on Robin's back eased. Something—or someone—slumped into the snow.

The bellowing rose again, more monstrous than ever. Robin wriggled forward and was free. Cords hampered his arms but they were not fully tied. He shook them loose as he ran. The bellowing seemed to have frightened the Sheriff's men . . . in which case . . .

Robin headed toward the noise. He plunged into a wall of the thickest, sharpest undergrowth—thorn and bramble clawing at his skin. He gritted his teeth and charged forward. Ahead of him the fearsome noise had stopped. Behind him he heard the rangers come back to life.

"Where's he gone?"

"Get after him."

"Where could he . . . ?"

"You let go of him? Treadfire, you—"

The undergrowth stopped clawing at Robin, opening up to allow him passage. He found himself on a steep incline. He tried to stand but low branches overhung the space, forming a tight tunnel.

He crawled onward and upward on hands and knees. The ground was rutted, frosted mud, cutting his palms. Behind him rustling slithering sounds made him imagine the tunnel closing behind him, vines and branches meeting and locking their limbs.

He kept crawling and he emerged into a flat, mossy space. He sat with his back against a tree, breathing hard, a cold sweat trickling down his neck. He listened for signs that the men had followed up the tunnel, but they were still thrashing around far below.

"Nolan . . . Nolan . . . you stupid son of . . ."

"Where . . . ? How could he have . . . ?"

"Stupid . . . Nolan . . . !"

From what they were saying it seemed one of the men had run off and was now lost. The others moved farther away, their voices fading. For now Robin was safe. But he thought about trying to find his way back to his camp, and to Narris, and he knew it was impossible. He was on his own.

He survived for almost three weeks in that place. He explored all sides of it with his fingers. It was a large, open glade, set in a natural bowl, ringed with oak and ash and hornbeam. Within the bowl was a smaller ring of seven yew trees, ancient by the feel of their trunks: hollow and knotted like rope. There was a stream, but it was locked up with ice.

For now the snow had stopped, but it was very cold. Groping his way back and forth, he began to collect fallen branches and to cut cordage from vines. It was painfully slow work, but eventually he constructed a small shelter with a tiny fire at its center. He slept on pine needles and moss to defeat the frost.

Hunger gnawed at him. He ate grass and bark just to quiet his twisting stomach. When he was lucky he would dig through a rotting tree trunk and find a devil's coach-horse beetle to crunch or a line of weevils to collect on his tongue.

The nights were growing colder. After five days, or perhaps it was seven, or nine, he woke and his fire was extinguished and the cold had sunk so deep in his bones he felt rooted to the forest floor. He felt so weak he was sure, this time, he would not be able to stand. But he struggled from the shelter, got to his feet, and the search for meager food began once more.

He imagined Marian was with him and they were children again and this was some game they were playing.

Feel under this rock for slugs, Marian was saying. *Come on, slow goat, you'll waste away to nothing at this rate. Don't you dare give up. Over this way, what's this? Mushrooms!*

She was right: a miniature village of fungi, wrapped around the base of an oak. Slimy to the touch. Robin was running a desperate tongue across dry lips. But still he hesitated.

Come on, eat up, Marian said.

"Remember, once, a mushroom almost killed you," Robin answered her, aloud. "These could be the same. I can't see if they're safe or poison."

Don't be such a baby, Marian said. *Anyway, you've got no choice. You'll die if you don't.*

"I might die if I do."

Then what have you got to lose?

He broke off a piece of mushroom and put it in his mouth. Just chewing now was hard work. But it was beefsteak fungus, and delicious. He feasted.

But that had been days ago. The last of the fungi was long gone. He dug in the ground with his knife, searching for worms, but they had disappeared far underground and would not reemerge until spring. There was no sign of any more bugs of any kind. He sat for hours, scraping moss from a log and licking the tangy iced slime from his knife.

His dreams and waking life had swapped places. When he was sleeping he could see the world in all its colors—he was in the dining hall back at Sir Bors's citadel, eating ducks' eggs and wheels of cheese and laughing with Bones and the others. And then he would wake, and his eyes would try to open, but there were only layers of blackness: the darkness behind his eyes and the weight of Winter Forest, stretching endlessly in every direction. An abyss as boundless as the hunger in his stomach.

The cold had become a numb presence that was eating him from within. When Robin woke this morning his fingers cracked with frost. There were flurries of snow.

Get up, Marian said. *Move around. If you don't, you'll freeze to the spot. You always were a slow goat, but you'll be a frozen-stone goat if you don't move around.*

"I'm too cold to move," Robin muttered.

You're too cold not *to move! You need to rebuild your fire. Get up, find an ash tree. Ash burns green and wet, your father taught you that.*

Robin used his knife to strip the bark from an ash branch and then to whittle wood shavings from the dryer wood inside. He rolled frosted moss between his palms to use as kindling. His frozen fingers did not want to grip the strike-a-light and it took him hour upon hour to get even one spark. When finally he did the moss only smoldered, failed to become flame.

Shuddering violently he repeated the process. Each time he thought this would be his last chance: If he failed this time, he would die. Once again he rolled the moss in his red-raw palms. He gripped the strike-a-light in his claw-like fingers. He tried again.

Eventually he smelled smoke and he cupped the flame in his palm and breathed on it and gently lowered the burning kindling onto the wood shavings. He nursed the fire and added ash twigs and crouched over the flame and felt some life returning to his veins. He laid moss next to the fire and when it was dry he stuffed it inside his boots and his surcoat to trap more of his body warmth.

There, you're winning, Marian said. *The cold will never beat you.*

"Winning?" Robin said. "Or saving myself for starvation?"

There was no food. He cut strips from the top of his goatskin boots, chewed the bits of leather. He was vaguely aware it was a pointless exercise, but he was desperate for anything to swallow into his stomach. If he could have peered into an ice-crusted pool, he would not have recognized his reflection: at the academy Sir Bors had made the squires keep their clothes clean and their hair short; now Robin's hair was wild and his cloak was torn on thorns and matted with mud and moss. His once stocky frame was shrinking; his cheeks thin and pale as winter.

Handsome knight, Marian was saying. *Sir Robin of the goat. Slow hood of the woods.*

His thoughts were becoming muddled and he was vaguely aware he was talking to himself. "You have to get up now, Robin," he was saying. "You have not frozen into the ground, it only feels as if you have. You are not a part of the earth, not yet. It's time for a homecoming feast. Suckling pig and pickled pears. Your parents are here, and Thane and Hal. Get up now or you'll be late."

Behind his eyes he sees a giant mushroom, dagger-shaped, growing and growing until it blots out the sun and turns the world pitch black.

He had stopped shivering, which he vaguely realized was a bad sign. *So that's that*, he thought. *Here's the end.*

Even Marian had given up. She had stopped screeching at him to find more food. He tried to keep his thoughts quiet so he wouldn't wake her.

An hour ago he had found a millipede amid the mush of leaves. He had killed it in his fingers and eaten it thankfully. But the effort of the search had exhausted him. He lay flat, wedging himself against a moss-quilted log, a deathly stupor washing over him.

He knew, for certain this time, that when sleep came he would not be getting back up. Half of him felt impossibly relieved; the other half was consumed by a deep cold sorrow connected to memories of home: his mother's singing drifting down the valley; his brothers teaching him to swim in Mill Pond. Marian, and their tower, reading stories by lamplight in their den. Their plans to explore together the far corners of the world.

All the things he had lost and everything that had lain in store but now would never be.

All of it fading. Finally to be washed away by this last bottomless sleep.

V. Robin's Cave

The log moved against Robin's back. He shifted his weight and lay still. The movement had barely roused him; he drifted once more toward oblivion.

Again the log lurched, more violently. This time he was thrust fully awake.

He dragged himself to his feet, stood away from this churning shuddering thing. The tree trunk—what Robin had thought was a tree trunk—shifted more forcefully than ever, making a noise like roots being torn from the earth.

Next came cracking sounds, and a rustling, and a sharp snap. All of which formed the strangest ideas in Robin's mind. He had the distinct impression that the log was uncurling itself: twigs unfurling into fingers, stumps breaking into gnarled feet, roots twisting into tendons. A moss-thick beard on a bark-wrinkled chin.

There was a yawning noise, which could have been human, or animal, or a tree bending in the wind. It seemed to Robin a figure had lurched upright and was stretching its old-man limbs.

"Has he been here . . . this entire time?" Robin muttered to himself. "Just lying here?"

"I dare say I have." The old man's voice was dry leaves,

scrunching. "What of it? How long have I slept? Perhaps I'm closer to the end than I thought. The merest task leaves me exhausted . . ."

A muffled thump, like a branch dumping snow to the ground.

"I can't entirely recall what I was doing," the old man said. "Ah yes, scaring away those creatures in metal skins. More tiring than it used to be. You're not one of them, are you? Oh no, you're the other one. We used to get plenty of your sort here, once. I hoped we were finished with all that."

It seemed the old man was now moving around the clearing, and as he did so there was a *clack-clack* sound, like branches coming together, or antlers clashing.

"I didn't know anyone lived in Winter Forest," Robin said. "Are you a vagrant, or an outlaw?"

"I'm an ancient discarded piece of the world, and nothing more. Leave me be, and I'll do the same for you. I won't be staying."

Robin lay down to rest. Nothing in this new life could surprise him for long. He drifted once more toward sleep. But something nagged at him. Something about all this was important . . .

This old man, whoever he was, had survived.

Robin sat up. "I need food."

"I dare say you do," said the old man. "The amount you crash around. Must be exhausting. The amount of noise you make. I was hardly able to sleep. Well, you're no concern of mine. You'll get no help from me."

Robin didn't have the strength to argue. He stretched out once more on the cold ground. Long moments passed before he felt a hard poke in his ribs.

"You certainly are a skinny thing. Nothing but bones. Your type, you do well enough in a group, but you're helpless on your own. But I won't help you. She'll fight me for you if I do. It's in her nature. I'll only make her worse. You're on your own."

Three more pokes in the ribs.

"On. Your. Own."

Another long pause. Snow beginning to fall. Robin thought the old man must have gone back to sleep. In that case, Robin would sleep too. It would be a relief. This frosted moss wasn't so uncomfortable, after all. And the snowfall was wrapping him in a blanket that wasn't so very cold.

He would sleep and let none of this trouble him any longer . . .

Another poke in his ribs.

"Oh, all right. Don't sulk," the old man said. "I'll help. I'm too soft. That's my trouble. Never could stand to see one of your sort in distress. If I hadn't been so soft, I probably wouldn't be in this mess. I don't suppose it matters, not anymore."

A lurching creaking sound, like a rotten tree falling.

"Come then. This way. Ah, yes, I forgot. Take my arm, there. Hurry now. Do you want my help or not? I can't have much time left. Come now, or you really will be lost."

He led the way to a cave. Robin crawled inside.

"It's damp," the old man said. "But it keeps out the frost and the wind. There's a spring for fresh water."

"What about food?" Robin said.

"Plenty of spiders under rocks."

There was a long silence. Robin realized the old man had gone.

Time passed in that cave.

Robin ate slugs and stinkbugs he licked off the wet walls.

Occasionally he thought he detected the musty, nutty smell of the old man, or thought he heard the shuffling of his feet.

Robin called out but got only his own echo in reply. He felt even lonelier here than he had done living in the glade. The feeling was so intense he even began to miss Narris Felstone.

He daydreamed he was back in Thuner's Fold, with his brothers, the three of them shooting arrows at baskets hung on poles. He remembered the day he tired of this practice— shooting at targets that never moved—and he took aim instead at a crow and hit it dead first time. Hal had laughed. "A penny says you can't do that again. Not in a score of arrows."

And he couldn't. It was beginner's luck. Shooting crows was hard. And so it became an obsession, Robin standing for hour upon hour in Thuner's Fold, until on a good day he could bring down one bird in every five. His mother baked the birds into pies.

See, said Marian's voice in the cave. *You can do anything if you try. That's the persistent goat I remember.*

"Leave me alone," Robin whispered.

No, I won't! You got us into this mess and you're going to get us back out. You said you'd kill him—the man who did this to us. A little bit of hunger and you've forgotten your promise.

"What do you want from me?"

I want you to stop feeling sorry for yourself and I want you to get up and explore and I want you to find better food. Bugs are one thing—you won't starve, I suppose—but you should see yourself. Like a coat hung on a pole to scare off crows.

Robin felt his way deeper into the cave. He found it was huge, with tunnels and chambers running in all directions, sometimes so low he had to crawl on hands and knees, sometimes so cavernous his voice came back a distant echo. He went a little farther each time, always counting his steps so he could find his way back to the mouth of the cave. In his mind's eye Marian went ahead of him, crawling through gaps, whispering for him to come through or telling him to go back, just the way she had when they used to explore the crypts and cellars beneath her father's manor.

On one of their adventures through the cave Robin found his own private larder. He brushed against something hanging from the ceiling. Maybe it was a stalactite: It certainly felt cold and dead as rock. But when prodded the dangling thing moved. When prodded harder it shrieked and began clawing at Robin's face. Soon the whole chamber was full of shrieking, beating, leathery wings. He retreated into a connecting tunnel, his heart hammering, summoning the courage to return.

Scaredy Mary, Marian's voice said. *Get back in there. What are you afraid of, the dark? Ha.*

Robin was quicker this time, grabbing one of the hibernating bats from its roost and ducking back out of the chamber before the creature could raise the alarm. He killed the bat and roasted it over a small fire. He took another bat the next day, and the next. Each one provided a morsel of meat.

What would you do without me? Marian said. *You're looking stronger already.*

"And what good will it do?" Robin said. "I might as well starve."

No! Marian screamed. *I can't do it alone. I won't make it without you. Our fates are tied, we've always known that. We've both got to dig ourselves out.*

Time passed. The cold, the damp, the loneliness.

And the fear.

Wind wafted through the cave and turned from stone cold to moist and hot, like breath. At the same time Robin heard a padding, clicking sound—claws against rock.

It's here! Marian hissed. *It's in the cave. Robin, run!*

But he couldn't move. His limbs locked with terror.

It's coming closer! You have to get away.

He fought to move even an arm, a leg, but he couldn't so much as flinch—his body impossibly heavy against the cave floor.

The Wargwolf moved nearer, its breath pulsing hot and putrid, a low rumbling in its throat.

Move! Marian shrieked. *Crawl into the low tunnels—it won't be able to follow.*

Robin struggled and struggled but he felt fused to the rock.

The beast moved closer, its giant nostrils tasting the air. The clicking of its claws stopped at Robin's side. Still he couldn't move. His heart hammering hard enough to break.

The Wargwolf was standing over him. Robin had the impression it had tipped its head. Then it was lowering its jaws, and he heard the wet noise of them opening . . .

From somewhere distant, echoing through the cave, came a woman's voice, shouting. The words were muffled, but the sound seemed to make the Wargwolf pause. And then it was turning, slinking away. The clicking of its claws faded and it was gone.

Time passed.

The cave was a place of weird noises and dreadful sensations. There was a hissing, which could have been water squeezing through a fissure in the rock, or could have been breath between ancient teeth. A clacking, like stones thrown in a game of snitch, or like bones grating in an old woman's neck.

Robin was sitting by his fire when suddenly he knew he was not alone. The old woman was here, at his side. She turned to face him, with that *clack-clack* sound of bones. In Robin's imagining she smiled, and even as she did so she became older still, her lips curling back like leaves in a fire, teeth dropping from her gums, skittering on the cave floor. She kept aging, her hair coiling from her head, skin flaking away, skeleton crumbling, until finally there was nothing left of her but dust, rising in the heat of the flames.

"There was no one there in the first place," he muttered under his breath. "These are the stories you were told growing up, and now your mind is making them real."

Sooner or later all the stories come true, Marian said. *All the monsters made flesh. I thought Arethusa was just a nymph from a myth until I realized I was her.*

"The ancient woman doesn't exist," Robin said. "There's nothing in this cave but me and the bats and the cold and the damp. And you're not even here, so I don't know why I'm talking to you."

Time passed.

Robin ate his daily meal of bat flesh and he felt some of his old strength returning.

He told himself, over and over, that he was alone in the cave. But he could never make himself believe it. Night after night he felt the hot breath of the Wargwolf and he lay pressed against the rock in fear. He listened to the old woman wheeze and her bones clack. He heard countless other uncanny things he could never begin to understand.

He thought, just once, he heard someone—a bigger heavier someone than the old man—moving through the cave, running his hands across the floor, turning over rocks, as if looking for something in the dark . . .

Time passed.

Robin lay down to sleep. As he drifted off he heard a sound that could have been the wind in the mouth of the cave, or could have been the memory of a song his mother used to sing, or could have been an old woman, whispering a ballad:

When the twelvemonth and one day was past
The ghost began to speak
Why sit you here, all day on my grave
And will not let me sleep?
When shall we meet again, sweetheart? When shall we meet again?
When the drying leaves, that fall from the trees
Are green and spring up again.

And then a hand gripped Robin's wrist, and he heard himself shout in shock and fear. Hot breath moved close to his ear.

"Finally, she's gone," the old man whispered. "Time to go. She'll return soon enough. I said I'd help you and I will. I stick to my word. But she won't like it. Not one bit. Come now, out we go. Before she gets back."

VI. The Weald Ones

Following the old man's voice, crawling from the cave, Robin heard the ticking of early insects. He smelled the sap rising in the trees and felt sunshine on his skin. From high above came the *tock, tock, tock* of a woodpecker calling for a mate. Winter was over.

The old man no longer held Robin's arm, yet somehow Robin found he could follow easily in his footsteps. He had the impression the old man had changed—he was no longer so frail. His movements were accompanied by a rustling, like the sweeping of a cloak of green leaves.

"We must teach you to find your own way around," the old man said. "The trouble with your kind is you never learn to look. You've got plenty of senses, but you barely put them to use. Under that bush, near your right foot, you'll find a hedgehog that failed to wake from hibernation. *Waste not want not*, the first and last law around here. The early days of spring offer even less food than winter, perhaps you already knew that much."

Robin searched with his fingers and retrieved the spiked ball from under the bush and he carried it carefully in a fold in his surcoat. He followed the old man.

"Why are you helping me?" Robin said.

"Because I said I would. I keep my promises, unlike you people. Besides, she has plans for you, which makes me suspicious. Perhaps I can teach you to see sense, before it's too late."

"What do I call you?" Robin said.

"Well now, let's see, it's been so long since anyone asked. I've had a great many names: Silvanus, Faunus, Herne, The Green Man, The Great Horned One. So many more I've forgotten. My favorite was King Cernunnos. Suits me, don't you think? *King* Cernunnos. A little respect for a change. Those were the days when—" The old man rustled to a halt. "They're here again."

"Who?"

"Those creatures in metal skins."

"The Sheriff's men? Where? What should I do? Where should I go?"

"Don't *do* anything. Don't *go* anywhere. All that wasted energy, blundering about. You ran last time—look how that turned out. They don't see much, these creatures. They look only with their eyes. Lie still and let them pass us by."

"Where are they?"

"On the southern edge of the forest. Half a morning's walk away. Heading in this direction."

"How do you know they're there, all that distance away?"

"They startled a fox, which left its usual path and frightened a hare, which disturbed a heron, which called out to its mate, which alerted a merlin, which . . . You get the idea. The forest is a pond, and every beat of a butterfly's wings forms a ripple. But those men in metal, thumping about, they are rocks thrown in this pond. Can't you feel the waves they've caused? How blind your kind can be."

Robin felt an overwhelming urge to run. But he didn't know which direction. He forced himself to stay with the old man. After a while they stopped so Robin could cook the hedgehog in its skin. He scooped out the meat with a sharpened stick.

They went farther into the forest, stopping to dig up edible roots. The old man taught Robin to know deadly enchanter's nightshade from its smell and how to find tubers from the feel of the soil. The day was warming toward noon when Robin heard the clinking of the soldiers' mailcoats and the crunch of their nailed boots. He crouched, his hood up, not moving a muscle.

"We should run," he hissed.

"No, no, lie still," the old man said. "Countless times you've walked past a fawn or a lizard, oblivious to their presence, simply because they didn't move. Invisibility is mostly a matter of patience."

"Which way are they coming?" Robin whispered. "How far?"

He got no answer. He was on his own.

He heard one of the rangers laughing. The crunch of boots. Those images flooded Robin's mind: bloodred cloaks, spiked clubs, blood misting with the rain.

Would the men stumble over him? Was he crouched on their path or just to the side?

The men moved nearer. Close enough to hear their words.

One ranger was saying: "So, a Friar and a Woodsman are being chased by a wolf, right. The Woodsman says: 'Father, we'll never outrun the beast. We'll have to hide.' The Friar doesn't answer, he just grits his teeth and runs faster. The Woodsman says: 'I know wolves. Believe me, we'll never outrun it. If we're quick, we can climb a tree. I'll help you, Father.' Again, no answer. The Friar just hitches his habit and keeps running. The Woodsman tries once more, getting desperate. He says: 'Father, we have to hide! The beast is too strong. We'll never outrun it.' Finally the Friar says: 'Will you shut up! I don't have to outrun the wolf—I just have to out-run you.'"

"Ha-ha, Damon, you're a funny man," a second ranger said. "Where do you get them all from? Let's have another."

The boots crunched past where Robin was crouching. He thought three soldiers had gone by, then four.

But the last pair of footsteps came to a halt.

"Captain," this last ranger called. "There's something back here I think you should see . . ."

Cold sweat at the back of Robin's neck. Overhead, a buzzard wheeled and shrilled *pew, pew*. To Robin it sounded like *run, run*.

Up ahead the other soldiers had come to a halt.

"What is it?" the shout came back.

"There's something here, Captain. I can't quite make it out but . . . it looks like . . . Well, I'm not sure . . . It's not moving . . . maybe it's dead . . . You might want to come and take a look."

"Get up here, Fitz," the leader shouted back. "Stop wasting my time. If it's not our quarry I don't want to know. I've got a life to get back to, even if you don't."

A twig snapped. The last ranger was pushing his way up the path. Robin let out a long breath. He didn't move until the last sound of the men had faded away.

The spring quickened.

Cernunnos began to teach Robin to know the forest through smell and touch. He taught him to hear the different tones below his boots: the *clump-clump* of stony ground; the hollower sound above a badger's sett; the packed-earth *tump-tump* of a deer track.

Several times Robin had to stay dead still while soldiers passed. Sometimes when they made camp he would crouch nearby, listening to them talk. They always spoke too loud, laughed too much—nervous but trying not to show it. When they had gone Robin would go and scavenge what scraps of food they left behind.

The spring warmed and the days lengthened.

Cernunnos taught him how to find woodcock eggs by the sound of his feet through the leaf litter. He showed him how to coax fish from the deep of the river using his bare hands. On a good day Robin feasted on smoked trout and wild garlic broth. Pheasant and chestnuts baked in a mud oven. He grew stronger.

And now it seemed to him he almost preferred it when he had been starving. Then his only desperate thoughts had been about food. Now, with a satisfied stomach, his mind began to torture him once more. He felt the white-hot tip of the lancing knife, pushing inside the jelly of his eye. He saw the man with the ruined face, and Marian in that cage. He heard her hissing: *They* did *follow you! You led them to me!*

Since leaving the cave he had heard nothing like the wheezing of the old woman's breath, or the clacking of her bones. Instead there were other uncanny sounds, like a baby crying, the noise drifting eerily through the trees. After a few weeks the crying stopped and instead he heard what sounded like a young girl, kicking through bluebells, giggling.

These noises, so deep in Winter Forest, so far from any town or village.

He heard something, or someone, creeping close to his shelter. The soft steps moved closer, then darted away, came back again, circling, a child laughing.

"Who are you?" Robin said. "What do you want?"

In reply, very faint, came the words of a rhyme:

Round and round the wheel turns,
Faster, faster, faster;
See the way the carriage burns,
Headed for disaster.
Show me where the wheel stops,
There! You're the master.

"What do you want with me?" Robin shouted. "Leave me alone!"

The girl of the forest said nothing. Instead there came an awful rumble. Searing breath washed into his shelter.

His anger had stirred something in the darkness.

It was out there too. The Wargwolf.

Robin scrambled from his shelter, meaning to run—

But it was too late. The beast was on him. It flowed forward, its fangs dripping, its jaws opening to engulf Robin's head.

VII. Hunting the Warg

So hard to tell now what is waking life and what is dreaming. It feels so real. The putrid heat of the beast's breath. The wet noise of its jaws widening.

And somebody screaming.

It is the girl of the forest—she is screeching and yelling—an incoherent babble. At the sound of her voice the Wargwolf becomes still, its dagger-fangs poised, about to snap shut. The girl continues shouting and the beast skulks backward, snarling, its top lip curled.

Robin's mind shows him the beast. It is colossal, black and silvered in the moonlight. But the most dreadful part is its shadow. Where the shadow is cast the dark behind Robin's eyes grows blacker still. It is a hole in the world, so abysmal that to step into it would be to fall and keep falling . . .

In Robin's imagining the girl of the forest has fox-red hair, spilling to her waist. She is smaller than the wolf-god's head, yet when she steps close it bends its neck to her and lowers its ears and its snarling subsides. She is reaching up to touch its muzzle, and she is whispering: "You can't, not yet. It isn't time."

And then in Robin's mind's eye the girl is turning and leading the forest god away, and as she goes she glances back

"And what would you hunt? Those creatures in metal skins? No. I'll not show you down that path. Anger is a forest fire. The more you feed it, the hungrier it becomes. So much I've forgotten, but I remember that clearly enough."

Something occurred to Robin. He still had his hunting pack, strapped across his back, and inside was the message from Sir Bors. Would this strange old man be able to read it? Could Robin know the full truth, at last? Why had his father abandoned him? Why did Marian say it all happened because of Robin? What did that phrase mean, *winter-born*?

Thinking all this, Robin had slowed, and Cernunnos had strode some distance ahead. Robin hurried after him, dark memories burning through his thoughts.

He felt as though he had been standing in exactly this spot for days. A little way ahead of him a heron was searching for a safe place to build a nest. Robin listened to the heron—he listened and he gripped his bow and he waited.

"The owl is the greatest hunter of the forest," the old man had told him. "Total awareness. Perfect patience. It will watch the movements of its prey for days before choosing the moment to strike. Its stillness makes it invisible. How many times did you hear an owl in the woods, and how many times did you *see* the bird behind the voice?"

Cernunnos had finally agreed to teach Robin to shoot his bow. But only once Robin promised he would hunt only for food.

"You are learning to sense your surroundings at last," the old man had said. "Eyes only deceive in the deep forest. Butterflies have ragged wings to look like autumn leaves; bugs change color to become the bark on trees; rabbits flash their tails one way and run the other. Everything here is illusion. Human hunters call deer 'fairies of the wood.' Did you

at Robin and wipes a tear from her cheek, and then they are gone.

Two people arguing, near where Robin is sleeping.

An old man saying: "I can see now what you're doing. How long you've had this planned."

A young girl laughs meanly. "Who's going to stop me, you?"

"You want to use him against our brother, don't you? These are not your playthings."

"Yes, you could try to stop me! Remember, like before? It'll be fun!"

"We've already lost so many. Where will your madness end?"

The girl laughs and squeals, and Robin wakes, his breathing quick and ragged.

He followed Cernunnos across a warm glade. By the feeling of the sun it was midday. By the sounds of the birds the middle of spring. The old man went to his knees and seemed to be uncovering something buried in the leaves. Robin could smell the object: the sharp tang of rust and caked blood. Cernunnos was poking at the thing with a stick. Steel jaws crashed shut. It was a wolf trap.

"The Wargwolf," Robin said. "That's what the soldiers are hunting, isn't it?"

"If that's what you choose to call him," Cernunnos said. "He's carried as many names as I have: Wightwolf; Fenrir; Scucca; Baal. I don't suppose he's particular. Not anymore."

"Why is the Sheriff hunting it?"

"A trophy?" the old man said. "Another head mounted on his wall? I gave up trying to understand your sort long ago. But he's not the first to seek my brother in these woods. There is a legend about wolves: When they die their shadows continue to hunt. If a person could possess one of those shadows . . . and if the wolf in question happened to be . . . hmmm, well . . . so many stories, I'm no longer sure which ones are true. Which are of the past, and which of the future. Not that it matters. Not anymore."

Robin listened to Cernunnos uncovering another wolf trap. A whiplash of air as the jaws slammed shut.

"Your brother? You said 'my brother.'"

"The last of my brothers," Cernunnos said. "There were many of us, once. Now see what we've become. My brother has fallen the furthest of all. Little more than instinct left. When I think what he once was . . ."

"What does it . . . What does he want with me? Why won't he leave me alone? I hear him at night, breathing outside my shelter."

"You've feared him all your life. He is drawn to fear, like a moth to a flame. I doubt he means you harm, or you wouldn't have survived this long. But stay away from him on clear nights and in open areas. You will want to avoid his shadow."

The *cla-clang* of a trap snapping shut.

"Why does he allow himself to be hunted?" Robin said. "Why doesn't he fight them?"

"That was never his way. Certainly, he can be terrible if he's provoked. But they never face him directly. He probably doesn't even know he's being hunted. He's sunk so low."

Cernunnos went on his way and Robin followed. More than once he had the uncanny impression that the old man had grown to a great size, his footsteps crunching like hooves through the undergrowth. The *clack-clack* of antler against branch.

"What about the other one?" Robin said. "The old woman in the cave, the crying child, the girl kicking through the flowers. They are one and the same, aren't they?"

"My sister," Cernunnos said. "She's the one you need beware. The strongest of us, by far. She remembers all the old shapes, and the rhythms. She won't be much trouble for now. But come late spring, and summer . . ."

"What does she want?"

"Want?" Cernunnos said. "Typical of your kind to think that way. I can't say she wants anything. It's in her nature to stir the mud, to watch the patterns turn."

They went on in silence. Cernunnos found three more traps. He came to a halt and sighed.

"They're back," he said. "No matter how many traps I find, they bring more. These people once worshipped us, then neglected us, now they spill our blood for profit and pleasure."

"Where are they?" Robin said.

"A few hours east. They've just crossed Silver River."

"Teach me to see the way you do."

"What do you think we've been doing? You've changed more than you know. No more blundering about, crashing into things. This is a powerful place, even now, and power always flows both ways. Winter Forest will destroy without mercy. But it will heal and renew with equal vigor."

Robin listened to a hedgehog, snuffling amid green shoots, sucking up slugs, and he realized Cernunnos was right: His other senses were growing sharp. He could not see the sky, or watch for the usual signs, but he knew from the taste of the air that a storm was approaching. He could tell from the smell of the bark that the trees here were beech, mostly, with some ash and hornbeam. The feel of the soil between his fingers told him this track led toward water. He was moving more swiftly and surely too. He had discarded his clumsy boots and his feet had toughened on root and thorn and bramble.

"You could teach me to use my bow," Robin said.

know that? They believe deer can disappear. But they are still there. They are just infinitely patient."

Robin listened to the old man and he stalked his prey. He missed, missed, and missed again.

"No, no, no," the old man had said. "Your mind is full of noise. I can hear it from here. And so can your quarry. Clear your thoughts. Sense the ripples in the pond."

Robin listened to the heron hopping closer.

And in the next instant everything else disappeared. There was only the forest, and this hunt, here and now. For the first time in months his mind was clear of Marian, of the Sheriff, of his parents. He listened to his own breathing, and to his heartbeat, and he heard those noises merge with the rhythmic click and ticking of the forest.

The heron flapped its mighty wings.

Robin released the bowstring, the arrow flew. The bird dropped dead.

"Tonight, a feast!" the old man said, and only now did Robin realize he was standing very close. "Perhaps you won't be a complete burden, after all."

Cernunnos led Robin back to the glade where they had first met. While Robin built a fire the old man plucked the heron and gutted two fish he had caught. Robin had gone days without a proper meal. He feasted on the smoked fish and the heron flesh. Fully fed, he lay down to sleep. The fork moss was soft and warm from the day's sun. The stream trilled across pebbles. Cernunnos had told him this stream was called Lethe and it was a stream of forgetting.

"It will help to wash away thought and memory," the old man had said.

Robin listened to the stream and he listened to the forest breathing softly around him and he felt something close to peace for the first time since he was seven years old. Hunting for himself, feeding himself, had felt good. Even better had been that feeling of clearing his mind completely. No room for those nightmares of the past.

Perhaps I could forget all that entirely, he thought. *Just hunt and eat and sleep and discard all those darker things. Become part of the wildwood, the way the old man has.*

Already he had abandoned his backpack, and the scroll it contained, casting them into the cave. Why would he want to torture himself with those echoes from the past? What use was the truth to him now, when there was nothing he could do to put things right? He curled himself amid the moss.

Yes, forget all that. Hunt and eat and sleep and forget everything else.

Everything?

Forget about Marian?

Don't you dare! her voice screamed in his head.

"I don't even know if you're alive or dead."

I'm not dead, stupid goat. I'm buried somewhere else. You've got to fight to dig us out!

"Fight?" Robin whispered. "I've only just learned how to survive. And where did fighting ever get me? Or you? I remember what Sir Bors said; I'll become the monster I fight against."

You're making no sense! Marian shouted. *Follow the path of the angels. Follow the girl with a thousand shapes.*

"Now who's making no sense?"

His thoughts were becoming disordered as he slipped toward sleep, Marian's voice fading with the breeze. Forget those painful things. Warm and well-fed and full of relief. Sleep.

VIII. Pieces of Old Gods

R obin had shot a woodcock and was carrying it across one shoulder, making his way back to the glade. He moved swiftly now through the forest-maze, guided by its shapes and its patterns. Here was a wren, singing on its boundary post; and nearby a hare, thumping the ground outside a bolt-hole. And here was a particular pattern of rutting rings, which Robin could trace with his fingers; and a familiar crisscross of badger paths and rabbit runs. Each of these was a waymarker, leading him on. Slowly, barely realizing he was doing it, he was building a map in his mind, as intricate as the roots in the soil. He followed this map and continued toward the glade.

As he drew near he sensed danger, and panic. Woodpeckers cackling in alarm, squirrels barking.

Something was very wrong.

In the distance an awful roar and a crash and splintering sounds. Robin turned toward these noises and he followed.

He stumbled down a bank of raw soil. Here was a fresh trench plowed through the forest—trees toppled on either side. He followed this furrow, groping his way through the debris: thousand-year-old heartwood splintered like kindling; ancient roots ripped from the earth; rocks tossed aside like marbles. What could have caused such destruction?

Robin thought he knew, and he quickened his pace.

From up ahead more roaring, thundering noises—something powerful was dragging itself though the wild-wood, carving this trail of devastation. Another bellow of pain. The clattering of countless wings, birds taking to the air thick as insects.

There was blood everywhere. So much blood. As if the trees themselves were bleeding. It dripped stickily on Robin's head; he slipped on it as he clambered over fallen trunks. Ahead of him the roaring, splintering sounds had stopped, but he could still follow easily by the trail of blood.

Eventually it led him to the cave. He crawled inside.

As he suspected, it was Cernunnos. The old man was barely conscious. Robin felt with his fingers and found the wolf trap was still clamped to his mangled foot—he must have ripped its chains from the ground and dragged it with him through the trees.

Someone else was here in the cave. She giggled. The girl with the fox-red hair. She giggled again and the old man groaned—she was poking a stick into his wound.

"Get away from him!" Robin lunged at her.

There was a sound like claws on rock as she scuttled from the cave, giggling.

Robin turned his attention to Cernunnos. He probed with his fingertips to establish the extent of the wound. He left the cave and he cut vines to use as a tourniquet, willow wands to make a splint. He collected moss and primrose to make a salve. He went back and used his knife to wind open the jaws of the trap. The old man came fully awake, bellowing loud enough to make the cave walls quake. Robin did what he could to stop the blood flow. He treated and wrapped the wound.

"Get away from me . . . ," Cernunnos mumbled. "Leave me

at Robin and wipes a tear from her cheek, and then they are gone.

Two people arguing, near where Robin is sleeping.

An old man saying: "I can see now what you're doing. How long you've had this planned."

A young girl laughs meanly. "Who's going to stop me, you?"

"You want to use him against our brother, don't you? These are not your playthings."

"Yes, you could try to stop me! Remember, like before? It'll be fun!"

"We've already lost so many. Where will your madness end?"

The girl laughs and squeals, and Robin wakes, his breathing quick and ragged.

He followed Cernunnos across a warm glade. By the feeling of the sun it was midday. By the sounds of the birds the middle of spring. The old man went to his knees and seemed to be uncovering something buried in the leaves. Robin could smell the object: the sharp tang of rust and caked blood. Cernunnos was poking at the thing with a stick. Steel jaws crashed shut. It was a wolf trap.

"The Wargwolf," Robin said. "That's what the soldiers are hunting, isn't it?"

"If that's what you choose to call him," Cernunnos said. "He's carried as many names as I have: Wightwolf; Fenrir; Scucca; Baal. I don't suppose he's particular. Not anymore."

"Why is the Sheriff hunting it?"

"A trophy?" the old man said. "Another head mounted on his wall? I gave up trying to understand your sort long ago. But he's not the first to seek my brother in these woods. There is a legend about wolves: When they die their shadows continue to hunt. If a person could possess one of those shadows . . . and if the wolf in question happened to be . . . hmmm, well . . . so many stories, I'm no longer sure which ones are true. Which are of the past, and which of the future. Not that it matters. Not anymore."

Robin listened to Cernunnos uncovering another wolf trap. A whiplash of air as the jaws slammed shut.

"Your brother? You said 'my brother.' "

"The last of my brothers," Cernunnos said. "There were many of us, once. Now see what we've become. My brother has fallen the furthest of all. Little more than instinct left. When I think what he once was . . ."

"What does it . . . What does he want with me? Why won't he leave me alone? I hear him at night, breathing outside my shelter."

"You've feared him all your life. He is drawn to fear, like a moth to a flame. I doubt he means you harm, or you wouldn't have survived this long. But stay away from him on clear nights and in open areas. You will want to avoid his shadow."

The *cla-clang* of a trap snapping shut.

"Why does he allow himself to be hunted?" Robin said. "Why doesn't he fight them?"

"That was never his way. Certainly, he can be terrible if he's provoked. But they never face him directly. He probably doesn't even know he's being hunted. He's sunk so low."

Cernunnos went on his way and Robin followed. More than once he had the uncanny impression that the old man had grown to a great size, his footsteps crunching like hooves through the undergrowth. The *clack-clack* of antler against branch.

"What about the other one?" Robin said. "The old woman in the cave, the crying child, the girl kicking through the flowers. They are one and the same, aren't they?"

"My sister," Cernunnos said. "She's the one you need beware. The strongest of us, by far. She remembers all the old shapes, and the rhythms. She won't be much trouble for now. But come late spring, and summer . . ."

"What does she want?"

"Want?" Cernunnos said. "Typical of your kind to think that way. I can't say she wants anything. It's in her nature to stir the mud, to watch the patterns turn."

They went on in silence. Cernunnos found three more traps. He came to a halt and sighed.

"They're back," he said. "No matter how many traps I find, they bring more. These people once worshipped us, then neglected us, now they spill our blood for profit and pleasure."

"Where are they?" Robin said.

"A few hours east. They've just crossed Silver River."

"Teach me to see the way you do."

"What do you think we've been doing? You've changed more than you know. No more blundering about, crashing into things. This is a powerful place, even now, and power always flows both ways. Winter Forest will destroy without mercy. But it will heal and renew with equal vigor."

Robin listened to a hedgehog, snuffling amid green shoots, sucking up slugs, and he realized Cernunnos was right: His other senses were growing sharp. He could not see the sky, or watch for the usual signs, but he knew from the taste of the air that a storm was approaching. He could tell from the smell of the bark that the trees here were beech, mostly, with some ash and hornbeam. The feel of the soil between his fingers told him this track led toward water. He was moving more swiftly and surely too. He had discarded his clumsy boots and his feet had toughened on root and thorn and bramble.

"You could teach me to use my bow," Robin said.

233

"And what would you hunt? Those creatures in metal skins? No. I'll not show you down that path. Anger is a forest fire. The more you feed it, the hungrier it becomes. So much I've forgotten, but I remember that clearly enough."

Something occurred to Robin. He still had his hunting pack, strapped across his back, and inside was the message from Sir Bors. Would this strange old man be able to read it? Could Robin know the full truth, at last? Why had his father abandoned him? Why did Marian say it all happened because of Robin? What did that phrase mean, *winter-born*?

Thinking all this, Robin had slowed, and Cernunnos had strode some distance ahead. Robin hurried after him, dark memories burning through his thoughts.

He felt as though he had been standing in exactly this spot for days. A little way ahead of him a heron was searching for a safe place to build a nest. Robin listened to the heron—he listened and he gripped his bow and he waited.

"The owl is the greatest hunter of the forest," the old man had told him. "Total awareness. Perfect patience. It will watch the movements of its prey for days before choosing the moment to strike. Its stillness makes it invisible. How many times did you hear an owl in the woods, and how many times did you *see* the bird behind the voice?"

Cernunnos had finally agreed to teach Robin to shoot his bow. But only once Robin promised he would hunt only for food.

"You are learning to sense your surroundings at last," the old man had said. "Eyes only deceive in the deep forest. Butterflies have ragged wings to look like autumn leaves; bugs change color to become the bark on trees; rabbits flash their tails one way and run the other. Everything here is illusion. Human hunters call deer 'fairies of the wood.' Did you know that? They believe deer can disappear. But they are still there. They are just infinitely patient."

Robin listened to the old man and he stalked his prey. He missed, missed, and missed again.

"No, no, no," the old man had said. "Your mind is full of noise. I can hear it from here. And so can your quarry. Clear your thoughts. Sense the ripples in the pond."

Robin listened to the heron hopping closer.

And in the next instant everything else disappeared. There was only the forest, and this hunt, here and now. For the first time in months his mind was clear of Marian, of the Sheriff, of his parents. He listened to his own breathing, and to his heartbeat, and he heard those noises merge with the rhythmic click and ticking of the forest.

The heron flapped its mighty wings.

Robin released the bowstring, the arrow flew. The bird dropped dead.

"Tonight, a feast!" the old man said, and only now did Robin realize he was standing very close. "Perhaps you won't be a complete burden, after all."

Cernunnos led Robin back to the glade where they first met. While Robin built a fire the old man plucked the heron and gutted two fish he had caught. Robin had gone days without a proper meal. He feasted on the smoked fish and the heron flesh. Fully fed, he lay down to sleep. The fork moss was soft and warm from the day's sun. The stream trilled across pebbles. Cernunnos had told him this stream was called Lethe and it was a stream of forgetting.

"It will help to wash away thought and memory," the old man had said.

Robin listened to the stream and he listened to the forest breathing softly around him and he felt something close to peace for the first time since he was seven years old. Hunting for himself, feeding himself, had felt good. Even better had been that feeling of clearing his mind completely. No room for those nightmares of the past.

Perhaps I could forget all that entirely, he thought. *Just hunt and eat and sleep and discard all those darker things. Become part of the wildwood, the way the old man has.*

Already he had abandoned his backpack, and the scroll it contained, casting them into the cave. Why would he want to torture himself with those echoes from the past? What use was the truth to him now, when there was nothing he could do to put things right? He curled himself amid the moss.

Yes, forget all that. Hunt and eat and sleep and forget everything else.

Everything?

Forget about Marian?

Don't you dare! her voice screamed in his head.

"I don't even know if you're alive or dead."

I'm not dead, stupid goat. I'm buried somewhere else. You've got to fight to dig us out!

"Fight?" Robin whispered. "I've only just learned how to survive. And where did fighting ever get me? Or you? I remember what Sir Bors said; I'll become the monster I fight against."

You're making no sense! Marian shouted. *Follow the path of the angels. Follow the girl with a thousand shapes.*

"Now who's making no sense?"

His thoughts were becoming disordered as he slipped toward sleep, Marian's voice fading with the breeze. Forget those painful things. Warm and well-fed and full of relief. Sleep.

VIII. Pieces of Old Gods

Robin had shot a woodcock and was carrying it across one shoulder, making his way back to the glade. He moved swiftly now through the forest-maze, guided by its shapes and its patterns. Here was a wren, singing on its boundary post; and nearby a hare, thumping the ground outside a bolt-hole. And here was a particular pattern of rutting rings, which Robin could trace with his fingers; and a familiar crisscross of badger paths and rabbit runs. Each of these was a waymarker, leading him on. Slowly, barely realizing he was doing it, he was building a map in his mind, as intricate as the roots in the soil. He followed this map and continued toward the glade.

As he drew near he sensed danger, and panic. Woodpeckers cackling in alarm, squirrels barking.

Something was very wrong.

In the distance an awful roar and a crash and splintering sounds. Robin turned toward these noises and he followed.

He stumbled down a bank of raw soil. Here was a fresh trench plowed through the forest—trees toppled on either side. He followed this furrow, groping his way through the debris: thousand-year-old heartwood splintered like kindling; ancient roots ripped from the earth; rocks tossed aside like marbles. What could have caused such destruction?

Robin thought he knew, and he quickened his pace.

From up ahead more roaring, thundering noises— something powerful was dragging itself though the wild-wood, carving this trail of devastation. Another bellow of pain. The clattering of countless wings, birds taking to the air thick as insects.

There was blood everywhere. So much blood. As if the trees themselves were bleeding. It dripped stickily on Robin's head; he slipped on it as he clambered over fallen trunks. Ahead of him the roaring, splintering sounds had stopped, but he could still follow easily by the trail of blood.

Eventually it led him to the cave. He crawled inside.

As he suspected, it was Cernunnos. The old man was barely conscious. Robin felt with his fingers and found the wolf trap was still clamped to his mangled foot—he must have ripped its chains from the ground and dragged it with him through the trees.

Someone else was here in the cave. She giggled. The girl with the fox-red hair. She giggled again and the old man groaned—she was poking a stick into his wound.

"Get away from him!" Robin lunged at her.

There was a sound like claws on rock as she scuttled from the cave, giggling.

Robin turned his attention to Cernunnos. He probed with his fingertips to establish the extent of the wound. He left the cave and he cut vines to use as a tourniquet, willow wands to make a splint. He collected moss and primrose to make a salve. He went back and used his knife to wind open the jaws of the trap. The old man came fully awake, bellowing loud enough to make the cave walls quake. Robin did what he could to stop the blood flow. He treated and wrapped the wound.

"Get away from me . . . ," Cernunnos mumbled. "Leave me

alone. I told you . . . a worn-out piece of the world . . . nothing more. You're too late. Leave me to die."

"No," Robin said. "Don't you abandon me too. Hold still. The worst of the bleeding has stopped, I think. Don't you dare die."

Cernunnos lay in the cave, drifting in and out of consciousness, while Robin hunted and foraged for them both. He sat with the old man for hours, telling him stories he remembered from his childhood with Marian. The old man never gave any sign he was even listening, but for Robin it was good to lose himself in the old tales.

It was several days before Cernunnos showed any real signs of life. He cleared his throat and asked Robin to help him sit upright against the wall.

"Wonder if she made this happen . . . all part of her plan," the old man said. "Stay . . . away from her, you understand? She will offer . . . attractive things . . . offer them for free . . . but they will carry a high price, in the end. Where's your knife? Give it to me."

He took Robin's woodsman's blade and there was the sound of sawing. He pushed the knife back into Robin's hands, along with something else. Something furry to the touch. A piece of antler.

"Pieces of old gods . . . ," Cernunnos said, "hold great power. Even now. This . . . this will help you see the ripples in the pond. Wouldn't be giving you this if I was thinking straight. The kind of shortcut she would offer. Take it, and promise you will stay away from her."

He rested his head back against the cave wall and soon he was sleeping. Robin turned the piece of antler in his hand. It was hollow and slipped over his finger like a ring.

*

239

He had climbed a tree and wedged himself into a saddle between branch and trunk. He had sat that way for a day and a night, his bow poised, feeling almost a part of the oak. Leaves stirred in the breeze, but Robin didn't move so much as a finger. Insects scurried past him, across him; birds landed on him and flew away, oblivious to his presence.

"Let the wildwood be your teacher," the old man had said, sitting against the cave wall. "Regard the hibernating creatures in their hideaways. They slow their heartbeats to a near standstill, so their body heat plummets and their scent disappears. They vanish."

With practice, and more practice, Robin found he could achieve this trick, just as the old man said, slowing his breathing and his heartbeat to the barest of tremors. Now he pictured himself as a cold blue shape, still and serene as the trees, while all around him and across him little red bodies scurried, leaving their scent trails.

The patterns began to change and Robin knew a large mammal was approaching. There were warnings. He heard the startled skittering of squirrel pups. His own pulse began to strengthen, but he focused and returned it to a whispered *ta-tump*.

The big mammal moved closer. It was a hind. Robin could smell her musty scent. She was relaxed, nibbling the heads off flowers. Her heart was a pulsing beacon of heat.

She walked toward Robin's hunting stand. She stopped, turned.

He drew, took aim, let loose. He shot the animal through the heart and she was dead before she hit the ground.

He clambered down and began skinning and gutting the hind, cutting and sawing, removing the heart and cooking that on a spit while he worked. From willow wands and fern fronds he built a smoking rack and he gradually cured the rest of the meat. With his knife he dug a pit and he used earth and leaves to cover what he couldn't carry, to return for later. The work had taken him all night and the morning's warmth was rising amid the trees.

He left some scraps for the scavengers and he headed back toward the cave. As he went he heard the footsteps of the vixen-child, running along behind.

My sister . . . , the old man had said. *She's the one you need beware* . . . *She won't be much trouble for now. But come late spring, and summer* . . .

Robin hurried on, trying to leave the girl behind, but she kept up easily, singing one of her rhymes, and she was still lurking hours later, as Robin tried to sleep in the cave, her voice skulking through his thoughts with a skittering noise like claws.

IX. No Way Back

Robin had been stalking a snake. He was becoming a good hunter with his bow, but he had lived long enough in the wild to know hunger is never far away. He knew never to turn down a meal.

And here was this adder, searching for a warm place to bask. He tracked it by the sound of its rough skin against rock. He crept closer, stealthy as a weasel, preparing to strike . . .

He lunged, seized the snake.

It hissed and twisted and bared its fangs. He slid his free hand up its body and held it tight at the tail and just below the head, then he sank his teeth into the rubbery flesh and he ripped strips from the snake until he was sure it was dead. He set about collecting wood and damp leaves, intending to smoke the meat.

He paused, listening to an unexpected noise.

Voices.

And these weren't the otherworldly voices he had grown used to in this place. And not the crude jeering of soldiers either. These were the voices of children. Shocking to hear the noises of ordinary children. He hadn't realized how close he had come to the forest edge. Only a few hundred paces away was a village.

The children were taunting each other, daring one another to set foot in Winter Forest. Robin remembered being very young, going to the wildwood edge with his brothers, teasing and testing one another in just the same way.

"That isn't true," the boy was saying.

"Yes it is," the girl said. "She was only five, like me. She slept three nights in Winter Forest, but when she came out she was ancient. Her teeth were falling out and her hair had gone gray and her village was empty because everyone else had died or gone away."

A sudden thought came to Robin: *I'm no longer lost in here. I could rejoin the world of people. It doesn't have to be just me and a crippled old man in a cave.* He could go to that village out there. Someone would take pity on him, wouldn't they? Somebody would give him a home. *I'm not helpless anymore. I wouldn't have to be a burden.*

He imagined freshly baked pies; stories near the fire; singing and laughter. Thinking all this, and listening, he had been moving toward the children. He moved so stealthily now that they hadn't heard or seen him. He was almost on top of them . . .

The girl started screaming. The boy was too frightened to make a noise—the boy just ran. Robin listened to them fleeing for the village, and finally he understood what he must have looked like emerging from the undergrowth: cruel crosses where his eyes used to be; hair long and wild; fingernails like talons. Skulking in a half crouch. He still had the snake dangling from one hand. He must have its blood around his mouth.

A true monster of Winter Forest.

Marian's voice rang in his mind: *Sooner or later all the stories come true. All the monsters made flesh.*

He listened to the children fleeing, the girl wailing, and he felt his anger rise. *The Sheriff did this to me. He cut me off from everyone, forever.*

That was when he realized the strange girl from the forest was there. The girl with the fox-red hair. She laughed, and he could hear she was older now: seven or eight years old. Aging with the spring.

"Silly little cross-eyes, doesn't know a thing. Thinks he can run away. Doesn't know he could run forever and never escape himself."

He turned away from her and went deeper into the forest. She followed.

"Those creatures are back, you know. The ones in metal skins. They'll never leave you alone, not so long as you live."

He stopped and listened, but he didn't hear any soldiers. It began to rain.

"Don't you get tired of being the hunted?" the girl said. "Don't you want to be the hunter for a change? I can show you how, if you come and play my games."

"Leave me alone!"

He turned, nocking an arrow to his bow. He drew and let loose. The girl giggled, far to the side of where the arrow struck the soil. Robin ran, all his old rage boiling to the surface, thinking of the Sheriff and Jadder Payne.

Bring me the boy's eyes.

The girl kept pace. Robin ran faster. And then, through the blood beating in his ears, he heard the soldiers. In his fury he had almost stumbled on top of them. They were below him, in a hollow, arguing and throwing dice; going on with their lives.

And these weren't just any rangers. One of them Robin had met before. This man was saying: "Shut your mouths and throw the dice. If I take enough money from you ladies, maybe I'll stop thinking about slitting your throats."

Once, a lifetime ago, Robin had watched this same soldier circling Marian's cage, making lolling noises with his tongue.

La, la, la.

Here was the soldier with wasp-orange hair and teardrop scars on his cheeks.

X. Deadly Games

Robin crept to the lip of the hollow. He nocked an arrow, anger throbbing in his ears. He steadied his hand and told himself to wait—to remember what had happened last time he attacked in a frenzy.

One of the rangers was saying: "I mean, so what if it *is* the last wolf in England? Why does the Sheriff care?"

"Why do you care why he cares?" a second man said. "Maybe he wants a wolf-hide disguise for All Hallow's Eve. Perhaps he's seen one too many wolves in his twisted dreams and he wants to wipe them out for good. The *why* doesn't matter a stuff. He says, 'Jump', we say, 'How high?'"

Slowing his breathing, teasing apart the tones and the textures, Robin begins to picture this scene in detail. The first man who spoke has a high-pitched voice and nervous hands. There is a clicking sound where he fiddles with rosary beads. He smells of the pig urine in his new leather boots.

The man who answered him is larger than the rest—he takes the heaviest gulps from the ale jug they pass between them. He smells of the hazelnut oil he has used to polish the wolf-head emblem on his breastplate.

But it is the third man who Robin can picture clearest of all. He is the smallest, youngest of them, yet appears to be in charge. He has a habit of scratching at a crush-scar above his left ear.

At this moment the third man is saying: "Throw the damn dice. You're so busy flapping your mouths your hands don't get a chance. I swear, Doggeskyll, if you don't stop fiddling with those beads, I am going to stick them somewhere less easy to reach."

Edric Krul. The ranger who tormented Marian in her cage.

Robin's rage surged, and the scene in the hollow became fuzzy, distorted by red noise. He took deep breaths and regained his composure and started again to tease apart the tones. The noises now were the glug of the ale jug, the patter of rain, the clatter of dice on the throwboard. The one called Doggeskyll had stopped clicking the beads and was now sprinkling a liquid on the steel of his dagger. Robin thought this was probably holy water.

After a while, Doggeskyll said: "Well, if you want to know what I hear. I hear it's not a wolf we're tracking at all. It's a mighty white stag that keeps its antlers year round."

"Then why wouldn't he say so?" the biggest ranger said. "Why would he have us checking these wolf traps, day after day? Why would he—"

"Shut. Your. Mouths." As Edric Krul shouted he made a violent movement, sending throwboard and dice flying. "Any more of your babbling and I swear I will slit your throats right here and I'll go back and say the Wargwolf ate your sorry waste of skin. Am I understood? Take your eyes off me, Gouger. You're a big man but I'll gut you like a fish. Get to your feet, both of you. Two more traps to check. God willing I'll never have to stomach you ladies again."

Edric Krul's outburst brought Robin's anger to boiling point. He could wait no longer.

In one movement he stood, drew, aimed, let loose.

He heard the arrow clatter off metal.

When Edric had stood he had taken his skull-helm from the ground; he was holding it at waist height when the arrow struck exactly that spot. Robin groped for another arrow, but his fingers were shaking with rage and he took too long to notch. By the time he shot again Edric had dived to one side. Two more of Robin's arrows sucked harmlessly into the soil.

"Up there," Edric screamed. "Get up that slope!"

Robin ran. Twenty paces away was an oak, its trunk hollowed out by fire. He scuttled inside and held still. He listened to the soldiers go crashing past on both sides.

"Gouger, that way, down to the river," Edric said. "You, go that way. He can't have got far."

Robin had taken his one remaining arrow from its quiver. Could he still do it? No. He told himself not to move—to remember what had happened before when his anger took control. *Stay hidden. Give yourself a chance next time.*

Eventually, the soldiers drifted back toward their hollow.

"Did you see that thing?" said the one called Doggeskyll. "What in Hades was it? If Edric hadn't been holding his helm—"

"Not another word," Edric said. "Get your stuff. Hold your tongue or I swear . . . Wait, listen. Do you hear that? What is it?"

"It sounds like . . . *singing*," the one called Gouger said. "A girl's voice. All the way out here. What the devil . . . ?"

Little robin red-breast, sitting in a tree,

"Come down," said the pussycat, "won't you play with me?"

The soldiers moved toward the singing; the singing was coming from directly outside Robin's hiding place. The men came closer, began circling Robin's tree. The *click, click, clack* of a crossbow being wound. The *swish-swish* of another man readying a throwing net.

The singing continued. The men edged nearer. No choice now. Robin ran.

Crossbow bolts made the air hum. One skimmed his arm, gashing the skin.

He slid down a steep bank, and darted along a riverbank and tucked himself out of sight among overhanging roots. He froze.

The men crashed about above him. One of them thrashed his sword like a farmer through wheat—wood pigeons flapping away in alarm.

"Find him!" Edric shouted. "I want him in that net. Filthy vermin. I'll skin him alive."

Robin held still. The men moved farther away. He was safe.

But then the singing started again, directly outside his hiding place.

Faster ran the pussycat, while robin chirped and sang,
Says little robin red-breast: "Catch me if you can."

The men moved toward the sound.

A sword came chopping down through the roots.

Robin darted away and slipped beneath a blackthorn bush and held still. He was bleeding freely from the gash in his arm and from a second wound in his foot. He felt dizzy, and didn't know how many more times he could run.

"Come out, come out, wherever you are," Edric said in a singsong voice. "You can't run forever. I've got your blood on my sword. I can take you apart slice by slice, drop by drop, if I have to. Come out, come out, wherever you are . . ."

The men were very close. Twigs snapping beneath their boots.

Something—or someone—slipped into Robin's hiding place. The smell was musty, like wet fur, but then she giggled—a girl's laugh. She rustled back out of the bush and darted away. The singing began again.

"Meow," said the pussycat, "won't you come and play?"
"Pleeeeease," said the pussycat, but Robin flew away.

"This way," Edric shouted. "After him. Bring him to me alive."

But this time the singing was nowhere near Robin's hiding place. The vixen-girl was leading the men astray. Their voices faded into the pattering of the rain. In the distance Edric Krul screeched and swore and thrashed his sword. Robin lay there breathing hard, fear and anger pumping in his veins.

"Not fair," the vixen-girl said. "You were too good at that game. Or those stinky men were too dumb. I'll think of something better next time. Blind man's bluff . . . ? Hee-hee."

"What do you want with me?" He lunged and caught the girl by the fox-red hair.

She screamed, and her scream became a snarl and Robin was holding a spitting, hissing vixen cub. Then fur became feathers—a bird of prey snapping at his fingers. In the next instant the kestrel was a snake, slipping from Robin's grasp to the ground.

From ten paces away the girl screamed again, louder and longer than before.

"You mustn't do that! You mustn't. Stinky little cross-eyes! Do that again and I'll never let you play my games."

With a rustle in the grass the girl was gone.

XI. The Price of Power

All through the spring the girl of the forest followed him, teasing him, taunting him. And all the time she was changing. Whatever it was she wanted, he didn't know how much longer he could resist.

Now summer's warmth was wafting through the trees. In his mind's eye she had become tall and lithe and graceful. Her voice was the singsong of a sunlit stream.

"The season is ripe, it's time to begin. Shed that pale husk, come claim your new skin."

"I told you to leave me alone," Robin said, turning to walk away. "I won't play your games."

She was perched on a high boulder. She hopped down and followed on soft feet.

"Games are all finished, time to grow up. Put down your toys, we've delayed long enough."

Robin stopped. She circled him, running fingers across his chest and shoulders. He breathed the perfume of her sun-warmed skin.

"I've carried your strength, deep down inside. Come taste it, it's yours: this power, your bride."

Robin forced himself to remember that underneath this new shape she was the same: She was the old woman of winter

251

who sat clacking her bones; the young girl of spring who skipped singing amid the bluebells; the stern woman of autumn who laughed to see Robin lost and alone.

She circled him again, pressing her naked warmth against him, nuzzling her mouth at the nape of his neck. Her breath was cherry-leaf and the hint of fresh blood.

"So many clues, leading us here. One final test: the hurdle of fear. No room for doubt; time to proceed. Come. Steal the wolf's hunger, and feed."

He raised his hands and pushed her away. "Leave me alone!"

She stood motionless. In his imagining her golden eyes were burning. When she spoke next her voice was as smooth as ever, but barbed. The sound put Robin in mind of an owl: fluff and feathers, but hiding razor claws.

"Beware my impatience; I won't wait forever. Who'll hear your song, if I turn to another?"

She was circling him again, running a finger across his face, tracing the line of his jaw. The finger was sharp, and getting sharper. It was a talon. Quick wingbeats and a falcon darting through the trees. Only once she was gone did Robin feel the sting of the cut and the blood running from his chin.

"We need to fight!" Robin shouted. "I'm tired of being the hunted. They're all out there, living their lives. The Sheriff. His rangers."

"You've been listening to her," Cernunnos said. "This will end in disaster." The old man had not long emerged from the cave. His wounds were healed but his movements were still lumbering, his speech confused.

"You're stronger than they are, even now," Robin said. "Why won't you help me?"

"Because you're scared!" Cernunnos had bellowed, and

the trees had quaked in their roots. "You're scared of the past. You're frightened of what you can sense lurking in the future. You're terrified of my brother. And I should add my strength to all that terror? When the fearful become strong, that is when the world burns. So much I've forgotten, but that lesson I have learned, and learned and learned. And now she has offered you a shortcut. Kill one fear and use it against another. And if you succeed? What price? I have lost you to her . . . I should have left you to die, grubbing after bugs . . ."

Cernunnos was standing at the highest rim of the glade. Robin's impression of him wavered—in his mind's eye he glimpsed snow-white antlers, the setting sun touching the tips.

"Such anger. Such dread. The worst of them. Should have seen that all along. Disaster. Too soft . . . always was too soft . . ." As the sun dipped farther the old man's voice began to splinter. "Go to her then. Perhaps this is the end. Perhaps you were the final test. One last failure . . ."

Robin's idea of him wavered once more, and the albino king stag was just a white-haired old man, frail and sad.

"I have begun to see the shape of all this. It ends in fire and with a journey across water. A journey shared by you and me . . . A firestorm. And a world of water. A story of the past, or of the future? So much I've forgotten . . ."

Now the old man's face was made of leaves, roots the tendons in his neck. But the leaves were fading to brown and the wind was taking him apart. A final gust, the last pieces scattered. The thump of falling fruit. Robin stood alone in the quieting glade.

The final blaze of summer. The forest quiet and drowsy.

For a moment she was all things at once: snake eyes, girl's smile, fox fur, hawk's tail. Then Robin's impression of her cleared and there was only this woman, with fox-red hair, stretching in the grass.

He moved closer. Her scent now was as rich as a wild flower meadow.

"Why me?"

"Does the river pick its path to the sea? I've felt you always, here, inside me." Her voice was honey, dripping. "You're not the first. Others will come. For now you're my only. My lover, my son."

"You'll help me kill the Sheriff?"

A soft, knowing laugh. "That is only the beginning, once we set the shapes spinning."

"I want to find Marian. And to claim our revenge. That's all. That's enough."

"Enough . . . ?" she said, as if tasting the word in her mouth.

He moved closer. The warmth of her body reached out to him, the way sleep lures a person in the summer shade.

He edged nearer, and she stirred. He moved to her side and she rose to her knees.

Long moments passed. Only the sound of the forest holding its breath.

Finally Robin said: "I'm ready. I'll do whatever is necessary. Tell me what I need to do."

The goddess of the forest sighed deeply as she stood. She took Robin's hand, and for once she spoke plainly.

"First . . . ," she said, "you must destroy my brother."

XII. The Wargwolf

The three hooded men led four horses into the stable yard of the inn. The last of the horses was a sturdy sumpter, yoked to a cart. On the back of the cart was a cage, its contents hidden beneath a black shroud.

A stableboy came to unsaddle the horses. He froze when he passed close to the cart and a rumbling rose from beneath the cloth. He glanced nervously at the strangers before going back to his work.

The mistress of the house came lumbering down the outside steps, her eyes coming to rest on the rumbling cage.

"Now, now, what's this? I won't have it, you hear! You can't just bring something like that in here. Even if we weren't full to the rafters, I wouldn't allow—"

She stopped abruptly. The three men were wearing travel cloaks against the dust of the late-summer road. Now they were taking off these outer garments and underneath was an emblem of a wolf's head, its fangs bared.

"Welcome, welcome," the mistress said. "A pleasure to host the Sheriff's gallant men. You catch us at a busy time, but we'll do our very best. We're already three to a bed. So long as you don't mind sharing with—"

Edric Krul lowered his hood, silenced the tavern mistress with his stare.

"Hay for the horses. Meat and ale and hot water for my bath, to be prepared at once. Two private rooms: one for me and one for these men."

Edric led the other two inside. The dimly lit common room smelled of stale food and fresh vomit. The rangers pulled up benches and a tall serving girl approached. Without meeting their eyes she put down a jug of ale, then lit a candle and shuffled away.

Edric blew out the flame. He didn't want to see this pit of filth any more clearly than he had to. Look at these people! Over there, young lovers, stuck to each other's faces—run away from their village, no doubt, heading for the city, about to breed and fill the world with yet more vile spawn. And that man, there, an idle drunk, passed out and snoring on a bench.

The serving girl returned, her bodice gaping at the chest, her flesh on display for the whole world to see. She put down three bowls of pale pottage.

"What's this?" Edric said. "Roots and grain? That man is eating fowl. Bring me what he's eating."

"Begging your pardon, we have no meat to sell and haven't had for weeks. That man arrived with his own bird. He shared it with Madam Alepenny and with his traveling companions. He is eating the last of it."

"Bring me what that man is eating. Now."

The girl took her apron in both hands, twisted it around her knuckles. "You want . . . *his* meal? The one he's already eating?"

Edric stared at her, his face growing hot. She turned, walked across the room. She lifted a hard-bread trencher— the man eating from it looked at her with his mouth open.

She hurried back, put the trencher in front of Edric, bowed her head and shuffled away.

Edric began picking at a chicken wing. He looked up and the man who had brought the meat dropped his gaze. The other rangers, Guy Oxman and Gunthor Bul, had their heads down, slurping the pottage from their bowls. They were sturdy, simple men. That was why Edric had chosen them for this expedition.

After a while the serving girl came back. "Begging your pardon, sire, your bath is prepared."

Edric pushed away the trencher. As soon as he left the inn he heard growling. The stableboy was standing near the cart with the cage; he had a stick and was using it to lift one corner of the shroud.

"Get away from there!"

The stableboy jumped back, ducked his head. "Didn't mean no harm. Was only looking, is all. Never seen anything like it! They sound hungry. Will you let me do the feeding?"

Edric jabbed a finger into the boy's breastbone. "Listen to me, you louse. You will stay away from my cage. They are *supposed* to be hungry. Feed them so much as a sparrow's fart and the next food they see will be your fingers pushed through those bars. Am I understood?"

The boy was staring at him, openmouthed. Edric continued through to the wet room. A lead vat stood steaming. He stripped off his clothes and climbed in. Immediately he felt the hot water begin to unyoke his muscles. His head began to clear. That long, dusty ride had left him angry. Anger was useful, but it was no good without focus. That was one of many things he had learned from the Sheriff.

Edric had almost let his anger get the better of him that day in Winter Forest—the day the wildling had tried to kill him. After the vermin got away Edric had been blind with rage, lashing out at his underlings. Finally he managed to control himself. He made his men retrace every step of the chase until they found what Edric was hoping they would find: a scrap of the wildling's clothing, torn on thorns. Now Edric was returning to Winter Forest, and soon the wildling's scent would be burning in the nostrils of his attack dogs.

He stretched his limbs and felt the water washing his anger clean—not diluting it, but leaving it immaculate and ready to use. He listened to the noises of the inn: someone being sick outside the stable doors; a woman singing a disgusting song about the King.

Edric breathed deeply. Ah yes, it did him good, occasionally, to come to places like this—a reminder of what he was up against. Perhaps, after his bath, he would teach one of these people a lesson. Who should he choose: the serving tart? The eloping lovers?

No. Not tonight; he was too tired. It would be done wrong. He had to save his energy for tomorrow's chase. In recent months he had risen quickly through the ranks of the Sheriff's Guard, but many unworthy men remained in his way. By killing the wildling tomorrow he would take another important step. Then onward and upward to greater things . . .

He climbed out of the bath, dried, and dressed. As he left the wash room he again heard growling. He ran and grabbed the boy by the neck.

"Wasn't doing nothing," the boy said. "Let go. Was just looking."

"Oxman! Bul. Get out here!"

The two older rangers came thumping into the yard.

"This boy thinks it is acceptable to disobey the Sheriff's Guard," Edric said. "He thinks the Guard is in the habit of making idle threats. Oxman, hold him still."

Guy Oxman glanced at Gunthor Bul.

"Don't look at him!" Edric said. "He has nothing to say about this. I am giving you an order. Take hold of the boy. Bul, go and make those people mind their own affairs."

Gunthor Bul went back to the tavern, shepherding the mistress of the house and another frantic woman back inside. Guy Oxman took hold of the struggling stableboy.

"Bring him this way," Edric said. "Closer. Right against the cage."

When the boy was in position, Edric gripped one of his arms, extended it, and pushed the boy's hand under the shroud and through the bars. Furious snarling and a wet cracking sound merged with the boy's screams. Edric fought to hold the arm steady while these noises grew louder and more frenzied. From inside the tavern there was shouting and a woman sobbing.

The boy passed out. Edric let go of the arm and Oxman managed to pull what was left of the hand free. Without looking back Edric strode away and climbed the outside steps to his room. He went inside, blocked his door with a clothes chest.

He smiled. He had proved one thing: The dogs were ready. What ferocity! What short work they would make of the wildling. He plugged his ears with beeswax to block the sound of snarling dogs and crying people. He slept soundly and dreamed of tomorrow's glorious hunt.

The goddess of the forest led Robin deep, deep into the wildwood, the tangle of vine and branch growing ever more dense and dark and cold. But finally they came to an open stretch of riverbank, warm in the sun. The river here was wide, the water slow and quiet.

The forest goddess removed Robin's clothes. Then she slipped into the water, and he followed. He felt the slow-moving river and the quick hands of the vixen-woman working across his body, washing him clean, helping to wash away his fear.

Her hands gripped the back of his neck and suddenly she twisted against him like a snake. Her legs coiled around him and he felt the shocking heat of her through the water. She moved against him, smooth and rhythmic as the river. He heard a voice cry out, and only afterward did he realize it had been his own.

When it was over she removed herself from him and splashed away, without a word. He heard her wringing her hair dry on the riverbank. Then there was a spraying sound, like an animal shaking water from its fur.

Silence. Robin thought she had gone. But when he dragged himself onto the bank he could smell her there, stretched out, sunning herself.

When she spoke next her voice had lost all of its playfulness. "Come. Bring your bow, your knife."

He pulled on his breeches but left the rest of his tattered clothing there on the bank. He followed the goddess of the wildwood. Her footsteps were almost silent; he tracked her instead by her scent, which now hinted at the heady fragrance of autumn decay.

They came to a stand of willow trees, and beyond the trees was a mud bank, and beyond that was a water hole.

"My brother comes here, every night without fail," the forest goddess said. "He is a child of winter, so now he is at his weakest. You will have only one chance. Once you strike, do not let go. Loosen your grip and all will be lost. Stay above him, at all cost. If the mist clears, and his shadow falls across you, it will mean your death, and our disaster."

With that she was gone. Robin moved toward the water hole, mud oozing between his toes. His father had taught him

260

that mud can help hide a hunter's scent. He scooped handfuls of it and spread it on his chest and stomach and face.

He stopped. *What am I doing? This is lunacy.*

He moved away from the mud bank. "I won't do it!" he shouted into the trees. "I won't be your pawn."

But then the smell of the mud delivered a memory: the day he and Marian met. They were in Hob's Hollow, hiding from her father's men, and she was spreading mud on her arms and legs to mask her scent from the bloodhounds. And that memory sparked another: Marian in that cage, shrinking away from Edric Krul's grasp. Robin's wrath surged.

He finished daubing his body with mud. He climbed a solitary willow tree that stood at the water's edge. He crawled along a high branch and held still, gripping his knife. He allowed his breathing and his heartbeat to slow and to slow further until they were no quicker than a hibernating creature, his body temperature dropping, the last of his scent lost beneath the mud.

He waited, and he waited, silent and still. Now it must be dusk because deer, foxes, badgers, stoats were all slipping beneath him on their way to drink. He felt the presence of the Wargwolf, moving steadily this way. A sinuous shape, weaving between the trees, its head lolling side to side.

This is madness, Robin thought. *I can't fight this creature of the shadows.* He began to climb down.

Don't you dare! Marian's voice screamed. *You need to take what the Sheriff has been seeking. This is the way. The only way. Stay where you are!*

"If I die here, it's over," Robin whispered. "I can't help you."

You won't die, not if you're quick and brave and stay away from its shadow. Don't you dare move, you have to fight and fight until this is put right.

261

Robin moaned in despair. He wriggled back along the branch. He slowed his heartbeat to a whispered *ta-tump, ta-tump.*

And now the beast drew near. Robin knew it did, because where the shadow of the wolf glides it sucks all light and sound into it, leaving a trail of nothingness behind. This void drifting closer, closer, and then stopping amid the willow stand.

The beast was here.

Robin's heartbeat quickened and strengthened. *Ba-boom, ba-boom*—it thumped so loud he was sure the beast would hear. He felt warmth pulsing through his body: heat that would carry his scent to the Wargwolf. And still his heartbeat quickened, panic rising . . .

Wind moved the mist and moonlight found the beast and laid its full shadow across the willow trunks. In Robin's mind's eye the Wargwolf was motionless—yet its shadow lifted its head. It turned one way, then the other, tasting the air.

Finally the shadow of the wolf turned toward Robin's tree, and its amber eyes were burning.

"Take a look at those eyes," Guy Oxman was saying. "I don't know which is meaner, the hounds or their master. It didn't feel right, what we did to that stableboy."

"Forget it," Gunthor Bul said. "You didn't have a choice. We did as we were told, is all."

Early that morning the rangers had stopped at a village on the edge of Winter Forest. While peasants looked on in alarm, Oxman and Bul had unloaded the attack dogs. They left their horses at the village and had continued on foot, deep into the wildwood.

Now they had stopped for a meal of stale bread and cider. Edric told the other two men to wait while he scouted for firepits or any other sign of the wildling. The dogs were chained to separate trees, snapping at one another and dripping drool.

"You know how he got so mean," Oxman said, pulling off his boots and stretching his legs. "Well, you know those scars on his cheeks . . . his father used to cut him there. In some shires folk do it to stop children crying. The tears sting in the cuts, see."

"Don't see how that's going to work," said Bul. "Those tears are going to breed more tears. Vicious cycle, that one."

"Anyway, that's not the worst of it," Oxman said. "Edric's father also used to beat him bloody, every single day, at dusk. Always the same time, so he knew it was coming. Not because of wild behavior, but just because Edric was small, and the beatings were meant to toughen him up. Well, it worked. One day he put henbane in his father's soup. His father slept. When he woke he found himself headfirst down the village well."

A little way off, Edric listened to the men speak. This was a ritual of his whenever he was on patrol: He would tell his underlings he was going to reconnoiter and then he would lurk within earshot. A man headed for the top needed to know exactly what the little people think.

And Edric was pleased with what he had heard. He had personally sown the seeds for that story about his boyhood. The basic ingredients were correct: yes, his father had been cruel, and yes, Edric had killed him. But there had been no henbane, and no well. In reality a knife in the neck had been the method of murder.

But there was nothing wrong with adding spice to a tale. That was something else the Sheriff had taught him: When it comes to the manufacture of fear, the devil is in the detail. And Edric knew that fear was important. The more men feared him, the quicker would be his rise.

And it was at that moment, crouching there in the bushes, that the idea first came to Edric. He saw, in that instant, where his rise would end: not as second-in-command of the Sheriff's Guard, but at the very top. He knew, at that moment, that he would personally depose the Sheriff.

What a bizarre thought: to kill your own idol! But Edric saw, very clearly, that this was the way it would happen. The Sheriff was not the kind of man to step aside. Therefore it would be up to Edric to seize command. Wasn't that the way of the world, for the old and bloated to give way to the young and vital? Didn't they say the Sheriff himself had been forced to kill his own father in order to rise to power?

Yes, yes, ruling this realm, becoming Sheriff, *that* was Edric Krul's destiny, and it always had been. He could see it now, as clear as daylight. He went back to his men, his whole body fizzing with the epiphany.

"No sign of the vermin," he said. "We move on. The dogs have its scent. It won't be long."

As Bul and Oxman unchained the harnesses from the trees, Edric allowed the dogs another sniff of the wildling's clothing. It put fresh energy into the beasts, and it was all the soldiers could do to keep their feet. They were beautiful animals, these mastiffs, almost as tall as Edric, and every inch of them muscle. Huge square heads, jaws like steel traps.

Many times Edric had gone to the kennels in the castle just to watch these dogs rattle their chains, their wrath awesome to behold. It was said that the same family of dogs had been with the Sheriff's Guard for twenty generations, and that in each litter the weakest, least vicious pups were destroyed. Generation by generation the dogs grew meaner, until now they were pure fury.

Edric followed the dogs, feeling almost sick with excitement, picturing what they would do to their quarry. That abomination had tried to kill him, and at last Edric was going to have his revenge. There wasn't much longer to wait.

This final stage of waiting was the worst of all. Robin was aware of every whisper of air through the trees. Every waft of the beast's breath.

It doesn't know you're here, he told himself. *If it did, it would have fled, or attacked.*

He concentrated on slowing his heartbeat. It was working: he could feel the warmth leaving his body, his scent fading away.

The mist swirled and the moonlight shone and Robin's idea of the Wargwolf wavered. For a moment there was no beast here but instead a man crouched amid the willows—a giant of a man, wrapped in a wolf-pelt cloak, his eyes an uncanny amber. Then the mist closed its grip and the man vanished and Robin could sense only the beast, poised on its haunches.

Finally the monster-wolf moved. It slid toward the water's edge. It stopped once more, to sniff close to the earth. It continued to the pool and lowered its head to drink.

It was directly below Robin.

He listened to its tongue hit the water and he told himself to remain still—to do nothing and wait for the beast to leave. *There must be a better way.*

But Marian's voice screamed—*You led them to me!*—and all the familiar images came flooding back: the cage, the lancing knife, the man with the melted face . . .

Do it! Marian screamed. *You have to fight!*

Robin's anger burning, but most of all his terror—every drop of fear he had ever felt for the Sheriff and his soldiers and Jadder Payne and Winter Forest and the Wargwolf—he was finally fully desperate to cast off his fear.

Shifting his weight, dropping from the branch, he fell onto the beast's back. He thrust his knife into the side of its throat.

A terrible, gurgling howl.

The beast bucked thrashed roared, bellowing blood.

Robin holding on—all he could do was hold on—trying desperately to grip fur already slippery with gore. The wolf snarling, flailing wildly with its claws and trying to bring its jaws around to snap off its attacker's head.

Another mighty howl. Robin gritting his teeth and holding tight, but slipping, beginning to slide from the beast's back . . .

The beast bucking and thrashing, a storm of claws. Robin's limbs feeling suddenly icy and slippery wet. Slicing pain and tearing sounds too frightening to think about.

Hold on! Marian screamed. *She said you would be lost if you lose your grip.*

Another long lance of pain. The right side of his body going numb. No strength left of his own—his only chance was to hold on and hope the beast defeated itself—thrashing its own weight across Robin's knife.

The taste of blood rising in his throat. Somehow still managing to keep hold. Outside his own body now: picturing a scrap of skin being flailed through the air, the way a cat shakes a dead mouse on the end of its paw.

But now something was changing. The thrashing had begun to slow. The howling replaced by a gurgling sound.

The monster-god was sinking to the mud. Dying . . . Robin was grinding it down. He was winning!

The beast slumping

Slowing

Gurgling—

And then raging, more violently than ever. It had only been gathering its strength. It howled, twisted its head fully and sank its fangs into Robin's flesh.

A wet sucking sound. A flood of heat and liquid flowing to the ground.

Robin lost his grip on the blade.

He was falling.

The beast still roaring . . .

Robin had lost. It was over, at last . . .

Another lurching, falling sensation, and finally a crushing weight on Robin's chest. The great nothingness that followed was as comforting as a good-night kiss.

XIII. Pieces of a Wolf-god

The goddess of the forest steps lightly to the edge of the pool. She looks down at the mess of blood and guts and ripped skin.

The man-child had proved brave. He had not let go—not even at the end. It is more than could be said for her brother. The Wargwolf loosened its grip to take a killer bite at Robin's neck, and in doing so had split itself open along the blade.

Now the Wargwolf lies with its mighty head on Robin's chest. They are both so torn and bloody it is hard to tell where beast ends and man begins.

The forest goddess goes to her knees. Time to do her work.

Blood is still pumping from the body of the beast. She collects some of the blood in three stoppered flasks. Next, she takes a knife with a shimmering blue blade and she cuts out seven of the wolf's teeth, using all her weight to lever them from the gums. Each tooth is the size of a dagger and they come loose with a crunch. She places them in a plain wooden box.

Lastly she crouches and watches the sky. Clouds part and mist swirls and moonlight spills through the trees. The moonlight reveals the shadow of the beast. The goddess bends with the knife and cuts away one last part of the wolf-god—this time without actually touching the corpse.

She bundles her prizes together. Only then does she turn her attention to Robin. She checks first—yes, a faint waft of breath and a tiny tremor in his chest. He is clinging to life, barely. She drops to her hands and knees. Her hair hangs forward and in the moonlight she now looks more vixen than woman. She begins licking Robin's many wounds. Between licks, it sounds as if she is holding a conversation with herself.

"Wasting time. Will die anyway."

"Have to try. Who will wield the pieces?"

"Taste him. Dying. Dead already? There will be others."

"Can't know that. He has destroyed so many."

"Even if he lives, will be too weak. They are coming. Too vulnerable in changing state."

"Will lead them astray. If we can."

"Waste of time. There are *always* others. Only the pieces are important."

"Have to try."

She licks and licks until Robin is a curled baby, bloodless and pale. Then she folds open the long gash in the Wargwolf's chest and, bit by bit, she pushes and heaves and rolls Robin inside the corpse. There is a sucking sound and steam rises from hot flesh. She pulls the fold of wolf hide closed, over Robin's head.

She gathers her prizes. Anyone or anything watching from the trees will glimpse, finally, what looks like a two-tailed vixen, fleeing into the night.

Robin is back in Wodenhurst, in the croft of his old home. His brothers and his father are here. They are digging a deep pit.

"Whose grave is this?" Robin says.

Hal turns to him and smiles. "Why, little brother, it's your grave."

Robin knows this is true. He is lying in a coffin. He can see the world above him, in summer colors. But then the lid slams shut and there is nothing but black. He feels the coffin being lifted, then lowered into the earth. He tries to scream but his mouth is full of fur.

"We'll be rid of him at last," he hears his father say, and his brothers laugh.

Sir Bors and Bones and Irish and Rowly have also come to stand at the graveside.

"You're dead to us now, Loxley," Sir Bors says.

The coffin comes to rest. Robin hears soil being scooped into the grave—wet soil, making a splattering sound on the coffin lid. The laughter of his father and brothers and the others becomes fainter through the earth. Fainter. Silence.

Robin is alone in the dark. He can barely breathe. This grave smells of rotting flesh. He has to get out. He begins to claw his way free. The coffin lid gives way and the soil begins to part. He is relieved to find his fingers are wolf claws, which help him dig. He is rising. But then he comes up against something solid.

It is something living. It turns its head and narrows its amber eyes. There is a wound in the wolf's throat that opens and closes when it speaks.

"You can wipe that wolfish look off your face," it says. "I never did you any harm." A scar in the shape of a teardrop falls from the beast's face.

"I didn't ask for any of this," Robin says. "It was them . . . It was . . . her. I'm going to walk my own path from now on. I can't breathe. I have to get to the surface."

"You're going nowhere," says the beast. "The least you can

do is stay here and keep me company. I bet eternity isn't as long as it sounds. We'll play games to pass the time. Wolf in Sheep's Clothing? Or is it Goat in Wolf's Clothing . . . ?"

Stay . . . ? Robin thinks. Stay down here? Why not? The surface is so far away, and it is surprisingly warm down here in the ground. But it's so difficult to breathe. Then give up breathing. Easy. Yes. Give up. What a relief.

He turns to tell the wolf the good news, but the beast is gone and in its place is a man, the left side of his face shining like wax.

"A blind bit of luck, seeing you," the Sheriff says. "I know we have not always seen eye to eye, but I wanted to assure you, you are making a wise decision, staying down here. I know what the Book says, 'an eye for an eye,' but these things can go on and on. I should know."

The Sheriff's clothes are black feathers and he has been pierced by a dozen arrows. He is pulling them out as he speaks. He removes the final arrowhead, made of jade.

"Must fly," he says. "Have you tried plucking the feathers from an angel's wings? The devil's own work, I can tell you."

Only as the man-crow flaps away does Robin notice two eyeballs dangling from its beak. He digs furiously, desperate to catch the man-crow. He feels himself rising. But then something stops him and he looks down. The wolf is holding Robin's ankles with pale pink hands.

"Just because I'm dead doesn't mean I can't still fight," says the wolf. "Doesn't mean I don't still have claws. Hmmm, matter of fact I only have these hands of yours. But they'll do. You're staying right here with me."

Robin gives up digging. The surface is too far away; the wolf's grip is so firm.

The Sheriff was right: better to stay down here, and sleep.

Yes, give up. Stop breathing. Relief.

Edric was relieved. At last they had the wildling. It was over . . .

The final part of the chase had been infuriating. Several times they seemed to be doubling back. Were the dogs leading them in circles? Surely a blind wildling couldn't be this quick on its feet?

The sun lowered and mist rose amid the trees. Edric's men became nervous, his dogs frantic. He could feel his own fury building. How dare that vermin lead him in this sort of dance? Edric had seen his glorious future, fully revealed. He needed to get this finished so he could progress to the next phase.

"This doesn't feel right," Gunthor Bul said. "I'm sure we just came this way."

"Look at the dogs," Guy Oxman said. "They're pulling in different directions. They don't—"

"Stop it!" Edric hissed. "Hold your tongues."

Once again they doubled back. Was that the flash of a fox's tail? The feathers of a hawk? Were the dogs becoming confused by other scent trails?

At times it seemed to Edric it was the *forest itself* that was leading them astray. The dogs suddenly turned, looked about to retrace their steps, but the track behind them had gone— forest paths closing in their wake. *These are just tricks of the mist*, Edric told himself. *You do not fear this place. It should fear you!*

The dogs and his men grew more skittish. Edric felt his wrath rising, threatening to erupt. He forced himself to remember the Sheriff's words: *Don't let anger be your master; shape it to your own needs.* He gave the dogs another sniff of the sheepskin and watched for any hint of the wildling.

And now, finally, they had him. Edric smiled.

Bul and Oxman had pulled up amid a stand of willow trees, looking down toward a wide muddy pool. The attitude of the dogs had changed—their eyes were fixed on something at the water's edge. They growled, low in their throats.

Through the thickening mist Edric struggled to make out what was lying there. It looked like the wildling, sure enough, wrapped in some kind of animal pelt. It wasn't moving. Had it fallen, exhausted by the chase?

"Is that blood?" Oxman said. "That darker patch, against the mud."

"It doesn't matter," Edric said. "Get this finished."

Glancing at each other, the two rangers unclipped the harness chains. Edric's smile widened as he watched the dogs lower their heads and race toward the water's edge.

There is a naked, angry angel with hawk-dark hair. One eye gray, the other eye green.

"Breathe!" she shouts. "You always were a stupid goat, but you were never so stupid you forgot how to breathe. Breathe. And dig!"

Are you dead too? Robin thinks. *If so, I'm staying down here with you.*

"I'm *not* dead. I told you, I'm buried somewhere else. We both have to dig ourselves out. Quick! Someone is coming." The Marian-angel screams and looks terrified. "Hurry, you've got to get out. He's a bad man with tears on his cheeks. Please, don't let him find you here like this." The angel shrieks. "He's here! By the pool. He can *see* you."

Just in time the angel flies free—dog jaws snap shut, ripping feathers from the tips of her wings.

Wait for me. Come back, please. Robin digs and thrashes, his lungs bursting, sucking the thinnest of breaths between the cloying flesh-soil. In any case, it is too late: The angel is gone. He lies still. Better to stay down here, safe and warm.

Safe?

He has come closer to the surface. He begins to make sense of what is happening above. He detects the frightened heartbeat of a badger, buried in its sett. He feels a fox bolt, terrified, for its den. He traces the complex patterns set in motion when one bird calls to another in alarm, and that bird calls to the next, and the next. These sensations intensify, the tones and textures emerging cleaner and clearer than he has ever known . . .

This is the connection Cernunnos spoke to Robin about—what the old man called seeing the ripples in the pond. Cernunnos had begun to teach Robin to sense the world this way. But now Robin knows those were glimpses, merely. Here it is in its full glory.

And now Robin thinks the old man was wrong. It isn't a pond; it is a spider's web. Robin is at the center, and he can feel where every bird and insect touches a strand. Every contact with the web lights a color in his mind's eye. It is beautiful, and peaceful, and Robin thinks he could stay down here forever, watching the shapes turn and listening to the slow language of the trees.

Except there is something happening, at this moment, that is twisting the shapes and leaving them deformed. There are creatures, nearby, that don't belong. They are so clumsy and cruel they are tearing the strands and causing Robin's mind to scream. The colors shatter and become shards.

The cruel creatures move closer. Robin feels a hatred for them as deep as the roots in the soil. *Why can't you leave me alone? Even buried here you can't leave me in peace.*

He detects a ranger with wasp-orange hair. And there are dogs, racing toward a water hole. The dogs start fighting over something, playing tug-of-war with bones.

Robin hears Hal's voice. *Why, little brother, those are your bones.*

Panicking, Robin digs, making a desperate lunge for the surface. He rises through the flesh-soil and he bursts free. He breathes fresh air. And he smells danger.

And he hears a cracking in his bones and feels a blaze of racking, roaring pain.

XIV. Hunter of the Shadows

In a lifetime of savagery, it was the most savage thing Edric Krul had ever seen. From the safety of the willow trees he was looking down toward the wildwood pool. The mastiffs had reached the wildling and now Edric watched them tearing it to pieces.

At his side, Bul was muttering something beneath his breath. Oxman had pressed a silver crucifix to his lips. Edric ignored them. He watched the attack dogs. They had gone days without food and now, as they worked, their muzzles sprayed lumps of muscle, sinew, fur . . .

Fur?

Edric beckoned to his men. Gunthor Bul and Guy Oxman glanced at each other before following him out of the willow stand, gripping their weapons. Slowly, they approached the dogs. The mastiffs were now playing tug-of-war with the wildling's entire spine. At least, it was big enough to be its spine. But it looked to Edric more like a single bone.

The mist was thickening. Edric tried to get a better look . . .

Mother of God. That stinking verminous . . .

"It isn't the wildling," Edric said. "Get your eyes open. We're still hunting."

"What do you mean?" said Bul.

"Take a look, genius. How could the wildling have a bone that big? What kind of animal . . . ? It isn't our quarry! That's all you need to know. You're not here to think—you're here to *do*. The dogs led us here, so the wildling must be near. It's not escaping me this time. Where's Oxman? Oxman! Where is he?"

Edric allowed himself one last look at the mess of blood and fur. It was an animal's carcass, wasn't it? But it was huge. And the way the flesh folded *outward* looked as if it had been killed *from the inside* . . . or . . . or, as if something had burst *out*.

"Oxman went back up that way," Gunthor Bul said. "He's been acting strange. Maybe I don't blame him. The way those dogs were behaving. And this mist. It's getting so I can't—"

"Be quiet," Edric said. "Oxman must have seen something. Find him quickly. No good disturbing the dogs now. Let them finish."

The two men moved away from the water hole, back toward the stand of willow trees. Edric called out to Guy Oxman but got no reply.

"Damn that man. Where is he?"

And then Edric spotted him, sitting slumped the other side of a tree. The mist was getting so thick they had almost stumbled past him. Edric pointed and they approached.

"What are you doing?" Edric said. "Resting? You idle waste of skin. You think you're the only one who's exhausted? When we get back to the city—"

He fell silent. They had walked around the tree and they stood looking down at Oxman. At first it looked as though he had been sick down the front of his tunic, some of the vomit still dribbling from his mouth.

But then they saw it was blood. Half of the arrow that had pierced his throat was still impaled in the tree trunk, the shaft snapped off where Oxman had slumped to the ground.

"Oh Christ, oh Christ, oh Christ . . . ," Bul was saying.

"Control yourself," Edric said. "A fluke shot. The vermin tried to kill me once but wasn't so lucky. We are going to find it, kill it, and leave its corpse for the dogs. Look at the angle of the arrow. It came from over there. With me." Edric edged forward, crossbow in hand. Behind him branches snapped where Bul followed, muttering prayers. The drifting mist made it look as if the trees were following them up the slope.

"Wait . . . ," Bul said. "I think I saw . . . over there . . . I can't be sure, but I thought . . ."

Edric spun and looked where Bul was pointing. He saw nothing but trees, stretching their limbs. Something skittered along a branch above; an owl hissed.

"Come on," he said. "Keep moving. Show some backbone." Edric clambered on, gripping his crossbow, the forest screeching and cackling around him. There was a piercing wail, and a gurgling sound, and the beating of wings. When he next looked back he saw Bul had fallen far behind. He was a small gray shape, standing upright against a tree.

"Keep moving," Edric shouted. "There's only one thing you need to fear in this forest, and that's me! Keep moving or when we get back to the city I swear . . ."

The other ranger showed no sign he had heard. He stood there, as if petrified. Edric snatched branches and thorns out of his way as he strode back to Gunthor Bul. The mist parted and he found himself looking into the ranger's eyes. A surprised look had frozen to his face.

He was still alive. An arrow had punctured his neck, and more were in his elbows and his knees. He was wearing chainmail but the arrows had found his unprotected spots. Between them the arrows had pinned him upright against the tree.

Edric shot his crossbow aimlessly into the undergrowth. He wound another bolt with shaking fingers. This could not be happening. *This* was not Edric Krul's destiny—he had seen his future and it was glorious and clear as daylight. It had nothing to do with death in the shadows—dark shapes in the mist. It had nothing to do with the pathetic gurgling sounds coming from Gunthor Bul's throat.

"No, no, I won't let this happen!" Edric shouted. "I will not let you do this. Hear me? *No!*"

A shadow slipped by him. Gray against gray. He loosed a quarrel. Reloaded. There it was again, closer this time. A flash of animal fur . . . ?

What *was* it? What was out here?

Another bolt fizzed into the trees. Each time Edric got a glimpse of the thing he let loose. But the glimmers were too quick—it was like trying to turn and stamp on the head of his own shadow. And now he was out of quarrels. He threw the crossbow into the trees. He ripped off his skull-helm and threw that. Then his gloves, his boots.

"*No.* You cannot do this to me! I am destined for greatness. You are just vermin of the woods. I will not let you do this!"

Crying, blind with rage, Edric saw nothing, heard nothing, barely even noticed when something ripped into his right hand. Another tearing thump, this time across his forehead. Still he felt no pain, but this last jolt did make him pause. He realized something had changed.

He stared. Someone—some*thing*—was standing in front of him, twenty paces away.

It was here. The wildling. Just standing there.

Horror and revulsion gripped Edric's heart.

What is it?

It was standing on two feet, half crouched, but it appeared more beast than man. A bloody pelt formed its hood and cloak—a pelt so freshly skinned it still glistened and steamed. Edric thought he saw the pelt bulge, or shift, as if . . . No . . . No . . . He was imagining things . . . These were merely more tricks of the mist. He had to focus. He was here to kill it. *It doesn't matter what it is. It will bleed and die, the same as everything else.*

And still Edric had a chance. The wildling was clearly in pain: It was gritting its teeth and making a hissing sound. The pelt rippled again and the wildling half stumbled, almost going to its knees. It was in agony, and disoriented—now Edric should attack.

Do it. Strike now.

But it was far too late. Edric's sword hand hung shattered at his side, impaled with an arrow. In any case, his arm wouldn't move. Neither would his feet. He couldn't even blink the tears from his eyes.

And only now did he understand they were not in fact tears, but were streams of blood. A second arrow had taken the top of his skull and had damaged something vital. He could still see, hear, think, but his every muscle was locked. He screamed inside, but no noise reached his ears.

The wildling appeared to recover from its latest bout of pain. It tipped its head; Edric stared into the dead amber eyes of that grisly hood.

What are you?

It came closer, its bow lowered. It sniffed at Edric and made a noise in its throat. It turned away, sweeping its bloody cloak.

It's going to leave me here.

The wildling loped away through the mist. A rustle in the leaves and it was gone.

Don't leave me like this!

Edric screamed noiselessly, and he struggled in vain to move his body of stone. He listened to his attack dogs snarling, somewhere close. The animals had scented newly spilled blood and now they were heading in this direction, prowling the forest for fresh meat.

Part Five

The Wearing of Skins

I. The Horror and the Glory

The leaves stir and a skin-feeling stops you in your tracks. Your head tips back, your limbs stretch toward the warmth. Ahead you scent a wild flower glade. You hear scaly creatures scratching across the rocks. You go and join them, finding a soft spot amid the moss, wriggling back and forth before finally lying still.

Biting things begin buzzing near your face—you swipe at them, growling low in your throat. The breeze strengthens and washes the biters from the air. You lie still once more, breathing slow and even, slipping toward sleep . . .

But something won't leave you in peace—something that stings worse than the insects. It drags you to your feet. You leave the glade and lope through the trees, lowering your head, sniffing for scent trails, listening for the heartbeat of concealed meat.

Something darts through the undergrowth and you follow, silent as its shadow. This creature had a name once—something like moooaaaausss—but you know it now as a red-brown smell and a warm-blood sound.

You stalk, pounce. The creature dies easily. You suck its heart dry and crunch its tiny bones. A guttural noise of pleasure. A swelling that might be called pride. But this meal does little to appease your appetite.

Back to your feet and off again, moving through the forest on swift strong limbs. More prey crosses your path and you are after it, dogging its steps. The creature hops across a clearing. The scrunch-scrunch *of its teeth ripping up green shoots.*

You glide closer, close enough to strike—

Another predator sweeps in from above, on muffled wings. The smaller creature shrieks and there is a death struggle. Your lips curl back from your teeth. But you don't make a sound. Instead, you string your bow and nock an arrow.

You draw, aim, let loose. The feathered thief drops dead, your prey still clutched in its talons. You go to collect your double prize. The floppy-eared thing is still alive—you shake it like a rag until its neck snaps and it hangs limp. You deftly skin the creature with your blade and you set about making a fire to cook the meat.

Something deep inside you remembers these tools—bow and knife and fire—and you use them unthinkingly, like extensions of your arms, your hands, your claws.

Claws . . . ?

Your hands go to your face and grope clumsily and bring blood to your cheeks. A silent scream rises in your throat.

What am I?

Your hands go to your head, your shoulders, tearing at the wolf hide. But it is futile—you could no more cast it off than you could discard your own shadow.

What have I become?

It passes. The same way it has before. You are up and running through the trees, following a fresh hunt, and the powerful predator stuff is flowing in your veins and those human thoughts are left lying in the litter, like snakeskin.

But it has only just begun, this new struggle. Until now your creature-self has been stronger. But winter is over. Flowers are carpeting the earth and birds are calling their song of rebirth and moths are drying their newfound wings. Spring, and everything is waking up . . .

Mutant memories that have lurked deep are bubbling to the sur-
face. You remember now. You remember . . .

Lying there by the willow pool, wrapped in the remains of the
Wargwolf, and you felt one last tearing surge of pain that could so
easily have been death but you are now beginning to understand was
the feeling of fur and flesh and sinew knitting together.

Aaaaaggggnnooooaaahhhh . . .

A howl rattles through the trees, snapping you back to the present.
Birds take wing and ground-creatures bolt for their burrows.

Naaaaarrrrraaggggggggaaahhhhhrrr . . .

There it is again, more desperate than before. You flee too, bound-
ing away with the frightened deer. But your running now is cramped,
your body twisted, and the noise keeps up easily. You feel yourself sink-
ing to the earth.

Naaaaaahhhhhhooooaaaahhhh . . .

Finally you understand: It is you *making these sounds. And only*
now do you feel the pain—a grinding torture in your limbs—hot
needles in your marrow. You fall to your hands and knees, your back
arching, your spine trying to burst free.

Aaaaaggggnnnoooooaaaahhhhh . . .

This body is still building itself: sinews twining tighter, creaking
like rope being wound. Wounds sucking themselves closed across bones
that are bulging, threatening to erupt once more through the skin.
Each burst of agony reaches the very limits of pain, and yet each new
spasm is more excruciating than the last. You slump forward, your
face in the wet earth, arms and legs thrashing—

It passes.

Your body ceases its quaking. You lie still, dreading its return. You
try not to make a noise, not wanting to wake the hot thrashing thing
within.

The thunder in your chest subsides, your fingers uncurl. You get
unsteadily to your feet.

The pain is gone. In its place is a gnawing void in your stomach.

You go on your way, uncertainly at first—these legs not feeling like your own—but then beginning to move more surely, and then to run, and then to sweep through the trees, the power flooding your muscles, the agony all but forgotten.

You go to the banks of the stream and to the crossing points, checking your deadfall traps. You find a snared creature, squashed flat. You scrape it from the rock and eat it raw, the blood coating your chin. Dropping the empty skin, you cut juicy morsels from the base of an oak, sniffing them for any hint of poison. They are safe—you stuff the meaty things in whole. You catch bugs and fish and flesh of every kind and you eat it all, greedily, but none of this can tame your raging hunger.

You sniff the air and follow an unusual scent trail. Here, perhaps, is something that can slake your appetite . . .

You move closer. There are five of these creatures, moving in a tight pack. You listen to their sounds: clinking noises, far too loud. The breaking of branches, the crushing of ground-nests, unseen. What kind of creature moves with so little stealth? What sort of animal destroys so much, without even having to try . . . ?

You listen to the noises coming from their mouths.

"Soopar luff roking lever mee joaki."

"Mender fare finlune geffer nit lep."

You know now every language of the forest. You know which pip means home and which whistle means food and which shriek means danger. But these alien glops and globs and lollings, they mean nothing to you.

"Ayrnyoo friitair inimat kool."

"Whitter winer, whitter froo."

A growl of self-warning rises in your throat. Steer clear of these creatures. They are unpredictable, and cruel. You turn and run and leave them far behind.

You check more of your traps and you hunt with your bow and you feast on more flesh. But your hunger only grows fiercer. Perhaps it is thirst. You stop at a spring and lap cold fresh water. You drink until you cannot drink a mouthful more, yet still the emptiness remains. You put your back to a tree and rub yourself against its rough bark. This provides a moment's distraction, but no real relief: As soon as you stop you feel the gnawing sensation, clawing at you from within.

You set off at a run, trying to outdistance this incessant yearning. It is working. You feel the mud and the mulch between your toes, the wind on your skin, the heat in your muscles. You run faster, swift and sure, reveling in the feeling of it—a squirrel pup, leaping through the trees, delighted to discover what its body can perform.

But you miss a step, stumble.

Nnnnnaaaaaarrrrraaagggggghhh . . .

The agony explodes and sends you crashing to the earth. Your limbs buckle backward. Your bones bend to their cracking point, then keep on bending, screaming like boughs in a storm. And still it intensifies, your every fiber shuddering fit to burst.

Nrrrgggggggaaaaooooahhhh . . .

This body thrashing warping rebuilding—

It stops.

You lie still, snorting sharp and shallow.

You make a hissing noise between your teeth.

The agony has departed, and in its place is that twisting emptiness in your chest and in your guts. It is more insistent than ever.

And you suspect now you know how to satisfy this urge . . .

In the distance you hear those creatures in metal skins. You move toward them. The hissing between your teeth becomes a gurgled yell. This noise isn't caused by pain, but by something deeper and older, red raw.

Gnnnrrrraooooooowwwwwwaaaahhh . . .

The creatures in metal skins have heard you. They are running, blundering even more clumsily than before.

"Whanafugaflet?"

"Whanaru? Gooogaar!"

Their shouting only fuels the fire coursing through your veins. You crash through the undergrowth, yelling louder. Your hunting instinct tells you this is wrong: You should be silent in your pursuit. But that last bolt of pain has left you beyond your own control.

The five creatures have separated. You go after the nearest one.

He is shouting, over and over, and his sounds are starting to hover close to sense.

"Weararryou? Gouger, ayemhere, where are yooo? Gouger!"

You descend on him. He turns, begins to scream, but your knife goes to his throat and turns his noise to a wet gurgling sound.

You lower the still-thrashing, blood-foaming body to the ground. You sniff close to the carcass, to see if this meat is good to eat. The smell makes you gag. No. You are not hunting these creatures for food. But you will hunt them, just the same.

You string your bow and go after the next intruder.

"What is it? What's out here? Yilman, Scragger!"

You have begun to understand their words.

"Yilman, is that you? It's me, I'm here!"

And their language twists in your mind to become questions of your own.

Why did he do this to us?

Where is he keeping her?

How long must I wait for my revenge?

You slip through the shadows, silently now, stalking your prey. Your quarry stumbles away, alone. You nock an arrow, draw and let loose—you taste this ranger's terror and you drink in his screams—and for the moment at least the twisting void in your stomach is appeased.

II. Into the Dark

The further Will Scarlett sank into the gloom, the more fetid the air became, the fiercer his self-loathing burned. *How long has she been down here? How long can a person survive, breathing this miasma?*

He released another length of rope and the pulleys creaked and the basket lurched deeper into the dark. All around him were the groans and pleading voices of The Forgotten—the noises swelling below him, passing close to his ear and echoing again above. *How long can a person stay sane, listening to this choir of the damned?*

He lifted his lantern and tried to peer into the tunnels and caves that formed the cells of this prison. Sometimes he caught the flash of eyes, but immediately the wretch would raise their hands to cover their face, would shrink from the light the way a leaf curls against the heat of a fire.

Will descended; the voices followed.

No, noooo. I didn't . . .

Help me.

Pleeeasse . . . What do you want with us . . . ?

He listened to the voices and he dreaded what he was going to find at the end of his descent. He fought the urge to pull on the opposite rope and hoist himself back to the light. *No. You put her here. You have to set this straight.*

He began coughing. He halted the basket and swung in midair, feeling the ache of fever at the back of his throat. He coughed and kept coughing. He suspected he was probably dying, and he found the idea held no particular fear. Not anymore.

He supposed he didn't look out of place here today—his beard unusually wild, his uniform splattered with mud and blood. He had spent the past ten days in the western shires, fighting running battles with a bandit company known as Hydra's League. Ten days of ambush and counterambush, of daylight raid and midnight skirmish, of rain and wind and no sleep. Finally Will's band had scattered the outlaws. But his enemies' arrows and the elements had exacted a heavy toll: He had limped back to the castle today with two of his men dead and another three dangerously ill.

Will himself was burning with fever, his body begging him to sleep for a week. *I'll rest once this is done. I won't put it off any longer.*

He descended farther into the pit and reached the deepest depths of the oubliette. The basket came to rest on solid rock. He broke into another coughing fit and waited for it to subside.

He stepped out of the basket—

A filthy snarling thing flew out of the darkness, tearing at his eyes, biting at his face. There was a stabbing pain at his shoulder and in his neck. He fell backward to the wet floor, his lantern clattering. He fought back, managed to reach out, to grab the object that was stabbing him in the neck—he threw the weapon away and in the same motion kicked his attacker, catapulting the wild-haired creature across the cavern.

He jerked painfully to his feet, threw himself on the prisoner. By the spluttering light of the lantern he looked down into a fierce dark glare—the same intense eyes that had once stared out at him while all around them a village burned.

Marian Delbosque.

Somehow she had gotten loose from her bonds, and in addition had managed to fashion a blade from a fragment of bone. Beneath Will she struggled and scratched and kicked. But she had been here a long time and suddenly the fight went out of her and she lay limp.

"Marian, I'm here to help you."

"Get. Off. Me."

Will untangled himself. He stood his lantern upright and checked it; some of the oil had spilled but it was otherwise undamaged. From his backpack he took a bandage and a phial of juniper water and, still keeping his eyes on Marian, he began treating the wounds to his neck and shoulder.

"I thought it was you who would need the curative," he said. "A fraction lower and you would have killed me."

"That was the general idea."

"And then what? You'd take the basket to the surface? There are locked doors up there, and armed guards. Could you get through them all?"

Marian sat back against the flowstone wall, hugging her knees to her chest, watching Will intently. Even all the way down here her gray-green eyes were luminous. She wore the same smoke-blackened cape and tunic she had been wearing the day they dragged her from that burning village. The memory of it came back heavy now and made Will wince.

Will Scarlett, child-catcher. How did you let yourself become this?

"There is a better way out of here," Will said. "I've come to help you see sense. I can take you back to the surface. You will have to stand in front of the Sheriff, make certain pledges.

But that's all. Afterward you'll be provided for. A life of luxury, almost."

Marian looked away, rested her chin on her knees. "Yes, they took me to that gilded cage," she said. "I failed to show sufficient gratitude, so they put me here instead. It makes no difference. A prison is a prison is a prison. If that's all you came to say, I'd thank you to leave."

"Marian, please. That's lunacy. You've been here too long. The air in this place—"

"It was fine until you arrived. You brought the stench. I'd be content here, if only the quality of the visitors would improve."

Will listened to the rattling of chains and the moaning voices falling from above. Now he could hear other noises too—even worse sounds perhaps for those trapped down here—people talking and working in the castle and its grounds. These were natural caves and many shafts and fissures ran to the surface. Some channels brought wafts of blessed fresh air, but some also brought the occasional faint laugh or echo of children's games.

"Marian, this place, if it doesn't kill you, it will break you. Take what the Sheriff is offering." He moved closer, knelt at her side. "It's up to you now—you can save yourself. Rejoin the world of the living. All that's happened, you can put it behind you. All wounds heal, given time."

Will wondered if she had understood—wondered if already her mind had slipped too far—but then she looked up and glowered.

"No, no, that's not it at all," she said. "Time doesn't heal wounds, it just drives them deeper, down into your bones, where you can't see them but where they can devour you from within, until one day there's nothing left but an empty skin, flapping in the wind. That's what I learned about you, Chief

Rider, from our friendly chat on the road. All those people you've killed, or left to rot in places like this—not all of them deserved their fate, did they?—but in any case you did what you were told, and the knowledge of it is eating you whole."

She pushed her tangled hair out of her eyes and smiled at him thinly. "You still don't have the first idea what all this means, do you? You don't have a clue what the Sheriff is searching for—what he's afraid of, what he wants—but still you go on following him, blindly, like an old loyal lapdog, barking when he says bark, wagging your tail for a treat. You don't even know why you're here. You didn't come to rescue me from this place—you're here to save yourself. If I go to the surface meek and mild, if I sit in his gilded cage and don't die, that's one less life weighing on your shoulders."

Will stood, feeling dizzy, steadying himself against the wet wall. "I can see I'm wasting my time."

"There's only one way you can put this right," Marian said. "One way to atone for all your crimes . . ."

Will went to the basket, fetched his backpack.

"I'll leave here with you," Marian continued. "I'll grant you forgiveness. The day you bring me the Sheriff's head."

Will closed his eyes. His throat burned, his skull thumped in time with the *plip-plip* of water dripping. He looked at Marian.

"You don't know what you're suggesting," he said. "The Sheriff's power is near absolute. There are hundreds who do his bidding, thousands more who follow his rule. What can I do, alone?"

Staying at arm's length he pushed his backpack close to Marian's feet. "There's meat and bread and fresh water," he said. "I'll be back soon with more."

Marian looked away from the pack, hugging her knees.

"There are fights that can be won," Will said. "And there are things beyond our control. Wisdom is knowing one from the other. The Sheriff is here to stay, that's a fact we have to live with. But we don't have to accept this torture. We can get you out of here."

He went back to the basket, climbed inside. He pulled on the rope, rose toward the open air, leaving Marian there below, knowing without doubt that tonight when he slept he would once again dream of her eyes, watching him from the gloom.

III. The Killing Mist

A knight of the realm, standing at the prow of a warship. He is sailing for home, triumphant, a golden sword at his hip, his cloak billowing. A young woman is there, on the shore, watching him, seeing all he has become . . .

But look closer. The knight's cloak is crimson, and glistening. It is made of flesh and blood. And its rippling has nothing to do with the wind. The cloak is still living. It is writhing twisting constricting . . .

Robin woke choking and frantic, feeling trapped in a body that was not his own. He took long shuddering breaths. His limbs came to rest with a final spasm and twitch, and he lay there gathering his senses.

He found he was in a natural shelter beneath a shelf of rock. He did not recall crawling in here. He searched his memory to see what he did remember and he found . . . something raw and dripping . . . voices screaming . . . the stench of . . .

He pushed these thoughts away, crawled quickly out of the hollow. From nearby came the trilling of a stream. He moved toward it, staggering slightly, his throat fiery, his head groggy. The feeling of rousing from the longest sleep. An idea nagged at him: Something had happened, close by, and it was important he remember . . .

He reached the stream and went to hands and knees to drink. Once again he searched his memory, but this time, to orient himself, he went further back, put everything he knew side by side, piece by piece. He had fought the Wargwolf at the close of summer. He knew that much for certain. He looked for the weeks and months that followed but found nothing. The whole of the autumn was still a complete blank. Winter was a little clearer. Winter had passed in a half dream in which Robin was fully a forest creature, roaming the snow-filled woods, slaking his thirst and his hunger, concerned with nothing else. Thinking back, it seemed a glorious dream and one he could happily have never left.

But now it was spring, and the paths were unblocked, the rivers unlocked. And the Sheriff's soldiers had returned in force . . . dragging Robin painfully, hazily awake . . .

He listened to the tinkling of the stream. And he listened to his own bones creak and groan—like the beams of a home as they settle among the stones. With the noise came a twisting in his joints, but it passed quickly: The worst of this physical torment was over. His major agony now was of the mind. What had he become? Had he taken possession of this second skin, or had it taken possession of him?

What had happened before he crawled into that shelter? Half-formed recollections rose once more, black and howling.

At the same time he tasted blood in the water.

He stood and walked upstream.

He found a wild flower glade, and a scene of slaughter.

It stank of death and was silent—even the scavengers had avoided this massacre. He moved around the clearing, feeling nauseous, smelling earth soaked with blood, bending to touch moss thick with it. He sniffed at the corpses and examined it all with his fingers, reconstructing events in his mind's eye.

It had happened recently, and quickly. One of the soldiers was slumped in the center of the glade, an arrow protruding from his spine, his head bowed as if in prayer. A second man, speared through both legs, had crawled some distance away, like an injured insect, leaving a slick slug trail. The third ranger had run as far as the stream, where he lay trailing one arm in the water. Occasionally he flapped, like a landed fish. But these were only ghost-spasms; he was dead, the same as the rest.

Robin stood perfectly still for a long time, numb with guilt and horror. *You did this, and you barely even remember. What else have you done? What have you become?*

Hazily he thought of his past life—his time with Sir Bors— all he had been taught about valor and the rules of war. These soldiers had not died facing their enemy. Their crossbows were still cocked, their blades unbloodied. They had been murdered from the shadows.

Consumed with remorse, still feeling thick-headed, Robin didn't hear the other soldiers until they were very close. There were three more of them, approaching the glade. Robin went to a king oak. Taking hold of creeping vines, gripping the rough bark with his toes, he scuttled up the trunk. He reached a high sturdy branch and ran along it in a half crouch. He stopped directly above the clearing—he suspected this was the killing stand he had used to attack the soldiers below. He listened to the three newcomers, drawing near.

"I still say it's a waste of time," one of the men was saying. "How long has it been? Months. No chance we'll find them alive."

"Makes no difference," said a second man. "You know his rules. Every ranger comes back, even if he's just bones."

"We won't find even that much," a third man said. "You know what I think—they never made it as far as the wildwood. Krul always was a mad dog. I say he killed Bul and Oxman himself, in some tavern over a game of dice, and now he's gone to ground."

"I've heard wilder theories," said the second man. "I tell you what Treadfire said? He swears blind that Edric Krul came—"

Pushing through the undergrowth, into the clearing, the men were swallowed into its silence. Several moments passed during which none of them flinched and they barely breathed. Finally a twig snapped and they were moving forward again slowly. A blade hissed from its sheath. A *click-clack* where another man wound his crossbow.

Krul and Bul and Oxman.

Did Robin take those lives too? He searched his memory and found more of those red smells and putrid sounds and he knew it must be true. Half of him sank further into remorse. But at the same time . . . another part of him felt a savage shiver of pride. The world was a better place without Edric Krul. And these other men who died, they each carried the Sheriff's blades. Robin had seen such men torturing farmers, burning homes. It was men such as these who put Marian in a cage and robbed Robin of his eyes.

And now here were more of them, below.

He strung his bow, took an arrow from his quiver. As he did so he fought an argument with himself.

What good will it do, killing these men?

Justice. Revenge.

They may not even have been there that day. It was the Sheriff. And Jadder Payne.

These are the same. Kill them all.

300

If I let them live, they might lead me to where Marian is being held.
Kill them.
What purpose will it serve?
Kill.

All other thoughts failed and this final command echoed over and over, *kill kill kill,* until the word became meaningless and was merely a sound, throbbing in time with his heart. Already he felt himself slipping beyond thought. Mindless rage rising.

He nocked the arrow. Every tremor of the forest had become perfectly distinct. Below him, tucked in a hole in the tree, he could hear a shrew crunching insect shells. Above, the footsteps of a wolf spider across bark. He was aware of each rustle and sniff of the men below. He could smell the sweat on their palms where they gripped their weapons.

"Derek Yilman," one of the rangers said, who was kneeling near the corpse at the stream. "And Wilt Scragger over there, and Samuel Topps. I suppose they were sent looking for Krul too. Weren't Rilke and Gouger part of this patrol? I guess they didn't make it this far."

"Yilman was a good friend of mine," another soldier said, winding his crossbow. "Whoever did this had better be long gone. If I catch up with them—"

"Over here is where they broke through," the third man said. "See these snapped branches. So they came running across, in this direction . . . and they stopped here, where Scragger is. But it doesn't make sense. There are no tracks following. Whoever did this must have had wings, or—"

This soldier had come to a halt in the center of the clearing. His heartbeat had begun to thunder and Robin knew he was looking up.

"What is it?" said the man at the stream.

With shaking fingers the man below was fitting a quarrel to his crossbow. "I'm . . . I can't be sure. Come over here, both of you. Take a look at this."

Robin remained so still a death's head moth came to rest on the bodkin of his arrow.

"Look, there," said the ranger below. "That part of the branch, see. The mist swirled, and I thought I saw . . . There! Look!"

Robin drew his bow. The death's head moth took flight.

The ranger was yelling, raising his crossbow . . .

Robin loosed his arrow—it sped toward the thundering pulse in the man's neck.

The second ranger stumbled, slipped, scrambled for cover. The third took a sharp breath and raised his weapon. But they were both too slow—Robin had already nocked another arrow and let loose. And even as the killing proceeded, he felt himself forgetting it, dumb fury descending in a thick mist, smothering the guilt and deadening the screams, leaving nothing but a numb nameless horror in their place.

IV. Darker Depths

William Scarlett lowered himself once more into the abyss. The basket jerked and creaked and swung, past the wailing voices and the shuffling of chains. This time Will was healthy and his clothes were clean, but if anything his spirits were even lower, having just made the most dreadful decision of his life. He felt the weight of his task fully as the walls of the oubliette slid past.

He found Marian in the same spot he had left her, sitting against the flowstone wall, hugging her knees to her chest.

"You again," she said, without looking up. "I thought I said I didn't want you here. I have the rats to talk to. They are less obnoxious company."

The words were as biting as ever, but the tone had lost some of its venom. She had slipped a notch since Will had last seen her. Soon she would accept his offer of help, of that he had no doubt.

"I thought you would want to know," he said. "You're right. I woke from my fever and I saw just how right you are. This has gone on too long, and he's getting worse. He has to be stopped."

He paused. Marian only watched him, in silence.

After a few moments Will said: "We're going to stop him, if we can."

Marian went on staring.

"There . . . there are three of us," Will said. "Two men I trust fully. Fellow crusaders who fought with me in the east."

He fiddled with the lid of his lantern, opened the spout to let through more oil.

"I . . . I thought you should know. We'll get an opportunity, sooner or later. We'll bring this to an end."

Finally Marian spoke. "Do you expect me to applaud? To drop my kerchief for Will Scarlett, the conqueror, parading the lists? You are not the hero of this tale, Chief Rider, you have blood on your hands—you have a *duty* to put this right. Do not come here expecting my praise."

"I thought you'd want to know. I thought it would give you hope."

"No! That is not why you're here. Once again you've come for your own sake, not for mine. This is one more attempt to set your soul at ease. So, finally you've opened your eyes, you've got two men on your side, you've done a lot of talking no doubt, but what have you achieved? Nothing! Go away. Come back when you've got something to show for all your brave intentions."

Will went to the basket and came back with a packet of provisions. This time Marian didn't hesitate; she snatched for the pack, reached inside, stuffed food into her mouth.

"You're wrong about me," Will said. "I've made mistakes, the same way everyone has. But I'm working to set things right. That's more than can be said for most."

He listened to water drip, the echo of it seeming to come from a thousand miles away. He sensed the weight of the earth above, and the depth of the darkness beyond the light of his lantern, and he felt a wave of despair. How awful would it be to stay down here for an entire day? How would it feel to be here for weeks, months?

"There's another reason I'm here," Will said. "Last time you talked of the Sheriff's aims, and his fears. You know about the divination. What do they call it, 'The Wyrdwood Dream'? I need you to tell me what you know."

Marian continued eating.

"The Sheriff takes this seriously," Will said. "And events . . . perhaps they're starting to turn the way he feared. I've been receiving strange reports. A patrol returned today from Winter Forest. They found . . . bodies. What is it the Sheriff has been trying to prevent?"

No answer.

"Marian, if we are to succeed in this we need every advantage we can get. I hear snippets of this thing. I overheard Bishop Raths reciting some of it. I think it went: 'Lock the son in darkness; the daughter in chains. Two shall meet; blood will rain.' What's the rest? And what do they mean by 'winter-born'?"

"Is that as far as you've got?" Marian said, her mouth full. "They don't breed you lapdogs for your brains. You're deeper in the dark than I am. And you came here to give me hope?"

Will sighed. He pulled his cloak close against the fetid air. He reached inside his tunic and took out the half-arrowhead amulet. He laid it at Marian's feet.

"I found one of the guards with it," he said. "I believe it belongs to you."

The jade amulet had already disappeared inside Marian's clothing, but she hadn't looked up. She was kneeling, stuffing more food into her mouth. Will went back to the basket. A noise caught his attention; he froze. At first he told himself it was one of the wretches above. But no, this new noise was coming from *below*.

That's impossible. There are no deeper caverns or caves—no depths more abysmal than this.

305

But there it was again, louder and more dreadful. Scraping, slithering, clicking sounds, filling Will's head with images that did not belong together.

What was it?

Marian had heard it too—he could tell by the slight straightening of her back, her brief stillness. But then she went back to eating, apparently unconcerned. Perhaps she had slipped further than Will thought, and there were no horrors left that could reach her.

You've got to get her to the surface, and soon. Next time you come here, she'll be ready.

He climbed into the basket and looked at her once more.

Just pray she lasts that long.

He pulled on the rope and headed gratefully for the world above.

V. Creature Fear

Murderer. Monster.

The wind breathed the words through the trees.

"No!" Robin shouted into the forest. "Those men . . . their deaths . . . it wasn't me. It was . . . the other. That's not who I am."

The wind snickered through aspen leaves, mocking him.

So then, who are you?

"I am . . . I was . . . a squire. I learned a code of honor. I was going to become . . . a knight of the realm."

The wind moaned through hollow trunks, and this time Robin heard the voice of Sir Bors.

You're dead to us now, Loxley.

Yes, the forest whispered. *Whoever you were, whatever you wanted to be, all that is lost.*

"I was raised in Wodenhurst. My father taught me to hunt. My mother sang to me at night. I am . . . a son. A brother."

The wind strengthened to howling derision.

Your family left you. You are none of those things. Who are you?

"I am . . . Squire Loxley . . . Sir Robin . . . I am . . ."

You are Robin Hood. You are the Sheriff's doom. Here are more of his men, listen.

Robin had been trying to ignore the soldiers: four separate

patrols thrashing through the undergrowth. They were coming now in ever greater numbers.

These are your enemies, the wind breathed. *They took everything from you.* And Robin's other, savage-self was rising. He headed toward the nearest patrol. As he strung his bow he battled with himself—finally he came to a halt.

"No! Not this way. It would serve no purpose."

They would kill you, if it was in their power.

"I am not like them."

You are the same. Only stronger. Accept your true nature.

Robin continued toward the patrol. He had the feeling this was the end: When he destroyed these men, Robin Loxley would die with them. He would lose himself forever inside this god-skin—and he found he was glad. He left the glade and headed toward the rangers at a run, sinking into dumb animal fury.

But then the wind whispered once more, softly.

Robin, come back to me.

It was a voice he recognized, vaguely.

Our fates are tied, we've always known that.

Marian.

It's not enough to be strong—you have to be clever. I can't do this alone.

Robin stopped on the path. Rain began to fall, drizzling across his face. He gripped the jade amulet at his chest.

"I am Robin Loxley. I am Marian's champion."

You are me, just the same as I am you.

"I made a promise. I will find her."

He stood there in the rain until the last of the killing rage had drained away. He began to think more clearly, and to plan. These soldiers did not need to die. Their murder would be cowardly, inglorious. What was more, their deaths would not help Marian.

The rain strengthened to a torrent. He moved off again through the forest, but this time he left his bow unstrung. He needed answers, and now he had an idea how to get them. He would employ a different sort of weapon.

"It's bandits. What else could it be?"

"You know what else. You've heard what they're saying."

"This phantom outlaw? I'll believe it when I see it."

"Gordon would know, wouldn't he? He was with them when they found the bodies. Bul and Oxman. He said they'd been *eaten*. Nothing left but gnawed bones."

All four rangers fell silent at that. Robin listened to the squelch of rainwater in their boots. He smelled the rust that had leeched from their armor into their tabards, and the first beads of sweat that had appeared on their foreheads.

Finally one of them snorted. "Eaten? They took attack dogs, didn't they? Oxman probably forgot to put them back on the leash. You sure we're on track, Finks? I haven't seen a waymarker for a while."

"There's one to your left, carved on that tree. We're still heading east."

"Yes, *but*," the second ranger said, "the skeletons were full of arrows. More spines than a hedgehog, is what Gordon says. What kind of dog kills with a bow? And they didn't even find a trace of—"

"Listen, all of you," a third man said. "I've heard enough talking. It doesn't matter who, or what, killed Gunthor Bul and Guy Oxman. One thing is for sure: It will die. And *we* are going to be the ones to kill it. All you have to think is—"

"Ssshhh, listen. What was that?"

"Shut up, Scutter, stop trying to—"

"Quiet, I'm serious, didn't you hear—"

Robin snapped another branch, this time on the opposite

side of the track. All four soldiers spun, their cloaks slapping sodden against their backs, their blades sucking from their scabbards. For a long time none of them moved. The only sounds were the dry swallowing in their throats, the booming of their hearts.

Finally one of them barked a laugh. "Ha, Scutter just wet himself. He's been listening to too many of Gordon's stories."

"Leave him here to chase shadows," another man said.

"Come on, the rest of you, we've got a job to do."

The men moved away, jeering at one another. But already their voices were not quite so loud; their strides not quite so steady. And distracted by Robin, squinting in the mist, they had missed their designated turning and were now blundering up the wrong path.

"What is it? What's out here?"

Robin dogged the soldiers' steps, walking behind them in silence, rustling a branch ahead, but always slipping out of sight when they spun with crossbows cocked and blades bared.

"Who are you? Show yourself!"

He scuttled overhead, rattling the boughs. He whispered close to their ears. He allowed them only the barest of glimmers—the shadow of a shadow.

"What was that? There!"

At every fork in the trail Robin was there to harass and confuse, shepherding the rangers deeper into the forest-maze.

"What are you? Come and face us!"

Crossbow bolts fizzed harmlessly into the trees. Swords swung wildly. One blade cracked against an oak. And now night was falling. The first bats had emerged for their reconnaissance flights. Robin listened to the *flutter-fluff* of their wings and the tiny clicking of their echo sight. And he listened to the soldiers' voices growing frantic, then delirious.

"Scutter? Where's Scutter?"

"I'm here! Finks, Brooks, I'm here!"

"Where is he? Brooks, he was right behind you!"

One of the soldiers had taken a misstep, followed by another, and now he found himself on the wrong track, alone. "Where are you? Stop. Wait!"

Crouched on a bough, listening to the soldiers below, Robin knew the missing soldier was barely more than an arm's length from his companions—but he was disoriented in the dark, and stupid with fear, and each desperate step was taking him farther away. His voice faded to ghostly wails.

"We have to go back," another soldier said.

"We're not turning again! You want to spend the night in here?"

"We can't leave him."

"His own stupid fault."

There was a scuffle, then silence. Finally the remaining soldiers continued through the forest, dragging their feet. Robin followed.

Not every weapon is forged of steel. Sir Derrick used to tell the squires that, back at the academy, a lifetime ago. *Your enemy's fear can be the blade that slices to his heart.*

Here was proof enough of that: These veteran enforcers had become children, whimpering in the dark. They had each lit a storm lamp—Robin could smell the tallow fat burning. Now one of the lamps had come to a halt. A soldier was staring into the mist. He pushed to his lips something that smelled metallic—a silver crucifix. Then he turned and went after the others. Except that glimmering ahead is not

311

lamplight but is instead fireflies beckoning him down a false path. And by the time he realizes his mistake his cries for help will be the merest of squeaks.

So now there were two, and Robin's work was almost complete.

The remaining pair came to a halt. One put his hand on the other's shoulder. "Greigor's gone," he said softly. "It took him. It's just you and me now."

"I think it's here," the other man said. "Standing behind you."

The first man did not turn to look. Eventually he said: "What do you want? If you mean to kill us, what are you waiting for?"

Robin remained silent. Finally the soldiers' lamps creaked on their chains and they were shuffling away, back the way they had come, retracing a trail they had walked a dozen times.

Their fear now was a tangible presence: It dripped through the leaves with the rainwater; it swirled thick as the mist. Robin could taste their terror on his tongue, the way a lizard scents danger in the air.

Their *fear*. It was glorious.

What exactly had Robin put on, together with this wolfskin cloak? He remembered what Cernunnos had told him about the Wargwolf:

He is drawn to fear, like a moth to a flame.

Had Robin inherited this too from the beast, its appetite for terror? *No*, he told himself. *Their fear is a tool. Nothing more. A weapon I can use.*

Yet still he put off bringing this sport to an end. He licked the rangers' dread from the air and he haunted them, just a little longer . . .

*

Finally they fell down, exhausted, in an old dried riverbed. The first ranger, whose name was Harcour Finks, began to gabble.

"I thought I heard . . . something . . . but it sounded like Greigor taking a breath. And when I looked back he wasn't there. Like the forest plucked him into the air. What did you hear? Why don't you say something? Anything!"

The other man, whose name was Graize Brooks, seemed to have passed beyond terror, into a place of dread acceptance. Despite his wet clothes and the settling frost he didn't even shiver. Harcour Finks shook him by the shoulder. "You must have heard *something*. What is it out here? Talk to me!"

It was Robin who answered, his voice still guttural from disuse. "You don't need to die here."

Harcour Finks scrambled upright, his sword jerking from its scabbard. "What are you? Show yourself!"

"Answer my questions," Robin said. "And I will let you live."

To his surprise it was the other ranger, Graize Brooks, who answered. "That is not in your power. You can't grant us life. We died the moment we entered this place. If we run from here, do you imagine the Sheriff will welcome us home with open arms? We're already dead."

"Quiet," hissed Harcour Finks. "He's letting us leave." He had dropped his sword and was trying to haul the other man to his feet.

"My questions," Robin said. "A young woman. Marian Delbosque. Where is he keeping her?"

"You think he'd tell us something like that?" said Harcour Finks. "We do what we're told, we don't ask questions. We don't know anything. Please."

"The Sheriff," Robin said. "When does he leave the city? How do I make him come here?"

313

"Come on, Brooks, come on! There's no point killing us, he knows that, we'll just go."

Robin's anger began to swell. He nocked an arrow. "Tell me what I need to know."

"Please. We know less than the scullery maids."

Robin drew his bowstring. If these men were no use to him . . .

He took aim at one man, then back to the other. His anger burned. They would kill Robin in a heartbeat, if the roles were reversed.

But I am not like them. I am still me, on the inside. No matter what I've suffered, no one can take that away.

He managed to relax his bow. He removed the arrow. *Let the forest decide.*

"Come on, Brooks, come on! What's wrong with you?" Finally Harcour Finks managed to haul the other man to his feet. They blundered away together.

Robin let them go. He had resisted the killing urge—proved he was once again master of his own actions. That was enough, for now. The rangers' fate was out of his hands. Running through here in the dark, Winter Forest would as likely swallow them whole as spit them out. *Let the forest decide.*

The soldiers had left behind their backpacks. Robin went through their possessions. He found a few coins and a bone-handled whittling knife and a copper flask full of a liquid that smelled of poppy seeds—a potion for pain relief, or perhaps for pleasure or for forgetting. He would take these things to the cave. Who knew when such objects would prove useful.

As he left the riverbed he heard footsteps following. She came closer, muttering beneath her breath, the words faltering, starting again. A child practicing a rhyme.

Spring. Everything has woken up. Including her.

He moved away from the girl with the fox-red hair, but she followed, singing her rhyme. He ran, she kept pace, and for the first time in months Robin tasted fear that did not belong to someone else but was his own.

VI. Monsters Beneath

Marian wriggled into the crawlspace that connected with the main cavern of her cell. She found the correct spot and she lay there in the dark and the damp. She waited and waited and finally it came: a ray of sunlight that found its way down a narrow shaft all the way from the surface. She closed her eyes and felt the sun on her face and she daydreamed she was back at Titan's Lake, lying next to Robin on the bank, her wet skin tingling in the summer breeze.

She lost herself so thoroughly in this memory that she didn't hear the basket descending into the oubliette. She didn't even hear the footsteps moving around her cavern-cell. The first she knew of the visitor was a noise that sounded eerily familiar.

Someone making lolling noises with their tongue.

La, la, la.

Marian opened her eyes. She squeezed herself deeper into the tunnel.

La, la, la.

It couldn't be, could it?

The lolling moved closer. And then came a singsong voice. "Come out, come out, wherever you are. I'll seek you near, I'll seek you far."

A head thrust into the crawlspace. Wasp-orange hair flamed in the shaft of light. Mad eyes rolled and bulged at her. Scarred cheeks twisted into a wild grin. "There you are!"

Marian didn't hesitate. From beneath her cape she pulled the blade she had fashioned from bone. She stabbed. The bone struck metal—Edric Krul had a steel plate sealed across one half of his skull. She struck at his eyes. This time she drew blood. Edric gasped and his head twisted back out of the tunnel. For a moment there was silence. Then a long manic laugh.

"If you won't allow me to come in, I'll wait here for you to come out," Edric said. "What is waiting to me, after all? Let me tell you of the trials I've known, Marian Delbosque, and then you will see what waiting is to me."

He laughed again, this time quietly, and when he spoke again it was like whispering a secret. "The wildling—this phantom outlaw—he thought he had killed me. He left me for the dogs. But death doesn't want me. The paralysis wore off—I climbed a tree. I waited up there for days, listening to the dogs eat the corpses of my men. The wildling had injured my hand and it was turning green. I had to remove what was left—I sawed it away with my sword—I seared the flesh with a lantern flame to stem the blood. A lesser man would have lost his mind. But in spite of all, I endured."

His head burst once more into the crawlspace. One eye was half-closed and bleeding. Marian stabbed at the other. He scuttled back out. A moment passed before he continued whispering his story.

"Finally the dogs went away. But little did I know my waiting had just begun. For weeks I wandered lost in the wildwood, often thinking I could see my escape, just beyond that next ridge, but reaching it only to find an endless sea of trees. Day and night I stumbled on. I was dead on my feet—there were

317

times I truly did believe I had died and this forest was my hell. But I kept fighting through the thorns and wading through the bogs and finally I arrived! Where? At the water hole, where else? Back where I'd started! A weaker man would have lay down then, having gone so long without food. But I said to Bul and Oxman: 'Do you suppose I fear starvation, after all I've seen? Do you imagine mere hunger holds sway over me?' My men had nothing to say, but they offered up their flesh, what remained of it. What? Did you imagine I would balk at such a meal? Surely you understand by now that death must not have me, no matter what price to be paid."

Once more Edric Krul invaded the crawlspace, but this time it was his arm that came thrusting in. At the end of his arm was not a hand but a double-pointed claw—a cooper's grapnel hook—its base forged shut around the stump of his wrist.

The claw thrashed and flailed, grazing her skin. She pushed herself even harder into the wall.

The clawing stopped and the arm scraped out of sight.

"You will have to come out, sooner or later," Edric said. "I have come to understand your purpose. You must help me cleanse the world of the wildling." He chuckled to himself, then put his face close to the crawlspace and continued to whisper his story.

"Finally the wildwood admitted defeat. It released me. But even then my waiting was not done. By now I was frozen to my blood and fevered to my bones. I stumbled across a hermit's shack. The old man took me in, gave me shelter and what succor he could. But all winter I was forced to wait in that sickbed, never strong enough to stand. The old man had barely enough food for one, let alone for both. In the end he too gave up his flesh, when he saw it was the only way I would endure. And so I began to see how the world is ordered. I started to understand that the rest of you—each and every one—you have all been placed here to serve—"

He fell silent. Marian knew why. Dreadful sounds were seeping up from somewhere below the cavern. Today it was a buzzing, like a thousand wasp wings, together with a rough slithering of tails, and a wet crunching, like children stomping snails. Beneath it all was that half whimper, half laugh. The noises grew louder; Marian couldn't help thinking the thing down there was rising, moving nearer.

Edric cleared his throat before he spoke, and for the first time he sounded relatively sane. "I don't need to wait here. I can return whenever I choose. I have other preparations to make. You will still be here, ready to fulfill your purpose, when the time comes."

Marian listened to the pulleys creak as Edric Krul left. The sun had moved on; the shaft of light had gone. She lay there in the total darkness, shivering in the cold, her mind full of monsters.

VII. Out of the Shadows

The soldier hung upside down, his cloak trailing to the ground. He laughed, and he kept laughing until it became a choking sort of sob.

"You're dead," he hissed into Robin's face. "One freak against the whole Sheriff's Guard! We'll skin you to the bone."

Robin tipped his head. This one was interesting. He had not been brave; he had been the first of his cadre to run. But now, captured and alone, his fear had bubbled over into a raving kind of courage.

"Whoever you are, whatever you want, you don't stand a chance," the ranger said. "I'll kill you myself! I'll crush you with my own bare hands." For the third time he pulled himself up and tried to free his ankle from the noose. He gave up and fell back. The rope creaked on its branch.

Bending young trees to the ground, Robin had built catapult snares—larger versions of the ones he used to hunt for food. When this soldier had run he had blundered into one of the traps.

"Marian Delbosque," Robin said. "Tell me where he's keeping her."

"Aha, ha-ha-ha. So that's it. A girl. The monster and the princess in the tower. That old one. Aha-ha-ha."

"Where is she?"

"What are you going to do, fight the Sheriff for her? Maybe you're the king of this place. Out there is his world. He's set up garrisons all along the forest edge. Hundreds of us! You step out there, you're dead."

"Tell me what you know."

"Aha. Aha-ha-ha-ha-ha-ha."

Robin turned and walked away, leaving the soldier hanging there, laughing to himself.

A snake slithered. The girl with the fox-red hair.

"Three gifts I have. The first is for you. Where is it hidden? I'll give you a clue."

"Leave me alone. I know what I need to do. You and I are finished."

"Finished? No, no, no. We've merely begun. Here's the next stage; so much to be done. We've planted the seed; now it must grow. Come, no more talk; let the deed show."

Robin was walking away, following the course of a stream.

The vixen-girl sprang alongside. "You defeated the wolf, took only the skin. The rest of the spoils are more . . . interesting. Three gifts I have, buried beneath. Which would you take: the shadow, the blood, the teeth?"

Robin drew his bow and aimed at the girl. She just laughed.

"Look, he's come far, his aim is so true. He could be so much more, if only he knew."

There was another slither in the leaves and the girl was gone. Robin told himself to forget her, he knew what he had to do next. He needed answers, and he wasn't going to get those here. Which meant he had to go out there. He couldn't put it off any longer.

*

321

He stopped at the threshold, where forest ended and open country began. Ahead he could smell a wild flower bank, warming in the sun. He felt for the vibrations in the web of green—above him a squirrel leaping, causing a jay to call in alarm, sending its mate into the air. Tracing these patterns and shapes, detecting the threads that weave within and beneath the visible world. His forest-mind seeping into the roots and the burrows—and then outward, pushing at the edge of the forest and beyond.

He finds with relief these abilities are no longer confined to the wildwood: His awareness trickles across the boundary, running through the rootlets and the water channels, nosing amid the bluebells. His awareness widens, like waves on a lake, tunneling through the topsoil with the beetles, mining with a badger's claws, warring in the bushes with the sparrows.

The creatures' senses become his own: A weasel explores a warren and Robin knows this black world through its whiskers. He picks up the chemical messages passed between ants, and he traces their labyrinth. There is a moment when all this is overwhelming in its complexity, but he breathes deeply and allows the pieces to settle and a kind of clarity is restored. He takes flight with a hobby hawk, pursuing a dragonfly; he prowls through the reeds with a fox, stalking a lamb.

And there—what he has been hoping to find—a manmade den. It smells of cold stone and old blood and it warbles with human noise. Robin examines closer, knowing this building through the swifts that nest in its roof, the rats in its rafters. It is a church, but it has been claimed by the Sheriff's Guard: It has been fortified, a lookout post in the bell tower, arrow loops punched through the stained glass.

Pulling all his senses toward the center, concentrating on the garrison, Robin sat back against a tree. He stayed there, motionless, while the day cooled in the evening and dew dampened the ground and night came and a frost settled. He wrapped the wolf pelt close and still he waited, observing. He learned there were twelve soldiers in this garrison church. During daylight hours other people came and went: a baker and an alewife arrived from a nearby market town; a forester delivered firewood. Once a messenger visited and another time a weapons trader.

The night deepened. Robin stood, gripping his bow. He waited a heartbeat longer at the boundary. He stepped out of the forest. Immediately he felt exposed and vulnerable. But he didn't pause; he ran down the bank in a half crouch, weaving between a copse of trees, a hillock, a hedgerow. He slipped down the final slope and into the graveyard, tucking himself between two sepulchers.

He strung his bow and listened to the two sentries rounding the church. He wanted to find his answers without further bloodshed, but he admitted now it was impossible. These sentries would have to die, quickly and quietly, before they could raise the alarm.

Part of him was horrified. *This ambush is cowardly. They should be allowed a fighting chance.*

Another part of him, nervous to be out of the forest, just wanted this over, by whatever means necessary. *It can't be helped. Marian needs you. Think of her suffering, not these men.*

The sentries were approaching the graveyard, fifty paces from Robin's hiding place. Forty. The clomp of their nailed boots, the clink of swords at their belts. Thirty paces. Twenty. Ten.

In one movement Robin stood, planted his feet, drew, let loose. The first soldier fell, his lantern smashing against stone. The second man gasped and reached for his war horn, raising it toward his lips. A second arrow appeared at Robin's bow and the string drew and snapped back and the arrow whistled through the night. It stapled the horn to the man's face.

This second ranger was making a low moan. Robin unsheathed his knife and ended the man's suffering. He moved to the nave door and used the hilt of his knife to knock five times: two short taps, followed by three long, the way he had heard the sentries knock.

His plan was vague—he knew only that he needed to find the garrison commander. Senior rangers must know where Marian was being held. He would tell Robin everything he needed to know, and then it could begin . . .

But how would he reach the commander, surrounded by guards? It was only at that moment, standing there waiting for the door to open, that Robin realized how stupid he had been. He had come here in desperation, without any real strategy, or any true chance of success. How could he fight ten men, out here, with only the darkness for cover?

He crept away from the door. It was not too late to bolt for the forest. But even as he took his first steps he heard a shuffling noise inside the church, and then a faint voice struggling through oak. "We heard a crash. Is all clear? What's the watchword?"

As the porter spoke, Robin heard other noises from behind the door: the shuffling of feet; the scrape of something steel being carefully lifted from stone; a man being shaken by the shoulder. The sounds of men trying not to make a sound.

He pushed himself against the wall, curling himself into a ball, his mind screaming *escape*. But where? He was caught in the open. How could he disappear in this place?

A crash where the nave door flew open. Soldiers pouring out.

No choice left but to run—Robin sprinting away from the garrison, up into the churchyard, slipping between gravestones.

"After them! Nets. Bolas. Take them alive."

Something clattering off a headstone. Robin running.

"Where are they? There! With me."

Robin's head down, racing up toward Winter Forest, his heart thumping, feeling again like that blind boy who first ran from men in nailed boots. Slipping through a hedgerow and sprinting for the tree line. The ground rumbling under hooves—at least five horsemen giving chase.

The forest was only a hundred paces away. But Robin wasn't going to make it. The mounted rangers were too close.

Still Robin ran. And he realized he shouldn't be running. In the shock he had forgotten everything Cernunnos had taught him. These soldiers didn't know their quarry—they appeared to think it was an entire bandit horde out here in the night—and they were thrilled by the chase, and dazzled by the flaming torches they were waving. All of which made them more than half blind.

Robin fell on his stomach and lay still.

In the wide open . . .

But perfectly still . . .

The hooves thundering . . .

The horsemen galloped past, the closest trampling just wide of Robin.

He got up and went back to the hedgerow and crawled into the undergrowth, feeling frightened and small. That ranger had been right: The wildwood was Robin's place of power. Out here, in the Sheriff's world, his new strength was not enough.

Something slipped into the hedgerow beside him. The girl with the fox-red hair. She didn't say a word, but he knew she was smiling.

Three gifts I have, buried beneath. Which would you take: the shadow, the blood, the teeth?

He listened to the soldiers at the forest edge, charging up and down, shouting at one another. Finally they rode back to the church. He left the hedgerow and slouched up the hill and slipped gratefully into the wildwood. And the vixen-girl was following behind and still she said nothing, only smiled.

VIII. Unraveling Threads

Marian was engaged in two important tasks, neither of which she could permit to fail or be relaxed, even for an instant. Firstly, she was marking the movement of time by the *plip-plip* of water dripping behind the walls.

Plip. Twelve thousand, four hundred, and four.

Plip. Twelve thousand, four hundred, and five.

Down here it was hard to tell otherwise if a day had passed or an hour or a year. It was true that sometimes she heard other temporal clues, filtering from the surface, echoing along the shafts of these caves. She heard mothers calling children in from play; bells announcing the hour of curfew or prayer; people laughing and arguing.

There was a time when she would have picked out each and every one of these sounds, grasped them to herself as fragile treasures, using them to build a picture of the world above. She did not do this any longer. She ignored these phantom noises altogether.

She focused on the single note of water dropping against stone.

Plip. Twelve thousand, four hundred, and ninety-eight.

Plip. Twelve thousand, four hundred, and ninety-nine.

Originally, Marian had maintained this count in order to

estimate when the jailer might appear: She needed to know when to pause in her other undertakings and to pretend she was still securely restrained. But at some point her marking of time had become even more vital. She understood now that this whole prison—the walls, the tunnels, the wretches above—all of it was held up solely by her vigil.

If she ever stopped counting it would bring disaster.

Plip. Twelve thousand, five hundred, and one.

Plip. Twelve thousand, five hundred, and two.

As she counted, she continued with her other task. When strands of her hair fell out—as they were doing more regularly—she collected them up and twisted them into threads. It was difficult work in the dark, but she kept at it, plaiting the threads together so they were forming a rope. Her plan was this: When the rope was long enough and strong enough to hold her weight, she would tie it with tiny yokes. Each yoke would harness one rat. The rodents would pull her up the sheer walls of the oubliette and propel her to the surface.

How many rat-steeds would she need? Fifty? One hundred? There were certainly enough here: She heard them scurrying in the gullies. To think how she used to hate the rats! She would wake, in the pitch-black, dreaming they were crawling on her face, gnawing on her flesh.

Now she knew the rats as her friends, most of them, although some were not to be trusted. She knew them individually by their squeaking voices: She knew which ones were cheerful or dyspeptic, which were tough and which ones weak and bullied. But more than anything she knew the rats as her salvation. It was merely a matter of time . . .

The first glimmer of a light descending and Marian looked up and she almost—*almost*—faltered in her counting. The ground lurched but she regained her place and the world held.

Plip. Twelve thousand, five hundred and eighty-four.
Plip. Twelve thousand, five hundred and eighty-five.

She watched the light descending. Was this Edric Krul, come to torment her once more? No, why would he return already? Then was it Will Scarlett . . . ? Yes, it must be—Will Scarlett was here to lift her out of the dark!

The part of her that was aware she was going mad—that knew she was losing her grasp—listened to the creaking of the pulleys and rejoiced. This sane part of her knew that this time she would return with Will Scarlett to the surface; she would do whatever was asked of her in order to escape this place.

But even as she was thinking this another part of her was screaming: *Too late! You can't leave. You have to stay and count, or the world will collapse.*

The light swung and dropped fully into view and dropped lower and came to rest. A figure stepped out of the basket, holding a flaming torch.

Marian missed a beat. The cavern shuddered.

"You're not Will Scarlett."

The walls began to spin; the sound of rock grinding.

"Where's Will Scarlett? He's coming to take me away."

The caves turning faster; a great crunching through the earth. Marian regained her place, continued counting. The world kept its shape.

Plip. Twelve thousand, six hundred, and nine.
Plip. Twelve thousand, six hundred, and ten.

It was Grust who had come, the giant jailer, a bunch of keys hanging in his fist. What was he doing here? It wasn't that time already. She could not have miscounted.

Plip. Twelve thousand, six hundred, and . . . thirty-three.
Plip. Twelve thousand, six hundred, and thirty-four?

Grust thrust in front of her a bowl of pottage and a jar of water. He turned to leave. But then he moved close to her once more and hung his face next to hers, making clomping noises through his gums. He held his torch high, reached past her, and picked up the iron collar.

She had forgotten to reattach it! She had thought it was Will Scarlett coming.

"Little woman. Big Trouble," Grust said. "No more visitors for little woman. Now only Grust come. Grust tell him. Will be angry."

He moved back toward the basket. Marian followed. "Don't leave," she said. "You have to help me. It's all going to fall!"

Plip. Twelve thousand . . . six hundred . . . seventy . . . two.

Plip. Twelve thousand . . . seven hundred, sixty . . .

Marian was clinging to the jailer. He lifted one arm and sent her sprawling across the cavern floor. By the time she ran again to the basket it was swinging up and out of reach, the light already fading into the heavens.

"No!" she screamed. "I can't do it on my own!"

Plip.

Plip.

She stopped screaming. She listened to the dripping. She tried to resume the count, saying it out loud. But it was no good, she had lost her place.

She began again from the beginning—"One. Two"—but this would not do. The caverns were falling. Cracking and crumbling above. The prisoners moaning as they began to plummet.

Plip.

Plip.

Marian screamed. She ran and collided with the wall and she ran again and fell, tasting blood. The caverns rumbling turning lurching, the sky itself pouring in to bury them all.

Plip.

Plip.

Marian screamed and kept running, feeling the rock burying her, grinding into her skull, blood running into her eyes and the caves thundering down with a deafening roar.

Her final thought, as the world fell, was of Robin, swinging from a high rope, the sun bright on the water. The sound of his laugh. Then this too gave way to blackness and she knew she had been buried here with the wretches and the rats and that this was the end for them all.

IX. Robin Hood, Arming

Day and night Robin paced, feeling caged in by the Sheriff's troops. He could hear them all along the forest edge, in their encampments, laughing and dicing and going on with their lives.

Weeks passed this way. He drifted and slouched, dragging his useless strength with him. He threw his weight down and slept fitfully, his restrained power choking him—a chained bear. He attacked lone patrols in spiteful fury and afterward loathed himself for it.

And then came the worst moment of all—the night he realized he could no longer hear Marian in his thoughts. Did that mean she was dead? Or was he just forgetting the sound of her voice and the kind of things she would say? Was their past life another part of the world he was locked out of forever?

Finally his desperation raged. He ran seething to seek the vixen-girl and he said, "Show me!" And she gasped and took his hand.

He followed the girl of the forest. She danced ahead of him, breathless, ran back to him, tugged at him to go faster, ran on again, laughing. She became a robin and hopped from branch to branch, leading him on with her song. She was a falcon, speeding ahead. She skipped back to him on human feet.

She led him to the far eastern edge of the forest, and to a hillock, thickly tangled with root and thorn. At least Robin thought it was a hillock, until he felt with his fingers two carved slabs of stone, with a space to crawl between. It was a burial mound, not unlike Beowulf's Barrow near Wodenhurst.

"Three gifts we offered, asked him to choose. He sent us away, he chose to be rude. Now he's frustrated, pleads with soft voice. He'll take what is given, no longer a choice."

In his imagining she was kneeling, stroking her hair between her palms. He could feel her watching him. Smiling. He paused at the entrance to the burial chamber. What was he going to find inside?

Three gifts I have, buried beneath. Which would you take: the shadow, the blood, the teeth?

He could smell on the air a storm approaching. Should he go and find shelter, turn his back on all this? No, this was the only way, he had no choice. He thought of how vulnerable he had felt outside the forest—he needed to build his strength, one last time.

He became aware that Cernunnos was moving nearby, his footsteps unsteady. Since his injury the old man had been more reclusive than ever, wandering deep in the wildwood, talking to himself. Now he limped closer, and his voice crackled between the leaves. "What price this gift?"

"Why shouldn't she help me, if you won't?" Robin said.

"Your anger is wildfire—never sated. It will consume everything in its path."

"You said yourself the Sheriff was hunting your brother. Should I leave the pieces for him?"

The vixen-girl gasped at that, and squealed. A rustling noise, where she sprang toward Cernunnos. Bellowing followed, and hissing and shrieks.

Robin told himself to ignore them both. Whatever old feud they were fighting, he would not be a part of it. He needed the vixen-girl's help, this one last time, but then he would go his own way. The quicker this was over the quicker he could begin.

He went to his hands and knees and crawled into the barrow. The air turned cold. A damp, rotten smell. He clawed his way through cobwebs, thick as spinning wool. He felt his way past holes in the floor that dropped away either side. The passageway narrowed and kept narrowing until Robin was squeezing himself forward. He thought about getting stuck in here. He thought about going back.

He could hear something now. The slithering of tails? He thought he had disturbed a nest of snakes. Something brushed against his neck. A wet thing touched his leg.

Too late to turn back. He pushed forward. The smell of powdered bones, and of gold and brass. There are ancient treasures buried deep in here. And what else?

The scraping slithering growing louder.

He wriggled out of the narrow space and into a larger passageway. He stood and moved forward, something brittle crunching underfoot. The passage was descending: He felt his way down ten, fifteen, twenty steps. At the bottom a round chamber.

Here the slithering slouching was loudest.

Hssst. Hsssssst.

It was here.

Or rather, it was *not* here. In his mind's eye this dreadful thing was not a presence at all, but an absence. A black so abysmal it is a hole in the world. An amorphous non-shape.

Hssst. Hssssssst.

And he could hear now this noise was not a slithering or a hissing or a scraping. Instead it was the sound of all sound disappearing—a void so profound even silence was swallowed into it.

He desperately wanted to go back to the surface and leave this thing down here in the dark. But he thought of the fortified church and how helpless he had felt when he left the wildwood. He thought of the Sheriff, and his army of men. He needed what the vixen-girl was offering. *She has already led you to power. You need this one thing more, to finish what you've started.*

He closed his hand around the jade amulet at his chest, feeling its coolness, its realness.

He stepped forward, reached out and grabbed at the shadow of the wolf.

He took hold of it.

Energy fizzed through his body. A chaos of emotion: elation and sadness and fury and fear. He relived the wrath he had felt looking at Marian in that cage. He tasted afresh her kissing him and the thunderhead charge when their bodies met. He felt the warmth of his childhood bed, his father stroking his hair, his mother singing a song of sleep. He felt all this and more—all in the same instant. He laughed again with Rowly and Irish and Bones. He heard the screams of each one of the men he had killed. He let out a wail of his own, but no sound reached his ears, the shadow-void devouring it. He dropped to his knees.

In his hand the shadow of the wolf writhed and whipped and bucked. It thrashed and flailed, the way the Wargwolf had as it sank to the mud. It curled in on itself, fitting the palm of Robin's hand. It shot out and circled the entire chamber. It twined around Robin's arm and pulsed. It swirled slower, slower. It began to settle.

Robin was able to get to his feet. He staggered to the back of the chamber. Up the steps, along the passageway, into the crawlspace. He wriggled and crawled onward and upward, desperate to reach the surface.

He smelled fresh air. He burst into the open, gasping for breath. He lay there on the earth for a long time, just breathing, a cold wind whipping across him, the sky crackling with distant thunder.

Slowly he stood. Cernunnos and his sister were gone. He felt the shadow of the wolf twining around his arm. It unwound to the ground and it writhed. It snaked back into his palm and pooled there, as heavy as fury, as light as laughter, burning like ice. It simmered in his hand and it curled tighter, a coiled whip, waiting to strike.

X. Survivors

The Sheriff sat deathly still, expressionless. Yet his fury was there, plain to see, lurking just beneath the surface. His eyes were intense, unblinking, staring at the figure slouched at the foot of the dais.

Will Scarlett had come late to the Throne Room; he had to push a path through the crowd.

"It's Harcour Finks," he heard one ranger whisper.

"Came back alone, on foot, raving . . ."

"Found him at dawn, slumped at the city gates . . ."

Will was not surprised the hall was packed. In recent months few soldiers had returned alive from Winter Forest; when one of them did a ripple of unease and intrigue spread through the castle. Everyone wanted to hear, firsthand, what this survivor had seen. Was it true, what they said about The Shadow of Death, The Killing Mist, Wolf's Head? Will had heard all these names used, and many more besides. And with every name came a different story. The outlaw could fly from branch to branch, some people said. He wasn't a person at all, but a shape-shifting demon of the forest. He was just a peasant boy, according to others—a boy who had fought the fabled Wargwolf, and won, and stolen its strength. Or he was an elemental, who could hear the growing of the grass and the tearing of a spider's web.

Will weaved closer and finally got a good look at Harcour Finks. The soldier had lost his cloak and his armor. He was shrunken and bowed. He could barely stand—it seemed to Will he was held upright only by the Sheriff's stare.

"Just two of us left . . . ," Harcour was muttering. "I . . . I must have lain down to rest . . . When I woke . . . Graize Brooks was . . . left his boots even . . . called and called . . . had to carry on, alone . . ."

Will elbowed his way closer and got a clearer view. Flanking the Sheriff's throne were Horor Conrad and Kluth Rogue, two captains of the Guard. And Jadder Payne, the torturer, was there, tall and skeletal in the background, half masked in shadow.

The Sheriff still hadn't blinked. He stared at Harcour Finks and the ranger babbled. "Kept walking, thorns like daggers, the bogs and the mist. But then there it was, the forest edge! I was free! Haven't eaten for . . . how long? Exhausted. But knew I had to get back here, knew I had to—"

"Why?" The Sheriff spoke so softly it was barely a sound, yet that single word sent a hush through the Throne Room.

"Wh . . . why?" Harcour said. "Why . . . did he let us go? I don't know. He said something about . . . he said—"

"No," the Sheriff said, even quieter. "Why did you come back here?"

Harcour Finks stared up at him, his mouth wide. The hall was almost silent: only the sound of breathing; rangers shuffling their feet.

Finally Harcour said: "I . . . we . . . *saw* it. No, I mean, not saw, you *can't* see it. But it spoke, and we listened. He talked about you, and about a girl, and I knew I had to get back here, to warn . . . to tell . . . to . . ." The ranger trailed off, looked about to drop, but remained suspended there, as if hanging from a noose.

"You were sent to the wildwood with a task," the Sheriff said. "You were told to find this phantom outlaw. To bring me his body, living or dead. Instead, you return here . . . like this. You bring back only your infection." The Sheriff raised his head, but he continued to talk in the same quiet tone. "Mark my words, all of you. This canker—*fear*—I will not allow it to take root within these walls. This man here, look on him . . ."

He lifted a finger. Harcour Finks began to shake.

"This man is riddled with it. Fear has entered his bones, and his marrow. It has wormed inside his heart. Jadder Payne. Take this man to your chambers. Find his fear, all of it. Cut it out."

"I . . . But . . . We couldn't . . . I thought . . . Back here . . . I . . . *No!*" Harcour Finks gabbled as two burly guards hauled him away. Jadder Payne walked wordlessly from the dais and followed.

The Sheriff looked up and raised his voice. "Let it be understood. Those who speak of fear, those who would spread this contagion, I will give them physic and see they are cured." He took out a handkerchief and wiped at his forehead and then at the ruined side of his face. He said: "Where is the other one?"

The crowd parted and Edric Krul came forward, showing his teeth. Two more guards formed his escort but they didn't manhandle him. Will was not surprised: ungodly stories had been circulating about Edric Krul since his return from the wildwood; mostly the other rangers kept as far from him as they could.

As Edric moved forward his skull reflected the flickering torchlight. It was said he forced a bladesmith to forge the metal plate directly onto his scalp, closing over a wound that had refused to heal. His right arm too was a hellish mesh of flesh and metal.

In any case, thought Will, *he won't be around to unnerve the other men very long. Only one question remains: Will it be a swift hanging or something more prolonged?*

Edric stopped at the foot of the dais. There was an audible intake of breath when it was the ranger, not the Sheriff, who spoke first.

"I need knives and nets," Edric said. "Twenty of each. And twelve barrels of poison seed. I'll use men of my own choosing. I'll have none of these innocents. I want the pick of the dungeons. There I will find men and minds prepared."

The Sheriff tipped his head. "You run from the outlaw. You return here with demands?"

Edric Krul stood onto the first step of the dais. He raised his claw. "I return with a promise. My suffering was the price, and it bought me potent knowledge. You, of all people, will understand. I have looked into the workings of this world. The outlaw has two weaknesses, and I have learned them both. He uses the forest as his eyes. Such petty insights, in fact, are the least of it."

The healthy side of the Sheriff's mouth twisted. "So then, enlighten us. How do you intend to capture the menace?"

Edric Krul leered around the room. He moved up two more steps and dropped his voice to a whisper. "There are unfledged children here. They would not even understand these truths, to hear them spoken."

The Sheriff said nothing, only stared. Edric Krul grinned at him and swiveled his eyes at the other rangers and licked his teeth.

"Very well," the Sheriff said. "Come to me in private. We will see what your wisdom is worth."

Edric Krul turned and left the Throne Room, leering. The other rangers muttered darkly but parted to let him through.

Without turning his head, the Sheriff said: "Chief Rider."

Will straightened. The few rangers in front of him gave way. Will walked forward.

"I am keen to return to our usual duties," the Sheriff said. "Prepare your men. Ten in total should suffice. I intend to inspect our working parties. We shall begin on the Sabbath, with Crowcote."

Kluth Rogue spoke at the Sheriff's side. "Have you been shown the charts, sire? Crowcote is on the edge of the Winter Forest. Two garrisons have not yet reported back. Would it be more prudent to—"

"You too, Captain? Has the canker of fear infected you too?"

Kluth Rogue lowered his head and took a step back.

"Chief Rider," the Sheriff said. "We have been distracted too long. Your men."

Will nodded and left the hall.

An hour later, his duties completed, Will headed across the Great Ward. He passed the Inner Keep, and the arsenal, with its roaring of furnaces and *clank-clank* of hammers and rasping of saws. He reached the dungeons and went down a flight of steps, and another, into the gloom. He stood at the first set of iron-clad doors and thumped three times with the hilt of his sword. Eventually bolts rattled and a hatch clacked open. The jailer's face appeared.

"I'm here to see the girl," Will said. "Marian Delbosque."

Grust the jailer made huffing noises through his gums.

"Little lady no more," he said. "Little lady crazed. Broke head on wall." His gums worked again, slurping. "Little lady tough. But hole break them all. Little lady fall to pieces. All done. Huff huff."

The hatch cracked shut and the bolts slid back into place. Will laid a palm against the dungeon door and pressed his forehead to the back of his hand. *This is your doing*, he thought. *Will Scarlett, child-killer.*

He thumped the heavy door and he kept thumping until his fist was raw. *No. This is his fault. Another life consumed by his mad obsession. This has to end, now.*

He turned and went up the steps, blinking into the light.

He checked all their usual haunts. The drinking dens were full of soldiers, whispering among themselves, or drinking stolidly in silence, but Ironside and Borston Black were not among them.

He came at last to the Sign of the Feathered Fox, at the southern edge of the city. He descended the steps into the common room, musty-smelling and dank, a single lamp on the counter the only illumination.

They were there, in the darkest corner, Borston Black stretched across a bench, his boots pulled off, Ironside resting his big frame against a mold-stained wall. Neither of them were wearing their crimson cloaks, but they were known as members of the Sheriff's Guard so no other drinkers sat close. In fact, there were only two other people in the tavern, sitting separately against a far wall, their hoods raised, their heads lowered.

"It's Black's fault," Ironside said, seeing Will peering around the room. "I told him if he didn't bathe this year, we wouldn't make any friends."

"What's up with you, Chief?" Borston Black said. "You look even gloomier than usual."

Will leaned on the table. "Listen, it's starting. It's time to make our move."

Ironside's flagon went down hard. Borston Black swung his feet to the floor.

"Just the three of us?" Borston said. "What have you been drinking? Can I have some?"

"We've been given a chance," Will said. "This Robin Hood. Whoever . . . whatever he is. If even half of what we've heard is true—"

"Taking sides with the outlaw?" Ironside said.

"I don't see we have a choice," Will said. "Is there a single ranger, beyond the three of us, who you'd trust? And we can't go on as we are. We've been doing as children do, squeezing our eyes shut, pretending it's not there. Time to look this horror full in the face."

"But . . . how?" Borston said.

"The Sheriff is riding out, to Crowcote," Will said. "That plays into our hands. Perhaps all we need do is make sure this Robin Hood gets his shot. Afterward, we'll be there to take the reins, put the Guard back on the right path."

Will glanced around the room; the other two drinkers had vanished. "Come on, drink up. I'll tell you about it on the way. Borston, go and get the horses, we'll meet you at the armory. This is our chance, and it might be the only one we're going to get."

XI. The Shadow of Death

Robin returned to the garrison church. He took cover between two gravestones. The storm raged, a powerful wind wailing through shattered crypts. Faint beneath the wind were the voices of the sentries, patrolling the grounds.

"You want to know what I hear," one of the men was saying. "He doesn't kill you quick. He takes you deep into the wildwood, still living. He sits you down while he prepares a woodland banquet."

"Can't you talk about anything else?" the second sentry said.

"He calls it 'feasting the Sheriff's men.' Once you've finished your meal he asks for payment. Ten pounds is his price. And if you don't have the silver you pay with your flesh. He strings you up and eats you alive."

"Can't you change the subject, just this once?"

This time Robin intended to wait for the changing of the guard—only then would he strike. But it wasn't easy to remain patient. In his left hand he gripped the vixen-girl's gift. It shook itself and a savage shiver ran up his arm.

A crack of thunder. The squelching of the sentries' boots. Robin's senses had become keener-edged than ever. One of the guards carried a bared sword—Robin could *hear* the lighting reflecting off its blade. He could *feel* in his skin the sentries' movements through the night air.

The shadow stirred again, tendrils of it flowing between Robin's fingers and encircling his wrist. It became suddenly scalding, then cold as winter-steel. Robin gritted his teeth—he didn't know how much longer he could wait.

"Changing of the guard," came a shout from the garrison at last, followed by the clanging of a bell. "Matins hour. Changing of the guard."

The nave door creaked open, then banged heavily where the wind took hold of it and flung it wide against stone. The sky rumbled. The two sentries hurried inside and their replacements trudged out. The newcomers put their shoulders to the door and struggled to heave it closed against the wind.

The shadow of the wolf fizzed and twisted in Robin's hand. It uncurled itself and swirled. It tugged at him and raged—a caged creature, desperate to be free.

Robin could resist no longer. The shadow hauled him to his feet.

Lightning flared just as one of the sentries turned.

"Up there! It's him! He's here!"

Robin's left arm came up. The shadow shape warped and flowed, bending into the form of a bow.

"Guards! Everyone. Here!"

Within the church sounds of men running, of crossbows being wound, of swords being drawn. The clanging of the bell.

One of the sentries came to his senses, reached for a throwing dagger at his belt . . .

Robin's right arm came up and drew and released, drew and released, and the shadow bow loosed twice—black arrows taking shape and flying—pieces of the night made murderous. There was a noise like the beast inhaling in the cave, devouring all other sound as the arrows flew. And quicker than thought both sentries were dead.

They fell without a splash of blood, without a whimper. As if they had died of pure fear. Or as if their lives had been sucked out. And already Robin was thinking: *Too much. Not like this.*

Shouting at the entrance to the church. More soldiers emerging.

"There he is. With me."

"Take him alive."

But the rangers did not rush at Robin. Because this time their quarry wasn't running. Instead he stood above them in the graveyard, his head tipped forward and to one side, the amber eyes of his hood flashing as lightning flared. He held the shadow bow horizontally at chest height, the weapon weaving and misting in front of the soldiers' eyes.

For a moment nobody flinched. The rangers just stared.

Then someone raised a crossbow.

"Wait," another soldier shouted. "Don't—"

But Robin's right arm was already on the move, drawing and letting loose. The shadow weapon expanded, contracted, expanded, contracted. Dread arrows flew—each one making that monstrous breathing noise—and three more soldiers fell.

Too much. No. Not this.

More rangers emerging. The baleful bow flexed and pulsed and kept shooting. With each killing its power grew. The next arrow took the form of a shadow serpent, flowing inside a gaping mouth; another was a comet of black flame, engulfing a ranger in dark fire; a third trailed legs, like a monster insect, wrapping itself around a man's neck; the next was a demon maw, roaring wide as it flew.

The soldiers slumped, their weapons falling noiselessly

against stone, their screams muted, even the storm silenced while the weapon worked, all sound swallowed into the shadow-void.

No, no. They don't all need to die. Not this way.

But it was too late to turn back—the shadow weapon would not allow it—it hauled Robin toward the church. He stepped over corpses, through the nave door, the storm raging at his back.

More men were inside, weapons drawn. But they were far too slow. The shadow bow breathed and arrows formed and flew and the men died—each of them in their last moment seeing the thing they feared most: a storm of fire; a childhood fiend; a father's face. And each time the shadow pulsed stronger, gorging on their fear.

Clattering sounds: the remaining rangers dropping their swords.

"We're unarmed," one of them said. "We'll walk away. On Christ's bones I swear, I'll leave my cloak here and I'll go back home. There's no need for this."

Robin moved forward; the shadow weapon simmered.

"Mother's mercy," another man said. "There are women and children here."

Robin knew this was true: He could hear them shuffling in their hiding places. A miller and his wife pressed against each other. Two forester's children. A ranger's wife and their baby son. Robin listened to their frightened breathing and he fought to lower his arm. But the writhing, twisting thing would not stay still. It tugged at him, and raged. It shook and seethed.

One of the soldiers made a sudden movement. The bow leaped in Robin's hand. It warped and flowed, flicking out and back, throwing death into the corners of the church. The amorphous arrows howled through pew and altar, stone and wood, to reach their targets. The remaining rangers died, one of them crashing through the rood screen, another slumping across a cadaver tomb, bones skittering across the floor.

They're dead. All of them, dead.

No, not quite all . . .

There were other living things in this church. Allies and friends and aides to the Sheriff's troops. The miller moving around his wife, trying to use his body as a shield. The children cowering beneath the pulpit. The clatter of a misericord where somebody else was trying to crawl away.

Robin took aim at each of these people in turn, the shadow weapon seething in his hand, demanding he finish this work. He fought, tried to force his arm down, his muscles screaming with the effort, his whole body shaking. The shadow raging, desperate to destroy anything that breathed, even the rats in the rafters and the miller's mangy old cat. Even the child in that woman's arms.

He fought and struggled to keep the weapon still.

He battled not to let loose.

Finally he won. Hissing through his teeth, he managed to lower his arm. The bow shuddered; its form fell apart. The shadow swirled and snaked back into his palm. He fell to his knees and stayed there, breathing hard, listening to the wailing of the infant.

Too much. Not this. Never again.

He dragged himself to his feet and staggered out of the church and went back the way he had come.

He lurched back to Winter Forest. He went to the water hole where he had fought the Wargwolf.

With a herculean effort he tore the shadow weapon from his arm. It came free in pieces, with a sucking sound, taking with it sheets of steaming skin. Flesh tore too, deep as the bone, blue and glistening. The pain was immense. He didn't care. He ripped at it and ripped, and the thing shrieked and howled—spewing its devoured sounds—and finally it shredded loose. He threw it into the water. It wriggled away, like a swimming snake. He slumped to the earth, clutching his mangled arm. Only then did he realize the girl of the forest was there.

"Casting it *away*?" she said, in a soft puzzled voice. Then: "No, no, no, you mustn't!"

She dived into the pool. Splashing sounds. Silence.

Robin was physically sick. Those soldiers had thrown down their swords. Yet still they had died.

But the worst thing had been the urge: that surge of power that insisted he destroy every living thing in that church—even the infant in that woman's arms. And the feeling that to have done it would have been a triumph . . .

He realized Cernunnos was there too, beneath the willow trees.

"I told you there would be a price. Did you think it would be paid by you alone?"

"Never again. It wasn't me, it was her."

"This is only the beginning. She will recover the shadow. She will offer you worse. She's told you of the blood and the teeth?"

"Never."

"You still have no idea, what you have become. The extent of your new form. It is so much greater than quick deed and violent action. It is limitless. But she will keep it all buried beneath rage and hatred. Such a waste. Such a waste . . ."

A noise like the cracking of old bark. The old man bowed his head, turned, and disappeared.

XII. Bearer of Bad News

Will Scarlett was halfway across the river when an arrow thunked into the log, narrowly missing his toes. "Go back," he said.

Borston Black shuffled backward and Will followed.

Thunk.

A second arrow landed where Will had been standing a moment before. They retreated faster, their boots slipping on the slimy log. They found themselves back on the bank. A third arrow sank into the soil at their feet.

"I guess that's a no," said Borston Black.

"I think he made himself clear," said Ironside. "So that's that. Time to forget this whole business."

Will looked at these two veteran rangers, both of them built like barrels, with fists like hammers. Two of the toughest, bravest warriors Will had ever known. Like him they had survived wars and ocean storms and a five-year crusade. Yet if Will didn't know better he would say at this moment they were afraid. And it wasn't plotting against the Sheriff that had unnerved them. Instead, it was this place: the wildwood, lurking the other side of the river. *Not that I can blame them*, Will thought. *But if I show fear now this is over.*

He unclipped the baldric from his back and laid his scabbard and Saracen sword on the ground. "I'm here to help you," he called across the river. "I'm coming over alone. Unarmed."

Borston Black laid a hand on his shoulder. "You know how this goes, Will. Rangers go in that forest, they don't come back out."

"I have to take the risk. I don't think he'll attack an unarmed man. Besides, I think we've met before."

I just hope he remembers me in a good light, Will thought.

He stepped onto the crossing. "We can help each other," he called.

An arrow landed just in front of his toes. He stepped over it and continued across the log.

I hope I'm right about this.

Another arrow landed; he stepped over it and continued. He forced himself to walk as tall and as steady as he was able, while he listened with dread for the whisper of the third arrow. He felt Ironside and Borston Black watching him, holding their breath.

There was no third arrow. He reached the far bank and pushed through the undergrowth, into the forest.

"If you had come here a week ago, you would be dead," a voice said. "I want one more life, then it's finished."

Will stared in the direction of the voice, but he could see no sign of Robin Hood.

"We want the same thing," Will said. "I've come to bring you information. In two days' time the Sheriff travels to a village. Crowcote. It's on the edge of Winter Forest. This is your opportunity—he seldom travels this far from the city. We'll help you do it, if we can."

Something moved in the undergrowth. High in the branches a jay shrieked in alarm.

"I recognize your voice," Robin said. "You were there, the day they took her."

Every sound in the wildwood became horribly distinct: the droning of a hornet, the shuffling of something in the leaves. The creaking of a bow being drawn?

"You tracked us through the forest. If it wasn't for you, Marian would have gotten away."

The hornet buzzed louder.

"I was following orders," Will said. "If I had refused . . . there were ten men ready to take my place. If it had been done by another guard . . . it might have been done crudely. She was not harmed, not so long as I was—"

"Where is she now?"

Will took a deep breath, gathered his courage. "She . . . is dead. I'm sorry. She was brave—braver than I could have been. But it was too much for her, in the end. She . . . chose to take her own life."

A choking sound drifted from the trees.

"I did everything I could," Will said. "I took her food and curatives."

The choking sound grew thicker and became a wailing noise—a sound of limitless anguish and anger. Will battled the urge to bolt from the forest.

"Marian helped me see what must be done," Will said. "That's all we can do for her now—continue as she would have wished. I believe we have a chance, together."

He used his cloak to wipe the cold sweat from his brow. He looked up—and finally he caught sight of Robin Hood. The outlaw was standing no more than twenty paces away. His body was shuddering, and it was this movement that caught Will's eye and made Robin faintly visible through the branches and the leaves. The animal pelt that formed his cloak was wrapped close and fell as far as his feet. The cloak was mottled brown and dotted with moss and buzzing with insects—just another part of the wildwood—so it was almost as though Will was looking *through* him.

Had Robin raised his bow? Or was that just another branch, crossing the figure at chest height?

The choking, wailing grew louder, then abruptly stopped. Robin became once more as still as a deer and Will had to concentrate hard to stop his outline fading from sight.

"You deserve . . . to die today," Robin said, his voice faltering. "But others have died in your stead. Leave this place. Never return."

Will lowered his eyes and let out a long breath. By the time he looked up Robin had disappeared.

Marian is dead.

Robin knelt on the cold earth, perfectly still, squeezing his arrowhead amulet, the jade cutting his palm. He was weathering a storm of horrendous visions: all she must have suffered at the hands of the Sheriff.

Chose to take her own life.

He rose unsteadily to his feet, went to the tree line. He listened to the soldiers riding away. Why had he let them live? Why should they continue with their lives while Marian had to die?

He drew a short-feathered flight arrow. They were three hundred paces away; if he was going to do it he would have to do it now. He nocked the arrow.

As he did so a creeping sensation began in his bow hand—the way cold liquid seeps through your chest, or when fear makes your blood run cold. The feeling grew more intense and began to spread.

Something was moving across his skin—no, *beneath* his skin. Black threads, thin as the veins in a leaf, were spreading upward from his left hand. He felt them flow quicker, up past his elbow, twining around his shoulder—he heard them making a splintering noise, the way an iced lake cracks before it gives way beneath your feet.

Robin thought he had discarded the shadow weapon, but now he understood a shard of it remained. It had seeped inside and lurked there, waiting . . .

The shadow veins continued to spread, at first gossamer thin, but then beginning to pulse and swell, like rootlets drinking in the rain. They rippled across his chest, down his right arm. He felt them leak deeper, into his muscles and his bones.

They tugged tight—a puppet master pulling strings—Robin's bow rose. His right arm drew the bowstring. He took aim at Will Scarlett.

The soldiers were four hundred paces away. Too late. Out of range. But the shadow threads twisted tighter, creaking as they became taut, adding strength to Robin's arms and chest. At the same time the shadow spread from his fingers into his bow, splinters of it encircling the point of his arrow, gifting power and weight and extra killing edge.

Five hundred paces away, yet *still* he could do it. It was no more than these men deserved. It would be a measure of revenge, for her . . .

The shadow veins bubbled up through his skin and snaked around his left arm. They shook and shivered, while his anger burned, urging him to shoot . . .

And that was why he didn't let loose. That was why he relaxed the bowstring and fought to lower his arm. He had to prove he was not the shadow weapon's slave.

Shaking, shuddering, he managed to remove the arrow and unstring his bow. The shadow threads merged and swirled and flowed like black mist, being drawn back across his body and down into his left hand, and then they faded to gray and were gone. At the same time he felt all his anger draining away, to be replaced by . . . almost nothing. A cold, deep emptiness.

She's dead. It's over.

And suddenly he knew, without question, what he would do next. In his mind rose the screams of all the soldiers he had killed—and worse, the silence of those who had died in that garrison church—and he knew he was finished with all this violence and death. It had all been for nothing, because Marian was gone, and nothing could bring her back. Even revenge now seemed an unreal and unimportant thing.

Nothing remained for him, in this world of man. So then, he would cast it off forever, go deep into the wilderness and shed the last scrap of his human skin. He knew he could do it because twice before he felt himself slipping into the quietude of the green. He would live deep in Winter Forest, the way Cernunnos had all this time, unconcerned with human things.

There was only one thing he needed to do first. He picked his way unsteadily through the forest, stumbling toward Wodenhurst.

XIII. Good-bye to Old Ghosts

Dazed with grief, Robin staggered toward the valley of his birth. He reached the wildwood edge and crouched there above Wodenhurst. Before he faded forever into the green, he felt the need to come back here. He couldn't say exactly why. To remember his family, fully, for the final time? To say good-bye to his old self, and to Marian, and the life they might have had?

He sank into the web of green, probing the details of the valley below, searching for a safe route—his forest-mind nosing through the grass with a vole, taking flight with the bees, sweeping down Herne Hill on the wings of a swift, scurrying into the village with the fleas on the back of a brown rat.

What he finds there is . . . his old village . . . and yet . . . what has happened here? Wodenhurst now is little more than a husk. A charcoal patch marks where the hayloft has burned to the ground; ditches and fences are rotting and overgrown; the waterwheel is silent.

Numbly, he discovers something worse, far worse. The Trystel Tree has been destroyed. The body of it lies twisted and shattered, houses flattened beneath. Even the tree's stump has been torn from the earth. *Why would anyone do that? And how? These are the ways of man. Leave it all behind.*

Probing farther, borrowing the ears of domestic cats that stalk the rats between the homes, he discovers no people. His forest-mind sweeps back out of the village, taking flight on the tattered wings of a crow, leaping with the grasshoppers in a wild flower meadow, finally shivering amid the barley on the opposite slopes of the valley. He finds the villagers there in the fields, every pair of hands pulling weeds.

So, a clear path to the house.

Leaving the forest, crossing the spirit fence, Robin went through High Field, and down Herne Hill, then through the orchard and the croft. And here he was, outside his old home, crouching beneath the window he had leaped through countless times when he was young.

He felt cold and hollow, his senses unusually dulled, so when he heard a clicking sound he put it down to a creature's teeth working in the thatch.

He circled the house, went inside. He was met by silence. The absence of his mother's singing, of his brothers' laughter, hung thickly in the air. The home he remembered smelled of crushed apples, and sweet woodruff in the rushes on the floor. Now this house had a deathly odor: a family of dead rats left to rot in the rafters.

Already he wished he hadn't come back here. Why he would want to torture himself like this?

Then another thought struck him.

The village was not deserted, after all.

There's someone here. In this room.

She was sitting still and silent in the gloom, the same way Robin had in the weeks after he had lost his eyes. Her one good hand gripped the distaff that had made the clicking sound Robin heard from outside.

"It's you, isn't it?" It was Mabel Felstone's voice, but thin as water. "You've returned to us," she said. "I knew you would, one day. I think it's kept me alive. The idea I would get to say sorry. Please. Sit with me. This creeping death has stolen my sight, but I know it must be you. Come closer. I'll know your face with my fingers."

Robin stepped back toward the door.

Mabel sighed. "I can't blame you," she said. "We pushed you away last time. We didn't want you here to remind us of what we did. What we didn't do. At least . . . before you go . . . let me tell you a story. Allow me to do that much for you. It is a tale you should have heard long ago."

Robin hesitated at the doorway.

Mabel sucked breaths that died wheezing in her chest.

"This story . . . ," she said, "is about a headman of a village. He was a farmer and a father . . . and a woodsman and a hunter. And he was the noblest man you could ever meet."

Robin came back into the room.

"One day . . . ," Mabel said, "while he was tracking a white hart through Winter Forest, the headman heard the crying of a child. He abandoned his quarry and followed the sound. Sometimes, when the crying was faint and his way faltered, there was a robin, hopping branch to branch, leading him on with its song. He came to a yew tree, hollow with age. Inside was an infant, barely hours old."

Robin stood above Mabel. "I know you're talking about my father," he said. "Why don't you just say so? You're saying he found me, in Winter Forest. You're saying he wasn't my father at all."

"Yes," Mabel said. "These are the truths we should have told you, long ago. Robert Loxley was not your father, by birth or blood. But in any case he brought you back to his home. He and his wife, Alma, cared for you as one of their own."

It was the strangest sensation, hearing this. The words cut through Robin—a physical shock. Yet at the same time the truth of these things settled, with barely a ripple, into Robin's story of himself.

Robert Loxley was not your real father, by birth or blood. Yes, it was true. The moment he heard it spoken, he realized a part of him had known this his entire life.

"So that's what it means," Robin said. " 'Winter-born.' It means I was found in the wildwood."

"Yes," Mabel said. "That is part of it, yes. Winter-born. Forest child. Named for the robin that helped lead the way to your crib in that tree." Her voice was growing quieter and by now was barely louder than the *blip, blip* of her heartbeat. "At first your arrival here was the cause of celebration. The people of Wodenhurst, they . . . we . . . regarded you as a blessing from the forest gods. The promise of bounty to come. But then . . . then we suffered our first failed crop. Some said it was your fault. When sheep caught the red death. When fields flooded. When cattle drowned. Time and again, you were blamed. There were those who said you belonged to the forest—that our fortunes would not improve until you were returned. These people began to fear you, and with fear comes hatred."

As Mabel spoke Robin was remembering the way he had been treated in Wodenhurst, particularly after his family disappeared. He pictured Narris Felstone and Swet Woolward and the others coming for him armed with sticks.

And it was only then Robin noticed the villagers were returning from the fields. Those in the lead had already crossed Mill Bridge.

"Finish the story," he said. "Tell it quicker. Does anyone know who my real parents are? Why was I left in the wildwood, as a baby?"

"Something you must understand, Robin, and never doubt it. Robert and Alma Loxley, and Thane and Hal. They were a real family to you. They fought for you."

"Then why did they abandon me? Where are they now? Are they dead?"

"The years passed," Mabel said. "You became the healthiest, strongest, quickest of boys. We began to hear stories about other winter-born, rescued from the wildwood, raised in other homes. We heard how the Sheriff was searching for them, destroying whole villages in his search. Some of the men from Wodenhurst, Nute Highfielde and Freeman Byeford among them, rot their souls, they—"

Narris Felstone walked into the house. He froze, staring at the man-beast standing over his mother. A gurgling noise broke from his throat as he staggered back outside and returned swinging a hand ax. Pots and bowls and candles exploded or were scattered. He was shouting now—an incoherent yell.

Robin kept the table between them. The ax thudded into the wood. Robin moved around Narris and out of the house. Others must have heard the commotion—the hue and cry was rising. Villagers were picking up dung forks, scythes, burning brands, and they were coming up the hill, stopping dead when they first set eyes on Robin but then running on, shouting, when they saw he was fleeing for the forest.

Robin felt their fury and their fear as a swarm of red noise. He was tempted to turn with his bow and send them scuttling back the way they had come. But no. No matter how they treated him, he would not act the monster. And already he had decided to leave the world of man. This was merely the final push. He had wanted to say good-bye to the happy times he had known, but even that had been denied him. He had almost heard the full truth, at last, but that too he would live without . . .

To the top of Herne Hill, across Woden's Ride, into Winter Forest, and not slowing down but rather running faster, heading deeper into the dark, never to return. The idea bringing with it release, but also further sorrow. Memories of his family—the people who were his family and always would be, no matter what. The river sparkling where he went with his brothers to fish. His father cutting him his first hunting bow.

But saving his final thoughts for her, of course.

Marian, I'm sorry.

I miss you. I failed you.

I'm sorry.

XIV. The Bait

The headman of Crowcote was still alive by the time the flames reached high enough to lick around his chest. The valley was thick with the sound of his screaming and the noise of the balefire as it began at last to fully roar.

Will Scarlett looked away. He had seen enough men die at the stake. He had seen the way the fat drips and bubbles from the ends of their fingers; he had watched their eyeballs begin to melt from their faces while they are yet still living; he had no desire to see another such death. And Jadder Payne was in charge of these executions—a guarantee of prolonged suffering. The torturer had ensured the balefires were built mostly from green wood so they would smolder and smoke and the condemned would be slow-cooked while their skins blackened. Jadder Payne stood now in front of the dying man, gauging his craft.

The executions were being staged at the eastern edge of the village. While the first man burned the other four waited, tied to their posts. One of them had twisted his head and was staring at the burning man, transfixed, eyes mad with horror. *Would the waiting be as bad as the pain itself?* Will thought.

Meanwhile, in the center of the village, the other peasants were even now being made to proceed with their work, sawing and hacking at their Trystel Tree. This labor had been going on for weeks, a garrison of guards stationed in Crowcote to oversee the work. And yet still the colossal oak showed barely a scratch. Many of the villagers, in contrast, looked broken. Even as Will watched he saw one exhausted farmer collapse, still gripping his blunted ax in a claw-like hand.

Crowcote stood on a slight incline, and was separated from Winter Forest by five or six oxgang of plowing land, freshly sown, dotted with green shoots. Several crossbowmen now stomped across these fields. Nearer the tree line pikemen patrolled, their shields raised. Longbowmen had taken up position in the village itself.

Twice as many men as I assembled, Will thought. It was not unlike the Sheriff to change arrangements at the last moment, keeping his real intentions obscured even from his most senior men. But still, Will felt a shiver of unease. *Is he more afraid of the outlaw than he's willing to admit? Or is something else happening here?*

Borston Black and Ironside were stationed among the guards at the western end of the village. Will felt them staring at him. He didn't turn to meet their gaze.

The death wails of the burning man were increasing in volume. One of his fellow condemned began calling from his unlit pyre: "I demand my right to trial by combat. I call the Sheriff a coward and a liar. If he isn't man enough to face me himself, let him choose a champion. Are all his men so frightened?"

The Sheriff sat unmoved by the man's entreaties. His black mare pawed at the soil and he stroked her neck with a gloved hand, clicked his tongue to calm her. Will waited with the Sheriff at the southern end of the village, next to a stone well-head that had been garlanded with dried flowers. Behind them three captains sat silently in their saddles.

"My horse has been unusually skittish," the Sheriff said. "Animals can smell thunderstorms, is that not so, Chief Rider? I have often thought they possess other faculties denied to people. They can taste fear, or hear betrayal, perhaps. She senses trouble of some sort, of that I'm certain."

"Most likely it's the smell of burning flesh," Will said. "I've not known a horse yet it won't unnerve."

The Sheriff smiled slightly. "Yes," he said. "Perhaps."

The wind changed direction, sending blue-black smoke billowing south. The Sheriff put one hand beneath his breastplate and took out a cloth pouch, stuffed with herbs and petals. He pushed the scapular to his nose and took deep breaths.

"I sense, Chief Rider, you have no appetite for our task here today."

This took Will off guard. A moment passed before he replied.

"Speaking plainly, sire, there are bandit companies running amok in the eastern shires. There are crime lords conducting their own private wars. And here we are, with a whole battalion, because these shire-folk chose to speak their prayers beneath a sacred oak."

"Others see matters differently," the Sheriff said. "Bishop Raths feels we are still being too soft in our war with the old gods. If he were here, he would be entreating me to burn every one of those peasants as heretics. The children included. However, I believe these five men will suffice. This smell will carry for miles, and will carry our message with it. And I agree with the Inquisitor on that point at least: The message is of vital importance."

The wind swirled again and brought the foul miasma to Will's tongue. The Sheriff breathed through his scapular, before clearing his throat. "After all," he said, "is it not our

God-given duty to keep order in this realm? If we allow every man to pick and choose his own idol, to worship a hallowed spring, to propitiate a sacred stream, how can we expect anything but pandemonium?"

Once more the defiant prisoner called out: "The Sheriff is a coward. Him and all his men. Spineless, every one. I demand trial by combat."

Will had to admire this man's courage. His fellow condemned had dropped their chins to their chests; two of them were visibly shaking and the other had gone deathly still. But this fourth man kept his head raised and continued to repeat his demands and provocations in a clear, even tone. *Little good it will do you*, Will thought. *You may as well try drawing blood from a stone.*

The Sheriff peeled off his kidskin gloves. He examined one perfectly clean set of nails and then the other. "But I anticipated your unease, Chief Rider. I know what sort of man you are, at your core. You are a man of sweat and blood and steel. You would rather be battling outlaws than keeping watch over peasants or hunting demons of the forest. But come, do you see no glory in this work? The Inquisitor believes we are on the verge of extinguishing the old gods forever. Think of that. Think how the scribes will record—"

He broke off. Something was happening at the edge of the village. The defiant prisoner had turned away from the Sheriff and had taken to cursing the rangers closest to him, calling them cowards and weaklings and worse. One of the rangers had snapped. Horor Conrad advanced on the unlit balefire. He took a stiletto blade from his belt and Will thought he was going to slit the prisoner's throat. Instead, he used the blade to sever the rope binding the man's wrists. He did it none too subtly and when the villager stumbled from the balefire and fell to his knees he was bleeding freely from his forearms.

Horor Conrad turned and spread his arms wide. "I declare myself champion of the Sheriff's Guard. I declare I will cut this worm into pieces and leave him for the birds. I declare that when I'm finished he will wish he had shut his mouth and taken the fire. You got anything more to say, worm?"

The villager had been tied to that stake for many hours and now it appeared to be a struggle just getting to his feet.

"My name is Much Millerson," he said slowly. "I declare myself champion of Crowcote. This is our home. I ask God, or the gods, whichever of them is listening, grant me strength to defend it." He looked at Horor Conrad and then at the Sheriff. "If I win," he said, "you must leave this place and never return."

Much Millerson had hands large as cartwheels and a face like a flattened boulder. *But his size won't help him,* Will thought. No farmer would be a match for Horor Conrad. The Prime Marshall was a born killer who had grown up knife-fighting in the city's roughest dens. He had the face to prove it: his chin and forehead were crossed with scars; he had half an ear missing and a patch over one eye.

The Prime Marshall took a second stiletto blade from his belt and tossed it at his opponent's feet. Much Millerson shook his head and left the dagger where it fell. Horor Conrad shrugged and showed his teeth. A boy, around ten years old, ran over from the village. He was holding two wide strips of leather. Much Millerson held out his hands and the boy began to wrap one strip around each set of knuckles.

At Will's side, the Sheriff had stiffened, his displeasure clear. "Horor Conrad was ever a blunt tool. I have watched him closely, to see if he might shape his raw anger to his advantage, but I must admit he never will. He will never understand himself well enough for that. A man who does not know himself is like a blacksmith who has not learned one tool from another. He spends his life thrashing around. All heat and no finished product. Is that not so?"

At the foot of the execution ridge, the boy was still wrapping Much Millerson's knuckles. Horor Conrad didn't wait for them to finish. He came forward, moving on the balls of his feet, flicking the blade from one hand to the other. Much Millerson raised a palm just in time to block a knife thrust to his face. He went into a fist-fighter's crouch, his big shoulders flexing. Horor Conrad stabbed at his stomach, then up at his eyes. He changed his grip to overhand, slashed at his opponent's ribs.

Much Millerson barely seemed to move, yet he must have been quicker than he looked, because most of Horor Conrad's thrusts were missing. Other attacks the big villager blocked with his open palm, the dagger glancing harmlessly off leather.

Horor Conrad's smile disappeared. He came forward in a frenzy, jabbing at his opponent's midriff. And in the next instant the Prime Marshall was on the ground, his knife flung to one side. Much Millerson had hit him just once, blood exploding from the ranger's nose.

Much Millerson allowed him the time to get up: He just stood there, swaying slightly in his scrapper's stance. The Prime Marshall lurched upright. He seemed to be looking for his dropped knife. He gave up and stumbled at his opponent with his fists raised. Much Millerson hit him twice more, once in the stomach and once on the jaw. Horor Conrad slumped to the ground, spread-eagled, and this time he didn't stir.

A hush fell across the entire valley. The burning man ceased his gurgling sounds and slumped senseless. Even the crows spiraling above Winter Forest stopped their raucous noise. Will felt the villagers holding their breath. A final moment of hope.

The Sheriff raised his voice but kept his words slow and even. "A fine demonstration. A diverting entertainment. But futile. The Sheriff's Guard does not recognize your old ways, it thinks nothing of your wildwood rituals, and it does not abide by your savage idea of justice. You were found guilty of heresy. You will burn. Marshall Rogue, tie that man to his post. If he resists, kill every man, woman, and child in Crowcote. Starting with the boy there."

Much Millerson was saying something to the crying boy and pushing him gently away as Kluth Rogue and two other rangers herded Much back to the balefire. There was the crack of a whip and the knocking of an ax as the villagers were put back to work. The crows had taken up their squabbling.

Will looked up at the wildwood. There had been no sign of Robin Hood, and now he could only think that was a good thing. There were too many rangers here; they would cut down the outlaw before he came within five hundred yards of the Sheriff.

Stay away, Robin Hood. Save yourself for a fairer fight. Even as Will was thinking this yet more soldiers were arriving, their leader nodding to the Sheriff as they passed. But it was what followed behind the soldiers that caught Will's eye and caused a lump to rise in his throat.

"Here now," the Sheriff said. "I hope this will speed proceedings."

The new squad was followed by a carter, the man at the head of four packhorses. On the back of the cart was an A-frame scaffold, and suspended from the scaffold by chains was a star-shaped gibbet: the type of hanging cage known as a crow's companion. Inside the gibbet, her arms and legs out-stretched, was a half-naked young woman. Her body was covered in savage wounds, her face was partially obscured by the crossbars that held her in place, but despite all this Will recognized her immediately. He recognized her lustrous dark hair; her striking angular features; her full lips and large eyes. Those eyes had turned a kind of milky white—perhaps from so long kept in the dark, or because of blood loss. But Will knew, as the lump thickened in his throat, what color those eyes had once been.

Varicolored eyes of gray and green.

"Marian Delbosque," he said quietly. "I was told she was dead."

The Sheriff turned in his saddle, his teeth grinning where the lips had burned away. "Come now, Chief Rider. You know, better than anyone, what effort I expended in capturing this girl. Did you think I would simply allow her to die in the oubliette? It suited my purpose to let people believe she had. But I did not imagine my own Chief Rider would be fooled."

The cart crossed the rutted common ground, the gibbet rocking on its chains. Will couldn't help staring at Marian, cataloging her wounds.

"Once more, Jadder Payne has done his work superbly," the Sheriff said. "She will not live much longer. But she will survive long enough to serve a purpose. It is not the role I hoped she would play. But a vital part just the same."

The cart reached the Trystel Tree. The four new soldiers threw chains up over a branch and began hoisting the crow's companion into the boughs.

"The King's Sheriff must have secrets, even from his Chief Rider," the Sheriff said. "The fact is, I did not come here merely to watch heretics burn. I have something more important in mind. This . . . Robin Hood. I hoped my presence here would be enough to lure him into the open. After all, he has been boasting of how he intends to kill me."

The gibbet rose to meet its supporting branch. Two magpies came immediately to investigate and began pecking at the bloody mess inside. Marian didn't scream at this fresh torment—a brace held her jaw shut so she was prevented from making a sound.

"But you know I never leave anything to chance, Chief Rider. So we will set our trap with double bait. And here she is. All we need do now is wait."

Will looked once more at the pikemen and archers. And he glanced again at Marian, before looking up at the wild-wood. *Stay away, Robin Hood*, he thought. *She can't be saved. Enough lives have ended here. Don't add your life to the pyre.*

XV. The Heartwood

You know this place—this realm of ancient darkness.
        Your wolf-self remembers. It calls to you.
    But there are depths here even you cannot fathom—like the pri-mordial reaches of the ocean—there are things living here never glimpsed by human eyes. What would they look like to you, if you could see them? What stories could you tell if you managed to return to the light?
    This is the realm of forgotten gods; the home of nymphs and naiads and faerie stuff. There is danger here, make no mistake. The black-ness of madness and forgetting. But even this is preferable to the ways of man, so you head deeper and deeper into the unknown, yearning for the seclusion and the silence; the regeneration and the nurture. The opposite of man and all his tortures.
    You keep going, farther and farther into the nameless dark.

Robin follows badger paths, thousands of years old, deep into the wildwood, past the glade where he first met Cernunnos, and deeper still, and now into realms where he is sure no other person has ever set foot.

It is midday, and the sun bright above, but here beneath the cathedral trees it is almost nocturnal and growing cold. Towering beech trees are wrapped in ropes of ivy and creeping vine; every inch of forest floor and rock and fallen log is coated with a deep carpet of moss. He keeps moving and the forest grows denser still. He can sense the wolf pelt changing, darkening to the black of shadows.

It is teeming with life here, despite the gloom. Above the water holes mosquitoes are so numerous Robin has to keep one hand clamped to his nose and mouth to keep them out. Flies and bees are noisy on the ivy and the rowan trees. They are busy too on Robin—the wolf fur is crawling with insects— nesting, burrowing bodies that Robin can feel on his skin and *beneath* his skin. He no longer brushes them away or crushes them; they are a part of all this and so is he. He feels them leaving their eggs, nurturing their grubs in him the way he is nurtured by this place, and all of this feels correct. He feels heady, almost mad, with the idea of surrendering to the wild- wood and never going back. Soon, just as soon as he finds the true heart of Winter Forest—a little farther yet—he will lie down and allow the wilderness to grow over him. He will feel its roots twining with his veins, his bones fusing with the stones of the forest floor. How easy it will be to cast off the last scraps of his human skin and sink into the green and be at peace.

He pushes on, hunting and foraging as he goes. A monster oak has fallen, and in the warm glade created a fawn hides in the grass while its mother feeds on flower heads. He hears the hind limping away, feigning injury, trying to distract Robin from her young. He ignores mother and baby and continues on his way, stopping instead to dig up the tuber roots of dead men's fingers. In fallen tree bark he finds wolf spiders, fat and juicy with their egg sacs still attached, and he is pleased. He sucks them down whole.

He moves on, seeking the heart of the wildwood. But even now he is struggling to forget all that has happened. Before

she was interrupted by Narris, Mabel Felstone had not finished her story—still he did not know who his real parents
were or what happened to the people he thought were his
family, or why they abandoned him.

It makes no difference, he tells himself. *They're gone. It doesn't
matter who did what. It doesn't matter if they deserved their fate or
not. Did I deserve all that has happened to me? There is no such thing
as justice, right or wrong, there is only the weak and the strong.*

Robin's family had been weak, and so they were unable to
protect him. Marian, for all her cleverness, was weak also, and
so she had suffered and died. That is the way of the world.
That is all there is.

The victors and the vanquished. The quick and the dead.

Listen here: a goshawk, imperious on its killing stand, the
feathers of a hundred songbirds littering the ground. It has a
fresh bullfinch in its talons and is ripping it apart in shreds.
And feel this: a fallen tree, still wrapped in the python-vines
that strangled it to death. *It is the same here*, Robin thinks. *There
is no justice, natural or otherwise. There is only the mighty and the
fallen. The weak and the strong.*

And then another thought rises. An idea he has long been
trying to keep buried. *I am the strong. I am the strongest.*

He stops near a beaver lake and he hears the beavers slapping their tails on the water, warning that a top predator is
near. In the trees jays shriek their two-tone alarm. Squirrel
bucks quit their games and head for higher boughs.

Everything here fears me.

And that is how it should be . . .

He turns and listens to distant noises he had been trying
to ignore. He sends his senses into the green, searching for
the cause of this disturbance he can feel rippling through the
roots. Yes, there it is: A village on the edge of the forest. There
is fighting there, and fire and death.

Robin senses one man in particular. A man dressed all in black, one side of his face like melted wax.

Here is the man who stole Marian and robbed Robin of his eyes.

Everything should fear me. That man most of all.

He probes further and he senses the suffering this man is causing. The fear and misery of villagers. A man burning alive. And . . . somebody else there . . . someone arriving on the back of a cart . . .

A person in a cage. A young woman, tortured and dying.

Dying because of Robin.

He runs, heading for that village, following deer trails and badger paths, the undergrowth opening before him, allowing him passage, blackthorn and bramble drawing in their claws. He runs faster, gripping his bow, stringing it as he goes, muttering a prayer to the forest that he won't be too late.

XVI. Mercy Killing

The four newly arrived soldiers, once they had finished hoisting Marian into the Trystel Tree, made their way toward the southern edge of the village.

"I must apologize, Chief Rider," the Sheriff said. "I have continued to keep you in the dark. In fact, there is a third matter we must resolve here today. Not as vital as the phantom outlaw perhaps, but significant, nonetheless." As he spoke he looked behind him and nodded. The three captains of the guard were stepping their horses forward. The four new arrivals were approaching Will from the front.

It all happened so fast.

Will was still reeling from the shock of seeing Marian, near death in that cage. By the time he realized what was happening, by the time he had reached over his shoulder for his sword, the soldiers were on him from both sides and he felt a wet crack at the back of his head and the world pitched forward and turned black.

Will blinked. His head throbbed and felt icy cold. He couldn't move his arms. Something hard was pushing against his spine. He found he was sitting upright against the stone wellhead, his hands tied. He looked blearily to the western edge of the village and he saw Ironside and Borston Black were similarly restrained. He looked around the rest of the village, getting his bearings. On the eastern ridge, Jadder Payne had lit the fire beneath Much Millerson's feet. Horor Conrad had regained his senses and stood in front of the smoldering pyre, holding a cloth to his ruined nose.

The Sheriff looked down at Will. "Good, you are still with us. If Marshall Treadfire had killed you, I would have been displeased. You and I are going to spend many days together before I allow you to die. For you there will be nothing so quick or merciful as a balefire." He looked up at the forest, before turning once more to Will. "I meant what I said earlier about anger, about how it must be molded to best use. My fury, at this moment, could not be topped even by God. And yet, would you know it? Do I not appear composed, on the surface? I shall need my fury when you and I arrive back at the castle. I do not intend a single drop of it to go to waste."

Will tried to speak, but his tongue felt too big for his mouth. "Let e uffersss go," he managed to mumble. "If aa nuffffin to do wiff em."

"Marshall Treadfire," the Sheriff said. "Give the traitor something to loosen his tongue."

Sansom Treadfire knelt and tipped a drinking bladder, pouring ale across Will's face. Will began to work some life into his mouth.

"Why are you holding Ironside and Borston Black?" he said slowly. "They have nothing to do with this. They tried to talk me out of it."

"Very noble," the Sheriff said. "But, no, I know their part, the same as I know yours. You should understand, better than anyone, that nothing happens in this realm without my learning of it. I have ears and eyes everywhere. I know those two traveled to Winter Forest with you, to make a deal with the outlaw. They too will pay the price of treason. But rest assured, their suffering will be as nothing compared to yours. You have not watched Jadder Payne at work, have you, in his chambers? I can tell you this: After the first few days his subjects begin to look at him with something like awe in their eyes. With something almost like love. The man is an artist. You will be his masterwork."

The Sheriff stroked his mare's neck. He bent to whisper something in her ear, but then straightened and stared, unblinking, toward the wildwood.

Something was happening near the tree line. One of the pikemen had sat down on his backside, like a petulant child. A second man went to the ground, and a third, crumpling like puppets with their strings cut. There was shouting, and metallic *ping* and *zip-zip* sounds.

Dark shapes were emerging from the forest, like startled birds. They appeared to rise slowly at first before accelerating forward at great speed. One of the flashes raced toward a crossbowman and he went to his knees, his weapon firing into the ground.

The forest, Will thought, his head throbbing and his thinking confused. *The forest is coming to our rescue.*

But then he saw the dark shapes were arrows. They had crow feathers as fletches: That was why they looked like angry black flashes.

Robin Hood is here. The trap is sprung.

"So, the waiting is over," the Sheriff said. "We reach our main order of business, at last." He stood in his stirrups and raised his voice. "An incentive for the man who kills the outlaw. Ten pounds in silver. If he comes to me alive, fifty pounds to his captor. Any man who runs will receive his reward in the company of Jadder Payne."

At the tree line more dark shapes were spreading their wings. A mounted ranger tumbled from his horse. Pikemen were advancing, huddled behind their shields. Longbowmen were loosing into the trees. But they were shooting blind— still there had been no glimpse of Robin Hood. And still his arrows continued to race down the slope. A crossbowman went to his knees to wind his weapon and stayed there, huddled around an arrow in his groin.

"He will have to show himself eventually," the Sheriff said. "And then we shall see the true face of this monster." He wriggled his fingers back into his gloves. "In fact, this Robin Hood may have done the Sheriff's Guard a favor. He has reminded me what a powerful tool fear can be. And people fear most what they cannot see, is that not so, Chief Rider? What do the rangers call our outlaw? The Shadow of Death. He steals life unseen, like the plague. What power! Power that should have come to me. When the outlaw lies at my feet, I intend to borrow his skin. I shall receive the boon that should have been mine all along."

Will looked toward Much Millerson. Flames now were licking the pyre, but the big villager still hadn't uttered a sound. At the gibbet, the magpies had been chased away by a gang of rooks, which now took their turn jabbing their beaks through the bars.

"Observe those pikemen," the Sheriff said. "Resisting their urge to run. Weighing their fear of the outlaw against their terror of me. The monster imagined, versus the devil they know. The outlaw will not be so frightening once he shows himself, that I can guarantee."

It was at that moment Will caught sight of Robin Hood. The outlaw had left the forest and was moving along the tree line. At first he was little more than an outline—a green-black blur against the green-black of the leaves. But then he came into clear view, moving down the slope, loosing arrows on the run.

Zip-zip sounds. Two more soldiers falling, their blood running in rivulets down the furrows of the field. As Robin ran he notched, drew, let loose, notched, drew, let loose. Two pikemen blocked his path and they fell, holding their throats.

At the sight of the outlaw, some of the soldiers had frozen, staring. The dead eyes of his hood glistened. His wolf-pelt cloak trailed the ground, obscuring his legs and feet so it looked as though he was gliding across the ground, moving in a zigzag, the way a fox stalks its prey.

A crossbowman came to his senses and let loose but his quarrel went wide. Another arrow appeared at Robin's bow and the air hummed and the guard fell. The outlaw continued down the slope, letting an empty quiver drop and drawing from another, slung at his hip. A pikeman spun to the ground, an arrow in his eye.

The Sheriff's smile disappeared. For the first time something like doubt crossed his face. As Robin drew closer, details of the battle were becoming horribly distinct. The outlaw was armed only with a shortbow, yet his next arrow removed a man's arm at the elbow. He loosed again and a mounted soldier was decapitated, the head rolling down the field, the headless horseman galloping away and fountaining blood.

Will could see now that Robin's left arm throbbed and pulsed—it writhed with what looked like tendrils of black mist. When he drew his bow the tendrils tightened and when he let loose they flowed forward, a wisp of the dark stuff flying with each arrow.

His next shot sliced off a man's leg. Another punched through a steel breastplate and into a soldier's chest. The range of his bow was also impossible. His next black-shrouded

379

arrow arced far into the village and left a longbowman slumped across a dung-cart.

This was the moment Will saw fear flicker in the Sheriff's face. Robin was still hundreds of paces away and yet that last missile reached almost to where the Sheriff sat. Others had seen it was time to retreat: Jadder Payne had mounted his horse and was hurrying away from the execution ridge; Horor Conrad too was galloping toward the Sheriff.

The Sheriff turned his mare. As he did so he pointed down at Will. "Marshall Treadfire, take the traitor and—"

The Sheriff screamed. An arrow had speared his leg, puncturing the platemail near his knee. A second shot glanced off his breastplate.

All was confusion then. Jadder Payne appeared at the Sheriff's side and took the reins of his mare and began pulling the panicking animal away. Sansom Treadfire and the rest of his troupe were helping to bustle the Sheriff to safety.

Robin had reached the northern edge of the village. But now he was out of arrows. He drew a knife. It flashed darkly and sliced away a sword hand. He swept across two more men, leaving fountains of blood in his wake. At this distance the black thing on his arm looked like oil, flowing and surging as he ran and attacked. His mouth was locked in a grimace, as if the black pulsing was causing him great pain—or as if the killing itself was torment.

He surged toward the Sheriff. But the gap was widening. Jadder Payne and Sansom Treadfire and the other soldiers had spurred their horses into a gallop and they were taking the Sheriff's horse with them, the Sheriff slumped forward, both arms locked around the mare's neck.

Robin stopped and pulled an arrow from a corpse. He sent it arcing high. It landed where the Sheriff had been a heartbeat before. He found another arrow and tried again but now the Sheriff was beyond even his prodigious range.

The outlaw became still, the black writhing of his arm pulsating slower.

The Sheriff had escaped, the drumming of the hooves starting to fade. The valley was loud with the sounds of injured men, and with the frantic efforts of the villagers to rescue Much Millerson from his burning pyre.

Robin stood a moment longer, his head tipped forward and to one side. Then he turned toward Marian. He moved closer to the Trystel Tree, and the crow's companion. He knelt at the corpse of a crossbowman and he twisted an arrow free. He nocked the bloody thing to his bow. He drew, took aim, sent a shot through the bars of the cage.

The arrow found its mark in her heart. Death would have been instantaneous.

Will watched this with disbelief. He could see Marian was beyond saving: her wounds were too severe. But he had expected Robin to try. After searching for Marian for so long, he had expected him to show some emotion at least . . . or to hold some kind of ritual or . . . something.

He looked at the crow's companion, rocking slightly from the impact of the arrow. *At least her suffering is over. It was all Robin could do for her, in the end.*

He looked back toward Robin—already the outlaw was approaching the wildwood, fading into the dark. And a moment later, as quickly as it spat him out, the forest swallowed Robin Hood and he was gone.

XVII. Outlaws

Will stood beneath the crow's companion, looking up. The resemblance was uncanny: the same shape to her nose and mouth, a similar figure, and matching hair. Her injuries made it all the more difficult to tell the difference from afar.

But from this distance Will could see what Robin Hood must have sensed all along: It was not Marian in this cage. This was some other poor wretch, dragged from her village no doubt simply because of her beauty—because she had the misfortune to resemble Marian Delbosque—then tortured close to death purely so she would serve as effective bait for Robin Hood. *But Robin wasn't fooled or distracted for an instant. The Sheriff underestimated his new foe.*

Will looked at the villagers. Most were gathering their belongings, preparing to take their chances on the road. Much Millerson and his son, Midge, had come to stand with Will and Ironside and Borston Black.

"Last chance to change your mind," Will said to Much Millerson. "You know what being outlaw means? It makes us lower than wild beasts. It will be the duty of every person in England to kill us on sight, without pause or question. Anyone who so much as offers us food or shelter will be outlawed themselves. If you go with the others, if you travel far enough, you might be forgotten."

"He destroyed my home," Much said. "He burned my friend and would have done the same to me. He would have deprived Midge of a father."

He didn't need to say more. Will nodded. "So, first we need to bury these men," he said. "And then we have to find cover. It's no good heading to a town or village—there's going to be a hefty reward on our heads. There's only one place left to go."

"Leave this place," said Robin Hood. "You don't belong here."

Will Scarlett had led them deep into Winter Forest, all the while with the feeling they were being watched, or followed. Now they were lost, and it would be soon be dark.

"We're not rangers anymore," Will said. "We're outlaws, same as you. We can help each other."

"I don't need your help."

Still they had seen no glimpse of Robin Hood. His voice seemed to emerge from all sides at once. It seemed to come out of the ground before whispering away through the leaves.

"He won't underestimate you again," Will said. "Next time he'll come with an army."

"Leave this place." Robin's voice howled heavy, making the aspen leaves tremble and the saplings bow their heads.

"You struck him a blow the way nobody has ever done," Will said. "Let us join you and others will follow. We have experience. We can organize weapons, training."

"This is your final warning." Robin's voice rumbled up through the roots and the trunks of the trees. Birds took flight, squirrels shrieked and magpies cackled and the entire forest seemed to take up the threat.

Leave this place.

Will ran his swollen tongue across dry lips; he weighed the danger against their desperation. He was putting the others at great risk. *But they have nowhere else to go. This is their only hope.*

"Think of Marian," he said. "The Sheriff talked of the role he wants her to play. I think she must still be alive."

At last he caught sight of Robin Hood—a faint shape standing against a king oak. He was wrapped head to toe in his cloak, the fur of it seeming to change color even as Will watched, streaking with white and gray as the mist thickened. He held his bow horizontally, at chest height. It was fully drawn.

Will sucked in a breath, tried to swallow. "We can help Marian, together. Or you can kill me now, and do the Sheriff's work for him."

There was a long silence. The bow shifted in Robin's hands. He was gone.

Robin crouched out of sight, listening to Will Scarlett and the others. They smelled of blood and scorched skin and one of them was shaking violently as the shock set in. They had made camp on a bank of the river, where the water was deep and slow. The one called Much Millerson had been bathing his burns and Will Scarlett was cutting him bandages from an old tunic. The one called Ironside had come to sit beside Much Millerson. Ironside was saying: "You were useful with those fists. Where'd you learn to fight like that?"

"He's the champion of the seven shires," blurted the youngest one, the one called Midge. "Northridge and Sothley and Sidbarrow and all the rest, they send their best fighters, every Michaelmas, and they go away beaten, every one."

"You didn't see anything today," Much Millerson said. "You should see Midge here when he wears the leathers. He's twice as fast as his father. Here now, son, slow down with that wine."

They had brought food and drink with them—supplies left behind by the Sheriff's men. Midge Millerson, shaking with shock, had been grabbing the wineskin every time it passed near.

"This Robin Hood," said the one called Borston Black. "He's watching us, isn't he?"

"In a manner of speaking," said Will Scarlett. "If we're lucky, he'll decide we're worth saving. None of us knows how to survive out here. This time of year we won't starve, or die of cold, but what about in winter?"

"I suppose we do as other outlaws do," said Ironside. "Move from village to village, begging what we can, stealing what we can't. Taking shelter in the cowsheds, amid the heat of the cattle. Not a pretty picture, is it?"

"And how many last long, that way?" said Will. "How long before somebody gives us up for the silver? We need to take root—make the forest our home and our fortress, the way Robin has."

Robin listened to all this with a rising sense of dread. He felt sick to the core, and drained, as he always did after giving vent to the killing rage. How many lives had ended in that village? And for what? The Sheriff was still alive.

And now Will Scarlett and these others wanted to add their strength to Robin's . . .

Let us join you and others will follow.

What had he started?

When the fearful become strong, that is when the world burns.

He moved away from these people. They were unimportant. Marian was alive: That was all that mattered. He would find her and free her; he needed nobody's help. He left Will

Scarlett and the others by the riverbank and he loped away, alone.

He became aware of the vixen-girl, moving nearby, watching him. In his imagining she was taking on a woman's curves. And as she moved closer he noticed something new about her. It was her heartbeat . . . no, her heartbeats.

Inside her was a second, much softer pulse.

He remembered those sensations in the river, and her words to him later. *We've planted the seed; now it must grow.*

He pushed the vixen-woman from his mind. He would have nothing more to do with her schemes. He refused to even think about this new development, and what it might mean. Only Marian mattered. She was out there, somewhere, waiting. He moved away to prepare for a journey, and to begin his search.

Part Six

Destroying Angels

I. The Garden of Angels

Bishop Raths looked through the spyhole at Marian Delbosque. At first glance he had to admit the Prime Warden was correct: She certainly looked harmless enough. Barely a spark of life left in her. She was alone in a circular prayer garden, beneath the shade of potted trees. Like the rest of the girls she was dressed in a simple gray smock. She was sitting upright on her knees, resting back on her heels, working at something in her lap.

At the Inquisitor's side the Prime Warden huffed and fussed with his mustache. "This is a waste of time," he said. "You won't learn anything from these girls. Especially not this one. The first time they brought her here she was a spitting demon. You couldn't go near her if you wanted to keep all your fingers. So they put her in the hole and left her there for three months. Three months! I've never known anyone last three weeks. And one day she just cracked. She tried to take her own life. Beat her head against a wall. That's how she got that scar, see it, near her eye? They fixed her up and brought her out tame as a kitten. She's barely uttered a word since. She hardly moves unless you move her. I assure you, she's quite broken."

"What is that around her neck?" the Inquisitor said.

389

"A talisman. Half an arrowhead, made of jade. In those early days we had a fight to get it off her. When we gave it back it made her calmer. But that was before. You could probably take it away now and she wouldn't even notice. Like I say, she's a turnip."

A breeze blew and lifted Marian's hair away from her face and Bishop Raths got a clear view of her numinous gray-green eyes. She was the most alluring of all the girls, without doubt. Even her single scar—her solitary blemish—managed to be picturesque. It was a moon shape on her temple, curving perfectly around her right eye. A wasp buzzed near her face but she didn't move to brush it away. Yes, it appeared the Prime Warden was correct: She looked quite docile.

And yet . . .

An idea began to form. The Inquisitor scratched his powdered chin. He folded his bony hands one across the other and he felt the pieces start to fall into place. *Ah yes. Now then.*

"This is a waste of time," Killen Skua said again. "You won't learn anything here."

The Prime Warden had been saying this over and over, ever since the Inquisitor arrived at this strange place. They called it the Garden of Angels. It was a fortified convent, five miles outside the city. Killen Skua had come to greet him at the front gates, and they walked together through the gardens. After a week of rain it was a rare sunny day; most of the young women were sitting in the open-air cloisters. Some stared silently into space, others took turns to speak passages from their Bibles.

There were angels everywhere, painted on the walls, carved into stone, hanging from the beams of the arcades. Messenger angels and avenging angels; angels of love and peace and war. The sounds were of doors closing softly, of slow footsteps and gentle conversation. Very quietly, out of sight, somebody was crying. There was a single peal of laughter, incongruous amid the hush.

"What's this all about?" the Prime Warden had said.

"I've been tasked with an investigation," the Inquisitor replied. "I don't suppose it's any longer a secret: The Sheriff is dying."

"Yes. Some news reaches us even here. An outlaw shot an arrow in his leg."

"No, not that. A flesh wound, merely. Perhaps it precipitated his decline. But, no, the Sheriff is suffering something more deadly."

"He is? Well, what do you expect to learn here? Whatever happens in the outside world, it has little to do with us. There could be war out there and we'd barely feel a ripple. You're wasting your time."

The Inquisitor smiled. "I presume you appreciate your posting here, Master Skua? A pleasant place to work, compared with guarding the labor pits, or the torture chambers? Like you, I have a lot to lose if the Sheriff dies. You will forgive me if I leave no stone unturned in my search for the would-be assassin."

"Assassin?"

"I believe someone is killing the Sheriff." The Inquisitor stopped to watch four young women who were plaiting one another's hair.

"Killing him?" said Killen Skua. "Who? How?"

"That is what I intend to discover."

"But why come here? These young women, they've been with us three, four years, some of them. They've not set toe in the world outside. What could they possibly know that we don't?"

The Inquisitor dropped the hood of his cowl. He studied the prisoners, one by one. He began to feel strangely sorry for

Killen Skua and the other guards: It must be an exquisite kind of torture, to be surrounded by such creatures, so close and yet forever out of reach. He gripped the hem of his cassock and continued through a fragrant bower. So far he had seen nothing to shed light on the mystery.

But then they had come to Marian Delbosque. And the Inquisitor felt a shiver of discovery. *Ah now . . . Yes, this is interesting.* He watched Marian working deftly with the thread and cloth in her lap, her needle flashing on and off in the dappled sunlight.

"And they can have anything they ask for?"

"Anything short of the front door key," the Prime Warden said. "The Sheriff says they should be occupied. They have the run of the gardens, and the grounds this side of the river. There's room enough to trot a horse. They do some archery, calisthenics of various sorts. A few of them even like to swing a practice sword. Silly, I know, but they seem to enjoy it. We have a set hour for each pursuit, of course. Some of the girls can be quite . . . willful. But not this one. Since they returned her to us Marian has done exactly as she's told. We've not once had cause to quiet her with one of our treatments."

"And how does Marian use her free time, when it's permitted?"

"She works in her garden, most days. And she does a lot of what she's doing now. Tailoring. Needlework. She's quite skilled, in fact, and it seems to satisfy what's left of her mind."

"I see. And I presume she dyes the clothes she makes. She asks for berries, roots for the dyes?"

"Well, I'm not certain. I think she—"

"I want an inventory of every item Marian Delbosque has ever requested."

"You do. Well, I'll have to check the pipe rolls. It could take some time."

"It will take precisely half a day. The details will be in my hands by prime hour tomorrow. The Sheriff will be notified as to reasons for any delay."

"I still don't see what any of this—"

"It seems to me, Master Skua, you don't see a great deal. Or rather you see only what this young woman wants you to see. You've noted her reluctance to speak, her vacant gaze, and you've concluded that Marian Delbosque has died inside. But take another look. What about her hands? See the dexterity, the tenacity. Do they not look like hands with a purpose?"

Bells began to chime, calling the girls to noonday prayers. The Inquisitor took one last lingering look at Marian, congratulating himself, confirming his impressions. He gathered up his robes and headed for the front gate.

"Watch those hands, Master Skua," he called back. "I believe those are the hands of a killing machine. A perfect, silent, invisible assassin."

II. The Search

A storm had raged for the better part of two days. Finally the winds eased and the soil sighed as it drank in the rain. Robin left his hillside shelter and went on his way, across open country, following the higher cart roads, avoiding the flooded paths of the lower slopes.

He kept his head bowed as he walked past a patrol of five soldiers. They had stopped at the roadside to repair a wagon wheel.

"You, old man," one of the rangers called after Robin. "You shouldn't be on this road. This is the King's Cartway. You need a permit to travel here."

"Get down to the packways, where you belong," another soldier said.

Robin shuffled on and the men made no move to stop him. It had been a halfhearted challenge. Already the rangers had gone back to staring at the horizon, lost in their own thoughts.

Before leaving Winter Forest, Robin had gone to the cave and dug through the horde of items he had taken from the Sheriff's men. He had chosen a horse shroud, big enough to cover himself head to toe. His unstrung bow, wrapped in an oiled cloth, he tapped on the ground in front of him, like a cripple's cane, or a blind man's stick. The quiver at his back, bulging through the blanket, formed the hump of his crooked spine. Trailing this disguise, keeping it pulled low over his face, Robin was just one more wretch of the road, unremarkable to rangers who had more pressing concerns. Robin understood from their urgent talk that all the garrisons had been emptied—every soldier ordered back to the city. The Sheriff gathering his forces close.

"So what happens if he dies?" he heard one ranger say as his troupe splashed through a swollen ford a little way ahead.

"Another man steps into his boots," another ranger said. "We all carry on, just the same."

"That's not it at all," a third man said. "I'm old enough to remember, not like you pups. Pandemonium, that's what happens. Crime lords go to war, barons take the chance to settle old scores."

"It's true," a fourth man said. "Hilltower has been in the far shires. He says even the peasants are forming militias. Whittling their dung forks into spears."

"God help them if they try that here."

For now Robin was only vaguely interested in all this. He cared about only one thing: finding Marian. He wrapped his disguise close, tapped his bow on the ground, continued on his way.

As he roamed the roads in his rags Robin recalled a daydream he used to have. It was a vision of his future self: He was a knight of the realm, standing at the prow of a warship, fifty bannermen at his back. As he sailed into port he turned to the shore and there she was, Marian, watching him, seeing all he had become . . .

What had happened to that vision?

That dreamed-of future had dissolved, like mist in the morning sun, to be replaced by this—here Robin was, alone, roaming these muddy tracks in a blanket crawling with ticks. A monster in an old man's clothes.

What would Marian think of him, if he managed to find her? And how would *she* have changed, after all this time, after all she must have suffered?

He dragged his mind away from all this. He focused on searching for any hint as to where she might be. He sent his senses into the green, searching the land through its roots and burrows, its streams and its creatures.

In an instant he becomes part of it all—rippling through the bushes with the shield bugs, circling with a flock of doves, thumping through a field with a fleeing hare. A formation of starlings twists high above, like a single giant shadow, and Robin sweeps the land with them, seeing in his mind's eye the shapes left behind by their acrobatics.

A peregrine arrows in and Robin shares the starlings' flash of panic—in the same instant he is with the bird of prey, tasting its hunting joy and seeing the world through hawk-eyes and listening with a raptor's sense of hearing. A dormouse stirs far below and through his hawk-sense Robin is aware of it. A cow coughs and a buzzard stamps its feet to bring worms to the surface and Robin feels every tremor and vibration.

But then—

He comes up against a void. A disconnection. If all this is a web, then here is a place where the strands are cut—where nothing grows and barely a worm moves in the soil. His forest-mind scuttles back to him, wounded.

What has happened here?

He moved closer. He smelled scorched earth. He crossed fields devoid of even nettles. He realized this wasteland had once been a village. It had been put to sword and fire. The fields sewn with salt so nothing would grow here again.

He moved amid the charred remains of homes. He examined

it all with his fingers: a scattering of animal bones, something that might be a human skull. The Trystel Tree was still standing but it was twisted, its skin blistered, like a dead hand thrust up from a shallow grave.

A little farther on, he found another of these dead villages, just a husk remaining. And here was a third, destroyed utterly, pulled out at the root so it would never flourish again. *This is the Sheriff's doing. Wherever that man walks he sows destruction. Why would he do this to his own land?*

Above Robin now, tumbling down a hillside, was another deserted village. But this was of a different kind—here the houses stood intact. He approached the ghost village. A heady smell was overwhelming: vegetables left to rot in the fields.

He moved between the empty homes. The wind fretted in the thatch. A sow crunched at something inside an old barn. The waterwheel creaked. But there was not a whisper of human sound. And there were no dead bodies or bones of people: This place had not died of famine or disease. *What happened here? Why did they all leave their homes? And so suddenly?*

This made him think of his own family. Where did they go, and why? Or were they dead? Was it the Sheriff's doing, as Marian had said? Robin's wrath shook itself and began to rise. Memories of Marian in the cage, and of the village burning around her, and of the Sheriff saying: *Bring me the boy's eyes.*

Rangers were approaching close behind, their wagon squelching through the mud.

"Step aside, tinker man," one of the men called.

Robin's fingers tightened into a claw, gripping his bow. The shadow veins crept up his arm. That slight splintering sound, like ice cracking.

"He said move, gutter-trout. Lest you want your legs broke beneath these wheels."

Robin kept his back turned and his head low. Beneath the horse shroud the black veins spread, running cold through his back and chest, seeping across his neck and face and around the dead sockets of his eyes.

"What's wrong with you? Are you a leper? Where are your bells?"

"We're talking to you. Turn to face us."

The shadow shard bubbled up through his skin. Tendrils of it twisted and squirmed. He kept his left fist gripped in his right hand and he fought to keep his bow still.

"Jesus, he stinks," a ranger said. "Disgusting, these road turds."

"He's moon-touched. Look at him, shaking. Probably can't even hear us. This will get his attention." This ranger uncoiled a whip and the sharp tip of it came flicking at Robin's back.

Kittissh.

"Ought to hunt them down with dogs, like we do with other vermin."

Kittissh. Kittissh.

The horse blanket and the wolf pelt absorbed the sting of the whip, but the sound of it twisted in Robin, made his wrath churn, and the laughing of the rangers made it worse. The black tendrils raged—snakes trapped in flames—he gripped his left fist and fought to hold it still.

Find Marian. Nothing else matters.

The ranger with the whip had seen no reaction from Robin; he had lost interest and coiled the weapon. The wagon squelched narrowly wide of Robin and the soldiers went on their way.

The shadow snakes unraveled, dissolved. The thumping of his heart slowed.

He continued with his search, spreading his senses into the web of green, widening his awareness.

And there, in the distance, is Nottingham. The Sheriff's domain.

The city is a hulking presence. And it is a whirl of merging sensations: black sounds and screeching smells and a cold endless weight. Already Robin felt repulsed by this place. But he didn't slow his progress. He knew this was where his path led. This was where he was likely to find Marian. And it was where he would face his enemy.

Tapping his bow at his feet, keeping his disguise pulled close, he shuffled toward the city.

III. A Gift

Marian walked into her sleeping cell and the Sheriff was there. He was sitting at the foot of her cot, picking at his fingernails with a knife. At her entrance he looked up and a thin smile creased his lip.

Marian continued into her chamber and went to the Sheriff and sat cross-legged at his feet, her back to him, her spine straight. Two rangers left the cell and stood outside the entrance, pulling the door half closed.

The Sheriff sheathed his knife and reached inside his surcoat and took out an ivory comb. He began combing Marian's hair, and as he did so he looked around the sleeping cell, at the tiny writing desk, clothes chest, the cornucopia of dried fruit and flowers.

"I envy you your life here," he said. "This sanctuary. To find a place of silence. Is that not what all of us are searching for, in the end?"

He turned to the wall and began coughing. He took out a handkerchief and pushed it to his mouth and made muffled hacking sounds. "There is no such place of peace for me," he continued. "My visits here are as close as I will ever know to quietude. But even now I hear my enemies scratching at the door. The little people meet beneath their sacred trees and they pray to their forest gods and afterward they plot my downfall. They are encouraged and armed by the barons. They imagine I do not know all this. But I have eyes and ears everywhere."

He broke into another coughing fit, more violent than before, causing candles to flicker in their alcoves, the cot creaking as his body shuddered. He stopped coughing and removed the handkerchief from his mouth.

"And now arises this new power," he said. "The atavistic threat of which we were warned. A small part of that larger doom perhaps, but significant nonetheless. If it is allowed to spread, it will prove seductive. Even my own Chief Rider has been drawn to its fold."

The comb hit a knot and he paused to tease apart the strands with his fingers. Then he said: "I understand the Chief Rider came to see you, in the oubliette. I would know what false words he spoke. And what you replied."

Marian answered without hesitation. "He said he was going to set me free. I told him I hated him and never wanted to see him again."

"Was that all? There was no talk of me, or of the outlaw, Robin Hood? No talk of the winter-born?"

Marian shook her head.

"And Robin Hood," the Sheriff said. "This . . . man who attacked me. What is your opinion of him?"

"I hate him most of all."

The Sheriff sat back, tucked the comb inside his surcoat. "And if you were given means to prove it . . . a way you could help trap the wildwood terror . . . what would you say?"

Before Marian could answer there was a knocking at the door and Killen Skua appeared at its edge. The Prime Warden's face was dark red and he was short of breath. "Sire, I was told you were here. I came as soon as I heard." He crept

401

a little farther into the room, but didn't loosen his grip on the door. "The Inquisitor. Has he . . . has he come to see you?"

"Not in recent days," the Sheriff said. "Bishop Raths is engaged in a task of utmost importance. He is not to be interrupted."

"Yes, as I understand. He was here, in fact, this morning. But I got the impression . . . I think he might be looking for you, as we speak."

"In which case, I am sure he will find me in due course."

"Yes, but . . . the things he was saying. It sounded urgent. I don't think . . . I'm not sure he would want—"

The Sheriff's weight shifted and the cot creaked. "If that was all," he said, "you may leave us."

Killen Skua hesitated at the door's edge, staring at Marian. His mustache was beaded with sweat; he lifted a sleeve to wipe it dry. His mouth opened, closed again. "Yes, sire," he said finally, and shuffled back through the door and was gone.

The Sheriff inhaled a long breath, which became ragged toward its end. He coughed so violently he was jerked to his feet. The room's two candles were extinguished. He continued coughing, a rasping rising from his lungs. Eventually the fit subsided. He steadied himself and adjusted his clothing, before moving toward the door, hobbling from the arrow wound in his leg. "I must leave you," he said. "This malady demands attention."

"Wait," Marian said, rising to her knees. "A gift." She reached beneath her cot and pulled out a pair of kidskin gloves. "Those are sapphires, in the knuckles," she said. "The most effective gem for health. They will help you get well."

The Sheriff took the gloves and examined them. He placed a hand on Marian's head. "All the girls here are jewels," he said. "But you, Marian Delbosque, you I treasure above all. One day, you and I . . . Well, all that must wait. Other matters, regrettably, take precedence. But soon I will return . . . and you and I shall talk of dreams."

He spluttered again into his handkerchief as he passed into the corridor, dragging his wounded leg. His footsteps and those of his guards became faint.

Marian remained there on her knees, staring at the half-open door, and she was still there, unmoving, long after the last light of day had faded from her cell.

IV. Heart of Steel

Sir Bors watched his men-at-arms struggling to subdue the boy's mother, he listened to the woman's wails, and he steeled his heart against that which must be done. *You have no choice*, he told himself. *What is one woman's pain, against all that is threatened?*

The mother was wailing: "Leave him alone! He is my son, born and raised. You would take a child from his mother. Monsters! Help me. Won't any of you help me? Don't let them do this. Please."

"See sense, Bearta," another villager shouted. "He is no more your son than that duck is my daughter. He has cast a spell upon you, and cursed the rest of us."

"He doesn't belong here," said a woman's voice. "You should have left him to the forest."

"Keep your nose out, Hogge," said someone else. "One more word and I'll—"

There were more raised voices, and a separate scuffle.

The boy himself stood apart, silent, his hood raised. He appeared resigned to leaving his home, as they usually were. He was perhaps twelve years of age, and for every day of his life he had most likely suffered the mistrust and vitriol of these villagers. He was now fully ready to leave this place, no matter the cost.

His mother, however—*his adoptive mother*, Sir Bors reminded himself—she was determined to fight to the end. She had broken free and had picked up a mattock and was swinging it around her head, screeching. A few other peasants were coming to her aid. One man appeared from a hut holding a clay pot. He smashed it over the head of Joscelin Tarcel. The chamber knight was wearing a skull-helm, but still the blow made him stumble to one knee. He regained his footing and lashed out with his fist, sending the farmer sprawling.

Sir Bors took a deep breath. He stepped his horse forward and he bellowed: "Enough!"

The mother froze. Another woman dropped a threshing flail. The entire village fell quiet; even the geese and the ducks stopped their chatter. From his belt Sir Bors took a purse. The coins clinked as they landed at the mother's feet.

"If the Sheriff had come here, in my stead, he would be taking more than the boy," said Sir Bors. "And he would not be leaving gold. Today is a hard for you, but understand this: It might have been far worse. Hawkwood, Warbrittle, get the boy onto a horse. I want this over with."

The mother resumed her wailing; the peasants took up their fighting, but soon enough the boy was sitting in the saddle behind Ralph Hawkwood. As Sir Bors led the way out of the village, he spared a glance back: The boy had lowered his hood and was watching his adoptive mother, a single tear on his cheek.

The boy turned to look at Sir Bors with a hard stare. Yes, he was one of them. There had been no mistake. Something in their eyes always gave them away. Sir Bors spurred his horse. At some distance he could still hear the mother's screech of pain.

You had no choice, he told himself again. *What is one person's suffering, when so much stands at stake?*

For many miles Sir Bors spoke to no one, lost in his own thoughts. He remembered that mother's anguish. He thought of Robin Loxley, and the other boy he had failed . . .

He half turned in his saddle. Behind him his men-at-arms were resplendent, their silver cloaks gleaming in the sun, the emblem of the golden arrow bold on their chests. He raised a hand, beckoned. Jack Champion rode forward and walked his horse at Sir Bors's side.

"That cloak fits you well, Sir Jack," the overlord said. "There were those who believed we would never see it on your shoulders. Sir Derrick once urged me to cast you out of my academy. Were you aware of that? He said you stirred mischief, and provoked sloth in others. He said we would never, in a thousand lifetimes, forge you into a fighting knight."

Jack Champion said nothing; he only twisted fingers through his blond chin-beard.

"Then came the day Robin Loxley disappeared," said Sir Bors. "I told you he was dead. It was dishonorable, that lie, and there were times I regretted saying it. But it had one positive effect, at least. Robin's rash act, and our falsehood, destroyed all traces of the fool in you. You became, overnight, dedicated to your studies, indomitable on the training field. On your first campaign, last summer, you were peerless. And so we see how our actions, and the actions of others, can send unexpected ripples through our lives. The lowest act can spark greatness, an intended kindness can bring misery—all such consequences impossible to predict."

Sir Bors maneuvered his horse so that one hoof came down upon an anthill, scattering soil and insects. "How do you imagine the ants conceived of that event? Are they at this moment inventing stories to account for it? Or are they simply laboring to repair their nest, and to guard, as best they might, against future catastrophe? We are not so different to the ants, Sir Jack. There are forces operating upon us that far surpass our understanding. You began to glimpse the truth of this, I'm certain, the day you were promoted to the Household Guard—the day I told you of your origins, and those of the other winter-born. I asked you that day to trust me, even when the wisdom of my actions seems opaque."

He paused while he and Jack Champion splashed through a shallow ford. A little way up the bank a fox froze, a gosling hanging in its jaws.

"I need to ask of you a hard task," Sir Bors continued. "I hear reports of a host, gathering in the wildwood. Will Scarlett, formerly Chief Rider of the Sheriff's Guard, is recruiting bandits and peasants and itinerant swords of every sort. I want you to join them. Pledge yourself to Robin Hood's cause. Take one other knight with you—the man you trust most in the world."

"You want Robin to defeat the Sheriff?" said Jack Champion. "Then why send just two? This time of year we could spare a score of men, couldn't we?"

"Something you must understand," said Sir Bors. "This war will not be as others. When Robin Hood and the Sheriff clash, fully, I am convinced there will be nothing so quaint as winning or losing. Nothing left to be called victory. You will not be there to fight, except for the sake of appearances. Your primary objective is to watch and to listen, to report back to me everything you learn."

Jack Champion stared straight ahead, twisting his beard.

"This . . . war," said Sir Bors. "I hold myself responsible, to no small degree. They were both of them, at separate times, in my care, under my guidance."

"Both?" said Jack Champion. "The Sheriff was your ward?"

"He was not always the monster he is today," said Sir Bors. "He was once a noble young man, and the best and brightest pupil I have ever known."

"Was he . . . like us? One of the winter-born?"

Sir Bors nodded. "That is why I fear what is coming. At my age, I have seen history repeat itself too many times. And this, I'm certain, will be worse than all. I cannot watch it approach and stand aside. But be warned, once you have joined the outlaws, I may ask worse of you than spying. In which case you must trust me, and know I act for the greater good. You must understand too that what I told you once has come true, in a way: Your friend Robin Loxley is dead. Someone else—something else—has taken his place."

He dismissed Jack Champion and the knight returned to take his place in the line. Sir Bors went back to his silence, and his thoughts. He saw landmarks that told him he was close to home. He looked around him at the rolling hills, the sparkling streams, the wooded valleys. This land that had raised him, that welcomed him home like a mother every time he returned from campaign. He studied this land now as if seeing it for the first and last time, and he felt a shiver of doom, and he steeled his heart once more against all that must be done.

V. Nottingham

Robin walked a ravaged land. The closer he drew to Nottingham the more dead villages he found, some of them razed to the ground, others intact but silent, farm tools left lying in the grass, children's games abandoned. Even the villages that were occupied had a deathly feel. Often their Trystel Tree had been destroyed, or their ancestral spring desecrated. Robin passed such places and he felt something was rising to the surface—something that had lurked beneath too long. From behind walls he heard dark muttering and sometimes a whetstone rasping across steel.

What had he heard that ranger say? *Even the peasants are forming militias. Whittling their dung forks into spears.*

Robin crested a hill and stopped. Extraordinary events were occurring below. Four soldiers had ridden into a village and were busy stripping it for their own supplies, filling their packs with what little food they could find. There was a squawk as one of them snapped the neck of a goose before tying it to the saddle of his horse.

But now the texture of this scene was changing. One of the soldiers had gone missing. He had entered a longhouse and had not come back out. Another ranger went looking for him, and as he stepped into the house there was a muffled shout and a repeated wet popping sound. Elsewhere in the village a cry of surprise and a gurgled yell.

Then all became quiet and still. The sounds when they resumed were of heavy objects being dragged across the ground, and the door of the slaughter-shed being closed and bolted, and the sharpening of knives.

Will Scarlett was right: Robin's attack on the Sheriff had changed everything. A mighty storm was about to break.

What have I started?

He told himself this was none of his concern, not yet. Marian needed him, and he must not be distracted. He left the village behind and continued on his way.

Finally, just before dusk, he neared Nottingham.

Still playing his vagrant act, tapping his bow, he shuffled up one of the approach roads, joining the procession of soldiers and traders heading for the city gates. A cutler with his wares clanking against his cart called out to Robin as he passed. "You don't want to go in there, cripple. You have any idea what the Sheriff does to your sort when he finds them in his city? Better to take your chances on the road."

Robin ignored him, shuffled on.

"So be it," the man called. "It's your skin."

Washing out of the city was a cacophony of noise—an almost physical presence as Robin drew near—the first curfew bells were clanging, and shutters were banging closed, watchmen rapping their cudgels against walls, shouting for all citizens to be indoors. At the river port, barrels rumbled and baskets thumped. And everywhere across the city the rattling of bolts as doors were locked against the gathering dark. Beneath these final day-sounds a nocturnal babble was rising: a low moan of laughter and lies and violence from the taverns and the dicing dens.

Robin stopped, overwhelmed. Perhaps he had imagined the city would not be so different to Sir Bors's citadel. But it must be ten times the size, to produce such a flood of noise. And so much of it was unfamiliar: scrapings and tappings and tickings he couldn't name. Had human habits and rituals become so foreign to him? Or did this place have rules of its own, which he could not hope to understand?

As he continued up the approach road he sent his mind into the green, trying to sense the city more fully. Above the gates, impaled on spikes, were the boiled heads of executed men—Robin riding with the crows darting in to peck at eyeballs. The *clatter-flap* of the crows' wings; the rasp of their voices. Robin trying to spread his awareness further, to fly with the birds across the city roofs. But failing to reach beyond the curtain wall. He tries again and is rebuffed once more. Finally he understands: There are no birds above the city. No buzzards or starlings. Not even pigeons. It is as though the impaled heads form a spirit fence, beyond which birds fear to venture.

No time to think about this further. The second round of curfew bells clanging now within the walls. On the approach road the wagons and carts clattering quicker, everyone anxious to be inside before the gates slam shut. Robin approached the walls—the cold endless weight of them stretching above. A stone bridge took him across the river, and then he was shuffling toward a guard house.

"State your name and your business," a sentry said.

Robin continued toward the open gate. The sentry stepped into his path.

"I need to go inside," Robin said. "Let me through."

"Not until you've shown your permit, or paid the entry tax. And not until I've seen your face."

"Get out of my way."

411

The sentry advanced, leveling his spear at Robin's chest. "Harold . . . ," he called over his shoulder, "we've got another one for the river. You stay here, I'll take care of it."

"I told you . . . ," Robin said. "Get out of my way."

He threw aside the horse shroud. His hand, woven with shadow, went to the hunting knife at his belt. The steel flashed up and out and the sentry's spear was shorn of its blade.

Robin fought to hold the knife still. The tendrils of shadow were frenzied, urging him to lunge again, to strike this man dead. The sentry was stepping back. He dropped the cleaved spear, stumbled and fell, scuttled away like a crab.

There were other sentries here, but Robin could hear in the racing of their hearts that not one of them was inclined to fight. They turned in silence and they ran.

Robin sheathed his knife. He left his disguise where it had fallen—he strode through the city gates and up through the cobbled streets. He strung his bow and nocked an arrow.

He kept expecting those sentries to raise the hue and cry, but no bell clanged or horn blew. No ranger came to face him. Perhaps the Sheriff's troops now feared Robin more than they feared their master. Perhaps they were willing to leave the Sheriff to his doom.

Well then, here it was, at the tip of Robin's arrow. The Sheriff would live long enough only to reveal where he was keeping Marian. And there it would end.

From the eastern edge of the city came the clanking of wood and rattling of chains and final *ca-clunk* as the first of the four great gates thundered shut. Robin didn't break his stride. He swept through the dusk streets, thinking of all he had endured, burning for his revenge.

VI. Angel of Mercy

The screaming began, and Marian was pleased. The noise brought with it a wave of relief and a smile sprang unbidden to her lips.

A warden hurried past—automatically Marian dropped her smile and lowered her gaze and shuffled on her way, once again wearing her blank mask.

The screeching continued, cutting through the cloisters.

"She's foaming at the mouth," Marian heard one warden say.

"Fetch the Apothecary," came another voice.

"And a priest," said a third guard. "She's possessed."

They were talking about Lyssa Brekehart. From the direction of Lyssa's sleeping cell came yelling and a strangled growl. Something crashing and shouts for help. Girls were looking up in surprise; on any normal day the loudest sound in this place was the muted bonging of a prayer gong.

Everything in the Garden of Angels was tailored toward peace and harmony. Set into alcoves in the walls were acoustic pots that caught the girls' hymns and their prayers and changed their pitch and carried them warbling through the arcades. Other background sounds were of fountains tinkling and the chirping of caged birds. Equally no noisome smells were allowed. The floors were scattered with sweet woodruff, mixed with dried rockrose. Censers of incense burned everywhere, along with fuminaries of lavender oil.

Marian hated it all. She loathed this place with a howling passion. The softness, the stillness, the stifling banality of every sensation made her want to scream. She daydreamed of running free in Summerswood, the wind biting at her skin; of clambering up a tree, filthy and scratched and smelling of bark and moss; of swimming half-naked in Titan's Lake, laughing and shouting and splashing from a high rope.

Today she felt more restricted than ever—there was a tightness in her chest and her breath came sharp and shallow. It was always this way following a visit from the Sheriff. In front of that man she struggled more than ever to wear her dumb disguise—to sit there with him and nod and murmur when what she wanted to do was put her fingers round his neck and squeeze and keep squeezing. The Sheriff's latest visit had been made even worse by Killen Skua. Why had the Prime Warden been so agitated? What was all that talk about Bishop Raths, the Inquisitor? *All that can wait*, she told herself. *Panic now and all this will unravel.*

The cacophony continued and guards were hurrying past. Nobody was paying Marian any attention; she could go about her work undisturbed. She would start with the easiest task first. She went to her sleeping cell and collected the Flemish mantel she had just finished stitching. She took it to the dining hall, where she found Peter Child, the chandler. Marian moved down the hall, the polished floor squeaking beneath her feet. Peter Child stopped his work and looked up. He tucked a strand of his black hair behind his ear.

"Did you find more?" Marian said.

The chandler glanced around nervously before putting a

wicker pot in her hands. It contained fly-bait mushrooms, red with bright white spots.

"I knew you wouldn't let me down," Marian said. "You're so brave, and clever. One day, when I'm free . . ." She trailed off. Peter seemed to be trying to say something but he only made clicking noises with his tongue. There were lines of pink beneath his eyes.

"I need more deadly nightshade," Marian said. "Just the fruit—the devil's berries. You remember what they look like, and where they grow? And you'll get this to your mother, I know you will."

Peter took the cape and hid it quickly among his tools. Marian leaned forward on her toes, as if about to kiss him. She froze, then glanced behind her, apparently startled. "I can't let them see me here."

She hurried away, leaving Peter stuttering something behind her. So far, so simple. But Peter Child always had been the easy one. Others today would prove more difficult.

She went to the service quarter, descended the steps into the scullery. It was gloomy down here, and cold, her breath misting. Norman Banes was waiting for her, pacing back and forth, clenching and unclenching his fists.

"You're late," the warden said, turning to her with bloodshot eyes. "Give it to me."

"You first," Marian said.

"No, that's not how it goes today. You think you can have everything your own way."

Marian turned to leave.

"Wait, wait," the warden said. "I've got it here. Look. I don't care. Just hand it over."

He took from within his clothing something flat and thin, wrapped in an oiled cloth. "One is the best I could do," he said. "Even that was a big risk."

415

Marian reached inside her smock and took out two stoppered phials, each containing a yellowish liquid. At the sight
of the drug Norman Banes's tongue appeared and worked
across his teeth. He was shaking and sweating visibly, despite
the chill. She handed him one of the phials. He snatched it,
and his eyes narrowed.

"And the other one," he said. "Give it to me."

"You brought half of what we agreed," Marian said, turning to leave. "You get half in return."

Norman Banes lurched at her, threw out a hand—she
sprang out of range. He went for her again and she twisted
away. They had ended up changing places, Norman Banes
with his back to the steps, blocking the exit.

The tall guard towered over her, his eyes crazed, his breath
stinking. "Evil little witch. Give me the rest or—"

"Or what?" Marian said. Her eyes burned into his. Her voice
dropped to a menacing hiss. "You really are more stupid than
you look. I am the last person in the world you ever want to
threaten. You've been taking this stuff from me for months, and
you'll have to keep taking it because you're its slave. You're more
of a prisoner than I am. At least I have choices. I get to choose,
for instance, what goes in these phials. Perhaps next time I'll
use less mandrake and fewer poppy seeds and I'll add a little
wolfsbane, or a slice of deathcap, and you'd have no idea, and
you'd barely care in any case, you'd swallow it down just the
same because you're so desperate to escape your sorry waste of
skin. How does it feel, taking this stuff? Like 'flying with the
angels,' you said. Any time I choose I can bring you crashing to
earth, and then I'll drag you lower still, until you're drowning in
Hell. How *dare* you demand anything from me. I'll have you
groveling at my feet, begging to be put out of your misery."

Norman Banes unclenched his fists and shuddered and
looked away from her eyes.

"Keep bringing me what I need," she said, as she stepped around him. "Raise your voice to me ever again and I will treat you to a death so slow and so painful you will wish you had never been born."

She walked up and out of the scullery, pathetic Norman Banes already forgotten, her mind turning to the third and final task of the day. The most difficult of all.

She went to her physic garden, a walled patch of earth just outside the main convent. She carefully cut a stem of burn weed, and she picked rosehip berries and sliced them open and scraped out the seeds. She put these ingredients in a mortar and she added some medical spirit and some honey to create a sticky consistency. She poured the mixture into a tincture jar. For a second jar she created an antidote, using butter dock and field balm. She stashed her equipment and left the garden.

She found Aimee Clearwater in her sleeping cell. She was hugging the underside of her thighs, her face turned to the wall, her red hair cascading around her knees.

"Did he come here again?" Marian said.

Aimee raised one hand to wipe at her cheek. "Why me? Why did he choose me? What have I done to—"

"Stop," Marian said. "I don't want to hear that again, ever. You've done nothing. It's his shame and his alone. It's that man, Gordon Sleth. Do you understand?"

Aimee began to rock. Marian sat and rubbed her spine.

"And I haven't given up," Marian said, placing both tincture jars on the cot. "I've brought you more. It's in the brown jar, and in the yellow jar is the curative. Remember which is which. I've made it stronger. By morning he'll have swelled up red as a berry. He won't dare come near you again."

"That's what you said last time. I used it the way you told me, and it hurt him, I know it did because I got some of it on

417

me and it burned and left a rash. For him it must have been much worse. But *still* he came back."

Marian sighed. "We're learning something about men, aren't we? They are slaves to their urges and their fears. We are stronger."

Aimee stopped rocking and turned. "We need to tell."

"No."

"They're not allowed to touch us, are they? None of the others do. If we tell the Sheriff what Sleth's been doing, then he'll—"

"No!" Marian shouted it and Aimee sat up straight.

"The Sheriff is *not* your protector," Marian said. "The moment you go to him for help, that's where it ends. That's when you're fully in his power."

Defiance had risen briefly in Aimee's eyes, but now she turned away.

"Real freedom," Marian said more gently, "with our nemesis dead. That is the prize. Your price has been higher than most, but nobody will be carried. That's why you've got this: to show you've suffered, for all of us." She touched Aimee on the underside of her right wrist, where there was an image of an angel above shattered chains—a tattoo Marian had drawn using a sewing needle and sloeberry ink. "Lyssa will wear one of these, after today," Marian said. "But not all the girls have earned the right, have they? Their time will come. We will all play our part."

Aimee had gone back to staring at the wall, her head on her knees. Marian sat for a while longer, rubbing her spine.

"I have to go," she said. "I'll be back soon. Remember, you are not alone in this."

She left Aimee's sleeping cell and she went to the northern end of the convent, where the tower stood. She went inside and spiraled her way up the five flights of steps. At the top was

418

a domed prayer room, its ceiling painted with a vision of paradise. She went to the window. Lyssa Brekehart's fit had grown quieter, but from up here she could still hear guards struggling to subdue her.

Marian's potion had worked better than she could have hoped. It was a recipe she had found in an ancient grimoire—fly-bait mushrooms soaked in wine—a potion the Vikings once drank to bring on their battle lust. Lyssa had agreed to test the berserker draft and it had proved a useful distraction.

But now the disturbance was coming to an end. Wardens were once again walking the corridors, their hands clasped behind their backs.

Marian descended the tower and she shuffled on her way, barely raising her gaze, while deep inside she screamed and screamed to be free.

VII. A Host of Devils

Will Scarlett reached over his shoulder, drew his Saracen sword. At his side Borston Black readied his own blade.

There it was again: a skittering in the leaves. The snapping of a branch. They were approaching from all sides.

So this is how it ends. As simple as this.

The first of them slipped from the undergrowth, stealthy as a fox. The others appeared, one by one, moving in that half crouch of forest fighters, dressed in black and dark green, their hands resting on the knives and stabbing swords at their belts.

Will's worst fears were confirmed: Hydra's League. And here, at their head, was Blodwyn Kage, gripping her short-bow, her eyes full of hatred.

Will lifted his curved blade. "I should never have got you involved in this, old friend. I had no right to expect—"

"Cut it out, Will," said Borston Black. "Just promise me we'll take a few of these devils with us, for old time's sake."

More outlaws stepped into the open.

"God's teeth," said Borston Black. "There are more of them than ever. I thought we killed half these dogs last summer."

It was true: Hydra's League had ever been well named. Will had battled this outlaw band all his life, so it seemed, but every time he managed to cut off a head, another two appeared to take its place.

"What are you waiting for, Blodwyn?" said Borston Black. "Don't be afraid. I'll keep one arm behind my back. Make it a fair fight."

Blodwyn Kage moved forward. Her armor was bits of boiled leather, mismatched, patched and repatched. Her bow, made of antler bone, rested at her side. "We're not here to fight you," she said. "Not yet. Not until we take the Sheriff's head."

You too? thought Will. *Even you?* He let out a breath and slid his scimitar into the baldric at his back.

Borston Black didn't lower his own sword. His teeth were gritted through his beard. He barked a laugh. "Are you going to tell her, or am I?"

"You might not like the new company we keep," Will said. "The White Crows are already with us. And so are Aks Arqua's men."

At mention of these names some of outlaws looked at one another, or muttered beneath their breath. But Blodwyn Kage only smiled. "You flatter yourself, Will Scarlet. Did you imagine I'd make an ally of you, but refuse to fight at Aks Arqua's side? Perhaps you men of the city underestimate what is coming. Our augur has given us glimpses of it, and we are in no doubt. The Sheriff must be stopped, no matter the cost."

Will looked around him at these hard, gnarled men and women, tough as roots, and suddenly they appeared a very welcome sight.

"Then we are of one mind," he said. "You'd better follow us."

"Hydra's League?" said Ironside. "They're the worst yet. They're cannibals."

"There's no way they'll fight together," said Borston Black. "They hate each other more than they hate the Sheriff."

"I thought so too," said Will. "Seems we were wrong."

But not by a large margin, he thought, turning to look over his shoulder. Hydra's League were still filtering into the broad clearing that had become the outlaws' main camp, and unrest was rippling through the other bands. The White Crows had lifted their shortbows; Doghead McGee's followers were muttering in low tones; Baphomet's Horde were silent and watchful.

"This is a mistake," Will heard somebody hiss.

"You going to tell him that?" whispered someone else.

"After all we've fought for, just to kneel at another pair of feet? And worse, to throw in with Hydra's League."

Give this wasps' nest the slightest shake . . . , thought Will . . . *and none of us will escape unscathed.*

"What about here?" he said, turning back to Ironside. "Any sign of him?"

Ironside shook his head. "Not a whisper. We're building an army beneath the banner of Robin Hood, and we don't even know where he is. How long will this merry band stay friends, do you think, once they learn their leader is missing? Well, what else? Any news from your travels?"

"We met my . . . associate, at the Sign of the Seven Crossings," Will said. "Dozens of rangers have passed through en route to the castle. They left behind plenty of rumors, not many of them credible. But we got confirmation, at least, of where Marian Delbosque is being held."

"Is she really so important?"

"She is to Robin Hood. And to the Sheriff. So she may be the flashpoint. In any case, we shouldn't make a move without

Robin. We need to sit on this wasps' nest until he shows himself."

Will took another look around the camp, he listened to the dark buzz of the outlaw bands, and he hoped Robin Hood wouldn't leave them waiting too long.

VIII. Dragon's Tongue

Bishop Raths gripped the hem of his cassock and he followed the maze of corridors that snaked through the castle. He passed through many sets of heavy doors, nodding each time to a pair of guards, standing to attention with their swords half drawn.

He reached the Sheriff's private quarters. He knocked, waited a moment, pushed inside. The stench of sickness was overpowering. Fuminaries burned in all four corners of the chamber, battling in vain against the miasma.

The Sheriff was lying, half-naked, on the four-poster bed, having just been bled. Jadder Payne stood over him, sealing a vein with a cauterizing rod, the smell of scorched flesh adding to the noxious vapors. On the ground sat the lancing knives and bowls of blood. Jadder Payne poured the blood into flasks and collected up his tools. He nodded once to the Sheriff and left the room.

The Sheriff was deathly pale and so thin his ribs were clearly defined. He was deteriorating visibly, day by day. "As you can see," he rasped, "even Jadder Payne's mastery is proving ineffectual. I am running out of time. And out of patience. This malady is not God-given. It carries the stench of dark arts. You should know this, Inquisitor: I will not suffer alone. I am considering drastic measures."

"The cause is as I suspected," Bishop Raths said. "You are being poisoned."

The Sheriff dragged himself upright. He coughed feebly, hung his head. "Impossible. Every morsel of my food is tasted and double tasted. Every drop of liquid. If I were being poisoned, half my staff would be on their deathbeds."

"There is a poison called Dragon's Tongue. It can be absorbed, very slowly, through the skin. Death occurs by agonizing degrees. Its exact composition can be found only in the most ancient of texts." The intensity of the Sheriff's stare made the Inquisitor pause. He took a moment to gather his composure. "Marian Delbosque," he continued. "I have a record here of everything she has requested during her stay at the Garden of Angels. Most items make harmless dyes for tailoring. But there are berries and oils and roots here that, combined in the right way, can be used to make Dragon's Tongue. Other ingredients she has grown herself, right under the Prime Warden's nose. She has worked to gain the confidence of several members of your household staff. The clothes she makes are passed hand to hand until they reach your garderobe. Other items, I understand, she has given to you directly, as gifts. For weeks now every garment you've worn has had Dragon's Tongue woven into the very fabric. Those clothes have been devouring you, from the outside in. Left unchecked, this venom would have . . ."

The Inquisitor trailed off, concerned with how the Sheriff was taking the news. He had swung his legs off the bed and now sat facing the wall. The Inquisitor could see only the half of his face that appeared to be grinning, as it always did. He could not see the expression on the intact side of his face but he had the shocking impression the Sheriff might even be *crying.*

The Inquisitor cleared his throat. "I . . . I have been thorough in my investigation. I hold here the names of Marian's aides and accomplices. Most have already been detained, and are awaiting your attention. I'm pleased to report that . . . that there should be little lasting damage. Have your clothes burned and within a few weeks you should—"

"Marian Delbosque," the Sheriff said softly. "Have I not been patient? Have I not done everything in my power, taken extreme pains, to safeguard her from the wilderness? And now . . . *this* is how I am repaid."

The left side of his face went on grinning. Bishop Raths folded his hands, one across the other. When he could stand the silence no longer he cleared his throat. "Shall I . . . shall I order Marian put back in the hole?"

Before the Sheriff could answer there was a thumping at the door. Horor Conrad and Kluth Rogue came into the room.

"The outlaw . . . ," Horor Conrad said, out of breath. "He's here."

At first it seemed the Sheriff hadn't heard; he went on staring at the wall. The captains stood there, breathing hard. They glanced at one another.

Finally the Sheriff spoke. "Were my instructions closely observed?"

"He was allowed through, unchallenged," Kluth Rogue said. "He's coming up Gibbet Street now. No one will approach him until you give the word. We have one hundred rangers, hidden in houses of the merchants' ward. By the time he reaches the castle walls he'll be surrounded."

"And Edric Krul's design?"

The Inquisitor caught the briefest of glances pass between the two captains of the Guard.

426

"We did what he told us," Horor Conrad said. "It worked the way he said it would."

"So then, we are ready," the Sheriff said. "Help me stand. We will go to the barbican tower, where we may greet our guest."

Kluth Rogue and Horor Conrad helped the Sheriff to his feet. They walked together toward the door. As he passed Bishop Raths, the Sheriff looked up, his blue eye shining.

"As to Marian Delbosque . . . ," he said. "No, the oubliette will not do, not this time. That one needs her wings clipped permanently. When we have finished with the outlaw, go back to her, without delay. Take Jadder Payne with you. He will know what to do."

With the help of the two captains, the Sheriff limped from the room. Bishop Raths followed them out and went to find Jadder Payne.

IX. The Dark Heart

The four portals of Nottingham were closing, one by one. West Gate had just shut with a resounding *ca-clunk*.

Robin didn't pause. He prowled the deserted streets, listening for the sound of his enemies' boots. Still nobody came to face him. Could they all be so frightened?

Spreading his senses into the green, seeking the Sheriff and his troops, he finds . . . almost nothing. He realizes something disturbing: Beneath the human heat and fury of the city there is a profound layer of . . . silence.

As he swept onward he understood the reason: so many creatures lay dead in the streets. Here the stink of a pig, rotting. And there a scattering of pigeons, and the carcasses of dogs and sheep. This is why there were no birds above the roofs: Those that had fed here were dead; only the crows were clever enough to keep their distance.

What has happened here? Are these streets always so pestilent?

Robin's forest-mind struggling on, seeking what few creatures remain, scuttling through cellars with the cockroaches, snarling with a bandog chained in a merchant's house. It is hard work, and slow, Robin's impression of the world splintered.

But his steps didn't falter—rather, he moved faster—

because his forest-mind has lurched on and has managed to trace the lines to the center: the Sheriff's castle.

And there, at the top of a tower, one image at last emerges cold and clear. A man is there, leaning his weight on the battlements.

A man with a half-melted face, glistening in the light of a watch fire.

The Sheriff tips his head, and Robin knows he is looking directly at him. Despite the distance, and the gathering dark, the Sheriff locks his eye on Robin and he stares.

And when the Sheriff speaks his voice is weak and distant, but Robin *feels* his every word, twisting beneath his skin.

"Robin Hood. Welcome. You will forgive my not coming down to meet you in person. Of late I have been . . . afflicted. But rest assured, soon enough you and I shall stand face to face, and we will talk of dreams and fears. You need only lay down your weapons so we may begin . . ."

Even as the Sheriff speaks, Robin is directing his awareness down, down through the tower, searching for a way into the castle.

Again his forest-mind proves unwieldy and it plummets too far, down through the cellars and the kitchens, and down further, tumbling through ancient roots and water channels, into the castle's dungeons. Searching these caverns through the rats and the lice . . . he finds prisoners chained at the neck.

Could Marian be down here, among these wretches?

His awareness lurches lower, into the bowels of the oubliette, and even deeper, into some forgotten depth, and here he finds—

What, exactly, has he found?

Here there is something . . . *other* . . . something scabrous and glossy and raw. An eyeless thing that lifts its swollen head and opens its bubbling maw and turns toward Robin and *knows he is here.*

His forest-mind whimpering away like a scolded pup—shivering up through the dungeons and out of the castle—Robin shuddering fully back into his own body.

What fresh horror was this?

But whatever it was down there in the earth, even this could not slow his steps. Because the Sheriff was still talking, his words burning at the base of Robin's skull.

"There will be no need for further hostilities between us. I will ask a payment from you, naturally—recompense for the injury you inflicted upon me. But then I will grant you peace, and sanctuary. After all, do I not bear a measure of responsibility? The day I spared your life, and took your sight, did I not usher you down this savage path? Is it not true to say, to some extent, I created you . . . ?"

Robin searching once more for a route into the castle. There *must* be a way: an unwatched postern gate, a service tunnel. But again his forest-mind shows him little, scratching across cold stone and lifeless timber.

The world fractures further. His senses scatter among flies above a bloated corpse; they stir thickly with maggots feasting on a dead horse.

Dizziness swirling, Robin stumbling. Regaining his balance and running on. Beneath his feet he could feel grain, scattered across the cobbles. He reached down and scooped some into his hand and sniffed at the seed—it was poisoned. This is what had killed the birds, and anything that ate their corpses had died in turn.

So, the Sheriff's Guard had deliberately spread this pestilence . . . they knew Robin would come here . . .

And, worse, somebody had understood that all this death would blunt Robin's sense of the world . . .

Part of him knew then that he had blundered into a trap. But the greater part of him was ravenous for revenge, and would not turn back. He readied his bow and he powered toward the castle.

From the northern edge of the city the third gate was crashing shut. *Ca-clunk.* At closer quarters a different noise was rising: a rasping, clanking cacophony. It put Robin in mind of the people of Wodenhurst, on the night of the Walking, clashing their sticks against pans, blowing reed whistles. This noise swelled louder, ahead and to either side.

Here then were the Sheriff's troops—hiding within these buildings. They were clanking their clubs against their shields and blowing war horns. And the din was making it even harder for Robin to get his bearings.

He collided with a fire barrel, the stagnant water sloshing. He slipped on the contents of a chamber pot, tipped onto cobbles.

He stumbled on, drawing his bow, taking aim at the Sheriff. The shadow shard twisted tight and sprang loose—the arrow flew with great power—but the shot whistled far too high. His next arrow broke against the castle walls.

The soldiers' cacophony was swelling behind him now, as well as to the sides. He tripped over something and went to his knees. But his rage hauled him to his feet and he lurched on.

He shot another arrow and it skittered across cobbles.

Still he charged onward.

But then, finally, seeping through all the noise and the rage, a voice slipped into his thoughts. *Robin, come back to me. I can't do this alone.*

He came to a halt. He gripped the jade amulet at his chest.

This is the most dangerous time, for both of us. It's not enough to be strong—you have to be clever.

431

He was suddenly furious with himself. This suicidal attack would not help Marian—no more than it had the first time his anger had taken control, when she had been locked in that cage. After all this time, after all he had endured, had he learned nothing?

Trumpets blared atop the castle walls; doors slammed; soldiers flooded out of the buildings, their boots thundering.

Robin turned from the castle and he ran.

Dozens of rangers were descending on him—the jaws of the trap snapping shut.

He sprinted away just in time—throwing nets swished narrowly wide, a single club struck him on the arm.

He ran toward South Gate, the rangers in pursuit, yelling and blowing horns and banging their clubs against their shields. He darted off the main streets, well-lit with hanging lamps, and he fled through the darkened alleys of the slums.

He stumbled over something dead at his feet. He collided with a wall but regained his balance and ran on. Rangers came at him from either side. He darted between them—spiked clubs caught him glancing blows or whispered wide.

There was no fizz of crossbow bolt or hiss of arrow: The Sheriff wanted Robin taken alive. He swept around another group of soldiers and they charged after him, shouting.

Ahead was South Gate, only fifty paces away. But it was closing with a grinding of wood and rattling of chains.

Thirty paces away, twenty, ten.

The portal clumped shut. *Cla-clunk.*

Robin ran close to the city walls, soldiers swarming around him, thick as flies. He slipped through their grasp and he leaped onto the steps that led to the ramparts. He fled to the top of the walls.

Without pause he flung himself over the battlements.

His heart lurched; his breath stuck in his throat. A long, frightening drop.

He splashed down in the cold, deep river.

He came to the surface, gasping, and he swam to the bank and dragged himself onto dry land. He crouched beneath a stone bridge, listening for the sound of soldiers in pursuit. There was only the blaring of horns within the walls, shouting from the ramparts. The city gates remained closed.

He crouched there, shivering, seething with frustration. How would he ever claim his revenge, with the entire Sheriff's Guard standing in his way? How would he free Marian if she was locked within that fortress? He would need an army, and siege engines.

Except—

Would I?

Or was there another way?

The black tentacles shifted in Robin's palm. He felt what power the shadow of the wolf held, even this fragment. He thought of possessing the whole of the weapon once more and his whole body fizzed with the idea of it . . .

This time I could master it, and not be its slave. Haven't I learned to wield the piece that remains?

He remembered what else the vixen-woman had offered.

Three gifts I have, buried beneath. Which would you take: the shadow, the blood, the teeth?

The Shadow. The Blood. The Teeth.

How powerful would a person become were they to possess all three?

Thinking all this, he found himself leaving the riverbank and returning the way he had come. He broke into a run, the black tendrils tugging at his arm, speeding him toward the wildwood, and toward the goddess of the forest, and her gifts.

X. End Times

All Marian's meticulous plans were starting to unravel. Something had gone horribly wrong, that was the only explanation.

She and all twelve of her fellow prisoners had been corralled into one place. They were all in the wash room, sitting on the tiled floor, amid the buckets and the ewers and the barrels. Four wardens flanked the only doorway. Norman Banes was there, sweating heavily, his crazed eyes rolling side to side. Gordon Sleth fidgeted, looking anywhere but at Aimee Clearwater.

"What's going on?" Ira Starr whispered at Marian's side.

"Why aren't they saying anything?" said Ena Agutter. "Where's Killen Skua?"

"Listen," said Alice White. "Hear the gates? Somebody's come. Who is it?"

Alice was right: Riders were being led into the Garden of Angels. Bishop Raths again? And who else? What could be so urgent that they had traveled here now, after dark?

"Marian, what is it?" said Elfen Goldacre.

"Something's not right," said Petronilla Coldish. "What do we do if—"

"Be quiet," hissed Minnie Reaper. "Can't you see she's

thinking. Everybody stay calm. Don't crowd so close." Black-haired Minnie, as tiny as she was fierce, elbowed and poked the others until they shuffled away and allowed Marian more space.

Now Marian could hear people approaching. One of them was carrying tools—they clinked as the person walked. Because of the enclosed cloisters and the acoustic pots the sounds became an ominous thump and rustle as they came to a halt outside the wash room.

"Be my guest." This was Killen Skua's voice.

The visitors came inside.

Sonskya Luz sucked in a breath. Alice White groaned. The visitor was not Bishop Raths; as far as the prisoners were concerned, this was somebody far worse. Here was Gideon Johns, the Apothecary. His apprentice followed behind, struggling under the weight of his master's casket. It was this that had caused the clinking sound.

Killen Skua came forward, smoothing his mustache with a finger and thumb of one hand. "As you all know," he said, "I like to think of myself as fair-minded. That is why you girls are granted certain freedoms and . . . privileges. But . . . recently my generosity has been abused. I have been forced to endure disobedience and disturbance." Here he looked at Lyssa Brekehart. His eyes flicked across the other girls, each in turn. "Worst of all are these markings that have appeared on some of your wrists. All of which is unacceptable. Whatever is going on here"—this time he stared at Marian—"*whatever* is going on here, it will stop."

"Your troubles are not in the least surprising," the Apothecary said. "A young woman's elements contain excessive fire. When quartered together, they feed off one another, until they are burning beyond control." He had opened his casket and was taking out phials and flasks, squinting at each

435

in turn. These were his purgatives: vile concoctions of linseed and salt soap and beetles' wings and wasp stings. "But fear not," he continued. "My art is equal to the task. And a full moon is rising—the most efficacious time to act. I will soon restore serenity to these troubled young souls."

Marian had witnessed this man's treatments: She had seen girls so racked with sickness that afterward they were mere husks of their former selves. During her initial imprisonment here, Marian herself had been bedridden by one of his potions and had taken weeks to recover her vitality. That is what the Apothecary meant by *serenity*.

"The remedy required will vary by individual case," the Apothecary said. "Naturally, each subject will need a purgative to begin, to cleanse the humors. We will follow with ministrations of water and ice, to dampen the excessive fire. But some of the afflicted will require the opposite: a treatment of intense heat. The malady, made to rage, will burn itself out, exhausted of fuel. So, since we are here and ready and able, you may bring forward the first subject and we will proceed." Gideon Johns turned. "Master Skua, I said I am ready for the first subject, if you please."

But Killen Skua was no longer listening. Neither was Marian. Her attention had been drawn to the rear of the wash room. Lusk Varg, a sentry from the main gates, had appeared at the doorway, short of breath. Killen Skua had gone to join him and the two of them were talking in low tones.

A creaking and rattling meant the gates were opening once more.

"Who is it now?" said Elfen Goldacre. "What can't wait until morning?"

Marian thought she heard Lusk Varg mutter two names: the first was Bishop Raths. The second was Jadder Payne. Other girls heard it too and a nervous whisper began to spread.

436

"Did you hear? The Inquisitor. Here."

"With the torturer. Why?"

Marian felt the Prime Warden staring at her. *The Inquisitor does know something. What has he uncovered?*

Killen Skua glanced up at Norman Banes and Marian felt her panic deepen. *How much do they know?*

"Marian," the Prime Warden said. "Come here to me."

She stood and shuffled mutely toward Killen Skua, her hands at her sides.

Killen Skua came forward. He reached out an arm. "Marian, come with me. I don't know what—"

Marian flew at him, screeching, her teeth bared—Killen Skua, startled, stepped back. Marian sprang to the side, raced around the Prime Warden, ducked the grasp of Lusk Varg. Two other guards closed together, the gap narrowed, the men reached, but they were too slow and Marian had dashed between them and fled out of the wash room.

She ran. Through the cloisters and the corridors. Skidding and slipping on the floor rushes. A warden appeared from a side door. She went to the floor and skidded beneath his lunge. Another warden lurched at her but she ducked and weaved and kept running. Other guards merely stood and stared at Marian as she went. They had known this slack-eyed girl for longer than a year, and in all that time she had barely shown a glimmer of life. Now she was a wildcat, hissing and scratching at any hand that crossed her path.

She ran through the gardens and the lashing rain and she reached the northern end of the convent, where the tower stood. She darted inside and started up, taking three steps at a time. The golden angels painted on the walls spiraled past and Marian grew dizzy—the stairwell inviting a thirty-foot fall. She put her hand to the wall and ran on. Breathing hard, she reached the top. The domed prayer room. She went to the window and looked down. Killen Skua was approaching, flanked by two rangers, the wolf-head insignia on their chests. And two other men followed behind. One was Bishop Raths, gripping the hem of his cassock.

The second was Jadder Payne.

He was holding what looked like a small pair of wool shears.

No, no, she thought. *Too soon. I needed more time.* She turned away from the window and went to the far wall. With her fingernails she eased out a single brick. She reached into the cavity and pulled out the smithing hammer she had hidden there weeks before. She used the hammer to smash at the bricks, the noise echoing down the tower.

Over many months, using a gardening trowel, Marian had spent her nights scraping away at the mortar of this wall. Now one brick gave way, tumbled out. A second leaped free. If ten or perhaps twelve of these bricks were removed, it might just be possible for a slim person to crawl through and throw themselves out and over the curtain wall and into the river beyond.

A third brick popped out, a fourth, the hammer beating the same rhythm as the soldiers' boots on the stairs.

A fifth brick. A sixth.

The final one.

A pair of boots had stopped. A second came to a standstill.

Marian looked to the doorway, the two soldiers there, rainwater running from their skull-helms. Behind them came Killen Skua, and then Bishop Raths, a grim expression on his leathery face. Finally appeared Jadder Payne, his expression blank, gripping the shears.

Marian put down the hammer.

So this was it. Time up.

XI. The Final Cord

Robin's forest-mind flies ahead, rustling the hedgerows. It ghosts through homes, making children stir in their beds. It stone-skips across ponds and puddles. It reaches Winter Forest and here it starbursts, sparkling through root and burrow, fuming with breath and spore, glittering away infinite as the heavens.

And instantly he finds her: the goddess of the forest. She is walking back and forth across a shimmering glade, humming softly to herself. Her skin is flushed in the moonlight and she has one hand resting atop her swollen middle.

We've planted the seed; now it must grow. No need for talk; let the deed show.

Where would this new development lead? What more did she want from him? But such thoughts did not make him pause. He forced himself to think of the shadow of the wolf, of possessing it entirely once more, and he quickened his pace . . .

But then he came to a halt. Because his forest-mind has also rippled backward, seeking any rangers who may be in pursuit. There is Nottingham, a shrieking void in the web of green, and there is something else, a few miles outside the city, which demands his attention . . .

A patrol of horsemen, traveling east, following moonlit paths. Six of these men cause barely a tremor in Robin's forest-mind. But the seventh rider is a distortion—a hot-steel noise and a red twisting taste. He is a tall, skeletal man, a holster of knives concealed beneath his cloak.

Here is the man who took Robin's eyes.

Jadder Payne.

Robin turned away from Winter Forest; he loped after this patrol. The vixen-woman would have to wait. Tonight Robin would, after all, claim a measure of his revenge.

His forest-mind nosing after these men, trying to sense them more clearly. They are approaching a walled town. At least, Robin thinks it is a walled town, or perhaps it is a fortress, or even a convent. Could it be a prison? His impression of this place is confused: It is quiet colors and musical aromas, but it is also hard tastes and a hatred that prickles the skin. All of this refusing to swim into focus.

Jadder Payne and the other men have reached the gates and are being led inside. Robin running faster, loping through field and copse and across stream and river, slipping through deserted hamlet and ghost village.

His forest-mind probing at the mystery place, thinking now that something has changed behind those walls . . . something has snapped, like a spring-loaded trap. There is running and shouting and violence.

And at the heart of this disturbance is a single blazing figure.

A wildfire force of nature.

And he knows he has found her, at last.

Marian.

His muscles burning, his heart thundering, sprinting to the limits of his strength and beyond, charging across scrub

440

and splashing through ford and running through rain now falling in torrents.

And then stumbling, almost falling to the mud. Because very faint, through the wall of rain, a scream.

He was too late. He had let them hurt her, again.

A second inhuman shriek.

They were killing her.

He flew across the ground—the shadow tendrils boiling through his skin—over hillock and across vale and through thicket. He crested a high hill above the mystery place—above Marian's prison. He powered down the lee slope, into a wooded valley.

More screaming, slicing through the night.

Robin kept running, but now it felt more like falling. The ground had opened up and the one final cord tying him to this world had been cut and he was spiraling through blackness . . .

A shout went up, and the blaring of a horn. The prison guards must have spotted him. He tried to make sense of how many men, and where, but his forest-mind was fuzzy through his pain and fury.

It made little difference, in any case, because Robin knew one thing with clarity: This would be a fight to the death. If this was the end for Marian, it would be the end for him too.

Our fates are tied. We've always known that . . . I am you, just the same as you are me.

Guards were coming toward him, their spears leveled, the slanting rain drumming against their shields. From behind the walls the screaming continued, raw and strange.

Too late. Failed.

Robin readied his bow. He nocked an arrow and powered toward the waiting spears. This was the end. A fight to the death and a measure of revenge. That was all he had left.

*

In those moments before the first scream, Bishop Raths studied Marian Delbosque, cowering in the corner of the prayer room. He felt a strange mixture of emotions for this girl. Desire, certainly. Respect, yes. To think she had almost succeeded where warlords and assassins had failed: to kill the Sheriff. And all from behind these walls! He felt a degree of pity. This was a cruel place, this painted prison, he understood that. And now Jadder Payne was about to cut her hamstrings. By crippling her they would be sending Marian to the cruelest prison of all—she would spend the rest of her life caged within her own body.

The Inquisitor looked at Marian and he felt one final emotion . . .

Fear.

Fear, truly? The idea shocked him. The girl was thoroughly at their mercy. Look at her, pushed into the corner, wearing only those ascetic rags, defiance battling panic in those gray-green eyes. How could he possibly fear this girl?

A jumble of thoughts arrived simultaneously, jostling for their correct position, trying to form an idea that was long overdue.

Marian had won help from beyond these walls . . .

If poisoned garments could be smuggled out, then other objects could be smuggled in . . .

He thought of all Marian had achieved.

An extremely resourceful girl, and ingenious. Yes, ingenious most of all.

What other resources does she have in this place? What else could she use . . . ?

He remembered the Prime Warden's words.

Some of the girls do a bit of archery. They even like to swing a practice sword.

A lump rose in his throat. He looked at the wall where Marian had been hammering. She didn't have a hope of escaping that way, not really. She would break her neck on the curtain wall. But the hammering had produced one tangible effect: the noise had brought the wardens and the soldiers running. They were all of them gathering here. All in one place. Leaving the other girls unwatched.

The idea hardened into its finished form. The Inquisitor took a step back.

The fear grew. So did the respect.

Clever girl. You're not just one killer. You've bred a whole flock of killers. Deadly little angels all.

But these thoughts, and this final realization, had arrived too late. Because Marian was already reaching into the space within the wall, and Killen Skua was walking forward, saying: "You've brought this on yourself, Marian. Don't make it worse than it has to be. If you don't struggle, it can be over quickly and cleanly. There's no point fighting. We've got you cornered."

And when Marian removed her hand from wall she was holding three short pipes of some sort. "Do you?" she said, those magnificent eyes flashing. "Or do we have you cornered?"

And she smiled. And in the next instant the screaming began.

XII. Angel of Death

From her hiding place Marian removed the three blow-pipes. She put the first of these to her lips and she spat the sticky liquid. Killen Skua screamed, clawing at his eyes.

Bishop Raths had already turned and was fleeing for the stairs. The two rangers were following his lead, bustling Jadder Payne to safety.

Marian stood. She walked past Killen Skua, writhing on the floor, and she followed the fleeing men onto the stairs. She put the second blowpipe to her mouth. The poison glob-ule struck one of the rangers across the back of his neck. He gasped, slipped, grabbed onto Jadder Payne—they fell together into the stairwell, the soldier screaming, Jadder Payne disappearing without a sound.

The next glob of poison hissed harmlessly off the second soldier's helm. He ran on, out of range. No matter—there would be no escape for these men. Bishop Raths and the sur-viving warden were reaching the bottom of the stairs and when they got there Marian heard noises that satisfied her. From elsewhere in the Garden of Angels came similar sounds: a muffled shout; a gurgled cry; a heavy crash and slump.

Marian continued to the foot of the stairs. At the base of the tower she found the body of the ranger who had fallen.

She looked for Jadder Payne but there was no sign of his corpse. Outside the tower Minnie Reaper and Ira Starr and Ena Agutter were waiting for her, gripping their hatchets and their stiletto blades, their smocks splattered with blood. At their feet were the twitching bodies of Bishop Raths and the second ranger who had fled.

"The torturer," said Marian. "Did he get past you?"

"We didn't see him," said Minnie Reaper, frowning.

"We'll find him," Marian said. "He's used up the last of his lives."

Ira Starr held out a shortbow and a quiver of arrows. Marian took them and strode off through the gardens, the other three at her back. The fires had already been lit. The smell of smoke and the crackle of flames. Marian smashed an oil lamp and started another blaze.

A panicked warden fled across their path. Marian drew her bow as she walked. She missed with her first shot, nocked and drew again, hit the man in the thigh. The warden went to the ground and other girls appeared and fell on him with knives. At the sound of hammering from the tower, all the prisoners had gone to their hiding places and retrieved their smuggled weapons. Now they were busy killing with garrote wire and poison dart and throwing dagger.

Another guard crossed Marian's path and she went to one knee and unsheathed an arrow over her shoulder. She nocked, drew, let loose. The arrow tore a gash in the man's arm. He cried out, stumbled, but managed to scramble out of sight before Marian could shoot again. It made little difference. These arrowheads—in common with all other steel wielded by the prisoners—had been doused in a poison made from wolfsbane. Any guard who escaped with a graze would only be saving himself for a death that lingered.

Marian moved on. She passed Aimee Clearwater. The

beautiful redhead had become a blood-soaked devil, a hatchet in each hand, still hacking down at the corpse of Gordon Sleth.

Thankfully most of the prisoners had remained more composed than Aimee. These girls had learned one skill above all else at the Garden of Angels: self-possession. How to remain pacific on the surface even when fury was raging within. Marian now saw that trait in abundance: Most of the girls were going about their grim labor wearing the same neutral expression they wore while saying their prayers or doing their needlework.

"Walk, don't run," Ena Agutter said with a straight face, throwing her hatchet and catching a fleeing jailer behind the knee.

"What have you been told?" said Minnie Reaper. "Lower your voices. Comport yourselves." She crouched to a shrieking warden and silenced him with her garrotte.

"Insolence will be punished," said Ira Starr, plunging her stiletto blade into another guard.

Marian moved through it all, feeling exhilarated, yes, but more than anything with a crushing sense of frustration. All this had come too soon: These events were not meant to unfold until she had received news of the Sheriff's death. Even after today, their true freedom would have to wait. *But for now, forget all that. Get this finished, quickly, and lead them to safety.*

On the ground amid smashed potted plants, Estrild Lunn and Elfen Goldacre were killing a guard with a chokewire. He was thrashing in his death throes, but the girls were patiently sticking to their task, shifting their positions and twisting the wire. Ena Agutter strode off to help Seren Child dispose of another recalcitrant guard.

Yes, they were performing admirably, Marian's Destroying Angels. Even the girls she feared might be a problem were proving resolute. Look at Petronilla Coldish. This willowy girl had only been here six months and had yet to develop a full loathing for her jailers. But here she was, ferocious, joining a pack of girls to hunt down a warden. He was trying to crawl behind a statue of an archangel, the girls hacking at any exposed limb.

Marian suspected her berserker's draft had played its part with Petronilla. The same potion she had tested on Lyssa Brekehart she later distributed to some of the more timid girls and told them to drink the moment they heard the fighting start. Perhaps the draft was working a little too well, in fact. Alice White went flying past, her lips curled back from her teeth, a blade raised above her head, the epitome of vengeful fury, but pursuing nobody as far as Marian could see.

"Minnie," Marian said over her shoulder. "Follow Alice. She's chasing shadows. Get her to the front gates. I'll meet you there."

Minnie Reaper flitted away, her raven hair flying. The flames now were visible on every side, crawling up buildings and along rafters. The rain becoming steam before it reached the ground. Marian and Ira Starr stalked the corridors, looking for survivors. Marian found one pathetic specimen clawing at the door of a chapel, as if he might find salvation inside. This one's name was William Blayde, and he had done Marian no particular indignity, apart from patronizing her with a fatherly smile every time he locked her in her sleeping cell. She supposed this one deserved to die quickly: She discharged an arrow into his heart.

The arcades were collapsing, fire eating through the timber frames, heat peeling the paint from the faces of angels. A statue fell and smashed. *Time to leave*, Marian thought. *Fire will finish the job we've started.*

But then she came across Sonskya Luz. Sonskya was the youngest and quietest girl in the Garden of Angels. A slight, almost skinny frame, with large blue eyes and skin so pale it was practically translucent. She was standing in a prayer garden, gripping a roundel dagger in both hands, the tip of it shaking.

"She won't do it," said Lyssa Brekehart. "She won't play her part."

"Sonskya was here first," said Avelina Sharpe. "He was hers. We helped her, but she refuses."

Harold Toor—a big guard and sadistic—slouched half dead against a fountain. Sonskya was standing well clear of the warden, holding the blade at arm's length.

"I-I . . . can't."

"Did you drink it?" Marian said. "The berserker draft?"

Sonskya shook her head very slightly.

Marian sighed. "That would have made this easier. I told you it would. Now you'll have to do it without."

"I . . . I . . . *can't!*"

"Then you've condemned us all. We're not leaving without you, and nobody is carried for free."

Sonskya's blade quivered. In the wide whites of her eyes tiny reflections of fire had appeared.

"It's all up to you now," Marian said.

The other girls were glancing around them at the fire.

"Come *on,*" hissed Avelina Sharpe. "Are you one of us or not?"

Sonskya took a step toward the guard, and then another. The tip of her blade came to rest on his chest.

"It's us or him," Marian said. "Your friends, and all we have done for you, or this man, and everything he did."

The other girls coughing. An arcade crashing, close by.

Sonskya's eyes now full of reflected fire. "I can't do it," she said. "Please, I can't. I—"

Lyssa Brekehart put her shoulder to Sonskya's back and shoved. Sonskya fell forward onto the broad hilt of the dagger. The pyramidal blade was designed to puncture plate armor and it slid easily into the warden's chest, making little more noise than Sonskya's gasp. Harold Toor's eyes opened wide and stayed that way.

"Good enough," Marian said. "Avelina, bring Sonskya."

Marian strode through the smoke-filled convent. Girls finished what they are doing and fell into step. The crash of a cloister collapsing. A whoosh of sparks rushing into the air. Marian headed for the main gates, sweeping up the last of the girls in her wake. Minnie Reaper and Alice White and some of the others were there at the exit, sentries sprawled at their feet.

All thirteen former prisoners emerged from the Garden of Angels together, an inferno at their backs. Marian led them a safe distance away and then took a moment to count heads. They were all here. Every one, safe.

"We have to get clear, and quickly," Marian said. "Avelina, keep hold of Sonskya. Minnie and Seren, follow at the rear, make sure nobody falls behind."

Marian scanned the hillside. Clouds were obscuring the full moon, and the smoke too was thickening the darkness. That would help provide cover, but it would also make their progress across country slower. They must begin at once.

She turned, preparing to lead the girls away. And it was then she saw him.

He was little more than a faint shape, half crouching in the dark, hundreds of paces away. Yet she knew it was him.

Robin.

She put her hand to the amulet at her neck, oblivious to the heat at her back, and she stood and she stared.

*

The closer Robin had run to Marian's prison, the more he felt like he was tumbling through the dark. He ran on and the dizziness grew worse. But he didn't pause. He stumbled toward the prison guards. He drew his bow, tried to steady his arm, took aim.

But then he realized something: These sentries were not running to meet an intruder; they were running *away* from something else. They were gripping their spears only through fear as they fled into the night.

He relaxed his bow, let them go. As he moved closer to the prison he smelled smoke. The rain stopped abruptly and he felt waves of heat.

Fire. The prison was erupting in fire.

And out of the fire came Marian.

He stumbled to a halt.

She's here. She's safe.

She had run clear of the inferno and stopped. She seemed to be gesturing toward the horizon, and saying something— her words lost beneath the roar of the flames, the crash of cloisters collapsing.

She turned, saw Robin, froze.

She's alive. She's unhurt.

She made a movement—maybe pushing her hair out of her eyes. She was holding something—perhaps a hunting bow. After all this time, Robin was dismayed to find his sense of her was fuzzy at the edges. Was this merely the shock of being near her once more? Or was it the swirling inferno that was muddling his senses? But then again, hadn't Robin's impression of this place been confused from the start . . . ? He knew he should be trying to explore this idea further, but he could think of nothing now except Marian.

She was here, at the bottom of this slope. He had found her, at last.

Several other young women were moving around Marian. Their smells were of sweat and smoke and blood. Blood on their hands and on their clothes and in their hair. But Robin's impression of them was fading—everything else in this world drifting to nothing and leaving only Marian, burning in the dark.

And still she didn't move.

Still she just stood there, staring.

Staring, the same way Will Scarlett had done when he first set eyes on Robin Hood. Staring, the same as those children on the edge of Winter Forest, before they fled for home.

Staring at the monster. Horrified.

And suddenly he knew: Marian was scared of him too. Any moment now she would turn and run. How could she stand to be near him, now? How could she even bear to *look* at what he had become? He felt stupid and angry for allowing himself to imagine they could one day be back together.

She was about to turn and leave him here, he was sure of it.

But then she made another movement—he thought she lifted a hand and gripped the jade amulet hanging at her chest. And when she took a step it was not away from Robin but toward him.

She edged closer, one foot slowly in front of the other, as if just learning to walk. She dropped her bow, both hands now clasping her amulet. Letting the rest of the world fade to black, Robin's sense of her was growing clearer. He thought she glanced down, frowning, and she seemed to be stepping over an object lying on the ground. She stepped over something else—it was the corpse of a cat. And here was a dead bird.

A shiver ran down Robin's spine. He realized what had happened here: Carcasses had been carried from the city and strewn all around these prison walls. That was why Robin's senses had lost their edge—just as they had back at the city.

This was another trap.

"Marian, run!"

But it was too late. Circling the prison, bursting clear of the inferno, swimming fuzzily into Robin's awareness, were a score of men, each of them raising a blade and descending on one of the young women.

And the man in the lead was rushing up behind Marian.

He was reaching his clawed hand around her neck.

And Robin smelled blood welling at her throat.

XIII. Under the Skin

Edric Krul held Marian at the throat, gripping so hard he had drawn blood. Marian shrieked and kicked but Edric twisted his claw and she became still.

Robin lurched toward them.

"You will stay where you are," Edric said. "One more step and this pretty thing loses her head, snip-snip. You will place your bow on the ground." He laughed—a lunatic cackle. "I ordered you to do that once before, the first time we met, do you recall? You chose that day to disobey. Let us see, at long last, if you have learned your place."

Marian gasped as Edric squeezed her throat tighter. Robin let his bow fall from his fingers. He shrugged off his quiver and cast it aside.

"The same goes for the rest of you," Edric said. "If you would rather Marian stay in one piece, throw down your arms."

Some of the young women had broken away, spun at their assailants with blades bared. But now as they looked at Marian they let their weapons fall.

"Shievers, Scale," Edric said. "Come here to me. Hold Marian close. Scale, press your knife here, beneath her chin. She is hellfire, this one, but observe, she obeys the blade well enough."

Two other men—half-naked and crazed like their leader—took hold of Marian.

"I am going to talk with the outlaw, and to claim what is mine," Edric said. "If he should raise an arm against me—so much as a finger—Marian will be the first to know of it. Are we clear?"

He left them and came toward Robin. Edric Krul reeked of metal and blood: The metal was the grapnel hook where his right hand used to be, and the steel plate fixed to his skull; the blood came from these dead dogs and pigeons that lay scattered about—he had smeared his bare arms and chest with their innards.

These smells drew closer, closer, until Edric was standing against Robin, toe-to-toe. He leaned in and his breath too stank of blood. He moved his mouth close to Robin's ear.

"We are brothers, you and I," Edric whispered. "We have both of us been through the fire. And here we stand, enlightened, on the other side. We possess truths the innocents would never understand. Truths that would destroy their minds to even try! Even the Sheriff is groping in the dark. He wants your skin, but he would be lost within it. He has endured much, so I have learned, yet his insight is naught compared to ours. No, he shall not have the skin. And you have owned it long enough. It is time it came to me."

He raised his sharpened hook and put it to Robin's shoulder. He raked it downward, tearing through the wolf pelt and Robin's flesh.

"Robin!" Marian shouted. She shouted something else but her words were stifled by a hand clamped across her mouth.

Edric raised his claw to Robin's other shoulder and drew it down once more, plowing deep as the bone. Robin gritted his teeth and he managed not to fight back or to cry out.

"Let Marian go," he said. "You have my word, I won't fight

you. Do what you will with me . . . I'm beyond caring. Only set her free."

In reply Edric only made a *tsk-tsk* sound with his tongue. He walked around Robin to stand behind him. The razor claw raked across Robin's shoulder blades. The cold sensation of blood flowing—but the pain was oddly muted—the wolf pelt must be absorbing the worst of this torture. The cloak felt alive, writhing, constricting.

Edric laughed, but this time there was anger in the cackle. "You have worn the skin too long," he said. "It is stubbornly bound. Well then, I will have to dig deeper."

He grunted with effort as he raised his arm high and brought it lashing down. The hook buried deep. Robin slumped to his knees. Edric wrestled with the claw and it sucked free. It went up and came down, driving deeper into Robin's back.

He fell to his stomach. The blackness spinning around him, numbness spreading through his limbs. He thought he could hear Marian screaming, but only vaguely. All sounds had become distant echoes, as if they belonged to a different life.

Edric jerked the claw loose. He brought it up and back down, grunting like a farmer hoeing soil. Robin heard tearing, slicing, and a wet thud—he thought Edric was removing whole strips of the wolf pelt and casting them aside.

Robin's world turning faster. Edric cackling.

The claw slashing, digging, tearing.

The ground giving way, Robin falling into the earth.

Hurtling further, and faster. Time beginning to fold.

He finds he is near a burning village; above him is a man with a ruined face.

Why the delay? The prescribed punishment is death.

Time folds further and he is a squire, riding away from a citadel, a warlord watching him go.

You're dead to us now, Loxley.

He is a boy, lying near a campfire, his father stroking his hair.

Find you I promise.

He is everywhere else from his past lives, all in the same instant: he is in his childhood bed, his mother singing a tale of a journey home; he is huddled with Marian in their den, reading stories by lamplight, while a snowstorm swirls outside.

These echoes pile up, layer upon layer. Here are sounds from more recent times: the wet popping of arrows striking flesh; the *schling* of steel against steel. Bellows of pain and violence.

Although . . . these new sensations . . . so close, and clear. Memories of the past, or events unfolding now?

It seemed Edric Krul had paused in his torture. He was shouting and shaking his claw toward Marian and the burning prison. More of those noises: the *zip-zip* of arrows; the crack of bone beneath a sword; a piercing scream. Robin shifted his weight, managed to drag himself to his knees.

He understood what was happening: Will Scarlett was here. Will Scarlett and Borston Black and Ironside and Much Millerson and many other outlaws besides. They had slipped down the wooded slope and charged out of the dark and taken Edric's minions by surprise. Edric's men were defending themselves, but they had turned their backs on their captives and the young women had retrieved their bows and knives and were putting them to work.

All this came to Robin fuzzily, but it was enough to clear his head and bring him to his senses. He lurched to his feet. Feeling came back into his arms and legs. Surely by now he should be dead . . . ? But he felt the wolf pelt warping, closing over his wounds, knitting his flesh.

He stumbled a few paces to his bow, picked it up. He staggered past Edric Krul, headed down the slope toward Marian. He trained his senses toward her, trying to pick out the two men who had been standing guard at her side. He could smell one of them lifeless on the ground. The other was wrestling with her, trying to plunge his knife into her throat.

Robin ran closer, still unsteady on his feet, disoriented. He drew his bow, trying to sense a clear shot.

Marian twisted, broke free. Her attacker went after her, raising his blade . . .

Robin let loose, his arrow fizzed, the man fell dead.

Robin stalked onward, hissing between his teeth. There were many more of these lunatic killers—these men who meant Marian harm. His bow sang again—a second body slumped. Another man came at him, screaming, swinging a club. The force of Robin's arrow lifted him off his feet.

Robin's rage did not reduce, but grew fiercer. He released two arrows at once and they forked apart and each found a man in the heart. The shadow shard was twisting cold through his muscles and his bones. The shard shook and another man died.

His enemies' fear and his own rage fed the shadow veins— he heard them sighing, like soil drinking in the rain. Each arrow flew faster, with a sharper killing edge. His next shot removed a leg. Another burst a head, like a berry squeezed between fingers. A third cleaved a man clean open, the way a child tears a leaf down the middle, leaving two halves shaking in the wind. Another man died in the far distance.

He became aware that all other fighting had stopped. Edric's surviving men were running for their lives; the outlaws had lowered their blades and were standing in silence.

It was over. They had won.

He fought and he fought and he managed to still his arm. He forced his bow down and held it at his side. *It's done. She's safe.*

He stood, and breathed, and the thunder in his heart began to ease. But then a noise behind him—Edric Krul, running down the slope, his claw raised.

"No! I will not allow it . . . Your purpose is to serve! I have seen to the heart of the world . . . I stand at the center . . . You are *nothing* . . . Kneel at my feet, give up your skin . . ."

Robin set his feet, nocked an arrow. He let his mind go dark, sent all the power of the shadow shard into his arms and his chest. He drew, let loose, the arrow thundered through the night. It struck Edric Krul and destroyed him utterly, leaving only pieces scattered in the grass.

Robin's fury surged, reenergized. He listened for more of these killers to slay. There must be more. Here's one: a huge man with bloody knuckles. He'd do. This man smelled of blood too.

Robin drew, took aim at the man's heart. The shadow shard snaked and raged. He almost, *almost*, let loose. He fought to control his arm, telling himself this was an ally. This was Much Millerson.

But what was the difference? Much was a killer now. A man of war. *All these people are bathed in blood.*

Here, Will Scarlett, his curved blade dripping with gore; and Ironside and Borston Black, stinking of all they had done in the Sheriff's name. And these other outlaws, all of them the same, reeking of death. Robin took aim at each of them, one by one, his fingers quivering.

The shadow shard shook and shuddered, ravenous for every one of these lives. Even these young women, bodies slumped at their feet, the taste of murder in their beautiful, silent mouths. The point of his arrow passed across one heart, then another, and the next, the shadow shard raging, demanding he let loose . . .

Robin fighting, shuddering, gritting his teeth, battling the killing lust . . .

Finally, fraction by fraction, he managed to relax his arm. He lowered his bow and removed the arrow. The shadow shard gave a final awful spasm before unwinding and dissolving back into his palm.

The flames crackled. A dying man moaned.

The outlaws were silent, staring at Robin. All the young women too. And Marian. She hadn't moved a muscle.

She was just staring.

If she wasn't frightened of him before, surely she was now . . .

For certain this time she would turn and run and leave Robin here.

But when she took a step, and another, it was toward him. She moved nearer, her hands at her side, as if walking in a dream.

Only twenty paces away, then ten, then close enough to touch.

Robin opened his mouth to speak, but no words emerged, all the things he wanted to say building up beneath his tongue—just the same as last time they were reunited, a lifetime ago. Marian too was silent, and still. He listened to her heart, racing fast as a squirrel pup's.

Finally she put two fingers to her lips, reached up and pressed the kiss to his forehead. Then her hand moved across his face, her fingers searching his cheek, his nose, his lips, as if she was the blind one. Her smell changed minutely and Robin knew there was a tear on her cheek.

"I thought I was losing you," she said. "After all this time, you'd come back to me, and I thought he was killing you. I could feel you slipping away. Everything I've endured, that was the worst." She wiped at her cheek. Then her fingers went back to searching Robin's face, and down to probe at his right shoulder. Robin recoiled.

"You must be hurt," she said. "Let me see, I can help." There was a dull pain in Robin's back, but it merely felt like muscles hardening after heavy work. In truth, he had never felt stronger. "It's nothing," he said. "It must have looked bad. Are you injured?"

"Just a scratch. I suppose we've both been through worse. And there's more to come, if we don't hurry. He won't like what's happened here. He'll send an army."

"I know where we'll be safe."

"Yes. Take us there."

And she locked her fingers with his, and they were turning together and running side by side through the night.

Behind them Will Scarlett was calling instructions to the outlaws: "Borston Black, in the vanguard with me . . . Blodwyn Kage, Ironside, watch the rear and round up stragglers . . ." And Marian's Destroying Angels were forming a procession, hand in hand. And all of them were following, away from the burning prison, back toward Winter Forest.

But to Robin all these other people were gray sounds, muffled smells. Because Marian was here, burning at his side, and nothing else mattered in this world.

XIV. The Lure of Vengeance

"**I** thought you were scared of me," Robin said. "I thought you were going to run."

"Silly goat, how could I be scared of you, of all the people in the world. You're still you, underneath, I can see that much. I've had to change too, but you're not scared of me, are you?" They were the first words either of them had spoken since leaving the Garden of Angels. They had run, with the others behind them, through hushed villages and silent fields. The moon was bright but sometimes lost behind clouds—Robin could tell when it was because the footsteps of the others slowed, and then he slowed too and guided their way, the girls holding hands and snaking single-file, Will Scarlett calling instructions up and down the line.

"Did you hate me?" Robin said. "After they took you from that village. Did you really think it was my fault?"

"No, never. I was frightened, and being frightened makes me angry, you know that. But I could never blame you. One man is responsible for all that has happened. He alone did this to us."

As she said this Robin felt his anger swell. He couldn't help sending his awareness rippling back, retracing their steps, and back further, to the Garden of Angels. Examining the

461

scene through his forest-mind, he finds many men are arriving there, gathering at the crest of the wooded hill. There must be fifty soldiers, at least.

And there—the Sheriff himself is among them. He is staring down at the smoking remains of his convent prison. Robin experiences a moment of distortion: a deafening smell, a screaming taste. The cause, he knows, is the Sheriff's anger: It is a monstrous, ravenous thing, howling through the night. It seems impossible Marian has not heard this sound. But in fact Robin knows even the men closest to the Sheriff do not understand the full extent of his fury. Outwardly he is pacific, sitting still and silent, his knuckles white where they grip the pommel of his saddle.

And then the Sheriff turns his head, the workings of his neck twisting, and he stares in this direction. Robin is sure, even at this distance, that the Sheriff is watching him.

And he is staring too at Marian.

Robin's anger howls, until it could almost drown the Sheriff's own.

"What is it?" Marian said. "Why are you slowing down?"

Robin wanted to say: *We're going the wrong way. He's there, in the open. We could end this, tonight.* But he managed to hold his tongue, and to keep running. Marian was here, at his side; leading her back into danger would be lunacy.

"What have you heard?" Marian said.

"It's nothing. We need to keep moving."

They ran on, the twelve other young women following behind, the mud squelching between their toes, running when the moon was bright, slowing and linking hands when the clouds bunched. Will Scarlett was moving up the line. He reached Robin and Marian's side.

"We need to rest," he said. "I've got two injured men—I need to see to their wounds."

Robin thought of the Sheriff, and his mutant anger. "A little farther," he said. "We can rest when we reach the wildwood."

"This ground is hard going on foot," Will said. "A few of those girls look ready to drop."

Marian said nothing, but evidently she agreed. She led the way into a deserted village. "We're not stopping long," she said. "But we need to dry our clothes. We didn't break free just to die of fever. Minnie, Lyssa, Ena, look for furniture—everything out here is too sodden to burn."

Some of Will's outlaws also went into houses and they came back with tables and benches and soon there were two fires burning in the open mouth of a threshing barn.

"Look what I found," said Ira Starr, returning with her arms full. "The smokehouse is stacked to the rafters. Here's badger ham and pheasant."

"Where are all the people?" said Ena Agutter. "Why did they leave all their food, and their belongings?"

"I haven't eaten for days," said Elfen Goldacre. "Too nervous."

"My mother used to make pheasant pie," said Seren Child. "It was famous, for miles around."

All the young women were talking now, quietly, as if testing whether all this was real and they could really be heard. Only two of the girls remained silent: Sonskya Luz stood a little way apart, hugging herself, looking into the night; Alice White was chewing her bottom lip and staring at the moon. Marian went to bring Sonskya closer to the warmth.

One of Will Scarlett's outlaws was approaching Robin. And when this man spoke his voice was a sharp stab from the past. "Robin, it's me. Jack Champ . . . Bones. Remember me, old friend?"

Robin said nothing.

"We . . . we were told you were dead."

Robin turned and walked away.

"I brought someone with me," Jack Champion called after him. "Ayala Baptiste. Remember him? He's become a good man, and a great warrior. We'll stand at your side."

Robin moved some distance from the fires. He sat with his head bowed, the wolf hide gathered around him. The color of it had changed, and the texture too: It was now a velvety gray, matching the moonlight through clouds. He felt Jack Champion still looking at him. He sensed too the young women glancing at him out of the corners of their eyes. It made him angry, this feeling of them all watching him—and, even worse, of them trying *not* to watch him. He got up and went farther off and sat in the shadows.

After a while Marian joined him. "I knew you'd come for me," she said. "You were too late, as usual, slow goat, but I knew you'd come. In a way you were with me the entire time, just like before. I could feel you at my side, helping me through. I wouldn't have made it without you."

Robin remained silent. He couldn't think of the right words—or he thought of too many words and they bunched up beneath his tongue. He sensed, in the far distance, the Sheriff, still staring in this direction. He battled that lure of vengeance, tugging at him, insisting he travel back there and confront his foe.

He stood. "We've rested long enough. Whoever is coming, they need to come now."

Without waiting for a reply, or even waiting for Marian's hand, he moved out of the village. And he heard his ragtag band of outlaws getting to their feet and falling into step, following silently and wearily behind.

XV. One Man's Truth

R obin's forest-mind is everywhere at once: it is stalking through the castle on feline paws; soaring with the buzzards above the shires; patrolling the coast with the gulls.

He observes a realm gearing for war.

The Sheriff has returned to his castle and he is limping down stone steps into his arsenal and he is ordering the construction of new infernal engines. And then he is journeying deeper, past even his deepest dungeons, and he is overseeing work of a different sort . . .

At the ports, mercenaries are already arriving. Hundreds of hired swords, drawn to the Sheriff and the gold he has promised. Robin senses these killers step ashore and he knows Edric Krul was as nothing compared to what now approaches . . .

Other fighters are flocking to Sherwood. A different type of army, ragged and makeshift, from boys no bigger than the axes they carry, to seasoned gangsters of the forest, they are all of them leaving their homes and their hideaways, lifting their blades and making their way here, to the wildwood . . .

A battlefield. A war roar. Robin's outlaws and the Sheriff's army are rushing to meet. They crash together in a thunder of hooves and scattered flesh and smashed steel. The sun is darkened by a swarm of arrows and a great howl rolls across the hills and Robin knows his forest-mind is no longer showing him what *is*, nor even what *was*, but *what is to come*. He feels the earth shudder and he hears the forest erupt in blood and fire, the flames engulfing the world edge to edge, leaving nothing behind but charred bones amid the ashes of ancient oak . . .

His forest-mind, overwhelmed, crashing back to the present.

Someone standing over him. Cernunnos.

"Was that real?" Robin said. "Is that what I've unleashed? How can I sense things that haven't yet happened?"

Cernunnos knelt with a stick and drew shapes in the mud. "Where the wind passes through grass, the bending of each blade depends on the movement of the last, and will help determine the movements that follow. The past is no different, nor the future."

He drew one last shape. Robin examined it with his fingers: two snakes, curled head to tail.

"You have barely begun to understand what you are," Cernunnos said. "You think you are the first to tread this path? You must learn to read the patterns, before you doom us all."

The branches shook themselves; the old man was gone.

Robin moved through the forest, heading across the outlaws' main camp. From above came the rasping of saws and the knocking of hammers: Fortress Sherwood rising amid the boughs.

Will Scarlett came striding across. "We're setting mantraps at the perimeter, and digging spear pits. All this would be quicker if the White Crows hadn't refused to work with Aks Arqua's men. Baphomet's Horde have taken off by themselves, who knows where. But we're getting it done slowly. No one wants to be caught unprepared."

Robin turned away without a word and continued through the broad clearing. He heard Ironside and Borston Black teaching a group of farmers the correct way to grip a spear. Much Millerson and his son were sparring with their fists. Jack Champion and Ayala Baptiste sat apart, talking. Robin felt their eyes on him as he passed.

And here, in a silent circle on their knees, were Marian's Destroying Angels. Marian was moving among them, addressing each in turn, speaking strange words. She appeared to be making marks on some of their wrists, and it sounded as if she was giving them each a new name. "Pitys . . . Dryope . . . Lotis . . . Syrinx . . ."

Robin left the clearing and he climbed to a higher glade, where a ring of boulders formed a secluded crown, like a natural hill fort. After a while Marian came to join him. Her hands went to his face, the same way they had before, her fingers searching his cheeks, his chin, his lips.

"It really is you," she whispered. "I keep thinking I'm imagining all this. But it's true, you're really here and we're together, at last."

She put her face to his, pressed their cheeks together, then their noses, then their lips. She was kissing him and the feeling was like lying near a lake in the summer shade, the warm breeze shivering his skin, the languid day stretching away forever . . .

Early autumn and Robin's cloak was taking on tones of copper and gold and shimmering with silver fork moss. Marian pushed herself into this soft coat and suddenly she was crying, and they were holding onto each other, the same way they used to when they were living in the tower, when the wind would howl and carry nightmare sounds from Winter Forest. Marian cried and they held each other tight, children again for the final time, just a boy from the village and the lord's daughter. She sobbed until she was almost choking, until finally the last of her energy was gone and she fell asleep.

Day gave way to dusk. The sawing and the hammering stopped. The outlaws broke into separate camps, each around their own fire, each telling their own stories and sharing their own jokes. Marian woke and detached herself from Robin, crawling out from under his cloak.

"It feels strange, being back in this place."

"You don't need to fear it," Robin said. "You're safe with me."

"That's what I mean, it's the weirdest thing, but I'm not scared, not in the slightest. There are always darker places, I suppose. But it's more than that. It's a feeling almost like . . . coming home."

Robin remained silent, strange possibilities rising in his mind. He set about building a fire.

After a while, Marian said: "I knew you'd come for me. I knew you'd stop at nothing. It's like I told you before: All the stories are coming true. Remember, in the tower, I used to read you the story of Sir Orfeo, whose wife was stolen away? He spent years wandering in the wild, sleeping on the bare earth, until he learned where his wife was being held, and he traveled to the Underworld, to bring her back. We've both been to the depths, haven't we?"

Robin sat back from the crackling fire. Marian curled herself against him. "We still have some distance to travel," she said. "But we'll make it, together. Once we destroy our enemy, then we'll truly be free."

Robin thought for a moment. "Those stories. Sir Orfeo. Orpheus. Lot. They all end the same way, don't they? They all say: 'Don't look back or you'll lose everything you've got left.' We don't need to go any further down that dark path."

468

"Yes, we do. We've got to follow it to the end—that's the only way back to the light."

"I've seen what revenge costs. It will swallow us."

An idea came to him. He got up and went to the cave and found his backpack. He returned holding Sir Bors's scroll, moldy now to the touch. Marian hesitated, then took the scroll and unrolled it. She began to read and behind her words Robin heard the voice of Sir Bors:

"Robin, there are no absolute truths in this world. That is one of the things we will endeavor to show you, during your time with us. One man's scripture is another man's legend, and a third man's lies. I want you to hold that in mind when you read the following lines. They are from a divination called The Dream of the Wyrdwood. Its complete contents are buried beyond my reaching, but over the years I have unearthed this much in full:

The tearing of an angel's wing
Harbinger of silent spring
Mother divine, mortal sire
Quickening of Gaea's pyre
A son in darkness, daughter chained
Two shall meet, blood will reign
Fenrir's lust shall be returned
Birth-rite of the winter-born.

"I shall not dictate what you should make of these words," Sir Bors's scroll continued. "I have made such mistakes in the past and the consequences haunt me still. Suffice to say this: There are powerful men in this realm who hold this script sacrosanct. It is the wellspring of all the harm they do. Each of us, Robin, when it comes time to face our enemy, can go armed with more than sword and shield. We can attempt to grasp our enemy's truths, and in doing so hope to guard ourselves against the worst of their hatred, and their malice."

Marian stopped reading.

"What else?" Robin said.

"Nothing. It ended there."

"There must be more. He was going to tell me why he made me his ward. He was going to tell me what happened to my parents."

"I told you what happened to them," Marian said. "Who do you trust, me or Sir Bors?"

As she spoke she rolled the scroll, placed it in the fire. The flames hissed as the moldy vellum began to burn.

"I told you . . . ," Marian said. "Your parents are dead. The villagers sent word to the Sheriff, telling him about you—how you were found in the wildwood—one of the winter-born. When Robert Loxley learned the Sheriff was on his way to Wodenhurst, he thought there was only one place you'd be safe. He took you into the wildwood and he left you there. He took the heart of a buck back to the village, told the Sheriff he had killed you himself—granted you a quick death. The Sheriff tortured him, regardless. Your brothers fought back and died for it. Your mother too. This is the truth. It is a part of you. You cannot hide from it, cannot run from it. You can only fight and fight until it's put right."

Robin listened to the scroll sigh as it curled in the heat, the unanswered questions twisting in his mind. Why did the Sheriff want to destroy the winter-born? What was that horror he kept chained beneath his castle? Who were Robin's real parents?

A line of the scroll came back to him, an awful idea taking shape.

Mother divine, mortal sire.

He thought of the goddess of the forest, and her words to him.

You're not the first. Others will come. For now you're my only. My lover, my son.

His forest-mind searching for her . . .

Here she is, exhausted and pale, walking toward the forest edge, a crying infant in her arms.

We've planted the seed, now it must grow.

Marian pushed herself against him, but this time he barely felt her touch. He was thinking of his family now—of how deeply he still missed them, and of all they had endured.

The Sheriff tortured him, regardless . . . fought back and died for it . . .

The shadow shard was running cold through his bones, bleeding deeper than ever, leaking to his heart, hardening around it and blackening it, like an oak scourged by wildfire. And as it did so an old promise returned to his mind, burning bright and fierce.

A man with a ruined face.

Robin's arrow buried in his chest.

Acknowledgments

I owe a great debt to my agent, James Wills, who was this story's first editor, and its greatest champion from the start. My deepest thanks also to everyone at David Fickling Books, particularly my mentors there: David Fickling, Bella Pearson, and Simon Mason. All that is excellent within these pages is due to their guidance and patience. Finally, and most importantly, thank you to my wife, Lizzie, who helped me find the freedom to do this work, who suffered its trials at my side, and who makes all the effort worthwhile.